The
Little Bookshop
ON THE SEINE

Center Point
Large Print

**This Large Print Book carries the
Seal of Approval of N.A.V.H.**

The
Little Bookshop
ON THE SEINE

REBECCA RAISIN

CENTER POINT LARGE PRINT
THORNDIKE, MAINE

This Center Point Large Print edition
is published in the year 2020 by arrangement with
Harlequin Books S.A.

The text of this Large Print edition is unabridged.
In other aspects, this book may vary
from the original edition.
Printed in the United States of America
on permanent paper.
Set in 16-point Times New Roman type.

ISBN: 978-1-64358-503-1

The Library of Congress has cataloged this record
under Library of Congress Control Number: 2019951862

The Little Bookshop
ON THE SEINE

For Claire Ellis

CONTENTS

The Little Bookshop
ON THE SEINE

ONE

October

With a heavy heart I placed the sign in the display window.

All books 50% off.

If things didn't pick up soon, it would read *Closing down sale.* The thought alone was enough to make me shiver. The autumnal sky was awash with purples and smudges of orange, as I stepped outside to survey the display window from the sidewalk.

Star-shaped leaves crunched underfoot. I forced a smile. A sale wouldn't hurt, and maybe it'd take the bookshop figures from the red into the black—which I so desperately needed. My rent had been hiked up. The owner of the building, a sharp-featured, silver-tongued, forty-something man, had put the pressure on me lately—to pay more, to declutter the shop, claiming the haphazard stacks of books were a fire risk. The additional rent stretched the budget to breaking level. Something had to change.

The phone shrilled, and a grin split my face. It could only be Ridge at this time of the morning. Even after being together almost a year his name still provoked a giggle. It suited him though, the

13

veritable man mountain he was. I'd since met his mom, a sweet, well-spoken lady, who claimed in dulcet tones, that she chose his name *well* before his famous namesake in *The Bold and the Beautiful*. In fact, she was adamant about it, and said the TV character Ridge was no match for her son. I had to agree. Sure, they both had chiseled movie star cheekbones, and an intense gaze that made many a woman swoon, but my guy was more than just the sum of his parts—I loved him for his mind, as much as his clichéd six-pack, and broody hotness. And even better, he loved me for me.

He was the hero in my own *real-life* love story, and due back from Canada the next day. It'd been weeks since I'd seen him, and I ached for him in a way that made me blush.

I dashed inside, and answered the phone, breathlessly. "The Bookshop on the Corner."

"That's the voice I know and love," he said in his rich, husky tone. My heart fluttered, picturing him at the end of the line, his jet-black hair and flirty blue eyes. He simply had to flick me a look loaded with suggestion, and I'd be jelly-legged and lovestruck.

"What are you wearing?" he said.

"Wouldn't you like to know?" I held back a laugh, eager to drag it out. So far our relationship had been more long-distance than anticipated, as he flew around the world reporting on location.

14

The stints apart left an ache in my heart, a numbness to my days. Luckily I had my books, and a sweeping romance or two helped keep the loneliness at bay.

"Tell me or I'll be forced to Skype you and see for myself."

Glancing down at my outfit, I grimaced: black tights, a black pencil skirt, and a pilled blue knit sweater, all as old as the hills of Ashford. Not exactly the type of answer Ridge was waiting for, or the way I wanted him to picture me, after so many weeks apart. "Those stockings you like, and . . ."

His voice returned with a growl. "*Those* stockings? With the little suspenders?"

I sat back into the chair behind the counter, fussing with my bangs. "The very same."

He groaned. "You're *killing* me. Take a photo . . ."

"There's no need. If you're good, I'll wear the red ones tomorrow night." I grinned wickedly. Our reunions were always passionate affairs; he was a hands-on type of guy. Lucky for him, because it took a certain type of man to drag me from the pages of my books. When he was home we didn't surface until one of us had to go to work. Loving Ridge had been a revelation, especially in the bedroom, where he took things achingly slow, drawing out every second. I flushed with desire for him.

There was a muffled voice and the low buzz of phones ringing. Ridge mumbled to someone before saying, "About tomorrow . . ." He petered out, regret in each syllable.

I closed my eyes. "You're not coming, are you?" I tried not to sigh, but it spilled out regardless. The lure of a bigger, better story was too much for him to resist, and lately the gaps between our visits grew wider. I understood his work was important, but I wanted him all to myself. A permanent fixture in the small town I lived in.

He tutted. "I'm sorry, baby. There's a story breaking in Indonesia, and I have to go. It'll only be for a week or two, and then I'll take some time off."

Outside, leaves fluttered slowly from the oak tree, swaying softly, until they fell to the ground. I wasn't the nagging girlfriend sort—times like this though, I was tempted to be. Ridge had said the very same thing the last three times he'd canceled a visit. But invariably someone would call and ask Ridge to head to the next location; any time off would be cut short.

"I understand," I said, trying to keep my voice bright. Sometimes I felt like I played a never-ending waiting game. Would it always be like this? "Just so you know, I have a very hot date this afternoon."

He gasped. "You better be talking about a fictional date." His tone was playful, but

16

underneath there was a touch of jealousy to it. Maybe it was just as hard on him, being apart.

"One *very* hot book boyfriend . . . though not as delectable as my real boyfriend—but a stand-in, until he returns."

"Well, he better not keep you up half the night, or he'll have me to answer to," he faux threatened, and then said more seriously, "Things will slow down, Sarah. I want to be with you so much my soul hurts. But right now, while I'm freelance, I have to take whatever comes my way."

"I know. I just feel a bit lost sometimes. Like someone's hit pause, and I'm frozen on the spot." I bit my lip, trying to work out how to explain it. "It's not just missing you—I do understand about your job—it's . . . everything. The bookshop sales dwindling, the rent jacked up, everyone going on about their business, while I'm still the same old Sarah."

I'd been at this very crossroad when I'd met Ridge, and he'd swept me off my feet, like the ultimate romance hero. For a while that had been enough. After all, wasn't love always the answer? Romance aside, life was a little stagnant, and I knew it was because of my fear of change. It wasn't so much that I had to step from behind the covers of my books, rather plunge, perhaps. Take life by the scruff of the neck and shake it. But how?

"You've had a rough few weeks. That's all. I'll

17

be back soon, and I'm sure there's something I can do to make you forget everything . . ."

My belly flip-flopped at the thought. He *would* make me forget everything that was outside that bedroom door, but then he'd leave and it would all tumble back.

What exactly was I searching for? My friends were getting married and having babies. Buying houses and redecorating. Starting businesses. My life had stalled. I was an introvert, happiest hiding in the shadows of my shop, reading romances to laze the day away, between serving the odd customer or two—yet, it wasn't enough. In small-town Connecticut, there wasn't a lot to do. And life here—calm, peaceful—was fine, but that's just it, *fine* wasn't enough anymore. I had this fear that life was passing me by because I was too timid to take the reins.

It was too hazy a notion of what I was trying to say, even to me. Instead of lumping Ridge with it, I changed tack. "I hope you know, you're not leaving the house when you get home. Phones will be switched to silent, computers forgotten, and the only time we're leaving the comfort of bed is when I need sustenance." A good romp around the bedroom would suffice until I could pinpoint what it was that I wanted.

"How about I sort out the sustenance?" he said, his voice heavy with desire. "And then we'll never have to leave."

18

"Promises, promises," I said, my breath hitching. I hoped this flash of longing would never wane, the sweet torture of anticipation.

"I have to go, baby. I'll call you tonight if it's not too late once I'm in."

"Definitely call tonight! Otherwise, I can't guarantee the book boyfriend won't steal your girlfriend. He's pretty hot, I'll have you know."

"Why am I jealous of a fictional character?" He laughed, a low, sexy sound. "OK, tonight. Love you."

"Love you too."

He hung up, leaving me dazed, and a touch lonely knowing that I wouldn't see him the next day as planned.

I tried to shake the image of Ridge from my mind. If anyone walked in, they'd see the warm blush of my cheeks, and know exactly what I was thinking. Damn the man for being so attractive, and so effortlessly sexy.

Shortly, the sleepy town of Ashford would wake under the gauzy light of October skies. Signs would be flipped to open, stoops swept, locals would amble down the road. Some would step into the bookshop and out of the cold, and spend their morning with hands wrapped around a mug of steaming hot tea, and reading in any one of the cozy nooks around the labyrinth-like shop.

I loved having a place for customers to linger. Comfort was key, and if you had a good book and a hot drink, what else could you possibly need to make your day any brighter? Throw rugs and cushions were littered around seating areas. Coats would be swiftly hung on hooks, a chair found, knitted blankets pulled across knees, and their next hour or two spent, in the most relaxing of ways.

I wandered around the shop, feather duster in hand, tickling the covers, waking them from slumber. I'm sure as soon as my back was turned, the books wiggled and winked at one another, as if they were eager for the day to begin, for fingers of hazy sunlight to filter through and land on them like spotlights, as if saying, *here's the book for you.*

Imagine if I had to close up for good, like so many other shops had in recent times? It pained me to think people were missing out on the real-life bookshop experience. Wasn't it much better when you could step into a dimly lit space, and eke your way around searching for the right novel? You could run a fingertip along the spines, smell that glorious old book scent, flick them open, and unbend a dog-eared page. Read someone else's notes in the margin, or a highlighted passage, and see why that sentence or metaphor had dazzled the previous owner.

Secondhand books had so much *life* in them. They'd lived, sometimes in many homes, or maybe just one. They'd been on airplanes, traveled to sunny beaches, or crowded into a backpack and taken high up a mountain where the air thinned.

Some had been held aloft tepid rose-scented baths, and thickened and warped with moisture. Others had childlike scrawls on the acknowledgment page, little fingers looking for a blank space to leave their mark. Then there were the pristine novels, ones that had been read carefully, bookmarks used, almost like their owner barely pried the pages open so loath were they to damage their treasure.

I loved them all.

And I found it hard to part with them. Though years of book selling had steeled me. I had to let them go, and each time made a fervent wish they'd be read well, and often.

Missy, my best friend, said I was completely cuckoo, and that I spent too much time alone in my shadowy shop, because I believed my books communicated with me. A soft sigh here, as they stretched their bindings when dawn broke, or a hum, as they anticipated a customer hovering close who might run a hand along their cover, tempting them to flutter their pages hello. Books were fussy when it came to their owners, and gave off a type of sound, an almost imperceptible whirr, when the right person was near. Most people weren't aware that books chose us, at the time when we needed them most.

Outside, the breeze picked up, gathering the leaves in a swirl and blowing them down the street in waves. Rubbing my hands for warmth, I trundled into the reading room, and added some wood to the fire. Each day, the weather grew cooler, and the crackle and spit of the glowing embers were a nice soundtrack to the shop, comforting, like a hug.

The double-stacked books in the reading room weren't for sale, but could be thumbed and enjoyed by anyone who wished. They were my favorites, the ones I couldn't part with. I'd been gifted a huge range from a man whose wife had passed on, a woman who was so like me with her bookish foibles, that it was almost like she was still here. Her collection—an essential part of her life—lived on, long after she'd gone. I'd treasure them always.

I wandered to the front of the shop. The street was coming alive. Owners milled in front of shops, chatting to early-bird customers, or lugging out A-frame signs, advertising their wares. Lil, my friend from the Gingerbread Café, waved over at me. Her heavily pregnant belly made me smile. I pulled open the front door, a gust of wind blowing my hair back, and fluttering the pages of the books.

"You take it easy!" I shouted. Lil was due any day now, but insisted on working. Times were tough for all of us, so Lil had to work, but claimed instead she wanted to spruce things up before she left. Nesting, her best friend and only employee CeeCee called it.

Lil tossed her long blonde curls back from her face. "If I take it any easier, I'll be asleep! Besides, how are you going to survive without your chocolate fix?" The wind carried her words to me in a happy jumble.

"True," I agreed. "I'll be there as soon as my tummy rumbles." It was torture, working across the road from the café, the scent of tempered chocolate or the yeasty smell of freshly baked bread wafting its way to my shop. I'd find myself crossing the street and demanding to be fed, flopping lazily on their sofa, while they flitted around making all my food dreams come true. The girls from the café were great friends, and often gave me a metaphorical shove in the back when they thought I should step from the comfort of my shop and try something new, like love, for example.

They'd set me up with Ridge, knowing I wouldn't take the leap myself. When I'd first met him, I couldn't understand why a big-shot reporter from New York would be interested in a girl from Smallsville. It wasn't that I didn't think I was good enough, it was more that our lives were a million miles apart, and the likes of him were a rarity in Ashford.

My girlfriends hadn't seen it that way, and

literally pushed me into his arms, at a dinner party the night of the infamous man crease fiasco. I wouldn't say that's when I fell in love with Ridge, my face pressed up against his nether regions after a "fall" on the uneven deck, but it was pretty damn close. My so-called friends had orchestrated the night, including the "whoops" shove in the back from Lil, so I toppled ungraciously toward Ridge, landing on my knees at his hip level. My breathing had been uneven, as his sweater rode high, and jeans had slung low, giving me ample opportunity to scrutinize the deep V presented to me. My lips a mere inch away from his tanned flesh, until he scooped me up, before I almost licked his skin to see what it tasted like. I had this strange burning desire to see what flavor he'd be. That's what reading too many romances does to a girl.

Recalling the evening still provoked a blush, because it was so unlike me. I mean, imagine if I *had* flicked my tongue against his exposed skin? He would have been running for the hills before the entrée was served. But that's the effect he had over me, he made my mind blank, and my body act of its own volition, including a thousand scenarios I'd never have entertained with any other guy. Dumbstruck by love was a real thing, I'd come to learn.

Lil's boisterous laughter brought me back to

the moment. "See you soon. I'll have a chocolate soufflé with your name on it."

"You'd tempt the devil himself!" I joked and gave her a wave before stepping back into the warmth of the bookshop.

My email pinged and I dashed over to see who it was from. That's how exciting my life was sans Ridge, an email was enough to make me almost run, and that was saying a lot. I only ran if chocolate was involved, and even then it was more a fast walk.

Sales@littlebookshop.fr

Sophie, a dear Parisian friend. She owned Once Upon a Time, a famous bookshop by the bank of the Seine. We'd become confidantes since connecting on my book blog a while back, and shared our joys and sorrows about bookshop life. She was charming and sweet, and adored books as much as me, believing them to be portable magic, and a balm for souls.

I clicked open the email and read:

Ma chérie,
I cannot stay one more day in Paris. You see, Manu has not so much broken my heart, rather pulled it out of my chest and stomped on it. The days are interminable and I can't catch my breath. He walks past

the bookshop, as though nothing is amiss. I have a proposal for you. Please call me as soon as you can.

Love,
Sophie

Poor Sophie. I'd heard all about her grand love affair with a dashing twenty-something man, who frequented her bookshop, and quoted famous poets. It'd been a whirlwind romance, but she often worried he cast an appraising eye over other women. Even when she clutched his hand, and walked along the cobbled streets of Paris, he'd dart an admiring glance at any woman swishing past.

I shot off a quick reply, telling her to Skype me now, if she was able. Within seconds my computer flashed with an incoming call.

Her face appeared on the screen, her chestnut-colored hair in an elegant chignon, her lips dusted rosy pink. If she was in the throes of heartache, you'd never know it by looking at her. The French had a way of always looking poised and together, no matter what was happening in their complex lives.

"Darling," she said, giving me a nod. "He's a lothario, a Casanova, a . . ." She grappled for another moniker as her voice broke. "He's dating the girl who owns the shop next door!" Her eyes smoldered, but her face remained stoic.

I gasped, "Which girl? The one from the florist?"

Sophie shook her head. "The other side, the girl from the *fromagerie*." She grimaced. I'd heard so much about the people in or around Sophie's life that it was easy to call her neighbors to mind.

"Giselle?" I said, incredulous. "Wasn't she engaged—I thought the wedding was any day now?"

Sophie's eyes widened. "She's broken off her engagement, and has announced it to the world that *my* Manu has proposed and now they are about to set up house and to try immediately for children—"

My hand flew to my mouth. "Children! He wouldn't do that, surely!" Sophie was late forties, and had gently broached the subject of having a baby with Manu, but he'd said simply: absolutely not, he didn't want children.

The doorbell of her shop pinged, Sophie's face pinched and she leaned closer to the screen, lowering her voice. "A customer . . ." She forced a bright smile, turned her head and spoke in rapid-fire French to whoever stood just off-screen. "So," she continued quietly. "The entire neighborhood are whispering behind their hands about the love triangle, and unfortunately for me, I'm the laughing stock. The older woman, who was deceived by a younger man."

I wished I could lean through the monitor and

hug her. While she was an expert at keeping her features neutral, she couldn't stop the glassiness of her eyes when tears threatened. My heart broke that Manu would treat her so callously. She'd trusted him, and loved him unreservedly. "No one is laughing at you, I promise," I said. "They'll be talking about Manu, if anyone, and saying how he's made a huge mistake."

"No, no." A bitter laugh escaped her. "I look like a fool. I simply cannot handle when he cavorts through the streets with her, darting glances in my bookshop, like they hope I'll see them. It's too cruel." Sophie held up a hand, and turned to a voice. She said *au revoir* to the customer and spun to face me, but within a second or two, the bell sounded again. "I have a proposal for you, and I want you to *really* consider it." She raised her eyebrows. "Or at least hear me out before you say no." Her gaze burned into mine as I racked my brain with what it could be, and came up short. Sophie waved to customers, and pivoted her screen further away.

"Well?" I said with a nervous giggle. "What exactly are you proposing?"

She blew out a breath, and then smiled. "A bookshop exchange. You come and run Once Upon a Time, and I'll take over The Bookshop on the Corner."

I gasped, my jaw dropping.

Sophie continued, her calm belied by the slight

quake in her hand as she gesticulated. "You've always said how much you yearned to visit the city of love—here's your chance, my dear friend. After our language lessons, you're more than capable of speaking enough French to get by." Sophie's words spilled out in a desperate rush, her earlier calm vanishing. "You'd save me so much heartache. I want to be in a place where no one knows me, and there's no chance for love, *ever* again."

I tried to hide my smile at that remark. I'd told Sophie in the past how bereft of single men Ashford was, and how my love life had been almost nonexistent until Ridge strolled into town.

"Sophie, I want to help you, but I'm barely hanging on to the bookshop as is . . ." I stalled for time, running a hand through my hair, my bangs too long, shielding the tops of my eyebrows. How could it work? How would we run each other's businesses, the financial side, the logistics? I also had an online shop, and I sourced hard-to-find books—how would Sophie continue that?

My mind boggled with the details, not to mention the fact that leaving my books would be akin to leaving a child behind. I loved my bookshop as if it were a living thing, an unconditional best friend, who was always there for me. Besides, I'd never ventured too far from Ashford let alone boarded a plane—it just couldn't happen.

"Please," Sophie said, a real heartache in her tone. "Think about it. We can work out the finer details and I'll make it worth your while. Besides, you know I'm good with numbers, I can whip your sales into shape." Her eyes clouded with tears. "I have to leave, Sarah. You're my only chance. Christmas in Paris is on your bucket list . . ."

My bucket list. A hastily compiled scrap piece of paper filled with things I thought I'd never do. Christmas in Paris—snow dusting the bare trees on the Left Bank, the sparkling fairy lights along the Boulevard Saint-Germain. Santa's village in the Latin Quarter. The many Christmas markets to stroll through, rugged up with thick scarves and gloves, Ridge by my side, as I hunted out treasures. I'd spent many a day curled up in my own shop, flicking through memoirs, or travel guides about Paris, dreaming about the impossible . . . *one day.*

Sophie continued: "If you knew how I suffered here, my darling. It's not only Manu, it's everything. All of a sudden, I can't do it all anymore. It's like someone has pulled the plug, and I'm empty." Her eyes scrunched closed as she fought tears.

While Sophie's predicament was different to mine, she was in a funk, just like me. Perhaps a new outlook, a new place would mend both our lives. Her idea of whipping my sales into shape was laughable though, she had no real clue how tiny Ashford was.

"Exchange bookshops . . ." I said, the idea taking shape. Could I just up and leave? What about my friends, my life, my book babies? My fear of change? And Ridge, what would he have to say about it? But my life . . . it was missing something. Could this be the answer?

Paris. The city of love. Full of rich literary history.

A little bookshop on the bank of the Seine. Could there be anything sweeter?

With a thud, a book fell to the floor beside me, dust motes dancing above it like glitter. I craned my neck to see what it was.

Paris: A Literary Guide.

Was that a sign? Did my books want me to go?

"Yes," I said, without any more thought. "I'll do it."

TWO

"You what?" Missy shrieked and her eyebrows shot up so high I thought she'd fall over backward. A handful of customers at the Gingerbread Café glanced over to see what all the fuss was about. I blushed ruby red, and squirmed. Missy shot the nosy parkers a look that said mind your own business.

I bit my lip, and threw my palms up. "It just kind of happened, and I said yes. *Yes.* It was as easy as that!" I shrugged apologetically. I was plain old Sarah Smith: introvert, bookworm, shy to a fault. Not a fan of change, a subscriber to the steady rhythm of routine. I found comfort in the familiar. The girls buoyed me up, and I could be myself, but my radical plan would definitely shock them, because it was so unlike me.

"I cannot for the life of me imagine you saying yes to such a thing on the spot like that, but you know—" she stopped to fluff her auburn curls "—I think it's a great idea, sugar. You've been skating along lately, without your usual sparkle." She crossed her legs, pulling at the hem of her leopard print miniskirt. "But, sheesh, this has come out of left field . . . you're *leaving?*" Missy's face contorted as she grappled with the idea of the bookshop exchange. Being my secret keeper, and my go-to person in times of need, the idea I'd done something so swiftly without asking for advice was a lot for her to reconcile.

"One hot chocolate, and one gingerbread latte. Pray tell, what's all this screeching 'bout?" CeeCee asked, and plonked down on the old sofa across from us, putting her feet on the ottoman. "Lil!" she hollered. "Come sit, there's somethin' goin' on over here." She clasped her hands over the spread of her midsection, and gave me a pointed stare, her sweet brown forehead furrowing.

"Well . . ." I tucked a tendril of hair behind my ear, waiting for Lil to join us.

Lil waddled over, her baby bump so big she balanced a tray laden with chocolate truffles and gingerbread men on it. She handed us each a plate and sat next to CeeCee.

"So," Lil said, gazing at me, curiosity in her big blue eyes. "What's the story?"

I rubbed my face, and took a deep breath. "I've agreed to exchange bookshops with Sophie in Paris. It all happened so quickly . . . she Skyped yesterday, and I said yes, without much thought."

There was an audible intake of breath from the girls. For the first time ever they were rendered speechless. Usually they'd chatter away and talk over the top of one another. I threw my head back and laughed. "Girls, I'm not going to Antarctica, or climbing Mount Everest. I'm going to Paris."

Lil cleared her throat, and composed herself first. "Wow, Sarah, just . . . wow. In a million years I would never have imagined you'd leave your shop. You *love* your shop. Your books are your *babies*." Her bright blue eyes were wide with astonishment as she emphasized each point. Pregnancy suited Lil, her complexion was rosier than normal, and her blonde hair seemed to grow overnight, falling down her back in effortless shiny waves. Her face though, paled at my announcement. Did she think I was making the wrong choice?

Lil hurried on: "It's not that I don't think it's a good idea. I just . . ." Her words fell away.

"Ain't nothing gonna change here. Youth is fleeting, I'll tell you that for free. There comes a time where you either fish or cut bait, cherry blossom . . . go on and do what you gotta," CeeCee, the warmhearted mother hen of our group, said.

Customers milled by the counter, waiting to order, but the girls were still too shell-shocked to notice. I pointed them out to Lil. "Won't be a minute," she said, smiling to them, her cheeks now pink from disbelief.

"What does that incredible hunk of a man . . . ?" CeeCee's eyes glazed over, as she lost her train of thought. "Mmhm, Mr. Rippling Abs, if I was forty years younger . . ." Her voice petered off and we all stifled giggles.

"Cee!" Lil said, faux scandalized. "Can you focus?" We giggled into our hands. CeeCee had pet names for all of our partners, and always threw in the same line about being forty years younger. She was at the pointy end of her sixties, and spritely as a teenager despite her plump frame. CeeCee was looking past us, lost inside her daydream. Her head snapped back. "What? Just 'cause I'm an old woman that don't mean I can't appreciate beauty! My eyesight still works plenty fine! And when I see that boy, and the way he struts up that street like he owns it, all smoldering-eyed, strong-jawed perfection, I just can't quit starin'. Then there's that sculpted body o' his, I say to myself, I says, 'Now, Cee, when it comes prayin' time tonight, you remember to thank the Lord for that fine specimen o' a man, it's the *least* you can do.' "

I almost spat out a mouthful of coffee, and tried my hardest to swallow it down without choking. Missy cackled like a witch and Lil gave Cee an astonished stare.

"I think," Lil said to me, trying to keep her belly-grabbing laughter in check, "you might want to tone down the bodice rippers you're lending to Cee. They may be affecting her health."

We lost our tenuous grip on our composure and laughter burbled out of us. "I don't know, Lil," I said. "I think she has a point. He's definitely not ugly."

Lil nodded. "Can't argue there."

"And then there's you," Missy said, surveying my face. "You even look French, Sarah—like a French ingenue with your beautiful black, bobbed hair, and big fathomless eyes." Missy had a thing about boosting people up, she only saw the good in a person and threw compliments around like confetti. Even if she thought Paris was a crazy idea, she would've supported me, it was just her way.

"Imagine you two in Paris, a couple of gorgeous lovebirds strolling along. That man is so in love with you, I bet he proposes . . . you'll be walking along, your hair wet by rain, he'll be gazing at you with those mesmerizing eyes of his . . ." Missy got lost in her imagination.

I laughed. "Admit it, you've been reading the books I gave Cee?"

Missy guffawed. "Yeah, who knew I'd become so addicted? But honestly, I think despite your outwardly quiet demeanor, there's a firecracker inside of you just bursting to get out. This will do you good, finding yourself in a place as romantic as Paris. And that man is the perfect match for you."

I smiled at Missy, unsure of what to say to such a thing. It was too soon to even contemplate marriage, but I did wonder about the future.

Ridge with his uber drive and ambition to succeed was at odds with my more gentle attitude. I was happy enough to float through life, book in hand, caught up in a fictional world. But was that my problem? The reason sometimes I couldn't sleep? There were times I worried that I wasn't trying hard enough to live in the real world. Everyone I knew had a goal, whether it was having children or expanding their businesses. And yet there I was, muddled by it all, so afraid that if I left the familiar I wouldn't be able to handle it on my own. I'd sleepwalked safely through life and it was time to wake up, and smell the . . . croissants.

"Ridge does his own thing, and it's time for me to find out what I want from life, other than reading, as much as I love it."

I wasn't sure if Ridge was completely comfortable in Ashford. He was a New Yorker through and through, and thrived on the hustle and bustle of big-city living. He was competitive and determined, speeding from one story to the next. Here, if you rushed anywhere people would think you were being chased by a killer plague of zombies, or something.

"You've come a long way from the girl who used to try her hardest to be invisible," Missy said, softly, remembering the old me, the one I was trying hard to shed. I'd had a range of issues growing up, all linked back to an incident in childhood, that like tumbleweed, rolled along gaining momentum until I was lost inside myself. The fallout from it still echoed. But it'd been these girls who pulled me from the safety of my books, and into the real world despite my protests.

"Ain't that the truth. We sure are proud o' you." CeeCee hefted her bulk from the sofa. "Let me serve these customers 'fore a protest starts."

"Good for you. If this is what you want, we support you a hundred percent." Lil had rolled into the dip in the sofa, in CeeCee's absence. She righted herself and pulled a cushion onto her lap, rubbing her big pregnant belly absently. In a wistful tone, she said, "It'll be so weird glancing over at the bookshop and seeing someone else there." Her voice caught.

Missy plucked a tissue from the table and dabbed at her heavily made-up eyes. "I haven't had a crying jag for the longest time, and I'm not gonna start again now. So hear me out, I'm gonna say it real fast . . . You leaving will be like a piece of our heart is missing, but that's because we love you. We know you'll flourish over there. Just don't stay there forever, OK?"

I gave her a grateful smile and moved to hug her.

"Golly," Lil said, her eyes shiny with tears. "Pass me a tissue!"

CeeCee trundled back. "Oh, glory be, I leave y'all for one minute and come back to a blubber fest!"

We settled back down, and stared at one another, before bursting into laughter.

"So," Missy piped up. "When are you leaving?"

I averted my eyes. "In two days." It was too soon, but maybe that was for the best. Less time to panic I'd made a mistake.

"*Two days?*" Missy said, her jaw dropping. We'd been best friends for the last decade—I'd miss her fiercely, and her baby Angel, whose first birthday was on Christmas Day.

"I know it's short notice, but Sophie needs to get away urgently. Manu left her for the girl next door. Can you imagine?" I said. "They're parading around in front of her, it's just too horrible to comprehend." The girls knew all about Sophie, I'd drop her into conversation regularly. To us, her life was exotic and utterly glamorous—a world away from our sleepy town.

"Oh, what a pig he is," Missy said, frowning. "Does Sophie know how small this place is, though?" she asked carefully. "I mean . . . swapping Paris for Ashford? *We* love it here, but will she?" In the background the fire crackled and spat, a comforting familiar soundtrack to so many of our conversations.

I toyed with the handle on my mug. "She knows all about Ashford. Her only stipulation was that there weren't a host of single men lining the streets looking for 'The One.' "

Our peals of laughter rang out. "Well then,"

CeeCee said, her brown face crinkling into a smile, "she's picked the right town. Single men so sparse around here, it's a wonder babies are still bein' made."

I giggled. While it was such a cliché, a small town with no single men, it was true for Ashford. The younger folk usually moved away to attend college or get jobs in bigger cities, and work here was hard to find. Each year the town population shrank.

Missy put her mug on the coffee table and stood. "I'm going to pretend you're just going away for the weekend . . ."

I tried to laugh it off, but it sounded hollow. It would be the toughest thing ever to leave my friends. They were like my security blanket, but the excitement of finally visiting the city I'd coveted for so long brought a fresh wave of butterflies. My eyes flicked to Lil's belly, as she put a hand to the sofa to ease her way upright. "Lil . . ." My voice fell away.

"What?" she said, searching my face. "Oh." Seeing the direction of my gaze she looked down at her belly. "Don't you go getting sad on account of the jelly bean . . . we'll be Skyping you every other day." Her voice wobbled.

I stepped toward her and placed a hand on the bump, and was rewarded with a little kick. "See?" Lil said. "That's the jelly bean saying it's OK to go!"

40

I kept silent, not trusting myself to speak without crying. I'd miss the jelly bean's birth, Lil and Damon's first wedding anniversary, and baby Angel's first birthday. Celebrations that meant a lot to me.

"Mom, seriously, it's only Paris. I'm not trekking up the Himalayas, or BASE jumping in the Grand Canyon. I'm going to another bookshop. I'll sip French wine, and eat macarons in every color of the rainbow. Wander down avenues where Édith Piaf once sang. I'll meander around the flea markets near the 18th arrondissement . . ." I'd grabbed every French travel guide in the bookshop, and soaked up the text, my heart hammering with all the beauty I'd find.

"But, darling. You'll be all *alone*. All by *yourself*."

"I get it, Mom. You don't need to emphasize it." It was hard to listen to the doubt in her voice. She acted as if I wasn't capable of traveling on my own, like I'd come home dead or something. "I'm sure I'll make friends, and Ridge can meet me there. And so what if I'm alone? I'll have more time to see what I want to see."

"Sarah, it's a jungle out there. I'm only telling you so you know. *Anything* can happen to you. You're not the kind of girl who waltzes off into the sunset . . ."

A jungle out there. Like I'd get swallowed up

whole. "What if you go back to that dark place again, Sarah? You're doing great here. You've got the best group of friends, a busy life . . ."

"Mom, my life is the opposite of busy. It's practically on standstill. I'm not going backward, I'm going forward. This will surely spur me on. I'm not seven anymore. All that's in the past, *well* in the past."

She clucked her tongue the way moms do. "I don't want you retreating again, that's all."

"I won't. Don't you see? This is a huge step forward for me. No one can accuse me of living in the shadows if I go to Paris." When I was seven, we went to a trade fair on the outskirts of Ashford, and somehow or other, I wandered off and got lost. I'd taken a walk into the nearby woods, and had gone too far. When darkness descended I'd felt real ice-cold fear that I'd die out there, being seven, every noise was amplified, every shadow a predator. A whole team of people with flashlights searched for me. They didn't find me until close to midnight. After that, nightmares plagued me, and I was scared to leave my parents' side. A side effect was developing a nervous stutter, and as you can imagine school life became impossible. Kids mimicked me, and teased me until one day I faded away, and dived into the world of fiction.

Books had been my only friends. My confidence had taken the almightiest of hits, and had never really recovered. That girl, the one who wanted to die of embarrassment was sometimes just under the surface. Years of speech therapy fixed my stutter, and by the time I was a teen I'd learned to be invisible. I didn't socialize, and didn't have the first clue how to change that. Once you've cut yourself off from people, it's so hard to find a way back in. My mom was certain I had developed depression, or agoraphobia, or a host of other medical conditions but it was fear, and the effects of bullying that left such a scar on my psyche. But that changed when I opened my bookshop, and Missy stepped into my life, and brightened it. Really, that was a million years ago, and the friendship with the girls, and falling in love had boosted my self-confidence.

Mom sat across from me, the chipped and faded Formica table between us. Nothing in Mom's kitchen had changed since I was a little girl. The spice rack was the same, the shelf displaying fancy plates still gathered dust, just like always. The silver kettle, dented, a boil-on-stove type, sat rotund, waiting. It didn't take a genius to see who I took after, change wasn't in either of our vocabs, yet here I was.

"Mom, my books have taken me around the world, but it's time I stepped from the pages, so I can see it for myself." I clasped my hands and leaned my elbows on the table. "It's a few months, and then I'll be safely home, and I'm sure I can pick up exactly where I left off because nothing ever changes around here."

Dad was out back in the apple orchard, having given me a bear hug and his blessing. He was a man of few words, but his actions always showed me he cared. Mom's black hair was streaked with more gray these days, and real fear was reflected in her eyes. She wrung her hands, a frown appearing, as if I'd told her I was going off to war.

"I just don't know how you'll cope." Her lip wobbled. She was worried, her only child heading off into the sunset.

My parents were salt-of-the-earth types. The only time they traveled was to sell the apples that grew abundantly out back. They worked hard, read a lot, and were quiet churchgoing folk, who lived softly in this world.

"Mom, I'll be fine. It's time I tried something new, that's all."

She shook her head, miffed. My mom was a lot like me with the *if it's not broke don't fix it* kind of mentality, so I knew she thought traveling was something frivolous, a folly. And dangerous to boot.

"What if something happens to you?"

"I hope it *does,* Mom. I hope I come back with a new vigor for life. I'm tired of being the same person, half-living, all this waiting for something to happen . . . I have to *make* it happen." The more I tried to convince her, the more I believed it myself.

The only sound was the tick of the clock on the wall, one that had been there since I was a skinny five-year-old. Eventually she said, "Is this because of Ridge? You feel like you have to go chase your dreams somewhere else? Following in his footsteps?"

I held in an exasperated sigh. "It's not that I'm mimicking his life, or wanting to change my values based on his. I want to experience somewhere other than Ashford. Just for a little while."

She took a deep breath. "Well, OK. But I'm going to worry about you until you're back on home soil."

"Try not to worry." I gave her hand a reassuring pat. "Try and be happy for me."

With an unsteady smile she said, "I am, darling. It's just Paris is so far away, and flooded with people. I've seen the TV shows, I know there's crime: bag snatching, people smuggling. Have you seen the movie *Taken*? I'm sure that was set in Paris . . ."

I hid a smile. Ashford was so small, no one was brave enough to commit any crimes. Here and there, a teenager would shoplift, and that was about it. The rest of the world seemed so fast, so downright hazardous to the quieter folk in our small town. "Mom, I'm not going to worry about being snatched off the street, or any of the million things that could happen. I'll be careful, OK?"

Falling into bed, the night before I was to leave, I dialed Ridge.

"Baby." His voice was soft with sleep. "We keep missing each other."

"It's our thing. Where are you?" I pulled the comforter up, and curled onto my side, wishing he was here, with his arms wrapped around me, his body pressed against mine. I closed my eyes against the empty feeling.

"At some sad little hotel at the airport. The empty spot on the mattress beside me a reminder how far away I am from you."

I hugged a pillow to my chest. No matter how much I tried to cuddle it during the night, the pillow was just a cold and aloof stand-in, until Ridge returned and held me tight. "And you'll be even farther away soon."

He sighed. "Yep. I fly out in a few hours. As always, when I'm in the quiet away from you, I wonder what I'm doing . . . is it worth it? Doesn't feel like it."

I smiled, sleepily. "What can I say? It's your job, and you love it. You'd get bored staying in one spot too long."

"I don't think I would, Sarah. I'd have you."

It was a sweet notion, and my heart swelled,

but Ridge thrived on the adventure of his job. The unknown of what he'd find. If he stayed in Ashford for any length of time, I'm sure he'd get itchy feet, and yearn to travel once more. His job suited him, he was as dynamic as his stories.

"You'll see me soon," I said. "Hopefully, you can get your story wrapped in a week."

A groan traveled down the line. "I hope so. That'll be almost a month I haven't seen you, the longest yet." He continued, "Sorry I didn't call last night. I had to file a story, and it was woefully late when I got back. I didn't want to wake you."

"You should have, I like hearing your voice, and then I would have closed my eyes and dreamed of you." Without any more preamble, I said, "Ridge, Sophie and I are doing a bookshop exchange. I'm going to Paris! Tomorrow . . ."

I heard the bed creak. He must have sat up abruptly. "What?" The word came out short and sharp.

Probably a lot for him to take in at a quarter to midnight. "Yes, it's sudden, and unlike me, but spontaneity is good, right?" That's what I kept trying to tell myself at any rate. Maybe it was a characteristic that could be learned.

"Sarah . . . you're leaving *tomorrow?* And you're telling me now?"

I frowned. "Well, I've been trying to call you . . ."

"Sorry," he said with a groan. "It's just a shock.

47

Your bookshop . . . you said you'd never leave it. I've asked you so many times to join me on an assignment and you've always said no."

"That's different, Ridge. You're working, and dashing here and there. I'd be in your way. Besides we always said we'd go to Paris one day, and this is our chance. I trust Sophie with my bookshop, she knows how I feel about it better than anyone because she feels the same about hers."

His voice softened. "Of course. I'm a jerk . . . you took me by surprise, that's all. Let's start this conversation again. You're leaving tomorrow. And what . . . you take over Sophie's shop as soon as you get there?"

Outside, stars twinkled in the blue-black night. "That's the plan. I'll leave a list of instructions for Sophie. Missy's going to drive me to the airport, and I'll get on my first ever plane!" I felt like a child on Christmas Eve. Without the anchor of my friends, my town, who would I be?

He blew out a breath. "How can you . . . ah . . . do you need . . . ."

I smiled. It was always awkward when we discussed money. Ridge, ever the hero, wanted to help out when I had financial woes, but I wouldn't allow it. "Sophie is paying me a small wage, because she claims her shop will be so busy, there won't be a minute for me to rest, let alone read. In return, she will treat her visit to

Ashford like a holiday, and enjoy the deadly quiet that is my bookshop these days. She will live at my place, and drive my car, and vice versa."

"So, after Indonesia, I'll join you there?" The question in his voice took me by surprise.

I rolled onto my back, and ran a hand through my hair. "Of course! We're going to stroll to the Arc de Triomphe. Meander through the Louvre. Read in the Luxembourg Gardens . . ." There was so much to see and do in the short time Ridge would be there, and I knew our desire to be wrapped around each other would take over. But part of me delighted in the fact that I'd have months to meander through Paris, and discover who I was when I was out of my comfort zone. It was all at once thrilling, and scary, in an electrifying way.

He let out a guttural moan. "You, me, and a bottle of Côtes du Rhône. In the birthplace of French panties."

I giggled at the lusty hint in his voice. "*And* French kissing."

He gasped. "How am I going to wait so long to see you? Remind me again why I'm in some musty hotel a million miles away from you?"

I laughed. "Because you're a workaholic. As much as I love reading you love writing, so what can I say?" What a pair we made. When Ridge worked, head bent over his laptop, I snuggled next to him on the sofa, happy to read the day away, content in being close to him, the silence a comfort as we both did what we loved best.

I'd had sporadic relationships in the past, where the guys in question didn't understand my voracious need to read. Some called it a waste, or said I lived in a perpetual daydream. Others implied that my bookworm state made me almost catatonic. The clamor of the death knell rang out loud and clear in my mind when they'd talked like that and I'd sworn off men unless I found a guy who loved me for who I was, foibles and all.

Ridge was happy to snuggle alongside me, and do his own thing, and also spent a fair amount of time with his nose pressed in a book, so I thanked my lucky stars for that.

"True," he said. "But lately . . . that buzz, it's waning. Work takes me from you, it's sort of like this annoying kid brother I have to humor."

"Well, how about when you get to Paris, you just say *no* when the next big story gets waved in front of you?" He wouldn't though. It was too hard to resist—a new place, a fresh twist, the way he'd spin the story. I respected him for the way he worked, his ethics. Intrinsically, he wanted to do the right thing, report honestly, when so many others concocted a headline that would sell, not a headline with the truth. Ridge had integrity, and was building a name for himself because of it.

"I promise, Sarah. When I get to Paris, it's you and me, for a few weeks at least. Enough time that you'll get sick of me, and push me to go back to work."

"Yeah right, Romeo. Just try me."

I wanted to clutch his hand while we strolled along the cobbled streets of Paris, the wind whipping my hair around, while Ridge whispered sweet nothings to me. The river Seine flowing languidly beside us as we walked without purpose, perhaps stumbling into the warmth of a bistro, where sensual French chatter would wash over me making me feel like I was living inside my own dreams.

"Oh, I plan to try everything, at least once."

I smiled into the quiet of the night. "Good . . . I need a tour guide after all, and you're the man for the job." Ridge had spent a few summers in Paris, working for a French newspaper. He spoke the language fluently, and knew a lot about the city.

"Tour guide?" he said huskily. "You're not going to see much except the inside of the bedroom, for the first few days at least."

My lips parted in anticipation. "I'm going to hold you to that."

"Fly safe, and call me when you arrive?" he said.

"You too. Be careful in Indonesia."

"I love you, Sarah Smith."

"And I you, Ridge Warner."

Before dawn draped its golden orange ribbons

across the sky, I was at my bookshop, enjoying the quiet, relishing the long goodbye. The lull before the town awoke. Soft yellow lamp light spilled through the shop, the novels basked sleepily in the warm glow.

Leaving my books would be like leaving a piece of me behind. Just the thought made me catch my breath, as though I'd done something audacious even considering it. I ran my fingers over their covers, murmuring farewells. How many would be missing when I returned? Their voyage into someone's home, someone's life, completed without me. There'd be no time to wish them well.

There was a slight rustle, a whisper-quiet mewling. I pivoted, hoping to catch a book moving, but I was too late. The stacks stood solemnly, fat with pride and perhaps a touch of melancholy. Did they sense I was leaving? I wanted to lock the front door, and let them all languish until I returned . . .

Would Sophie's shop be this alive? With stacks of leather-bound books peeking from a wooden shelf so high, I'd need a ladder to investigate? Or hidden hutches piled with old letters and diaries, penned by some of the writers who'd escaped from their lives and scribbled away there, their words flowing in such a famous place. Would I arrive and hear whispers from the past? The murmur of authors long since gone from this world? Their ghostlike presence hovering in the place they wrote their very last masterpiece. The place they were happiest—a haven for word lovers.

I wanted that . . . that feeling of being wholly alive, surrounded by like-minded souls. Bibliophiles who reread a book because it was so damn good—it had become a friend, one you turned to for comfort. The intimacy, the quiet, where words washed over you and made you smile again.

And to befriend other bookworms whose lives were left in tatters after falling in love with a fictional character. Unable to eat or sleep, and sad that you'd never met *him,* because he wasn't real, except in your mind. But you still looked for him in the faces of people on the street anyway, you'd recognize him anywhere. It would take weeks, sometimes years to stop yearning for that character who'd virtually jumped from the page and smothered you with kisses. Would I find people like that in the bookshop on the Left Bank where the cherry trees stood?

With a nervous flutter in my belly, I said goodbye to my books, and silently wished them well, hoping that if a customer stumbled upon them while I was absent they'd be cherished.

THREE

The sun bobbed in the blue sky, making me squint. For October, it was warmer than I'd expected, more so than Ashford. It was as though the city of love had pulled out all the stops on my first morning here. The air was fragrant with promise. I rifled through my backpack, searching for sunglasses. My face was split with a cheesy grin.

I was really here! Paris!

And so far, I'd hadn't been snatched, mugged, or even scammed, as Mom had warned me about four million times before she kissed me goodbye. Rolling my suitcase along, stifling a yawn, I made my way to a ticket booth to ask where the train station was.

I had to catch the RER train to central Paris, but I'd been swept along in a throng of people, and unsure of which way I was meant to go. Somehow I'd ended up outside, and couldn't contain my joy. I wanted to jump in the air, kick my heels together, and screech *Bonjour, France!* Instead, I smiled and trundled forward. Fatigue tried to catch me, I'd stayed awake for most of the flight, as excitement pulsed through my veins, making sleep impossible. I shook the lethargy away, promising myself a nap before starting at the bookshop. The time difference made my head spin—but I was here, and that was the only thing that mattered.

A raven-haired woman, chewing gum in the same repetitive pattern, *click, blow, pop,* eyed me with feigned disinterest as I approached the counter. *"Oui?"* she said.

I dropped my backpack to the floor, and leaned close to the glass.

I hastily found the train timetable, and pointed. *"Où est . . . ?"* Where is . . . how did you say train station? I flipped through my French phrase book.

Before I could find it, she popped her gum and said in English, "The train station is that way." She looked over my shoulder to the next person, signaling she was finished with me. I wanted to laugh, she was so French!

"Merci beaucoup," I thanked her, feeling foolish that my accent was so jarring compared to the words that fell from her tongue in a silky cadence.

Hefting my backpack on, I wheeled my suitcase in front and made my way to the platform. The sign was a maze of different colored lines crisscrossing all over the place. *Shoot.* It was a complicated web. How on earth would I pick the right one? I'd expected one freaking train! My research hadn't stretched to public transport, and again the size of the place hit home.

Overhead on the PA a French voice rang out, announcing something, but speaking so quickly I couldn't untangle the words. I blew out a breath. Maybe Sophie's French lessons wouldn't be enough here—unless people spoke to me like I was a five-year-old, with laboriously slow enunciation. Behind me people hurried along, bumping into me and jostling me out of the way. A train approached, its motor screeching, and brakes grinding, so loud it was like a drawn-out scream. I turned in fright, but no one took any notice. Openmouthed, I watched crowds exit the newly arrived train, and others elbow their way on, in one big gorging mass of bodies, and bulky accoutrements.

As fast as a click of fingers the doors shushed closed, and the train was off again. I double blinked. Why was everyone in such a hurry? Where did they all come from? One minute the station was empty, then full of bustling bodies, then empty again. Somehow I had to pick the right train to head into central Paris, and then squeeze into the damn thing.

Could I push my way forcefully like everyone else including grappling with my heavy suitcase and backpack? Why did I smuggle so many books into my bag? The weight of them slowed me right down, despite the wheels on the bottom of my case. It's not like I was going to a place bereft of books! I couldn't face some of my favorites being sold, though, and had taken one, then two, then a stack of them, just in case. They were my talismans, a reminder of my shop.

When the next train arrived, I gave myself a silent pep talk, and mimicked the people ahead of me, lunging myself and suitcase onto the train with a cry of *eee!* When the doors closed, I surveyed my limbs; all intact! I hadn't been snatched, mugged, scammed, and now I could add hadn't been squashed to death on the train. I was one step away from potentially booking a trek up the Himalayas . . . *Settle down, Sarah. You've been here all of five minutes.* My bucket list was a little fanciful for a newbie tourist, I must admit.

Eventually the crowd thinned, and I snagged a seat. I pushed my face against the glass, and tried to calm the erratic beat of my heart. Since I was a little girl, I'd dreamed of visiting Paris, and here it was before me—breathtaking, glorious, and everything I imagined. Apartments as far as the eye could see, window boxes with bright red flowers spilling out, like lackadaisical smiles. White shutters were flung open to welcome soft sunshine inside. Cars zoomed up roads. Abbeys were dotted here and there, their gothic facades awe-inspiring. I was goggle-eyed with the beauty surrounding me.

The city sprawled in every direction; even though I'd spent many a night dreaming of Paris, and gawping at photos, I hadn't expected this. The sheer enormity of what I'd done gave me pause, and I was proud of myself, for the first time in ages, for leaping from the monotony of my life and doing something that scared me.

The train sped on. Graffiti scribbles marred brickwork on a row of identical apartments, in front a cluster of elderly women held shopping bags, long skinny baguettes poked their heads out, eavesdropping on their chatter.

Between buildings, I saw snatches of it. The metal gleamed under the sunlight like the fingers of God were pointing to it, showing me the way. It was so much bigger than I'd expected, its middle higher than the tallest buildings, as it stretched for the clouds. The Eiffel Tower, the heart and soul of Paris. A young woman standing near me inclined her head closer to the window; like Sophie, she was coiffed to perfection, her barely there makeup expertly applied. I felt unkempt in comparison, and nervously ran a hand through my hair.

"First time in Paris?"

"*Oui*," I said, darting a glance back at the Eiffel Tower. It was magnificent, the way it stood proudly in the center of the city. I couldn't wait to see it up close. It would dwarf me—what an architectural marvel.

She gripped onto the handrail above, as we shimmied along with the rocking of the train. "Go to the Sacre Coeur for a good view of the whole city, and then you'll see how truly *magnifique* La Tour Eiffel is. Lots of steps to get there, but worth it." Her voice was almost musical, sensual. I didn't think I'd ever tire of the way French people spoke, whether it was in their native tongue or heavily accented English.

"*Merci*," I said, giving her a shy smile, knowing my accent must have sounded brash compared to hers. "There's so much to see and do. I can't wait." I fell back into English, feeling less inhibited with my own language. Though I'd promised myself to try and speak as much French as possible, when it came time to speak, I was embarrassed; I sounded clunky and disjointed compared to the lovely lilt surrounding me. The words that fell from commuters' lips were almost poetic.

"Find the real Paris," she said, fluttering her hand toward the window. "Away from the tourist spots. Look for the forgotten avenues. They're full of hidden gems." And with that she spun on her heel, leaving me with only the citrusy scent of her perfume.

What would I discover in lost laneways, and veiled gardens? So many literary greats had lived and loved here, and stepping where they once did thrilled me in a way I'd never felt before. I wanted to wander until I was lost, find fresh food markets, take a boat cruise, run my fingers along

spines in the Bibliothèque national de France—
the grand old library of Paris . . . exactly the kind
of place where secrets abound, if only you search
hard enough.

The train slowed. Passengers stood, pushing
forward to the doors, the usual frenzy ensued.
With a deep breath, I slung on my backpack and
grabbed the handle of my case, ready to jump off.
It was like being in the middle of a rugby scrum.
When the doors slid open, I jostled and shrieked
my way out, onto the dank, dim platform, not
caring I was drawing wary glances from other
passengers with my yodel-like squeal.

Whoop! I resisted the urge to fist pump, and
instead took a few lungfuls of Parisian air. I
was smiling like a loon, but I couldn't curb it.
A meek, shy bookworm from a small town had
navigated her way to the heart of Paris without
getting lost once! It was worth celebrating, so I
promised myself a big glass of sauvignon blanc
later that night.

Dragging my suitcase, I followed the lead of
the other commuters, shaking my head in awe.
It was one thing to dream about Paris and quite
another to actually be here. Fatigue was trying its
hardest to slow me down, but I shrugged it off,
wanting to see everything at once and soak up
every single Parisian thing.

Outside I glanced at the view ahead, and then
my map. My heart sank. Wasn't there supposed to

be a bridge? Frowning, and being gently nudged when people rushed past, I swayed and sighed as I took in my surroundings. I'd gone the wrong way, or had I? The Eiffel Tower . . . Somehow I'd ended up in what looked like an industrial part of Paris.

The sunshine dimmed, as though it was disappointed in me, as I tried to make sense of my map. The train had been an adventure, but I wasn't too keen to get back on it. It would take some getting used to, all that rushing and the threat of plunging into the gap between platform and carriage.

My feet ached from the shoes Missy insisted I wear. Note to self: travel in comfortable footwear next time. I was a ballet flats kind of girl, and the wedged boots—which Missy had demanded I teeter in—had taken their toll.

No one will guess you're American! she'd exclaimed. As though in order to be accepted here, I'd have to first fool them that I was French, and that could only be done by wearing the right shoes. I smiled, remembering the conversation. My heart tugged for my friends who were so far away, not only in miles, but in spirit. Would I find friends here? I couldn't imagine anyone being as lively and animated as the girls, but I hoped I was wrong. I didn't want to spend months here pining for them and the only way around that would be to mingle, and pretend I was a chatty, outgoing explorer. It was time to stop hiding, and start participating in real life.

I glanced up. The sky was different here; it was smudged white and baby blue, and somehow brighter, more vivid than Ashford. The air was richer, sweet and pungent, and wholly new.

Right, there was no more time to dither. *"Excusez-moi?"* I said to a woman pushing a stroller. She glared at me and kept going. I tried again with a young man, who shook his head, phone jammed against his ear, and pointed to the train. I tried not to take it personally, everyone was busy. I was due at Once Upon a Time; in fact, I was overdue. Mild panic set in, as I pictured myself catching trains back and forth, and never getting anywhere. Gulping, I grabbed the suitcase handle and spun to go back to the station, but instead banged heads with a man passing by. I clutched my forehead, eyes watering with the sting of the collision. "Oh, my God, I'm so sorry," I mumbled, wanting to dissolve into the pavement.

His eyes were scrunched closed. He blinked a few times, and then gazed at me. "American?" he asked.

The shoes hadn't fooled him. "Yes, is it so obvious?"

"You spoke English," he said, "with an American accent."

Kill me now. "Right. I did. Sorry about the bump." There was a small red mark where we'd collided. I'd certainly made a mark on Paris, or more specifically, Parisians.

He waved me away. Embarrassment made my cheeks flush, and now that I had someone to ask directions, I wasn't brave enough to. He must think I was some kind of village idiot. His lips turned up, as if he was amused by me. Which no doubt he was in an *I'm-laughing-at-you,* not *with-you,* way.

"Are you OK now?" he asked, as if the bump on the head dazed me.

"*Oui.* I'm fine."

Super.

Peachy.

Lost.

He tilted his head. "Where are you going?"

I forced a smile, all the while wondering if he was about to snatch me. Why was he so nice, when everyone else wouldn't give me the time of day? Was he going to try and snaffle me into a taxi? How exactly did someone pinch a person in broad daylight? Would he take my bags too? If I was going to be abducted, I'd still like to read. Scenes from the movie *Taken* flashed in my mind. I shook my head to dislodge them.

"Don't look so afraid," he said, laughing. "I'm not going to kidnap you!"

A kidnapper wouldn't mention kidnapping, surely? My mother had a lot to answer for, putting this crazy fear into me.

"That's a relief." I relaxed my shoulders. "I'm trying to head into central Paris . . . but the maps, there's so many different lines."

Running a hand through the gray shock of his hair, he chuckled, like he encountered this kind of thing every day. "You've gone the wrong way. Go back to the platform, but catch the train from the other side." My face fell. "It's OK. You'll get lost many more times. The trick is, to embrace the drama of it all." And with that he bid me *adieu*, his wise eyes sparkling, as though he'd been sent to stop me from feeling sorry for myself. Didn't I say I wanted to get lost? And here I was. Lost in Paris. *Check!* And not kidnapped! *Check!*

Feeling adventurous, I dragged my bags and myself to the front of a little bistro, with red cane chairs that faced the busy road. A glass of *vin blanc* would give me some liquid courage to face the manic train dance again.

A waiter with a flirty smile walked over.

"*Bonjour. Oui, madame?*"

I smiled. It was the accent, especially pouring from the lips of someone resembling a male model who'd just stepped from the front cover of a magazine. With as much confidence as I could muster I said, "*Bonjour, un vin blanc, merci.*" The first thing Sophie had taught me was how to order wine. She must have known it'd come in handy.

"One white wine, of course," he said and

64

winked before walking away. I resisted the urge to giggle. *He winked.* My friends would be rolling on the floor by now, pointing and gesticulating at his retreating back. I felt very sophisticated sitting alone, in some unidentified quarter of Paris. If only my friends could see me now.

FOUR

My mouth hung open when I gazed at the building before me. *once upon a time,* the sign read, which was pinned to the top of the building, weathered and faded. I'd seen countless photos, and Sophie had taken her laptop out the front when we Skyped to show me the facade and the view of the Seine. But seeing it in real life—its faded sepia brick, with the murky tea-colored river across the road—was something else entirely. The way the building leaned softly, as if time and the elements had warped it.

Time slowed, while I gawped in every direction. A world of accents chattering away only just registered. There was the scent of the Seine; earthy, fathomless. The bustle of waiters at a busy bistro, glasses clinking together, the *tink* of cutlery on plates. Shielding my eyes from the glare of their white shirts, and silver trays held aloft, I spun, taking in the three-hundred-and-sixty-degree view, like a panorama.

Cars honked and parked in spots that looked far too small, their expert drivers negotiating the tight space, without much maneuvering. Along the sidewalk was a cluster of cherry trees; naked without their perfumed blossoms. They stood tall and proud like watchmen out front. Off to the side of the shop was a little wooden house, on stilts like a letterbox, filled with picture books and marked with a hand-painted sign that read *kids' library*. A line of children waited patiently for their turn to open the tiny glass door and select a preloved book. Behind them, parents snapped shots of the Notre Dame looming in the distance, or the Pont Saint-Michel to the right. Others held maps, their faces scrunched in concentration.

I laughed at the sheer craziness of it all. It was so *busy!* I was like a dot in the jumble of people going about the business of living.

Turning back to the bookshop, I stepped closer and peeked in the window. It was just as I imagined; dark wooden shelves wound to the ceiling, books were double stacked, the ones higher up were beige with dust. On the main floor, rickety old tables bowed with the weight of colorful new editions.

A towering pile of the latest bestsellers were displayed by the front door in an unapologetic heap. Which books would sell best here? I couldn't wait to find out. In Ashford, romance was my biggest genre, the women in my small town kept me afloat with their purchases of sweeping love stories. Would it be the same here, in the city known for romance and passion? I hoped so. I could usually tell what genre a person favored after a quick once-over and a study of their mannerisms—it was a gift I was proud of, and I delighted in pairing up a book with its owner.

Somewhere above was Sophie's apartment, and the thought of a quick snooze on crisp sheets was too tempting to resist. I'd say a quick hello to the staff, and then sleep. Adventures would be so much better once I'd rested. I studiously avoided gawping into the window of the *fromagerie* next door, out of loyalty to my friend. I'd be living on French cheese—that much was certain, but I wouldn't buy it there, lest it taste like despair.

I pushed open the door of Once Upon a Time, and got stuck in a crowd of people. "Sorry, can I just get . . ." No one would move an inch to let me past. I didn't think they could see me, or hear me, amid the chaos. "Excuse me," I said, my words fluttering above unheard.

Sophie had said to find Oceane, a French girl who'd worked here for years, and she would show me to the apartment, and instruct me on exactly what I needed to do for the bookshop.

On tiptoe, I tried to find the counter. It was stifling inside with so many bodies. How did Sophie cope with so many fingers touching her books? A man in front picked one up and flipped it carelessly open. I winced when I heard the crack of its spine as it split. It took all my might not to snatch the book from his hands. I supposed it would be just as hard letting books go here as it was at home, though this might be tenfold worse, by the size of the crowds. "Umm, can you please let me past?" No response. Damn it to hell, being five foot nothing!

Off to the right there was a small nook, the right size for my suitcase, so I wheeled it in, squished my backpack on top, and draped my jacket over it. Determined, I elbowed my way to the counter, through the mass of slow-moving traffic, yelling cries of "Sorry. Excuse me." Golly, it was hard to breathe. Finally, I found some space near the counter, and fell against it, making a mental note to wear bright clothes, and maybe carry a megaphone next time.

A girl with fiery red curls stood serving customers, stamping the inside of their books with the famous Once Upon a Time logo.

The queue, long and snakelike, drifted right back to the dark recesses of the shop. Sophie had given me a rundown on the staff, but the journey had been a long one, and my mind blanked. What were their names?

"I'm Beatrice," the redheaded girl said without glancing up. "You must be Sarah." Her tone was flat, almost neutral, and she had a posh British accent.

Customers frowned as they were ignored. Where were the rest of the staff? I was momentarily distracted by a crystal vase that displayed long-stemmed roses so vividly red and fragrant that I had to pause and sniff them as their scent twirled in the air. "I've never seen such beautiful flowers . . ." Even the petals smelled love-red.

Beatrice gave me a half smile. "Americans aren't as subtle as the French with their declarations of love."

Was that a dig? "What does . . ." My voice petered off. Nestled among the blooms was a tiny envelope with my name on it. Ridge! I hastily ripped it open, heart racing, and speed-read it so I could get back to Beatrice and then dash upstairs for a nap.

Sarah Smith,
I can't wait to whisper to you in French, the wind carrying my words away, as we wander in the rain through forgotten avenues of Paris.
Oceans may separate us but know you're in my heart, now and always.
Je t'aime,
Ridge

That guy. Little fireworks exploded inside my heart that he'd think of something so sweet for my arrival in Paris. He always knew what to do and say when I most needed it. I put the card in my pocket knowing I'd reread it until the words smudged. The anticipation of Ridge arriving soon was almost too much to bear, so I blanked my expression and focused on Beatrice. The line was growing by the second. There was no sign of any other staff.

"Do you have anyone else here to help?" I asked, gazing around thinking maybe they were stacking shelves, and could be called to help.

Beatrice pulled a face. "Oceane is sick, or so she says. Convenient, since Sophie isn't here. She was probably up all night with her latest conquest and has a cracking champagne headache. TJ floats in later, and that leaves you. Mind serving?" She spoke with a hint of annoyance, but her smile softened it.

"Sure, I'll help," I said, as airily as I could. I rolled up my sleeves, and went behind the counter, trying to push the vision of a nice comfortable bed away. Once we'd caught up with the queue I could escape for a few hours, and bliss out in bed, mouth hanging open as I snored my way to slumber. The flight had been too exciting to miss one single second, but I regretted now that I hadn't forced myself to rest at least some of the journey.

Rookie travel mistake number 234.

"*Oui?*" I said, to the tall, thin man next in line.

"I've been waiting over an hour to be served," he said, and drew his mouth into a tight line.

"Sorry," I mumbled. Not the best start. "Let me ring these up for you," I hastily added, trying my level best to ignore his scowl.

He blinked rapidly down his spectacles at me, and handed over three books, keeping his palm over the cover to hide the title. Lots of people did the same thing. They didn't want to be judged on their reading habits, so as swiftly as I could, I took the bundle and bagged them, taking note of the price on the inside page. My face remained neutral, but inside I smiled. Even Paris wasn't immune to the popularity of *Fifty Shades of Grey*.

"For my wife," he said, hastily licking his lips, his eyes darting around.

"How sweet." I took his money and made change, knowing Sophie would probably be happy one more set of the trilogy was sold. Even in sleepy Ashford, I'd been inundated with requests to swap the trilogy for other books once people had read them, and in the end, I had to turn people away, or my shop would have been full of the erotic novels. I was glad their popularity made so many people rediscover their love of reading again.

He blushed. "She just wants to see what all the fuss is about . . . late to the party, but still."

I gave him a benevolent smile. They were definitely for him. "I hope she enjoys them. If not, there are plenty of other books here that I'll be happy to recommend."

"I'll keep that in mind," he said, taking the bag. "I mean . . . I'll let her know that." I tried to decipher his accent, maybe Australian? Once

Upon a Time stocked mainly English books, and only had a small French section.

"Happy reading," I said, watching him retreat fast as if he was carrying something illegal. Readers and their quirks never failed to amuse me.

Glad he'd softened about the wait, I said more confidently to the next customer, *"Oui?* Can I help you?" A ponytailed mom blew escaped strands of hair from her face. She grappled with a chubby baby, who was shrieking and trying his best to escape her arms. Somehow, she managed to free a bottle from the bag over her shoulder and said, in a desperate American accent, "Can I please heat his bottle?" The baby let out a scream so loud, Beatrice scowled and covered her ears.

"Err . . ." Heat up a bottle? Did we even have a kitchen here?

I turned to Beatrice for guidance. She pursed her lips, before saying to me, "This is a bookshop . . . we sell *books.* You know, things you read?"

I blanched at her sharp tone and was mortified for the mother in front of me. Traveling with a baby must have been tough. A small giggle escaped Beatrice, as if she was joking, but it certainly hadn't come across that way.

I whispered to her, "Is there a kitchen here? Maybe she can just pop in and use the microwave?" People fidgeted in line behind, sighing, and becoming impatient with the wait.

"Afraid not." Beatrice smiled at the woman, but it didn't seem to reach her eyes. "It's only for staff. Sophie's rules."

I blushed crimson. If this were Ashford the bottle would have been heated up, the mom given a cup of tea, and the baby snatched by someone for a cuddle. This wasn't right, ignoring a person in need. I deflated a little, as a headache from the earlier glass of wine, and the bedlam in front of me, loomed. My new adventure paled a little.

"I'm so sorry," I said to the woman, torn about what I could do. Behind her, the queue of people grew impatient, glancing at watches, and sighing, or outright mumbling *hurry up*.

"So this is when you say, 'Next,' " Beatrice said, her voice sugary. Surely I could tell Beatrice to march to the kitchen and heat the bottle up? But the queue was growing, and in my exhausted haze, I was unsure of my footing.

"Maybe you can try the bistro a few doors down?" I bit down on my lip, hoping the young mom wouldn't get upset.

"Yeah, thanks for nothing," she muttered and shot Beatrice a glare.

I said sorry to the woman, as she scrunched her face in anger, and spun on her heel. Then I turned to Beatrice and said quietly, "I feel for her."

"Why?" Beatrice knitted her brow. "This isn't a little fairy-tale village, Sarah. This is Paris, and a *very* busy bookshop. People here will try everything they can to take advantage. You'll see. It might sound harsh, but we have to follow certain rules or else we'll be overrun."

A little fairy-tale village? "I see," I said, but didn't really. Beatrice spoke calmly and confidently, but it was as though she was speaking down to me. Maybe I was reading too much into it, or being a touch sensitive. Of course there must have been certain rules and regulations here. Sophie was a very organized person.

Ridge's love-red roses were almost like a hug, their half-open buds like a countdown, and I only hoped when they bloomed maybe he'd be here.

The next customer approached, an athletic guy with sandy blonde hair. "I'm looking for some books about orchids." He took a piece of paper from his pocket and read the title.

"Upstairs," Beatrice said, pointing.

"Do you have that book though?" he asked.

"Only one way to find out," Beatrice said. "Trundle upstairs and take a look."

He frowned.

"I'll go," I said and brushed past her.

"Don't make a habit of it," she tutted. "We don't have time for that."

I double blinked. *No time to help them find books?* Just what kind of bookshop was this? "I'll be fast," I said, bamboozled by the ethics here. It was obviously busy, so if the other staff hadn't arrived for whatever reason, why hadn't she called for backup? I couldn't imagine telling a customer to go find his own book if he specifically asked for a title.

I had no idea which rooms housed what genres, but I did know the conservatory on the top floor was where the horticulture books were kept, because Sophie had mentioned it to me once before. It was her favorite room, and the place she sat at night to watch the Eiffel Tower sparkle under the moonlight.

I dashed up the rickety stairs, and went down a hallway, following hand-painted arrows that pointed the way for each different room. Once we reached the conservatory, I quickly found the orchid section.

The guy ran a hand through his hair, slightly puffed from rushing up the stairs two at a time behind me. After a quick flick through dusty old tomes, I found a selection of books about orchids, including the one he'd asked for. "Thanks," he said. "I'd never have found my way up here. This place is a lot bigger than it looks from the front."

"It is," I agreed, "and you're welcome."

He took the proffered books, and bounded back downstairs with a wave.

Hands on hips, I paused to catch my breath. My heart was hammering from the pace and the confusing start to my time here. The conservatory was aptly named, sunlight filtered in from a glass ceiling, which connected to the picture window that overlooked Paris. It was like being in a dream, the room luminescent with light, landing on the books in soft shards, making them almost ethereal, as they lounged in the glow of weak sunlight.

I started. In the corner, like a penumbra, a man sat hunched over a laptop. I hadn't seen him sitting there, in the only spot the sun didn't seem to shine. It was like he was trying to be invisible, back turned to the view outside of the Notre Dame in the distance, staring at his screen silently. I thought it better not to disturb him, but darted a quick glance as I edged out of the room. His side profile, blonde hair, blue eyes, full lips, seemed familiar somehow, but I couldn't place him. Stretching his arms, he turned to me, catching me staring. We exchanged nods, and I rushed back into the hallway. With one last centering breath, I headed back into the fray, worried to see the line was longer, and that still only Beatrice was serving.

Evening fell, and I hadn't managed to steal away for a nap. The customers eventually slowed to a trickle. I yawned and stretched, numbed from the unexpectedly long day, and ready to crawl into bed. My legs were jelly-like from exhaustion, and I longed for sleep.

I'd known Sophie's bookshop was busy, a hive of activity, but I hadn't expected high-pitched chatter, and incessant queues. It was more like a book factory: *wrap book, take money, point them in the direction of the nearest public toilet, make change, repeat.* Some customers were surly, others awed to be in such a beautiful bookshop, and they lingered, not wanting their visit to end.

Beatrice tossed her hair, and stretched her arms high above. "I hope I didn't come across badly," she said, with an amiable smile. "It's just that we have to follow protocol for things to run smoothly."

Smoothly? That was the worst kind of chaos I'd ever stepped into. I'd wanted to ask about the lack of staff, but thought it best to tackle the big questions the next day when my brain was firing on all cylinders. I was so bone-tired, my words would probably fall out in a garbled mess. "We can chat tomorrow, properly. You can fill me in on the things I need to know," I said.

An ebony-haired guy crept into the bookshop. He was shadow thin and fidgety. He nodded to Beatrice, and was rewarded with an eye roll from her. His black suit was crinkled and frayed at the hems, like he wore it a lot.

"Finally, he's here," Beatrice said, her voice sharp.

"Poor Beatrice," he said, real concern in his voice. "Rolling her eyes to make sure her brain is still there. Find it this time, did you, dearie?"

What now? A rift among the staff? Sophie had

told me that there were often petty squabbles, and I'd have to really pull them into line to make this place run efficiently. But did they snipe at each other just for the heck of it?

Beatrice crossed her arms, and said, "Go write some unpublishable poetry. Oh, wait . . . you already have." She smirked, and tossed her red curls once more.

My shoulders slumped a few degrees south. My lofty dreams of hanging out at the bookshop chatting about favorite novels were in tatters. Where was the booklovers' paradise I'd imagined? Us curled up on crinkly leather sofas, talking into the early hours of the morning about writers we adored, novels that changed our lives? I could fix it, I was sure of it, by injecting some fun into the monotony of day-to-day bookshop life.

"You must be TJ?" I said, holding my hand out. He had the tortured poet look perfected: mussed hair, perpetual frown, and secretive, dark eyes. His disheveled appearance was compelling, as though he lost himself in the business of living, and didn't bother about anything else. I recognized that attribute in myself too. Many a time, I wandered from my reading cocoon, hair a bird's nest, cheek with a thick pillow wrinkle, dazed, as my world had changed once again because of a book that had taken me on a journey, depositing me back on earth with a *bang* once I was done.

TJ cocked his head, and surveyed me for the longest time. "Sarah Smith. Romance reader. Book blogger. Owner of The Bookshop on the Corner. Twenty-nine. Loves metaphors. Hates mushrooms. Believes in love at first sight. Dates a roving reporter who resembles a Mills & Boon cover model, but that's not the only reason she loves him. Yes?"

My eyebrows shot up. "Umm, yes . . . ?"

His gave me an impish grin that made him look almost boyish. "How do I know? I'm a details man . . ."

"Stalker, more like," Beatrice interjected.

He flicked a hand to dismiss her. "Thanks for your input, Beatrice." His words poured out honeyed with sarcasm. He pasted on a smile, and took a notebook from his satchel. "Now if we're all caught up, I have some unpublishable poetry to write. I'll lock up, Sarah."

I yawned. "That's music to my ears. I haven't slept since yesterday. Can you point me in the direction of Sophie's apartment?"

TJ leaned over the counter, opened a drawer and took a bunch of keys out. "These are for the apartment, and the gold ones are for the bookshop," he said. "Go up the stairs, third door down is Sophie's apartment. Do you need help with your bags?"

"Thanks, TJ, but I can manage." I only wanted to shower and sleep. There'd be ample time to get to know everyone tomorrow. Though I was dead curious to find out their stories and how they found their way to Once Upon a Time, it would have to wait. "I guess I'll see you both tomorrow?" I went to the front door, to the little gap where I'd stashed my bag and backpack— only to find my jacket in a crumpled heap on the carpet. I spun around, searching the entryway desperately, but there were only books, no bags. *No!*

"What is it?" TJ said. "You've gone lily white."

I rubbed my hands over my face, hoping I'd wake up from a bad dream and find my things where I left them. "They're gone! My suitcase and my backpack. My passport!" I groaned.

TJ loped over, and surveyed the empty spot where my jacket lay like an empty promise. "Are you sure someone didn't move it?"

We both looked to Beatrice who shrugged. "This is what I meant by people taking advantage. It's why I'm tough with the customers. Sorry, Sarah, but this just proves my point."

A strangled hiccup escaped me. TJ rubbed my back. This was the never-ending day from hell. It was impossible to believe it was still my first day in Paris. It had been interminable. Bag snatch, check. Heck, I hoped my mother wasn't right. Was this a sign of things to come?

"Go upstairs," he said. "Use Sophie's phone. You'll have to report it all missing, I guess. Not that you have any hope of it being returned." His voice was soft with empathy.

I frowned. Bed was still out of reach. It was my own damn stupidity, I'd have to spend the next hour on the phone. *Way to go, Sarah.*

With heavy legs, I stomped up the stairs fighting tears. Paris was supposed to be perfect. A magical, romantic city where I'd discover a whole new me. Maybe I wasn't great at driving my own life outside of Ashford. I'd made a mess of things. Money, credit cards, passport—gone. That would make the coming weeks difficult when it came time to, you know, eat. And my suitcase, my precious books—gone. Clothing—gone. The only pair of shoes I'd have now were the borrowed clodhoppers on my feet, and the thought of lugging myself around on those all day in the store had me *and* my back at breaking point.

Why would I leave my bags right near the front door? I may as well have left a note on them saying: *steal me!* Back home we didn't even lock our houses at nighttime, but I had to learn quick smart I wasn't in Ashford any more.

Pushing open the door of Sophie's apartment, I lifted a little. It was an elegant space, pretty, and feminine and I knew I'd be comfortable. Grainy wooden floorboards were polished to a shine, a huge bed was made up with fresh white linen. A floor lamp lit the room from under its ruched vanilla shade. A bouquet of flowers scented the air sweet. Near the bed was a bookshelf that took up an entire wall; I was happy to note it was filled with romance books. I took in their titles, and anticipated making my way through them. Instead of diving into bed with a dusty well-read romance, I grabbed the phone and tried to sort out who I needed to call. My eyes were hanging out of my head by the time I hung up and fell into a deep sleep.

FIVE

The next morning, I woke groggily, forcing myself awake, fighting the need for a few more hours' shut-eye. My head spun like I was hungover from lack of rest. After a quick shower I pulled on the same wrinkled clothes I'd traveled in.

My travel insurance would replace the cost of my luggage, but it would take a couple of weeks for them to courier travelers' checks, at the earliest. *At the earliest?* I'd cried. Another travel fail; read the fine print.

I'd contacted the American embassy about my missing passport, and scheduled an appointment. I remembered what the elderly man on the street said, embrace the drama, so I tried to think of it all as part of the journey, and not that I was a hopeless, hapless tourist.

The bookshop was due to open, and there was no time to call Ridge or the girls—with the scattered time differences, I was sure they'd be asleep. What could I say anyway . . . *Hey, it's Sarah. In the first five minutes of my trip I've managed to lose everything you're supposed to lock away safe! You'd be so proud! I haven't been mugged, but the day is young! Au revoir!*

Time to switch on and become bookseller Sarah. That persona, I knew well.

With a liberal spray of Sophie's jasmine perfume, I headed downstairs, ready for another day. I was determined that I would handle things better, now that I'd had some sleep and I knew how hectic the shop floor was. Beatrice could show me the ropes, and hopefully a few more staff might materialize. There was something a little off about Beatrice, but she'd been under a huge amount of pressure in the busy shop. The back-and-forth with her and TJ might have been just the way they bantered. Who knew what friendships were like out of Ashford and beyond the pages of my books?

The stairs groaned underfoot as I rushed down into the maze of the bookstore. I couldn't wait to stumble around the nooks and crannies, and find some joy between the pages. The shop was layered with dark wooden shelves, which curved and bowed with the weight of books. There were lots of little hidey-holes, and I knew I'd find some treasures in among the disorderly piles. "*Bonjour!*" a sultry French voice greeted me as I made my way through the laneways.

When I stepped into the main room, the open lower level, a girl with cropped blonde hair and China blue eyes greeted me, giving me a gentle handshake. Her nails were manicured pale pink, and a spectacular diamond ring glinted under the lights. "*Désolé*, I heard all about the theft! I wish I'd been here to welcome you as promised. This is my fault. Beatrice should have warned you not to leave anything personal lying around. It only takes a second for things to disappear, as I guess you found out." She gave me a quick hug. "I'm Oceane. Do you need to borrow clothes? Money?"

She wore a tight knitted cobalt blue dress, and a cashmere cardigan. Her clothes screamed designer label, in a chic, classic French way. Compared to me, her outfit was downright glamorous, and I rued the fact I was wearing the same travel-wrinkled jeans and sweater.

"Thanks for the offer, but it's OK. I had some money in my jacket, which was thankfully left on the floor, and I'll make do with these clothes, or maybe borrow some of Sophie's until the insurance is paid." What if I spilled coffee down the front of one of her elegant outfits? Sophie's were just as elegant too. I cringed a little, picturing myself wearing something so form-fitting, and French, worried it would look like I was trying too hard to fit in. Oceane even walked differently, with an upright posture, poised as if she inhabited the space around her better than most.

She crossed her arms, and pulled a face as though she was annoyed at herself. "I feel responsible, I told Sophie I'd meet you and show you around. Why don't I treat you to a shopping trip later? Then I can show you where to do the banking, and where the post office is, so we can tie that in with a wander down the Champs-Élysées?"

After the disaster that was day one, Oceane's warmth was a godsend. "There's no need to do that," I protested. From my research I knew the boutiques along the Champs-Élysées were expensive, and I wouldn't let Oceane treat me because she felt guilty. The blame lay squarely at my feet.

She smiled. "Well, perhaps we'll window-shop until you're ready."

"Maybe," I said, laughing, relieved that she was open and friendly.

Outside, the sun was splintering the sky, the river lapped swiftly in the distance. After my shift I'd wander by the Seine and hunt out a pâtisserie or two. Or maybe take a book, and people-watch from one of the cafés along the avenue.

"Aside from the stolen bags, how was your first day in Paris?"

"Busy," I said, remembering the chaos of the previous day.

"It's always like that," she said, with a small laugh. "It takes a while to get used to the noise, and the tourists. I'm supposed to show you the office. It's where you'll do the paperwork, the wages, and all of those complex things that make my head throb."

My stomach knotted. Sophie had bombarded

me with emails about the paperwork side of things *after* I'd agreed to the bookshop exchange. She wanted weekly updates about the sales, and monthly profit and loss statements done. Besides all of that, there was the book ordering, the staff wages to do, and a stock take of the store at the end of December. Plus, I was responsible for her online shop and mailing whatever orders came from that. How on earth I could do all of it, and work in the shop during the day still concerned me.

I wasn't as mathematically inclined as her, but Sophie was very clear about increasing the sales, and keeping a close eye on the figures. From what I gathered from our flurry of emails, the cost of the building maintenance was frightfully expensive. Being such an old place, and the inevitable barrage of foot traffic, there was always something that needed to be fixed. Competition with other bookshops was fierce and her novels were priced lower to sell, leaving a dent on profits.

Budgets and sales projections made my brain hurt, but I'd have to learn how to do it, and make sure I didn't let my friend down.

"We're glad you're here," Oceane said. "I thought perhaps Beatrice would take the management position when Sophie announced she was leaving."

"Oh?" I asked, an uncomfortable coolness

running through me. Had I stepped on her toes, by taking the job she wanted?

Oceane nodded. "Sophie had mentioned a few times she wanted to slow down, let someone else take over. But, at the last minute she couldn't trust her baby to anyone. Except you."

My heart dropped, wondering how Sophie could have dangled it in front of Beatrice, and then given it to me. Is that why I detected a sharper undercurrent when Beatrice spoke? I'd have to see how she acted today, because I was here for the long haul. Sophie had even said if I wanted to stay indefinitely, I could. I had a lot to learn, and not much time to do it. Already, I adored the labyrinth-like rooms, the promise of adventures to be had.

"So, is Beatrice OK with me being here?" I didn't mention her abruptness the day before. There was obviously a system of doing things here, I just had to work it out.

"I'm sure she is. Just note that the staff will walk all over you, unless you're up-front. They can be merciless with new people, but we've never had a different boss before, so I really can't say how they'll act."

I had no staff, and never had, and hoped they'd be amenable to any changes my appearance made without making a fuss. The closest I'd come to confrontation was when the local book club dissolved into a heated argument, their opinions divided, and someone had to stand in and mediate. But I'd known those ladies my whole life, and all I had to do to calm them down was threaten to take the wine away.

Here they didn't know me though, and I was ready to inject some good old-fashioned fun into the workplace. My answer: team-building sessions! Sunday-night baseball at the gardens or something. I'd yet to work out the finer details. Apparently, big corporations did that to inspire their employees, make them collaborate as a team. It would be a great way for us to get to know each other, and I was sure it'd lead to a more harmonious working environment. We'd have staff meetings, and sit around a table so they could air their grievances. I felt like I had a secret up my sleeve and was well prepared for them. Perhaps trying new things would spark their enthusiasm once more.

Oceane surveyed the perfect shine of her nail polish. "The staff are young, determined in a way those Generation Z kids are without actually putting in the effort. It's just that sort of place. People come and go, Sophie only has one stipulation—that they love reading above all else. She can forgive them anything, as long as they read."

"OK," I said, confidently. Sophie mentioned a range of issues, but after reading *How To Be The Boss 101*, I was sure I could knock any drama on the head before it burst into trouble. Sophie was burnt out, and tired of refereeing. This exchange would help us both grow into different people, and I couldn't wait to get started.

Oceane took her jacket off and hung it on the coatrack behind the counter.

By the front door, a small queue was forming. I glanced at my watch, quarter to nine, almost time to open up and be caught in the rush of another day. "Where is Beatrice, I thought she was working today?" It was *at least* a three-person business. Just to keep an eye on the crowds, and replenish, and restack books would take a couple of people. Sometimes the line was four deep, even though a majority of those customers only had queries about Paris itself, the gaggle of people didn't seem to shrink no matter how fast we worked.

The casual staff had fluttered in yesterday afternoon and it took some of the pressure off, but not enough that I could catch my breath. Forget assisting people, there was virtually no time to step from behind the counter. The way we served people was almost robotic, and it took a little of the shine away.

Oceane played with the diamond on her finger. "No one ever works when they should. The roster is more like a suggestion. I work every weekday, and Beatrice does most days too. TJ is supposed to work days, but usually does nights. The casual staff come and go. When they come in, we escape for lunch. There's always someone here to help, you just never know who."

My mind boggled. How could Sophie run a business like that? For someone so thorough with spreadsheets—it was strange to allow the staff to flit in when they wanted, considering they're the ones who were most needed in order to achieve the projected targets and keep the sales ticking over at the rate Sophie expected. It was madness. Yesterday had been mayhem with only me and Beatrice on hand through the peak times.

The roster would have to be ironed out. Hopefully, I wouldn't ruffle too many feathers— maybe it would actually improve things if everyone knew when they were supposed to work. They'd probably praise me for it—they could then plan their social lives, knowing exactly when they had to work, and it would stop us being short-staffed.

Oceane patted my arm. "Before the hordes descend, let me show you around the shop properly. I bet you didn't get a chance to check it out yesterday."

"What about the customers outside?"

"They can wait." She gave me a flippant shrug. "It's not nine yet." She grabbed my hand and walked briskly to the back of the shop. "So the rooms all run into one another, like a sentence. Once you start, you just keep going . . . and you'll eventually end up in the courtyard outside, unless you take the staircase to the left, and then you'll end up lost. It's a rabbit warren."

The main open floor of the bookstore led into the first room up by one step. It was stacked floor to ceiling with books, some shelves leaned so far forward they were almost curved overhead like the crest of a wave. A huge mirror hung from the ceiling, reflecting everything in a warped Alice in Wonderland kind of way.

On the floor, a once ruby red rug lay almost threadbare, its colors dulled to a faded rose, indelibly changed by foot traffic, but at the edges, you could make out how truly vibrant it had once been. Old armchairs, their leather like wrinkled faces, sat solemnly. How many readers had wandered into this room, pulled a musty book from the shelves, and spent the day absorbed in a tale, every now and then glancing up, the scent of the Seine blowing in like a whisper as it had done for generations?

Oceane smiled. "And next, we have the lending library." She led me through an archway, where someone had scrawled in thick, black permanent marker: *this way to paradise.*

The lending library was ripe with the thick stench of old tomes and the lemony scent of new novels. Their fragrances mingled together in the space, almost like a perfume, a heady combination of past and present.

Sophie's bookshop was so alive it hummed. Dust motes danced, and I had to fight the urge to flop on a chair, and snatch up the nearest book.

An antique grandfather clock stood to one side of the room, its chimes long since stopped, the golden hands paused on the witching hour. "Who runs the lending library?" I asked.

Oceane leaned against the wall. "Bertie, François, and Phillippe. They organize their shifts between them, and keep track of the loans. You don't need to do anything for it. Sophie's pretty lax about the whole process. There's index cards, and stamps, it's very old school. The lending library is hallowed—it's been available for locals since the doors opened here back in the twenties. During the Great Depression, no one could afford much of anything, especially books, so strangers found their way here, and knew they could take whatever they wished. They became members, friends, and weren't faceless or nameless anymore."

"This history practically seeps through the walls." I was in awe of the shop. It had presence, almost like it was a character unto itself. "Do you ever wonder who sat here a century ago, and rummaged through these boxes of books?"

Her eyes grew bright. "Of course. I imagine people back then stopped past with rumbling bellies, their lives grim because of the Depression, until they found their way here, and they could forget their troubles, escaping into the pages of a good book, a warm drink in hand. What could be better than that? Sophie's grandfather opened the store. When he first started, he only used the front parlor, but as time went by his reputation spread, he grew more successful and expanded into the other rooms, eventually buying the apartments above. He never changed his principles . . . everyone was welcome here whether they had money or not. It was popular among American writers back then, a meeting place for literary transients."

"I get goose bumps, thinking about the stories they could've told. Do you think when they finally settled, back on home soil, they remembered their time here fondly?"

"*Oui,*" she said, crossing her arms against the chill in the room. "A lot of them were young. Traveling after the war or just because they were free, who knows? And when it was time to move, or go back to reality, they always had this place in their heart. Sophie has a thick folder of correspondence, letters sent over decades, people thanking them for their hospitality, some dedicating the books they wrote here to Sophie's grandfather. Others saying they searched their whole lives for the simple happiness Paris provided, but never found it again. Over a bottle or two of *vin rouge*, I read each and every one of them. I've told her she should publish them . . . an epic love story of people and place."

"That would be an amazing book . . ." Taking in the room, I thought of the people who once inhabited this space; I pictured the scene in black and white, like an old photograph. "The room has a sense of timelessness to it." As if time had truly stopped, just like the grandfather clock. And those people long since gone from this world had found the place just as it was now, a sanctuary for word lovers.

"The store has a rich and famous history. It's why people come here and don't want to leave." Oceane spoke in reverent tones, gazing wistfully around. The rooms were weathered, the furniture battered, the shop's once former glory dimmed, faded like late afternoon sunlight through a dusty window, which made it one of the most beautiful places I'd ever seen.

"Why would you want to leave?" I said. It was like a grand old dame, this shop. Once haughty, now a reflection of its past, and all that happened here.

She laughed and surveyed me. "Your face is flushed like you've fallen in love too."

I promptly closed my mouth, and scraped back my hair. "How could you not? It's like nothing I've ever seen before . . . almost like their ghosts are still here, those readers. Maybe that's why the sign says, 'This way to paradise'?"

Her gaze softened once more. "Like heaven?

Well, why not?" Soft laughter burbled out of her. "If I died and had to choose a place to spend eternity, it would be here."

"Yes," I said. It was different, surveying the shop when it was empty of people, as if the old building had settled in on itself while it waited.

Oceane consulted her watch. "I'll have to show you the rest later, the crowds are getting thicker. But that—" she pointed to the next doorway "—is the piano room, and where all the music books are kept." I snuck a peep, a shiny ebony baby grand piano stood earnestly. I couldn't wait to creep around the bookshop, and discover what else was hidden here, after all these passages of time.

We walked back into the main area and I was stunned seeing so many faces peering through the window.

I hurried to the door and pulled it open, the gray October day chilling me, as the sun hid behind clouds, not eager to show its face just yet.

SIX

The phone trilled, and I raced to answer it.

"Once Upon a Time."

"Sarah Smith, I thought I'd lost you to Paris already. That it swallowed you up whole."

Butterflies fluttered as his velvety voice hummed down the line. "Not yet," I said, laughing.

"I tried your cell so many times, and it rang out and then died, and I thought, that's it—some suave Frenchman has swept the delectable Sarah off her feet already." I fell back on a chair, and motioned for TJ to take my place behind the counter.

"You won't believe it—my bags were stolen. I lost my passport. My purse." I groaned. "Didn't you get my emails? My cell phone was stolen too." It'd been hidden away in one of the pockets of my backpack, ironic really.

"What a welcome," Ridge said. "I haven't seen any emails from you, or I would have called no matter what the time difference to make sure you were OK."

"Weird. Maybe your email thinks I'm spam . . ." I explained the dramatic first day, including the fact I'd been dead on my feet and thrust into working as soon as I walked over the threshold.

"I hope it gets better for you," he said. "I wish I was there."

"Me too." There was no point going down that path; he had to work, and so did I. "You should see the stunning display of roses in front of me . . ."

"Oh, yeah?" His voice came out husky. "There's one for each time I kissed you in my dreams the night you left."

What can I say? The man knew how to tug at my heartstrings. "Twenty-four kisses? I'm a lucky girl."

Hearing the steadiness of his voice calmed a part of me only he'd been able to reach. There were times I felt I could do anything, having him by my side, metaphorically or not. "So . . . how's Indonesia?" It was a million miles from me, in every sense, and I hoped he wouldn't stay too long.

"Hot. Balmy. It would be a damn sight better if you were here in a bikini beside me."

I laughed at the huskiness in his voice. "One day, we'll go there together. But first, Paris! I can't wait for you . . ."

"One sec, sorry," Ridge said as the soft voice of a woman purred down the line. I couldn't make out what she was saying—*something, something, I ordered room service . . .*

She ordered room service?

My cheeks flushed crimson, and my stomach clenched. Surely Ridge wouldn't be sharing a room with another woman?

He muffled a reply and then said, "Sorry. Where were we?" I waited a beat, hoping he'd explain who he'd been speaking to. He didn't.

"Who was that?" I asked, hating myself for the twinge of doubt.

"That? Oh, the girl? That was Monique, she's my photographer. We're working together again."

"Again?" I said, prickling. "And she's ordered you room service?"

"Baby—" his voice was so smooth it was almost silky "—there's a bunch of us, and we order club sandwiches, and go hang out together to eat, before we head back to our own rooms to write. Monique is the best in the business, and I'm lucky to have her. Why? Do I detect a touch of jealousy?"

I rolled my eyes at my stupidity. This was Ridge, he wasn't that kind of guy. But still, *lucky to have her?* "Who would have thought long-distance relationships were so hard? I'm picturing some blonde bombshell, dressed in a teeny-tiny bikini, teetering on spiked heels . . . and then she all huskily says, 'I've ordered room service, *stud . . .*' "

He let out a roar of laughter. "She could be all that and more, and it wouldn't matter a jot to me. *No one* compares to you, Sarah. You have my heart, no matter where I am or who I'm with, so look after it."

A few of the casual staff scampered in before lunchtime, different faces to the day before. They were a scruffy gaggle of college students who worked for a few hours each day. Sophie allowed them to borrow books, and sleep upstairs. At closing time they'd snatch a lumpy sofa and quickly convert it to a bed for the night. It struck me as crazy they were happy to live like that. I couldn't imagine pulling up at any old space to sleep each night, and then packing my belongings away each morning, escaping into the daylight when the shop opened.

They were exotic with their unruly bed hair, and quick smiles. Their glowing youth and adventurous spirits were enviable. They spoke fast, like machine-gun fire, bumping and jostling each other as they discussed their latest reads, trudging past, backpacks slung over skinny shoulders. They gave me a wave, as if it wasn't anything extraordinary to find a new person behind the counter. *I'm your new boss,* I wanted to chortle, but that may have come across too cheesy. They were all stylish in that *I'm-a-ragamuffin-hipster-traveler* kind of way.

I desperately wanted to chat to them and ask how they ended up here, their accents as varied as the books around us, but Oceane pulled me by the elbow and dragged me into the brisk autumn day. "You'll have plenty of time to talk to them later, though they'll speak in riddles and pretend they're literary snobs. I'll show you where the bank is, and while we're out we may as well stop for lunch."

Oceane walked quickly, despite wearing high-heeled boots. I struggled to keep up, my feet still aching from the day before. She looped her arm through my elbow. "I'm taking you to my favorite café, on the corner of Rue Jacques-Callot. It's called Café La Palette. You know Picasso used to frequent it?"

"He did?" I wanted to pinch myself, to make sure it was all real—the thrilling view before me, the Eiffel Tower in the distance, the Seine with boats chugging along, and now a new adventure to explore a historic café. Yes, day one hadn't been ideal, but day two was shaping up to be a heck of a lot better. Oceane was serious in that studied, French way, but she was sweet, and seemed to like me. The people I'd met so far were three-dimensional, vivacious, so sure of themselves; I felt like a cardboard cutout in comparison and hoped some of their confidence would rub off on me.

"It's where the art crowd mingle," she said. "But first we must cross to the other side where the bank is, and I'll show you the post office too."

"OK." I tried to match my steps to Oceane's. Her hurried pace was enough to send my heart racing. "Are you engaged?" I puffed, pointing to the blinking diamond on her finger.

She tutted and shook her head, her blue eyes

shadowing. In the distance the Notre Dame loomed, formidable with its heavy archways, and gothic facade.

"*Non*," she said, "I bought it for myself. And why not? Why should I wait for a man to buy me a beautiful diamond?"

"I like your style," I said, smiling.

She held her hand up, and gazed at the sparkly precious gem. "It was a present to myself. Unfortunately, I'm a magnet for the Mr. Right Nows. Mr. Right, well, he must be on vacation, because damned if I can find him."

Oceane was stunning with her high cheekbones, and full lips. Her cropped hair only emphasized her startling features. I bet men fell at her feet, but I agreed with the idea of finding The One and waiting for the happy ever after.

When we got closer to the famous church I stopped and craned my neck, taking it all in. Stone gargoyles leaned from the structure, almost lifelike with their piercing eyes and open mouths, as if they were ready to pounce.

"Impressive, *non*?" she asked.

"I don't think I'll ever get used to the beauty here." Hard to imagine that those gargoyles perched above like watchmen had been gazing over the city for almost a thousand years. I was intoxicated by the scene before me. Goose bumps riddled my skin as excitement fluttered through me. I'd left my home, my routine, and I was here where ancient beauty was abundant. I'd made the right choice, I could feel it in my bones.

"I can take you inside later. We won't have to line up." She winked. "I used to date a guy who works there."

Oceane grabbed my hand and we continued down the street, ambling through groups of people, dodging children who were running through the open space in front of the church, before crossing over. I shrugged deeper into my jacket as the wind whipped past.

"What about you? Is there a man who's stolen your heart?" Oceane asked.

"There is." My pulse quickened, as Ridge's face flashed through my mind. Missing him was like being in a heavy fog sometimes. "He's a freelance reporter, so he's always off on some exciting adventure. Once his latest story is submitted, he'll come to Paris."

She tapped my hand. "So you don't see him much?"

"Not as much as I'd like. At the beginning it was almost every weekend. And then he moved to my town, but the stories came thick and fast . . ." My voice faded. Was the thrill of new love waning for Ridge? These days, he hunted for stories zealously, almost like he was happy to escape the humdrum of Ashford. It had been different in the beginning, when he'd turn down work in favor of staying with me.

"Maybe you need a vacation romance while he's away?" Her eyes glittered with mischief.

I gasped, scandalized. "I would never . . ."

She shrugged. "So, my pretty American friend, you *have* found Mr. Right I see."

"Yes." I smiled. He was my Mr. Right, there was no question about that. It was just a shame he wasn't Mr. Right Here.

She flashed a grin. "That's the bank." Oceane pointed to a building that was far too pretty to be a bank—with wide columns and a balcony up above. "And the post office is down that laneway. And now I'll take you for lunch. If we see a celebrity like Julia Roberts, please don't do that gushy tourist thing where you rush up to them for a photo. We're not fans of the 'selfie' here."

I laughed at Oceane's frown. There would be no chance I'd run to a celebrity, in case I made a fool of myself. "Julia Roberts?" I asked.

"She loves it here," Oceane said. "But it's better to act like she's a regular girl. She likes that anonymity. And we don't go gushy over celebrities, they're just regular people who happen to earn a lot of money, you see?"

She was deadly serious, so I held in my smile. "I do see."

We arrived at Café La Palette, trellised roses rich out front. Oceane strode briskly inside, zigzagging through tables and finding us a spot in the front salon. There was a bevy of waiters standing to attention behind a bar that shone like burnished gold, and above it hung an oversized artist's palette. "It's made from zinc," she said, following my gaze to the bar.

She motioned for me to sit. Even the floor was a mosaic of tiles, so many touches and textures made the space almost art gallery worthy. Kaleidoscopic colors and materials had my gaze bouncing here and there, trying to take it all in. A waiter appeared and kissed both Oceane's cheeks before saying, "*Bonjour, ma cherie.*" He took her hand, and brushed his lips across her skin in an intimate way. My eyes widened in surprise, but Oceane paid zero attention to him.

"The usual," she said, finally giving him a half smile. His face lit up under her attention, and as quick as that she turned back to me, snatching her hand back.

"*Bien sur,*" he said, and spun away.

"He's smitten," I said, fidgeting with the cutlery on the table.

Oceane pouted. "We dated once. But he was not for me."

I smiled. Oceane had no shortage of suitors, yet claimed they had all been Mr. Right Nows. "Why?"

"I want someone who makes my heart sing. Someone that lights me up from inside. Laurent—" she motioned into the space the waiter had gone "—was sweet, but after a few weeks that fire fizzled out. I don't want to settle for ordinary, I want fireworks, enough to last me my whole life."

"Spoken like a true romance reader," I said. I'd been the very same before I met Ridge. I wanted the book boyfriend to come to life, to make a gray day blue. Otherwise what was the point? Why shouldn't we strive for what our fictional friends had? Why did they get the grand love affairs and we settled for second rate? That's why my love life had been virtually nonexistent before Ridge had wandered into town. My expectations were high, I wanted a once in a lifetime love.

"Exactly," she laughed in that quiet gathered way of hers. "I want a love affair like the books. And until then, guys like Laurent are just good practice."

Laurent returned, expertly balancing two glasses of wine and two plates of food.

When he placed the plate in front of me, my hand flew to my mouth. Were we supposed to cook this ourselves? I surreptitiously glanced around for some kind of grill, or a hot plate, but found nothing.

"*Bon appetit*," he said, giving Oceane one last hungry look.

I snatched up the glass of wine, and sipped to delay the inevitable.

"Enjoy," she said. "Steak tartare, my most favorite dish."

I eyed her dubiously when she picked up a fork, broke the raw egg yolk and mixed it through the raw meat. All I could think was, raw, raw, RAW!

"Eat," she said between mouthfuls. "Don't you like it?"

I sucked in a breath before responding. "Well, I've got the makings of a very fine burger here, raw mincemeat, raw egg, spices, capers . . ."

She giggled, and waved her napkin at me. "Trust me. You'll love it. You're not vegetarian, are you?"

"No." Though I suddenly wished I was. But in the arty café it seemed absurd not to give something new a try. Had Picasso come here for this dish? Once again I was opening up to life as it opened up to me. I gave myself a silent pat on the back for embracing a wholly new culinary experience, and only hoped my stomach didn't revolt against it.

I made a show of grinning, like I'd always wanted to eat steak tartare, and picked up my cutlery. Maybe it would be mind-blowingly brilliant and I'd wonder why I'd ever wasted time actually barbecuing meat back home. *It could happen.* I took the fork and broke the yolk, trying not to inhale the pungent smell.

Clenching my jaw, I mixed the ingredients together, wondering what Lil and CeeCee would make of this meal. I could almost hear Cee, "I didn't fall off a watermelon truck yesterday. What you mean, you eat it raw?" She'd have one of her conniptions if she saw what was in front of me.

I scrunched my eyes closed, and took a mouthful, trying my best not to gag. The texture was all wrong, the mincemeat like slime in my mouth. I swallowed without chewing, and waved my cutlery victoriously. Until I remembered I had many a forkful to go.

"Delicious, *non*?" she asked.

"*Magnifique*," I said, loving the feeling of total sophistication I had when trying things with the likes of Oceane, and took a huge swig of wine to get rid of the awful mouthfeel. After a few more forkfuls I put a hand to my belly. "If only I weren't full," I said, and promptly put my knife and fork together. Oceane didn't buy it, I could tell by the lift of her lips, but she let it slide.

After lunch we set off at Oceane's usual brisk pace; she talked while I listened. "Twice a day, you have to deposit the takings. Then enter it all into the computer. Sophie is fanatical about it," Oceane said. "The mail, well, that's almost a full-time job in itself. Open, sort, and file it. Purchase invoices are to be entered into the computer too."

"Right." I walked fast to keep up. "What else?"

"The book orders. The biggest sellers are all kept in a storeroom out back. Go through the spreadsheets and see what's selling best, then reorder what we need. The online shop, too, though, that's usually Mills & Boon books.

Romance is huge here. Whatever books are ordered online need to be mailed out. You can always get someone to help package them up. Use whoever you can to get them wrapped and mailed or it'll spiral out of control."

I blew out a breath. "It's so much work. I hadn't expected it to be so . . . frantic."

"It'll get worse as Christmas approaches. You'll have to assign jobs to certain people and double-check they're doing it. Everyone loves the shop but a lot of them are young, and unreliable, and get caught up with the social aspect."

"OK." Sophie really neglected in telling me the finer details when I first agreed to exchange. "Why doesn't Sophie assign some of these jobs to other people?" It didn't make an iota of sense for one person to do so much work.

"She doesn't trust anyone enough. Sophie's traditional."

I fell silent, worrying I'd make a mess of it all. There was so much to consider with the various aspects of the business, if there were any disasters it would fall squarely on my shoulders.

Suddenly I pined for my own bookshop, the simplicity of it. And I wondered when I'd snatch time to read, which for me was as essential as breathing.

"One moment," Oceane said, stopping as we arrived in front of a little flower shop. The pastel green front was chipped and faded in that shabby chic French style that people the world over tried to recreate. A slatted wooden bench sat in front of the window, filled with cane baskets of brightly colored blooms. Petals had fallen to the ground, like a scattering of confetti. I bent to the bouquets, their sweet, feminine perfume mingling in the air. I wanted to gather them in my arms, and take them all back with me, to wake to the sight of them, and breathe in their evocative scent like a tincture.

"Oui?" A French woman appeared, dressed well, similar to Oceane. Were jeans and T-shirts not a thing here? I'd have to rethink my super casual wardrobe when the insurance checks arrived. I felt downright bedraggled in comparison to the smart, French way of dressing.

Pointing to a bunch of pale pink peonies, whose petals were folded in on themselves like a secret, Oceane spoke quickly to the woman. My best friend Missy loved peonies, she had pots full back home, and crooned to them lovingly as if it would help them live. She was a real green thumb, and these little flower shops that were hidden down cobbled avenues would have sent her into a tizzy.

I pointed to a bunch of peonies too. I wanted to wake to their pinkness, and remember that there was beauty everywhere here, even if I was cooped up in the bookshop, counting endless piles of books, or wrangling the paperwork.

We paid, and cradled our tissue-paper-wrapped purchases like they were babies, wandering out of the avenue and back into the filmy light of day. I checked my watch. We'd been gone almost an hour. "We better head back," I said, worry catching me as I thought of all I had to do.

"Oh, there's no rush," Oceane said. "French people take long lunches. I usually go home, and sit on the balcony for a while. Besides, my flowers need a vase and some water."

I followed blithely along, hoping the bookshop wasn't being overrun, as guilt at being absent gnawed at me.

Oceane's apartment was on the Quai Voltaire a few doors down from the Musée d'Orsay. The museum took up a fair expanse of street. The facade of the building was magnificent. Inside was full of priceless art, and I itched to wander in. I wasn't an expert on the arrondissements but I could guess that this part of Paris was expensive to live in. I wondered how she could afford the trappings of her lifestyle on the salary Sophie paid her, but thought it rude to ask.

"Do you spend a lot of time at the Musée d'Orsay?" I asked.

"*Oui.*" She nodded. "I adore art, especially the greats. Van Gogh, Monet, Renoir . . . I pretend they're alive and we're neighbors." She blushed, as if she hadn't meant to admit that.

"Which is your favorite?" I asked.

"It's impossible to choose, and like books, sometimes one appeals to you more, depending on what kind of mood you're in or which draws you when you most need it. Let me show you," she said. "We don't need to line up. You need to see them for yourself." She shook her head. "I could never tire of staring at them, Sarah."

Sure enough, we bypassed the queue and went in another entrance, Oceane giving the security guard a fluttery wave. How did she do it?

With a laugh, I caught up with Oceane and her breakneck pace, and stopped short. The ceiling above was vaulted, almost like a tunnel, with intricate patterned glass and gold panels. Arched windows funneled in bleached light.

"It used to be a train station a long time ago," Oceane said, pointing upward.

"That explains the height. It's stunning, the way the light filters in."

We spoke in hushed tones, with a certain reverence that the building prompted. We hurried along, until she stopped abruptly. "Here's Vincent."

I gasped, astounded that I was standing in front of a Vincent Van Gogh painting. Like, it was right there. Vincent. Van. Gogh. It spoke to me in such a way, I promptly burst into tears. Oceane patted my back. "His work has the ability to do that," she said softly.

The painting was *Starry Night over the Rhône,*

and the famous blue and yellow loops and swirls on the canvas were so detailed close up they pulsed. The reflection of lights on the water was startlingly lifelike, so golden, it glowed under the daubs of moonlight. I'd read many a biography about Vincent, and the sadness that followed him. Seeing his work brought back all those memories, and the picture I painted in my mind about him and his complex life. I'd felt a real empathy for him, like he was too good for this world.

We went back to Oceane's apartment; I was dazed by what I'd seen, and I vowed to return to the museum at a later date, giving myself a full day to explore. Seeing Vincent's work had touched me deeply. I felt different when I walked outside, as if I'd added a layer to my life. By stepping away from my fears and visiting Paris, I'd just clapped eyes on a masterpiece, and I was indelibly changed by it. It would probably sound dramatic, trying to explain to my friends back home, but it was almost like I felt a vibration from Vincent himself, as though he was still alive through his work. What else would I find here?

Bustling around, Oceane arranged her flowers and murmured to them. I sat on one of the chairs outside, the sun warming my cheeks. The balcony had a selection of planters filled with fragrant herbs. Oceane said she enjoyed cooking and liked having fresh ingredients on hand. She filled a watering can and gave them a quick drink. She was in no hurry to get back, retreating into the spacious apartment, returning with a bottle of wine and two glasses.

"Don't be so concerned," she said. "We all take long breaks. It's the way it goes."

I didn't want to be a wet blanket but felt the shop pull me back. The thought of staying up into the night in front of the glare of a computer monitor galvanized me. "Take your time, if that's what you normally do. But I better return. I'm worried about the five thousand things I need to do."

"OK," she said, sitting on the chair beside me and pointing her face to the sun. "I'll be back later. You'll see, Sarah. That shop will swallow you up, if you don't step out from time to time."

I gave her a quick hug, feeling slightly woozy from daytime wine. This French lifestyle would take some getting used to. But I had to make a start on the to-do list for the shop. I'd need to escape the following day for my passport appointment, and I only hoped it didn't eat too much time out of my day.

SEVEN

"You'll have a new passport in three weeks, Miss Smith, at the earliest. Please be more careful. Passports are *not* like train tickets. You should know where it is at all times." The consulate official tutted, and signed the paperwork with a flourish.

His colleague steepled his fingers and reiterated, "You *have* to be careful, Miss Smith. We suggest you read our website when it comes to travel warnings and how to be safe. Paris is a beautiful city but you must take precautions . . ."

I forced a tight smile. They were speaking to me like I was a child, and it grated. Did I have a sign on my forehead saying, "Kid trapped in adult's body"? "Yeah, it was an *accident,* a split-second decision, so it's not like I plan to repeat it."

"Just be careful. Treat your passport like it's priceless, OK?"

Steepled Fingers joined in, "Like . . . it's the *Mona Lisa.*"

I willed my eyes not to roll, it was a good twenty-second battle. "The *Mona Lisa.* Got it." I smiled to soften the sarcasm that poured from my mouth and donned my most innocent expression.

"Three weeks, so no international travel until then, OK?"

I slapped a hand to my forehead. "No international travel? Are you sure? Can't I use my train ticket in lieu of a passport?" I couldn't resist acting like the imbecile they took me for. "Joke," I said to their startled faces. "I'll lock myself safely in my room so no harm comes to me."

When I finally found my way back to the bookshop, phones were left ringing, the counter was staffed only by Oceane, and customers grumbled to one another about the wait. I dashed behind the counter and stowed my bag, ready to help.

"Next." I smiled brightly, hoping to ward off any complaints. "Where is everyone?" I asked under my breath.

"Who knows?" Oceane muttered. "It's like with Sophie gone everyone's in holiday mode. I don't get paid enough for this kind of treatment. I've been screeched at a hundred times already."

I nodded in agreement. The next customer approached. "You're in all the Paris guidebooks as the best bookshop, yet you don't even have the latest Cathy Kelly book here! What kind of bookshop is this?" The woman plonked some romance novels down, and glared.

"I'm sorry," I said. "The Cathy Kelly's only just arrived and we haven't had a chance . . ."

She held up a hand. "I've waited an hour to be served. I just want to pay and go."

"Sorry," I said lamely. Where the hell was everyone?

Once we'd caught up, I rushed to the storeroom and unpacked the latest delivery of books. Really, we needed someone in charge of restocking. You couldn't sell books if they were hidden in a back room. I raced to the computer and made up some quick flyers, advertising "Buy three books, get the fourth half price." People loved getting a bargain, and I was mindful of keeping the sales figures healthy. When I had more time I'd introduce other bundle deals to inspire people to buy. Already, I could tell the difference between a customer who truly loved books, and paid for one, and a tourist who just wanted to cross another sight off their list. Somehow, we had to convert those sightseers into customers.

Ridge and I had become masters in phone tag. It was like we instinctively knew when the other one was busy or sleeping, and seemed to call at that moment. I missed him like crazy, and still got a little thrill when I heard his voice mail greeting, even though it meant he wasn't available to chat. A week on Paris soil, and I still hadn't managed to tee up a time that was convenient to speak to Ridge, or the girls back home. It was so odd to think they were sleeping, while I was racing around the shop, the days whooshing by in a blur.

When there was a lull in customers, I dashed

outside to call Ridge, calculating the time difference and hoping I'd catch him before he left his hotel for the day. "Morning, beautiful," he said, in that rich, husky just-woke-up way. I could see him in my mind's eye, lying with crisp cotton sheets tangled around his taut, tanned body. Him running a hand through his shock of black hair. That sexy, dazed gaze of his as if he'd awoken from a nice dream.

"Morning, mister. Still lazing in bed?"

He let out a gruff sigh. "I am, and it's not half as much fun without you."

"I hope not." I strolled down the street to René Viviani Square, and walked through an arbor covered with climbing roses that gave off a musk scent. I sat under a canopy of leaves, bracing myself against the strong winds. As cold as it was, there was something magical about the rain hitting my flushed cheeks, and Ridge's silky voice.

"How's it going there? A booklover's dream?" A rustle of sheets, and the splash of running water filtered down the line.

What could I say that wouldn't make me sound like a timid little mouse? "Oh, you know, I'm still having a few teething problems, but I'm sure I'll get there. The little hurdles are nothing when I have Paris outside waiting . . ." I big, fat, lied. He was so self-assured and dynamic, I didn't want him to worry that I couldn't handle myself in the so-called big bad world.

"Sounds like you've got a handle on things there."

"Yep, having a blast. I cried when I saw Van Gogh's—"

He interrupted, "Wait one second, baby."

My mouth promptly closed as someone spoke out of hearing range. When he came back to me, his voice was firmer, more businesslike. "Sorry, I have to go. You can tell me all about Picasso later."

"It was Van Gogh . . ."

He spoke to someone again. Whoever it was, their voice garbled through in an urgent tone. "Gotta go, baby. It looks like the story might have just broken. I'll call you as soon as I can." With that he hung up, leaving me with just the pitter-patter of rain for company. Was he really that busy, he couldn't spare five minutes?

A few days later I was still reeling from the awful experience at the passport office, they'd been so belittling—I bristled every time I thought of it. Why didn't I speak up for myself better? Their warning rants had continued on for another thirty minutes until I was mute with anger. And then there was Ridge's abrupt hang-up. He hadn't managed to call me back, so the story must've have been breaking like the slowest wave on earth. I'd left a bunch of messages for him, and then vowed no more. It was hard not to take it personally. Surely he ate? And slept? Showered. He could spend a minute on the phone to me. But perhaps, like so many times, he was out of range, or something. My life was hectic here anyway, and I always had so many things vying for my attention.

Still trying to familiarize myself with the shop, I worked on stacking shelves while TJ manned the counter. It was a gloriously quiet moment, one where we scrambled to get as much cleared up before the next wave of tourists and booklovers swarmed in. The door gusted open and the man I had caught a glimpse of in the conservatory on my first day walked in. The one who hid in the shadows like he didn't want to be seen. Again, his blonde-haired, blue-eyed looks seemed familiar, but how could they? I didn't know any French men, I was from Smallsville.

"Who *is* that?" I asked TJ, in a whisper. For some reason I was drawn to the mysterious man who sat upstairs for hours on end and yet I had never seen him buy a book.

TJ shrugged. "Haven't stopped to speak to him before. But every day like clockwork he's here. He's been here ever since I arrived." He moved to fix a fallen stack of books. "I'm going to tidy the blue room."

The blue room was yet another little piece of perfection in the store. It was stacked with blue-bound novels. Sophie's idea of a private joke because of the amount of times she had been asked for a book, the only clue given was that it had a blue cover. The blue room had an old locked armoire in the corner filled with the manuscripts of writers who'd left them with Sophie as a gift when their books were published. An antique rolltop desk stood proudly in front of the window. "OK," I said distractedly.

The blonde man intrigued me. I hadn't seen many people with such expressive features before, but instead of happiness, his face was lined with pain. I wanted to know why. He was one of many that regularly visited the store. People often came to sketch, or read, they traipsed in as if they were at a friend's home. He was different though. It was as though he was searching for someone when his eyes scanned the counter, and always came up missing.

TJ strolled over, his boyish grin in place. "Hectic day. You want me to lock up?"

I yawned, which produced a chain reaction— TJ joined in, and so did Beatrice who'd wandered over, leaned her elbows on the counter and cradled her face in her hands.

"Would you mind?" I asked TJ, grateful he'd even offered. My legs were jelly-like from standing so long, and my lower back twanged each time I bent to restack shelves.

"I know men aren't supposed to say things like

this, but you don't look so great, Sarah. Maybe an early night's in order?" He patted my shoulder in a big brother kind of way.

I groaned and covered my face. Even at dawn when I first awoke I had shadows under my eyes, and my complexion resembled Casper the ghost. Too many late nights with only the glare of the computer screen for company. "I'm shattered," I said, managing a small laugh. "I could sleep standing up. Though I think I may be developing some buff arms." All that book heaving and carting of boxes was doing wonders for my tiny frame.

"I promise by week four things improve. It's all about snatching those break times, and getting some distance between you and the shop."

"Week four, you say?" I held onto that, hoping he was right and that somehow after a month here, I'd learn to cope better.

Beatrice chewed a nail, surveying me. "Don't forget Sophie'll expect the end-of-month reports soon."

"Urgh, the reports. I'd forgotten."

Beatrice smirked. "All part of the management fun." Was I imagining it or did she gloat a little when she said that?

"Great," I couldn't even pretend to be chirpy. "I'll take the till, TJ, you can start a new cash drawer." Time to count the takings, and add everything into Sophie's difficult computer program.

Hours later, nursing another coffee, I squinted hard at the screen. Had I made a mistake somewhere? Sighing, I rechecked the figures again. And once more, flicked through the euros, securing them into piles with rubber bands. *Please no!* I had triple-checked, and the same figure popped up every time.

Money was missing. And not small change either. I'd have to tell Sophie.

My stomach clenched at the thought. She'd think I was completely incapable of running her shop. Worry gnawed at me, and like the coward I was, I put off calling her until the next day.

Glumly, I gathered everything up, stowing the money in the safe, and headed to bed. No shower, no dinner, just an overwhelming need to pull the quilt cover over my head and sleep. Fatigue hit me like a brick, and I fell into a fitful slumber, jarring awake when anxiety dreams tumbled into my subconscious.

Midafternoon, I finally corralled Beatrice to man the front counter, so I could do the banking. Soon, Sophie would be starting her day in Ashford, and I'd have to call about the missing money. A quick breather would steel me for the dreaded admission that things weren't running smoothly.

With the Parisian air against my face, and slivers of autumnal sunshine breaking through clouds, I was happier outside. How people walked along here without stopping to marvel at each and every little thing was beyond me. I crossed the Pont Neuf, and headed into the little island in the Seine, the Île de la Cité. I loved the idea that in such a bustling crowded place, there was an island like a refuge between both sides of the city, and the river flowed freely, like a fork in the road on both sides before joining in harmony once again. Quirky me found it metaphorical, somehow. In a totally whimsical way, it was like me and Ridge—parting, going about our lives until the tides changed and brought us back together again.

I hurried along, soaking up the detail of the buildings—their gray slate roofs; the wrought iron balconies, small pots filled with plants; shutters, opened to the day; and even the naked trees, their roots spilling out squid-like as though they were searching for something—it all captivated me. The age, the history of the buildings and every magnificent little feature caught my eye. A rush of sentimentality hit as I imagined Paris changing over generations, from black and white to full Technicolor.

Time raced away, and before I knew it the banking was done and I had to return and call Sophie, my stomach knotting at the thought.

"Sarah, if there's money missing, you have to do something about it. I'll tolerate almost anything, but not that." Sophie's French accent sharpened, and I cringed, glad we were on the phone and not on Skype so she couldn't see mortification color me red.

"I've recounted so many times. And triple-checked the sales figures. We're four hundred euros down. I'm so sorry, Sophie. I thought it may have been a mistake . . ."

My toes curled thinking someone was stealing, and most likely because I was here, and they thought they could get away with it. "It's not your fault," she said. "You didn't take it, but just be aware. Watch them. We can't have that, and the sales dropping too."

I wanted to roll into a ball and cry. So far, the sales had plummeted significantly, and money was going missing every few days, sometimes fifty euros, sometimes a heck of a lot more. "I'll fix it," I said, squaring my shoulders, determined.

"I know you will. In other news, your sales have almost tripled. Well, I'm guessing by your hastily scratched sales sheet here."

I was the opposite of Sophie. My meager sales were handwritten in a ledger by the till. "Tripled?"

"Yes," she said. "I've added a few tabs to your online shop. They can now buy romance bundles by subscription, and all sorts of things. I blogged about it for you, and almost immediately there were orders. I hope it's OK, that I shuffled things around?"

"Of course," I said, imagining complex charts and graphs when I returned home—my sales figures proudly in the black after Sophie had taken over. A tiny part of me was a little put out. Only because she was increasing my revenue, and I was decreasing hers, despite my efforts. Nothing was going as planned, and I felt a lot like a failure compared to the together types.

"Anyway, darling. I must dash, the girls are waiting for me at the Gingerbread Café. They've baked some heavenly French dessert to curb a homesickness I don't have."

My friends. I could picture them all squashed together on the sofas in the café, the fire crackling next to them. I double blinked at the sudden hit of jealousy I felt. Sophie was living my life, and probably better than I did. And I was here, trying my best, but failing at hers. "Tell them I said hello, and I miss them." I swallowed a lump in my throat. Perhaps November would bring better things.

"I will, *ma cherie. Au revoir.*"

I turned my back to the counter, and leaned against the brickwork, taking in the glorious view outside. Being able to ogle the Eiffel Tower from any vantage point in the bookshop was enough to produce a smile. No matter what was happening inside, when I gazed at the beauty of Paris, a thrill ran through me. The shadow of the Notre Dame falling on the bank of the Seine. The boats that chugged past, their passengers slightly dazed from the wind on their faces, and the weak sunlight in their eyes. The crazy way in which the French drove, with lots of gesturing, arms out of windows, the bleeping of the horn. Arches of the bridges in the distance. I loved it all, and wanted to soak it up, meandering lost laneways, snapping pictures so I'd never forget. But for now, I had to sort things here, otherwise my time in Paris would be spent squarely in the bookshop.

My email pinged. I didn't dash for it like normal. These days, my inbox was filled with orders, staff queries about their pay, and a wealth of bookshop related messages. Reaching for my pot of tea, I poured a cup, and then settled back to read the message:

Sarah Smith,

My cell phone is in and out of reception here, as is the Wi-Fi. I'm crossing fingers that you receive this. Today we're heading into Java, moving as the story does. I'm sorry to say I won't be in Paris as quickly as I'd hoped. But trust me when I say I will be there eventually. It can't come soon enough. I miss the way you laugh, the flutter of your hands when you're nervous, and those deep, dark soulful eyes of yours. Most of all, I miss holding you in my arms, while you drift off to sleep.

May Paris carry you in its embrace until
I can.

All my love,
Ridge

I snapped the laptop closed. He sure had a way with words, my roving reporter. When he wrote love notes, or whispered sweet nothings, they were always flowery and poetic. Even with his declarations a knot of impatience settled. How much longer would Indonesia beckon? Was it safe in Java? My mind spun with worry, until I shut it off. Ridge wasn't stupid, he'd avoid trouble. And hopefully get the goddamn story submitted and fly to Paris. I was doing it again, the waiting thing. An email was all I'd had since the hastily ended phone call. And I couldn't help thinking he wasn't living up to the book boyfriend, but then there was me who wasn't exactly heroine material either. If this were a romance novel, he'd be in almost every chapter, sure there'd be misunderstandings, and crossed wires, a few conflicts thrown in, and lots of makeup sex. I had to remember my life wasn't a romance novel, no matter how much I wanted it to be.

Before the day could get any worse, I summoned the staff over. If I nipped the stolen money issue in the bud it'd be one less thing to angst over.

"Guys," I yelled out. "Can you come here for a

sec?" There was a lull in customers, so it was now or never. I threw them a winning smile and went to the counter, spreadsheets at the ready. They wandered closer, some not hiding the boredom on their faces. TJ loped over, and motioned for Beatrice to join.

"Thanks," I said, gripping onto the paperwork so they didn't see my hands shake. It was nerve-racking with all eyes on me. "Just quickly . . . there's quite a bit of money going missing." I gulped. They stared at me like they wanted to eat me for dinner. "I'm not pointing the finger at anyone." Their eyes narrowed, and I fumbled. "But . . . but we can't have that. It's happening more and more often, which makes me think it's not an accident like giving out incorrect change, or something."

"You're accusing *us?*" Tyler—one of the American exchange students—said, not hiding his huffiness.

"Yeah, what're you implying? We work our asses off here, you know!" said Joey, who I'd only met a handful of times. As much as he tried to be hostile, his voice wavered, as if he was only copying Tyler's attitude.

I blushed. Gosh, this wasn't going well. "I know you all work hard . . . when you actually come in, that is, but the thing is . . . "

Tyler interrupted me. "What did you say?" he scoffed.

"What?" I said, miffed at how this was panning out. My book, *How To Be The Boss 101*, was severely letting me down here. I'd expected them to act contrite, worried even. Not hostile. Was Tyler the thief? He certainly had the opportunity to do it, working behind the counter when I hurried out for lunch.

"The way you said, *when you actually come in*. I can see a passive-aggressive person at a hundred paces, and I don't like your tone, Sarah."

My jaw dropped. "Erm, I wasn't being . . ."

TJ piped up. "Tyler, watch your mouth. You're being rude. Sarah's simply saying there's money missing, and it's not going to be tolerated. Makes me wonder why *you're* being so defensive . . ." He gave Tyler a pointed stare. "Got something to admit?"

I threw TJ a grateful smile. And hoped my skin wasn't as beet red as it felt. If Ridge was here, and in charge, he would have belted out missives and had them shrinking back, and here I was getting told off! What was I doing so wrong? Maybe I had to be harder, sterner?

"Don't try and turn this on me!" Tyler spat to TJ and then faced the others as if leading a battle. "She's basically calling all of us thieves! We work for next to nothing here, and then she's got the gall to accuse us? I'm not having it!"

Beatrice crossed her arms and gave me a pitying down-turned smile. "Sarah, look, there's certain ways to go about sensitive issues like this. Guys—" she faced the staff "—she's new, I don't think she knows yet how this place works. Maybe give her the benefit of the doubt, just this once?"

They flashed me daggers, and it was all I could do not to shake my head, and cry out WHAT! What the hell just happened? Give *me* the benefit of the doubt? I was in bizzaro-land, I was sure of it.

I pressed on: "What I'm trying to say is . . ."

Tyler rolled his eyes, and cut me off. "Save it, Sarah. Until you know what you're on about." He stomped off, and the others followed suit, leaving just TJ and Beatrice. I blew out a breath, my heart racing at the conflict and my meaning being so misconstrued.

TJ patted my shoulder reassuringly. "It might be better to chat individually next time. Not that anyone will admit they're taking the money. But then you won't have everyone following Tyler's lead."

Beatrice gave me one of her smiles, which somehow came across a little condescending. "I did tell you, Sarah. There are certain rules here. It's a busy place, and staff come and go. It's about the experience for them. You can't strut in here and try and change things. It won't work."

I frowned, completely baffled by how I'd done the wrong thing, when really, they had. I made

132

my voice as even as possible. "I'm not trying to change anything," I said, hating the slight wobble that betrayed my inability to stand up for myself. "I'm just saying money going missing won't be tolerated. What kind of place is this, that I can't say that? Sophie knows, she's really disappointed."

"Perhaps she should have to put more thought into who she hired to run the bookshop then," Beatrice said. "If she's disappointed in you, I mean."

"I didn't mean in me, I meant that the . . ." My words fizzled out, as I stared at Beatrice's retreating back.

I rubbed my face, willing myself not to well up. Honestly, this was such a bizarre and confusing situation. "Don't worry," TJ said. "They're testing you. Like toddlers do to their moms. Pushing the boundaries to see how much give there is."

I nodded, dumbly. Too surprised to speak.

The blonde man who spent his days upstairs in the conservatory watched the exchange, and gave me a sympathetic look before retreating outside. I envied him his freedom to come and go.

The girls' faces sprang to mind and I yearned for home. Whenever I was upset, we'd gather at the Gingerbread Café. They'd ply me with cake, and make jokes until I snort-laughed my way to happiness, knowing they were on my side, always. CeeCee would've doled out some of her no-nonsense southern advice that put things into perspective. My fingers itched to call them, but I wanted them to be proud of me. Not worried that a few weeks in, I was a stressed-out mess. So, I'd approached the staff the wrong way . . . it was time to rethink my strategy.

Once the shop was mercifully shut, the front door closed against the chilly breeze and the promise of customers, I escaped. The paperwork could wait an hour or two. Paris at nighttime was like a canvas waiting to be captured by the nimble fingers of a painter. Stars glittered in the blue-black night, the moonlight casting its yellow hue across the Seine, and I thought of Vincent Van Gogh and the way he'd been able to bring such scenes to life, that lived on long after him. Shoving my hands into my coat, I breathed deeply, the freshness like a tonic for my soul. Happy to stroll without any plan, I found myself in front of a church. From my back pocket I took my guidebook, and flipped until I found the description. Sainte-Chapelle, famous for its stained glass windows. Before I could dither about going in, the most haunting music rang out, freezing me to the spot. Classical notes drifted into the night, so melancholy and poignant, I wanted to cry out at the sound. Someone tapped my arm, and spoke in French, *"Rapide, quick, ou vous allez manquer."*

Quick, quick, or you'll miss it. I followed along, not sure if I was supposed to pay, but feeling the music deep down in my soul. When we stepped into the main part of the chapel, my mouth fell open. The rich colorful stained glass windows pulsed under the lights, ornate gold shone down. I'd never seen anything so glorious, and coupled with the music, it was one of those moments that made me understand how precious life is, and how I was finally, really living it. And a few dramas along the way were par for the course, I supposed. It couldn't all be rainbows and butterflies. Inside the church, I understood how people believed, whether it was religion or love, or friendship. Being in the heart of the Sainte-Chapelle, surrounded by such artistry I knew anything was possible. The stranger, an elderly woman who'd led me in, pointed to a pew.

I fell in love with Paris, and its people, and the creative souls who'd made it this way. If only Ridge were here to experience this with me.

EIGHT

I was stacking the front table with some newly arrived romances when Oceane called to me. My plans to find someone to be in charge of replenishing the books were forgotten, since I'd offended them when I asked about the missing money. "Phone call," she said. "From America."

"I'll take it in the back room," I said, wanting some privacy, knowing it was one of the girls from back home.

I picked up the receiver, out of breath, and said "Hello?"

"Well, there you is! Cherry blossom, how's the city o' love treating our girl?"

I wanted to shriek at the comforting, familiar tone of CeeCee's voice. "It's . . . good." I was careful how much to say, but CeeCee with her so-called second sight would know anyway. She was intuitive like that.

"You gotta give it time, my darlin'. Till then, know we're thinkin' of you, and missin' you like crazy."

I took a deep breath, and sat on the edge of the paper-strewn desk. "I miss you all so much! How is everyone?"

"We're all good. I'm calling to tell you Lil's not just five minutes ago had a little baby girl . . ."

The dam broke and tears rolled down my face. I wished so much I was in Ashford, with my friends, with people who treated me well. Already, I'd missed a huge event, the birth of Lil's baby. They'd all be hanging out together in the waiting room, nursing mugs of watery coffee, waiting on news about Lil. I felt a dull ache in my heart, being so far away. "A little girl!" I cried. "What's her name?"

"Her name's Willow, and she's as sweet as anythin'. Bald as a badger with one tiny tuft of blonde hair at the front. Damon's gonna email you a photo. Lil said she couldn't get on with trying to feed her until you'd been told, and the photo sent!"

"Awww." I didn't trust myself to speak. My friends knew instinctively that I'd be miserable missing out on such a special occasion, and they'd included me anyway. "Tell Lil I love her, and I'm so proud, and give Willow a kiss from me. I can't wait to snaffle her up for cuddles, and smell that new baby scent."

"She be waiting for you, don't you worry 'bout a thing. Like a click o' the fingers, you'll be back again, so enjoy the time you have there. Lil says she'll Skype you as soon as she's home and settled in. We thought we might all head to her house too so we can see your pretty face, and know you're OK."

After I caught CeeCee up on my adventures, I

hung up and opened my email. I clicked on the picture of Lil gazing at baby Willow. Lil's eyes were full of love as she stared at her little girl. Willow slept soundly in her mom's arms, her expression peaceful as if she knew she was right where she belonged. And here I was, a million miles from home, when I wanted to be there with my friends so much I ached. Even if I wanted to go home, give in and say it wasn't working, I couldn't because I still didn't have my passport.

I printed the grainy picture of Lil and baby Willow. My email pinged, and another attachment came through—a photo with the girls gathered around Lil's hospital bed. CeeCee held baby Willow, and Lil and Missy had a handwritten sign propped in front of them saying, *"hello aunty sarah, love willow xxx."* I printed that one too, and retreated upstairs to one of the quieter rooms so I could be alone.

Precious photos in hand, I climbed the rickety steps, willing myself to hold it together until I was out of earshot. In the quiet of the map room, I finally let the tears spill. I gathered my legs up on the battered velour sofa, and tried to stare at the photos through glassy eyes. Was I a failure? Who comes to Paris and doesn't enjoy it? When I was strolling through the cobblestoned streets myself, I adored it. But in the bookshop it was like I was trying too hard and making mistakes, upsetting some indistinct balance between shop and employee. Ridge flashed through my mind, and I was tempted to call him and pour my heart out, but he was a man of the world, a seasoned traveler who'd have whipped the shop into shape. Would he pity me, not being able to handle it like the sheltered girl I was?

Footsteps worked their way up the stairs. I hastily swiped away at my tears and hoped whoever it was wouldn't venture into this room. It was filled with dusty old maps and a mishmash of globes in various states of disrepair, old compasses and barometers. Like an adventurer's cave, a place to come and dream about the next voyage. Boats in bottles sat on hutches. The thought of not being one of those types, someone who takes the reins and sets sail, made the sobs start anew. Goddammit, I was losing it. I wasn't a blubberer usually, but here my emotions were heightened, and I felt silly for it.

A blonde head peeked through the door. "*Bonjour.* Are you OK?"

I started. The guy who spent most days hunched over a table in the conservatory. His intense blue eyes marred by melancholy, or so I imagined. "Sorry. Yes, I'm fine. Just . . ." I grappled with what to say that wouldn't make me seem like a fool. A little lost without the routine of my old life.

"Homesick?" His features softened.

"Umm . . . yes," I said. "Is it so obvious?"

He gestured to the sofa beside me, as if asking for my permission to sit. I nodded.

"It's not for the faint-hearted, this place."

I must've looked like some doddery, faint-worthy girl. "It's a contradiction, sometimes, I suppose." Wrapped up in its embrace, tottering along a forgotten avenue, I felt alive, and present in that very moment. But seeing a picture of my friends, and sweet baby Willow, a part of me longed for the simplicity of life back home.

"That's what makes it such a great place," he said, smiling.

"What do you do all day in the conservatory?" I hadn't meant to be so blunt, but he was still a mystery.

I'm sure he flushed a little. "I write."

"Books?" *No, Sarah, he writes the telephone directory. Sheesh.*

"*Oui.*"

"What type?"

He shrugged as if it was nothing. "Love stories."

He ran a hand through his hair, and stood abruptly. "I hope you let Paris show you its beauty. What you don't find in here—" he motioned around the room "—you'll find out there. Just give it time."

And with that he strode out. I wanted to follow him into the conservatory and ask him what his name was so I could find his books, but his sudden need to retreat stopped me. Maybe one of the staff knew who he was.

November

When November rolled around, I was still struggling to adjust to the hectic nature of my job. By afternoon, I was reaching for the Tylenol, as the chatter in the bookshop reached fever pitch, and so did the buzzing in my brain. It was a culture shock, getting used to the crowds, and the noise, and the fact there was never time to take a break. Back home, it was nothing for me to amble across to the Gingerbread Café and chat to the girls for an hour. Here, I could barely take a minute to dash to the kitchenette for a drink. I could see why Oceane stepped out for long lunches, because the days were endless; to the credit of the staff, they stayed as long as was needed, but you just never knew when they'd deign to work.

There was no pattern for peak times, the ebb and flow of people changed without warning. When the shop was empty of crowds, we scurried along, righting piles of fallen books, and restocking tables of the bestsellers, scooping up trash, and taking a deep breath before the shop filled again.

Lunchtime was approaching and I found myself eager to get outside, away from the mob of customers. There was only Oceane with me. Beatrice had stepped out to run errands, and TJ was due in, not that that actually meant he would be.

Callie and Jorge arrived, two of the casual staff, and I almost wept with relief. The claustrophobic nature of the packed bookshop was getting to me. "Hey!" I said, a little too exuberantly. "Can you take over? I need to run to the bank, and . . ."

Jorge held up his hand. "Nope. Just stopping by for some books."

I threw Callie a desperate look.

"Same," she replied. "Besides, we worked yesterday." As if a shift every few days was enough. They walked through to the piano room without a backward glance. I had to do *something* for things to change. It was absolute mayhem, and I was red-eyed from fatigue.

TJ loped in with Beatrice in tow. "Guys, finally!" I said. "Look, I need to go to the bank, and ship some of the online orders. But I wanted to run something past you. I've been meaning to do it since I first arrived, but there hasn't been a moment spare." I sent up a silent prayer this would go better than when I corralled them into a group about the missing money.

Beatrice smiled, the same one that didn't seem to reach her eyes. "Sure," she said.

"The roster . . . it's not working. No one turns up when they're supposed to. It makes it hard when I have to cover so many shifts. But instead of coming here, and just making these huge changes, I thought I'd approach it differently. No one wants a new person to boss them about, so what do you think of team-building sessions?" Their faces dropped, like I'd just suggested we work for free or something. Part of the plan was that I'd also know who was on what shift, and could nail down the thief better.

"Erm," TJ said.

I wasn't selling it well enough. "Perhaps we could take a macaron baking class, and discover deep down, we're all soft and squishy on the inside?" I nodded emphatically to convince them.

TJ narrowed his eyes. Beatrice tried her hardest to smile, but it came out more like a grimace.

I hurried on: "Chocolate making classes, even? A wine and cheese walking tour?" My words tumbled out in haste.

The air in the room cooled. TJ coughed into his hand, and mumbled something about being too busy. With a flick of her red curls, Beatrice studied the carpet intently. No one was making eye contact.

"Guys, like, imagine being free of the shop for a few hours . . . we could talk books, and get our hands dirty, bake bread, or . . ." my mind whirled with ideas " . . . climb the Eiffel Tower, I think there's seven hundred and four steps! We'd feel alive! Like we'd achieved something together!

As a team!" I was exclaiming too hard, I knew it, but I was desperate for them to see I meant well. Callie and Jorge returned, their hands filled with books. "Did you say team building?" Jorge asked, his lip quivering with held-in laughter that finally spilled from him in one big shriek. Callie stared at me like I was speaking a foreign language.

"Well . . . yeah, I did." Was it that ridiculous a thing to suggest? Was I making a mess of things again?

Oceane appeared and moved toward me. Under her breath she said, "Darling, just no. *No.*"

"But, but . . . surely, together, doing something fun, we could really bond. Really become friends, as well as colleagues . . ." My voice petered out, as Oceane grabbed my arm. "We're off for lunch," she said loftily, and dragged me into the light dusting of rain, ignoring TJs protestations that he wasn't staying long.

"But I'd almost convinced them. And the banking—"

"Leave it," she said. "Let's have a minute to chat."

We turned right from the shop. My mind was a jumble—I couldn't understand why no one would take me seriously. The farther away we were from the bookshop, the quieter the buzzing in my brain got. Strolling around Paris had the ability to comfort me in a way only books had done before. I loved finding the street signs, like this one—Quai de Montebello—and rolling the words on my tongue. They were always exotic-sounding compared to little old Ashford, where our streets were more predictably named, like Main Street, Second Avenue.

"You're an adorable American," she said. "But that's just the thing. You're a little *too* American, sometimes. Here, people are more reserved. Team building will not work. It's the way you project yourself that will make them respect you. Being a sweetie pie, cute as a button, group hugger, will not work. And trying to get them to become the same—no, just no, Sarah." Her expression was fervent.

"I'm not a group hugger!"

"I meant metaphorically," she said. "But I can just see you now, a group—what did you call it— bonding session. Next minute there's high-fives, and we're wearing baseball caps or something. *Non. Non, non, non.*" She shuddered.

My shoulders slumped a little south. *I was too American?* Or too small-town girl, maybe? "We're not hitting sales targets, and someone's pilfering money. All I wanted to do was inspire them so we could work together to improve things. Otherwise, I'm letting Sophie down, but I can't do it alone."

She laughed. "You will get better at this. I know it seems like there's no order, but that's the way it's always been, and people don't like change. The money, well, that's a different story. We do need to get to the bottom of that. But pushing them to agree to certain times and days, it won't work. They flit in when it suits them."

I stuffed my hands into my pockets. "I can't understand it, that's all. Sophie is so formal about the paperwork, the endless spreadsheets, but then so lax with the staff. It's mind boggling. Maybe it's just that I'm not used to such a hectic job. I'm exhausted by nighttime. I was searching for some balance. I thought if they became my friends, they'd understand. They'd try harder, follow some simple rules. Freeing me up to have a day off, here and there. Help hit the sales targets."

Oceane clucked her tongue. "It's been hard for you. I know you've worked too many hours. You need to take charge, and take a day off when you can, otherwise you'll never see Paris."

I crossed my arms, considering it. She was right. I'd seen a few sights as I raced my way through the day, but so far most of Paris was still a mystery to me. "That's one of my greatest fears, missing out on sightseeing, because there's no time. Who comes to Paris, and doesn't explore? I want to spend a morning in the Louvre, and gaze at the *Mona Lisa*. Read in the Tuileries Garden. But I can't even think of doing that, until I know things aren't going to combust when I'm not there."

"When your man arrives, you can escape, and do those things together. TJ and I will help you more. But do take some time for yourself, Sarah. Otherwise this time will pass you by. When is he coming, by the way?" She stared me down.

I shrugged. "Soon, I hope. I haven't got a clue." It was radio silence again, and beginning to wear thin. My emails were left unanswered, and calls went straight to voice mail. My dreamy romance had turned into dinner for one, and late night chats with the stray cats who made Once Upon a Time their home. Not ideal, but at least they listened when I asked advice in the dead of night, mewling, I'm sure, when they agreed.

"I see," she said.

Cars honked and sped down roads. Tourists milled, sitting by the Left Bank, eating croissants from white paper bags. A wave of envy washed over me that they didn't have to work, they could just meander around Paris, snapping endless pictures and enjoying each different vista. How many places on my bucket list had I crossed off since arriving in Paris? Not as many as I had wanted and already a month had passed.

"Anyway, back to the bookshop. You have to be more forthright. Take those long lunches. When you see staff wander in, grab your things and go. Don't *ask* them, *tell* them."

I thought about it for a few minutes as Oceane and I continued walking, weaving in and out of the foot traffic. It was hard for me to be that person, the one who spoke the loudest, spoke up first, but I could see her point—if I didn't take charge they'd continue to stomp all over me. And perhaps I needed to stop thinking like an American and start thinking like a Parisian. I vowed to throw away my well-read copy of *How To Be The Boss 101* as soon as I got back to the apartment.

Continuing at Oceane's usual breakneck pace, we came to a bridge that was covered in padlocks. The love locks! I'd read so much about the famous place where lovers stood, in my guidebooks. This was where they would make promises, and secure their engraved padlocks to the wire, for all eternity. Something that could never be destroyed or tainted. A pure sign of true love.

"Pont de l'Archevêché," Oceane announced, as she smoothed down her mussed hair that had been ruffled by the light breeze.

The long row of gilded padlocks shone in the gray day, like a holy place. Thousands of locks, layered one on top of the next, thick and almost rotund as they found any space to secure the link. It was like something out of a love story—I had never imagined there would be so many. I stepped forward to read some of the inscriptions, wondering if I was crossing some invisible boundary by reading the couples' messages scribbled on the locks, some with text, some expertly engraved.

"Aren't they beautiful?" I sighed. Romance seeped from the bridge. That so many couples came here to seal their love, and kiss under Parisian skies, made me smile. Farther along, an old man sat on a crate playing an accordion, and the whole experience felt so Parisian I wanted to laugh out loud. This was the Paris I had always imagined, afternoons languishing in the moment.

"Very beautiful," Oceane said. "You know my friend Anouk has a lock here somewhere, but we'd be hard-pressed to find it. The man in question broke her heart, anyway, so it's probably been snapped open and thrown into the Seine."

I wanted to ask what happened but we edged closer and the man playing the accordion called out: "What song would you like?"

"Ummm." I glanced at Oceane, who shrugged in her usual noncommittal way. It was such a strange moment, as if time had stopped, and it was just us three here. The bridge was quiet, even the Seine was empty of boats in this spot. I wanted to feel Ridge's arms around me, as I snapped closed our own love lock. The scent of him, and the city whipping around me would make me giddy. Yet, here I was with Oceane and a man with blackened teeth, and a rheumy-eyed smile.

Would Ridge understand the symbolism?

"For you," the old man said, " 'La Vie En Rose.' "

I hugged myself against the wind, as the first few notes of the iconic song drifted out to me, creating a bittersweet moment where you're living in the small space of time and nothing else mattered. As the familiar song came to the ending, I couldn't stop myself from clapping. I threw some coins in his accordion case as Oceane pulled me along, down another avenue toward a café where she promised they served the most heavenly café au laits. The tune played over in my mind, as I hummed it long after the accordion player was out of sight. The haunting notes provoked a loneliness I had all but been hiding from. Ridge. I needed him. Simply because I loved him. I'd be up-front, and tell him.

When I returned to the shop, I took five minutes to compose an email, hoping his response would be swift.

Ridge Warner,
The city of romance is lonely without you. We could secure a love lock on the famous bridge. Or sip champagne, its bubbles like stars, while we whisper promises to each other at the foot of the Eiffel Tower. Can you come soon? Paris is truly spectacular and I want to hold your hand and get lost here with you.

Yours as ever,
Sarah Smith

NINE

I checked my emails for what seemed like the hundredth time, still no response from Ridge. What would it be this time? No internet connection? A remote posting in some tropical jungle? Phone lines down? A typhoon? Locked away somewhere with the photographer?

TJ and Oceane were at the counter, bickering over a book.

"You can't just end the story like that," she said, her eyes blazing. "It's too ambiguous. We need to know if he made it in the end, if he survived. To say the girl wrapped her arms around him as his breath shook and eyes squinted closed . . . that's it? He died? Or did they rush him to hospital? Unless there's a sequel, which it clearly states there isn't, I think it's the cheat's way out. I need to know! Did he make it? Urgh, I threw the book in a fit of pique!"

TJ shook his head. "It's leaving it up to the reader to decide, to map out their fate."

Oceane fluffed the crop of her hair. "Boring. The author was stuck and ended it lazily. Let the reader decide? It's not a Choose Your Own Adventure book!"

TJ, ever the diplomat, said, "We'll have to agree to disagree." When it came to the missing money, my instincts told me, it wasn't either of these two. TJ was too sweet a person, and Oceane had more money than anyone. Fifty euros here and there wouldn't be enough to pay for her swishy lunches, let alone her shopping trips down the Champs-Élysées.

I laughed quietly at their bantering and went upstairs. This was more how I had imagined life in Once Upon a Time, if only I had time to join in their literary discussions. With a stack of files hugged to my chest and the laptop under one arm, I planned to work where I'd have a view. When I got to the conservatory I stopped in my tracks, I'd forgotten the blonde-haired guy had arrived when the doors opened earlier that day. He was always so quiet, I worried sometimes we'd lock him inside by mistake. Though there were worse things than being stuck in a bookshop like Once Upon a Time for twenty-four hours.

With my bundle of work in hand, I teetered on the threshold, not wanting to disturb the writer who rushed in each morning.

He must have heard the cogs in my mind ticking over because he turned to me. *"Bonsoir."*

"Bonsoir," I replied, "I'm Sarah." We had crossed paths so many times, and I hadn't thought to introduce myself until now.

"Luiz Delacroix." He stood, and did up a button on his coat before holding out a hand.

I shook it and tried not to gasp. No wonder

his face was so familiar! "The writer?" Luiz Delacroix was one of my favorite authors. He wrote about love in such a way, I pined for the characters long after I closed the cover. His stories, sadly, never ended in a happy ever after. And I'd always wondered why. They were tragic tales of love gone wrong, but they swept me away nonetheless—even though I always hoped they'd end differently. Not only that, but he also wrote his stories in the bookshop I just happened to be running . . . it felt like fate.

He tilted his head. "Guilty. I am he," he said with a shy smile. I was so starstruck that I couldn't form words. Luiz was famous the world over, men and women alike swooned over his prose, and his intense good looks. His picture adorned the back of each dust jacket. I must have stared into those blue eyes of his a million times, after closing one of his books, and trying to figure him out.

"Wow." I blushed, so tongue-tied I didn't dare try to speak again. Sometimes my brain ran away from me, and I knew whatever words tumbled from my mouth would be too intense and too soon, as I wanted to pepper him with questions.

He surveyed me, and lit a cigarette. Was smoking allowed in here? So many French people lit up in cafés and bars, maybe it was another Parisian quirk. On him it seemed elegant, somehow. I was going crazy. *Smoking was elegant? No.*

In the old, slightly mildewy room, the smoke sailed out the crack of the window, mingling with the thousand other scents that made the perfume of Paris.

"So you write your masterpieces here?" I finally managed to bumble out some words and was overjoyed they were in order and made sense.

"Most of them, yes. I've been writing here since Sophie took over."

Sophie knew he wrote here and didn't tell me! There were probably a handful of famous poets, and painters as well, who used the upstairs rooms for their crafts. It was that kind of space where everyone was the same, no matter who you were, and that was one of its draw cards.

"I better let you get back to it. I don't want to interrupt the flow of your writing." I hovered there like a fool, wanting to loll about in the room and watch the world go busily by from the comfort of the conservatory.

He blew out a puff of smoke, and grinned. "I'm finished for today. The end of the book is close. So I will leave something for tomorrow."

I smiled. Behind me the fire cracked and spat like it was in its death throes and fighting back once more. "Do you write at home, too?" I said, not wanting an awkward silence to fall.

He nodded. "Sometimes. I'm too manic, and I forget to eat, forget to sleep. It's like falling in love, everything else fades, and I am lost to it." His eyes blazed with a kind of ardor. It was evident he loved his work, and put his soul in to it, and it translated on the page. When I read his novels the rest of the world ceased to exist, it was just me and the characters on those black and white pages.

"An intense way to live."

He stubbed the cigarette in a half oyster shell that was littered with butts. "It's the only way to live," he said. "I cannot control it when it begins, so I must write or I can drown in those feelings."

He was intense, the way he spoke, the things he said. "Why don't they ever end in happy ever after?" I double blinked and instantly wished I could take the words back. I shouldn't have asked. I knew from speculation about Luiz that he was a private person. He was almost reclusive, or so I'd been led to believe. He'd been hiding in plain sight, and no one was any the wiser.

"Why should they?" he asked, as his eyes shadowed. "Does life really work like that, Sarah?" His words were slightly sad, a touch morose, like he was talking about himself, not his books.

I weighed up how to answer. "Not always, but shouldn't we hope it will?"

"I don't write fairy tales. People expect a certain level of truth from me. I write what I know, and that is that love doesn't always last."

I raised my eyebrows. "In your books, there's always a reason why they split up, and it's usually something that's come between them, not always another person. Doesn't that leave room that one day they might find each other again, and find their happy ever after?" I wanted to pinch myself that he was discussing something so private with me, he was well known for being reserved and elusive. And I almost applauded myself for sounding knowledgeable, even though a part of my heart chipped away when I thought of Ridge and our love affair that was on ice, our happy ever after paused for now, or so it seemed.

"You're a hopeless romantic," he said.

"I guess you could say that, but I've never understood that term. Like what's hopeless about believing in something so beautiful? Yours are the only books sans HEA that I read. But I do rewrite the ending in my mind. I pretend they sorted it out, otherwise, I kind of can't cope . . ."

He crossed his arms and leaned against the desk, a small smile playing at his lips. "And where do you take them?"

My palms were beading with moisture at the thought of telling him—was I being rude implying they should finish differently? "OK, say for Emile and Isabelle, in your most recent book. You said she could never love him because of his past, and the fact he'd been damaged by it, so much so. He couldn't leave his home, for fear that he'd have flashbacks of the war and do something crazy. But Isabelle *could* have lived with him. She trusted him. And she wanted to be with him, no matter what, and you took that from her." I felt a passion roil through me as I expressed myself. I'd been heartbroken when the last sentence of that book was goodbye.

Luiz pulled his eyebrows together. "But Emile couldn't control those flashbacks, or what he'd do when they happened. What if he hurt her by mistake? Don't you see? Doesn't he love her more if he walks away knowing he can never harm her? That she's free of the violence that plagues his dreams."

"His dreams were violent, and toxic from what he'd been through, but they had nothing to do with Isabelle. Real love would see past any character flaw, surely? They could have had a plan for those times when he wasn't himself. He could have taken medication, or had a counselor come and visit. Could have locked himself in the bedroom . . . anything, so they could be together."

"In a perfect world, they could have done all that and more. But it's not a perfect world, is it?"

I smiled. I wasn't convincing him. His popularity around the world proved that people loved the shocking endings, the twists, the various plot devices used so you never knew what was coming. "Being a heart-on-sleeve type, and a romance fan to boot, maybe it's just me, but I want them to end up together, no matter what they have to do in order for it to happen."

Outside the day had come to an end, as night slipped firmly across the sky. "I hope you'll continue to read them, even if the love never works out."

"I'll happily read them, and hope one day, when I'm all the way back in America, I'll pick one up and find you've surprised us all with a love affair that lasts a lifetime."

"Never say never, but in this case . . . never."

I couldn't help wondering if there was more behind his opinion than just notoriety and success. Was he haunted by love gone awry? I narrowed my eyes as he shuffled his papers on the desk. "Does life imitate art as they say?" I broached, gently.

He spun to face me, a truly tortured expression darkening his features. "Art imitates life . . ."

Did it though? Or did we usually try and recreate what we read in a good book, like making the book boyfriend come to life? Or wishing those circle of friends we read about were ours?

We said our goodbyes, and I stood in the blue room for an age, wondering what had happened to Luiz to make him write the way he did. I was certain he'd lost someone. He said, *art imitates life* and not the other way around. Art imitates life . . . so he writes what he knows, and that is that love doesn't last. I hoped we'd get to chat again soon. I wanted to pinch myself; I'd just conversed with *the* Luiz Delacroix, and found out more about him in twenty minutes than I would have ever guessed possible. Ridge would get such a kick out of it; he too loved Luiz's fiction. We'd spent many a night bickering good-naturedly about how his books should have ended. I sat at the table by the window, and flipped open the laptop. And emailed Ridge.

Roving Reporter,
Should I send out a search party? I'm worried you're dead, injured, or in love with someone else.
Please reply at your earliest convenience, or I will take a French lover.
P.S. I met Luiz Delacroix! And I'm going to convince him to write a HEA!
Love,
Your Parisian bookseller

A few days later not only did my mail have the usual bills and invoices for the shop but it had my travelers' checks. I let out a squeal and before I could say anything, Oceane's eyes lit upon them. She did her usual arm grab thing, ready to pull me outside to go shopping. "Wait," I cried out. "Sophie's about to email me back. I just sent her a load of reports, and she's not impressed with the figures." I slumped. "Which are, you guessed it, down some more. If I can't turn things around, she'll come back, I know she will." And it struck me I didn't want to leave. Paris and its charms had wooed me and I hadn't seen enough yet, or found what I was searching for. Did that sound like a cheesy song lyric from the nineties? At any rate, I wasn't done yet.

"Sarah, you need some new clothes. You've been waiting forever. Sophie's email can wait an hour, I'm sure. I'll get TJ to watch the counter, and supervise the staff."

She had a way of galvanizing me, and the thought of finally having new clothes to wear, something other than Sophie's, did excite me. I dashed to the computer to email her, and explained that I'd call later. I was only buying time, and eventually I'd have to face the same disappointed tone in her voice. But I was determined to turn things around. TJ had been a godsend with ideas, and we were slowly implementing them—I was sure we'd see results soon. I hit send on the email, and gave TJ a wave as he took my place.

Oceane chatted incessantly as we made our way to the Champs-Élysées.

"Cold today, *non*?" she asked, wrapping her mink coat tighter against the bluster.

"*Oui*." I was dressed in one of Sophie's outfits, another flowy, layered ensemble, and

I could barely wait to find some jeans, and simple sweaters. We headed deeper into the 8th arrondissement.

"Avenue des Champs-Élysées," Oceane said.

"Wow." Sculpted chestnut trees lined the edge of the long avenue, and at the end, the Arc de Triomphe stood proudly, the arch colossal in comparison to everything around it. Even the detail carved into it stood out from our vantage point halfway down the avenue. Cars raced around it in a speedy procession on what must be the world's biggest, zaniest roundabout.

"Look at those fools." She pointed to a bunch of teens trying to make their way across the busy circle, dodging cars whose horns beeped incessantly. "There's an underpass. You go underneath and come out right below the Arc de Triomphe."

"Maybe we should tell them." My heart was in my throat watching them try and escape the mad traffic.

She waved me away. "First we need to eat. Ladurée." She pointed to a pâtisserie, its name glinting in ornate gold. There was a long line of people, a motley bunch with a range of accents, as Oceane led me straight past them, and up to the front where a man stood holding the door as if it was an assembly line.

"Oceane," he said, kissing both cheeks. "Your table is at the back." I followed her meekly, hearing the cries from the front of the queue that we'd pushed in.

"Seriously," I said to Oceane. "How do you get in everywhere?" I was beginning to think the "I've dated a guy here" thing was a ruse. Everyone seemed to know her, and be semi starstruck when she waltzed by, leaving them gasping after the scent of her perfume.

She motioned to a table, before sitting and throwing me a playful look. "You think I've slept with the whole town?"

I laughed. "Well, at first I thought they were old boyfriends but now I'm not so sure . . ."

A waiter came over and Oceane ordered a selection of macarons, and two café au laits. "My family is well known. That's all. Now," she said, resting her chin on her palm. "Tell me about this man of yours. How do you cope being alone all of the time? If he's 'The One' where is he?" she said, arching a brow.

I toyed with the buttons on my jacket. "It's not easy, that's for sure. I wasn't looking for love, but it found me, and here I am. While it's not perfect . . ." I thought of the abruptly ended phone calls, and how it had made me feel second-best to some indistinct thing he was chasing " . . . it's real. And he chooses to work, which takes him away from me." Girl talk, this I could do. Without my friends, it was the poor bookshop cats who had to hear my laments.

She frowned. "But why doesn't he choose you?"

I didn't want to own up to the fact that on the love lock bridge I had been wondering the same thing. My instant reaction was to defend Ridge, and explain it was pure circumstance. But sitting in the bustling little pâtisserie, it hit me anew— once again, *I* was waiting for him. I'd been in Paris for over a month, and his trip here was delayed time and time again. Our phone calls had been becoming shorter and shorter. If I really admitted it to myself I'd almost given up hope he'd get here at all.

"I don't know, Oceane." My heart constricted confessing it out loud. "I guess he's addicted to the chase of a new story, the competitive nature of it. His work is important for other people too." Ridge had given countless people a voice, a way to get their stories out there for the world to read. His work wasn't selfish, I had to admit, it truly did help people.

"Are you sure that's all it is? Some men, they have a girl in each port." It was a quirk of Oceane's to be direct, like she didn't have a filter for how that would make me feel, but she wasn't malicious, just curious, and up-front about whatever popped into her mind.

Still, my stomach flipped at the thought. "He's not that kind of guy. It's purely his work that drives him. And I guess that I knew from day one

163

he was ambitious." Visions of the photographer, Monique, Mona, or whatever her name was, flashed in my mind, which I blinked rapidly away.

"So, you wait?" she said, while sipping her coffee.

"I wait." It struck me how ridiculous I sounded. What kind of relationship was this? Short of flying all over the world with him, what was the solution?

"I hope he's worth it. Paris is beautiful when you're in love. Better though, when your lover is actually *in* Paris."

"In a perfect world, he'd be here."

"Here are the macarons," she said, squeezing my hand in support before thanking the waiter, giving me time to consider her take on it.

I bit into a hot pink macaron, the biscuit pillowy, like air, until I tasted the tart raspberry center. Between mouthfuls I said, "I always wondered how on earth they get so much flavor into such a small biscuit."

Oceane waved a finger. "*Non, non.* They're petit cakes, not biscuits. Ladurée has been famous for their macarons for over one hundred and fifty years. They're the experts."

"You can taste it," I said smiling. Lil and Cee from the Gingerbread Café would get such a kick from seeing the vivid little cakes in front of me. The greens were almost teal, the yellows saffron bright, fuchsia pinks mottled with another flavor. I hadn't tasted anything like it before. I would have to buy boxes to take home when the time came, and I was sure it'd send Lil and CeeCee straight into the kitchen trying to recreate the flavor combinations.

An hour later, with a full belly and on a sugar high, we walked past boutiques with windows full with mannequins wearing stunningly chic clothing. After feasting on macarons and sipping strong coffee we hadn't mentioned Ridge again, but it was still playing on my mind. I'd come to Paris for an adventure and here I was stuck in the same position I had been back in Ashford. Waiting for something to happen to me, rather than changing things myself. I could get lost here among the crowds, I didn't stand out, I was one of thousands, and that made it easier to blend in and enjoy it. I liked being nameless, anonymous in a busy stream of people. It helped me delight in every small thing. Back home, everyone knew every single thing that had happened to me since I was a child. The small-town grapevine had a lot to answer for and was like living under a microscope at times. Here I was free.

"Sarah, I think you have a chance to reinvent yourself," Oceane said, a little gleam in her eye. "You could try some different styles. I know what would look great on you."

Did she sense I wanted to change? It was like

she'd read my mind. Oceane had an eye for all things stylish, and I trusted her judgment but I feared her budget was significantly more generous than mine.

"I'm more of a casual dresser," I said, wondering how I'd get away with any shred of dignity if I couldn't afford it.

"*Oui*, but you're here now. And I can find some outfits that suit your budget, and *you!*" Her face shone happily, and I almost flopped with relief that she knew money was scarce, and the insurance would only go so far.

"Don't look so worried!" She gave my arm a pat. "Here, you can dress like you're rich, if you know where to find the right boutiques." She pulled me to a stop and swiftly looked me up and down. "Navy, and red, maybe some black and white stripes would suit you. Nautical. It's easy when you know how. A blue blazer, a white T-shirt, and a scarlet-red scarf, and voila! You're so slim, we'll look for some skinny leg jeans, and that way you're still you, just more French!"

"OK," I said laughing, her enthusiasm contagious. "Let's see what we can find."

With one last look at the Arc de Triomphe, Oceane pulled me into a smaller avenue, to a tiny boutique at the end of the lane. She spent the next thirty minutes tossing clothes over the top of the change room curtain, and speaking rapid-fire French to the assistant.

With a flourish she pulled back the curtain and surveyed me.

"What do you think?" she asked.

I stared at my reflection, too surprised to form words. Oceane had picked a range of garments I never would have pulled from the coat hangers, but somehow they worked. With a tight pair of dress pants, she matched up various pieces I could mix and match.

"It's all about classics," she said, smiling. "And finding those basics, so you can just switch a cardigan or scarf to give a whole different look."

She'd given me a chili-red sweater, and teamed it with a polka dotted black and white scarf. With black fitted pants, and a black blazer, I still felt like me, just with a bit more *oomph*. Paired with a pair of leather ankle boots with a medium heel, I was totally comfortable, and not at all like I usually was shopping for clothes, which was gangly and awkward. In the pile of yeses on the chair were various color combinations of similar garments, with patterned scarves to swap and change. Form-fitting clothing was more my friend Missy's thing, but on me in those classic combinations, it actually worked.

"Scarves are a French woman's secret," she said touching her nose. "Anything can be fancied up with another scarf, and don't be shy when it comes to colors. Lemon yellow in summer, and plum purple in winter, burnt orange in autumn . . .

add some gold earrings, bright red lipstick, and you don't need to spend a fortune. Just change those basics, and every season you're *en pointe*. You have the jeans, the dress pants, blazers, and then you simply accessorize."

"Yes," I said quietly, unable to drag my eyes from the girl in the mirror. Who'd have thought clothes would give me such a boost? Perhaps this is why women were addicted to shopping. There wasn't much of a selection in Ashford, and it had never appealed to me before. What Oceane had shown me had blown my mind, and thankfully not my budget.

"OK," she said, scooping the clothes into her arms. "I'll have her ring these up. Get dressed and I'll take you to the next shop. Then you'll really have to pick that jaw up off the floor."

I laughed, and changed back into Sophie's clothes, which seemed elegant in their own way, but not suited to me. How did French women know this stuff? I smiled once more at the eager-eyed girl in the reflection before rushing out to pay.

"We're going to the Little Antique Shop under the Eiffel Tower. Under its *shadow* to be specific. When afternoon sunlight hits the tower it casts its zigzag pattern over Anouk's shop."

"An antique shop?" I asked. What did I want with antiques?

"Your outfits are sorted, but you need some *va-*

va-voom. Not cheap supermarket jewelry, *non*. Not acceptable. You can find something there with history, something no one else has, see?"

"Right," I said, glancing down at my cheap supermarket bangles, and instinctively covering them. "Is that where you bought your diamond from?"

"*Oui*. Now Anouk is rather . . . quirky. She believes each piece tells a story, she researches, knowing where it originated, who owned it, and how it came to her. Whatever you do, don't touch anything. She'll decide if she wants to sell to you, or not."

The clack of Oceane's high heels sounded as we hit a patch of cobblestones. The Eiffel Tower came into view, its magnificence as always taking my breath away. "Wait, what?" I asked. "She'll decide if she wants to *sell* to me or not? Isn't it a shop though?"

Oceane tutted as if I was dense. "It's the French way, Sarah. Some shopkeepers are very particular about who their prized possessions go to. And Anouk is fussy, more so than most. She treasures her things, and will only part with them if you're the right person. So don't slouch, don't fidget and for God's sake don't do that snort laugh thing you do when you're nervous."

I giggled. I was sure no one had noticed my unfortunate snort laugh because I'd covered it up with faux hiccuping fits. Damn it! I couldn't help but fidget. What if Anouk turned me away? Would that sully Oceane's reputation with the owner? Nerves fluttered in my belly at such an unusual but utterly French predicament.

We came to the Little Antique Shop. It was pastel pink, and had a planter filled with peach roses giving off a rich, fruity scent. How were their flowers always so fragrant? A table out front housed a range of trinkets: small silver candelabra, an old typewriter, gilded photo frames. My fingers itched to pick them up and observe them closely, but I merely leaned over, gaze alighting on an old tea tin, full of fake pink peonies.

"Not too close," Oceane hissed.

I stood ramrod straight, my eyes wide, fighting the urge to snort. What was this? How did she make any money if she wouldn't part with her wares?

"She's coming. Stop playing with your buttons."

Golly. There were so many rules.

"Oceane," Anouk greeted her in a sultry drawl. She was vivaciously dressed, forties style with a tight woolen dress, cinched at the waist with a wide belt, accentuating her curves. Her blonde hair was a mass of big curls, her face heavily made-up with smoky eyeshadow and scarlet-coated lips.

"Anouk, this is Sarah, an American book worshipper."

I bit down on my lip. Laughter was so close it tasted like sunshine.

"Oh, really?" She gave me a slow once-over, like she didn't believe it.

"Yes," Oceane said with a touch more authority in her voice. "She's a lot like you. Doesn't want books to go to any old person. They have to *match*, you see."

Anouk raised a perfectly plucked eyebrow, and continued her scrutiny. It was impossible not to squirm so I blanked my face, and thought about all the words starting with Z I knew—a technique I used when I was nervous in social situations. After all, nothing stupid can spill from my mouth when I'm deep in thought with the rhythm of words like zigzagging, zippered, erm, zucchini . . .

"Go!" Oceane shoved me in the ribs, and squinted at me.

"What?"

"Inside!" she whispered. "She said you could view the jewelry."

"OK!" I tripped up the front step, which drew the ire of the diminutive French shopkeeper. With a sigh she continued to a glass counter. The shop had an aura about it, almost like I'd stepped back to nineteen-twenties Paris. Old lampshades in muted pinks and beiges hung from hooks above, their tassels waving in the wind. On a section of wall old metal irons hung, their paints chipped and faded, exposing their flat metal underbellies.

Ornate mirrors clung to walls, reflecting the contents of the shop, and my wide-eyed stare. Overhead, brass pots and pans, dented with dimpled bottoms, shone fingers of gold to the floor.

"What are you searching for?" Anouk asked me, her cool stare making me bumble under my breath.

Before I could answer, Oceane spoke up. "She's after a ring, something with a blue gem perhaps? Or a ruby. Some gold hoops, and maybe a pendant of some sort, small, delicate."

Anouk whipped out a felt box that housed rows of antique rings. They were exquisite, from thin silver to chunky gold, and everything in between.

"This one," Anouk said. "It suits the complexity in your eyes."

Searching my face, she waited for a response. I nodded, enjoying the sheer solemnity of the situation. It was as though I was about to handle the crown jewels, or something priceless. With the utmost care, she took a gold ring from the display, its gem winking like a secret.

Oceane stiffened beside me. "Green?" she pointed to the gem, a hint of doubt in her voice.

Anouk rolled her eyes heavenward. "It's *olive*. Peridot aids matters of the heart." She gazed at me like she could read my mind, and a shiver of comprehension ran through me. "You'll see," she said and flipped the display case closed, as if it was the only ring she would offer me.

"Try it," she said, haughtily. "I bet it fits you perfectly."

I slipped the dainty ring over my finger, and sure enough, it was like it was sized especially for me. On the soft flesh on my pinkie finger, it sparkled, like Oceane's diamond, only much more subtly. I understood why Anouk was fastidious with her treasures, it was much like me with books. You wanted to be certain they found the right homes.

"That ring belonged to a woman who lived in Provence. She had an olive farm. Can you imagine the trees?"

I could envision their leaves fluttering in the wind, the breeze scented with lavender from fields beyond. This was certainly one shopping expedition I'd never forget. "Yes," I said, casting my gaze back to my hand.

"And that's why the ring is right for you. Come back," she said, staring into my eyes like she was trying to read me. "You don't need an introduction next time."

Oceane nudged me, and tried to contain her smile. I paid swiftly, and when we were safely outside under the shadow of the Eiffel Tower, laughter finally burbled out of me.

"What did she mean about an introduction?" I asked.

Oceane had her hands on her hips and was breathing hard like she'd just run a marathon.

We'd been coiled tight in the little antique shop, and the tension was eking out of us as we stood far away enough to talk.

"There are a number of French businesses where you cannot shop unless you have an introduction from someone they trust, someone who is a regular customer of theirs. She has another room out the back with her most valuable possessions, but you won't be allowed to go there, not for a while. It's the way things are done. There's a piano shop on the Left Bank, and he is the same. You could be a billionaire, and they won't sell to you without the recommendation of a friend who they know well. It's a way to preserve our heritage."

"I've never heard of anything like it."

I'd passed some kind of test though, and the thought made me stand a little straighter. Perhaps a small part of me was becoming French, if the likes of Anouk approved of me purchasing a ring in her beautiful little shop.

TEN

After the arrival of the travelers' checks, I felt light as air, and a tiny bit French. I was even mistaken for a native at the market stalls where I bought my fruit and vegetables—managing to have the whole transaction done in sleek French and I hadn't stumbled once. Perhaps Paris was opening up to me . . . however, the shop was another issue altogether.

I had snatched a few more minutes before nine a.m. to recheck the balance in the books again, while TJ replenished the front tables. It was peaceful in the shop and I was coming to love these mornings, standing at the counter near the front door sipping on the strong black coffee TJ had gotten into the habit of making for us. I wasn't looking forward to having to call Sophie again and was interrupted from bashing my head on the table when a courier arrived, setting the doorbell pinging so loud I had to lean over to switch it off.

"Sarah Smith?" he asked.

"*Oui?*"

"*Parcelle*," he said, and propped it on the bench before scuttling outside.

TJ and I looked at each other. We weren't expecting a delivery today.

"Well, open it!" TJ said, jolting me into action.

Laughing I reached for the note. The handwriting was the same loops and swirls I'd come to love in the letters he wrote me and used to leave secreted around my house so I'd find them at various times when he was away. Something to stave off loneliness. Even though I felt a rush of pleasure at seeing his handwriting I couldn't help the little voice in my head that was still worried about our lack of connection, with almost zero communication aside from snatched conversations here and there, and the odd email, or two.

Whatever the small box contained, I only hoped it wasn't a gift to let me down softly that he wasn't visiting Paris anytime soon. He'd promised me two weeks in Paris, no work calls, no chasing stories. I ripped it open, to find a note on top:

Sarah Smith,

Would you allow me to steal you away for one magical day in Paris? Please wear these under something warm, and meet me out the front in an hour. Perhaps, organize someone to cover your shift tomorrow, I have a feeling you won't get much sleep.

Love always,
Ridge.

I peeked under the pink tissue paper so TJ wouldn't see, because I knew Ridge, and bet it was some kind of racy undergarment.

"What is it?" he asked, craning his neck.

I blushed crimson and shut the box. "It's . . ."

TJ donned a wide smile. "French panties, right?"

"Erm." How the hell did he know that?

He shook his head. "Men. Step one foot in Paris, and it's always about the underwear."

I laughed, thrilled that I was a mere hour away from wrapping my arms around Ridge and French-kissing him, clichés be damned! Finally, the story was done, and he was here. Would things be the same, after all this time? We'd never been apart for this long, and doubt crept up. Oddly, I was first-date nervous.

"What're the chances of someone covering my shifts today and tomorrow?"

The dreaded paperwork would build up, but there was no way I was going to miss out on time with Ridge. Somehow I had to make it all work. While he slept, I'd catch up.

"Sorry," he said, averting his eyes. "I have to—"

I remembered Oceane's warning, not to ask, or dither about it, to just tell people.

With a deep breath, my words fell out in a rush. "Gotta go, TJ. You're in charge until tomorrow night. Don't let me down."

I bit back a smile as the shock registered on his face and flounced off. The only thing on my mind as I raced up the back stairs, was what outfit I'd wear that would match the lacy little surprise Ridge had sent me. And the joy of knowing he was out in the chilly Paris day somewhere close.

Thirty minutes later, dressed in another of my new outfits, I thanked the heavens for Oceane's jaunt in the boutiques along the Champs-Élysées. With chic clothes on, I felt like I'd cast off a piece of me that was redundant, and replaced it with a brighter, more modern version of myself. My peridot gem blinked under the lights, and I wondered if Anouk from the Little Antique Shop was right, and it was a good omen for matters of the heart.

I managed to stop ogling the new me, and raced downstairs into the hive of the bookstore. TJ whistled appreciatively. "Who is this and what have you done with Sarah?"

I giggled, like a schoolgirl. "I left her back on the Champs-Élysées . . ."

"Paris agrees with you. And . . ." He ducked behind the counter. "Another love note has appeared. He's good, I'll give him that."

Anticipation sizzled so hard I thought I'd faint with excitement. He sure knew how to woo a girl.

The note read:

Sarah Smith,

Would you allow me to escort you for a cruise down the river Seine? The champagne is on ice, and the musicians are waiting . . .

Ridge.

A shriek escaped me. *Calm down, Sarah. Do not start snorting.* Throwing the note on the counter, I ran my hands down the length of my jeans, suddenly nervous because it had been so long since I'd seen Ridge, and what if things had changed?

Beatrice walked in, bringing the icy November winds with her. She pushed her weight on the door to close it, against the gust. "I need to chat," she said.

"I'm just about to leave," I said. "Can it wait?"

She frowned. "Not really. How long will you be?"

I grimaced, feeling guilty at the stung look she gave me. "I'll cover the night shift tomorrow."

She folded her arms. "Right. Well, it will have to wait then." She stomped off, angrily. What the hell? The one time she actually wants to chat, and it was right then, the worst timing ever.

"What was all that about?" I asked TJ.

TJ shrugged. "Probably got a headache from all her eye rolling. Who knows, none of us hang out with Queen Bee."

179

I couldn't shake the feeling I should have heard her out. I was torn about whether to go find her and listen, or walk outside into the blustery day, but what if she wanted me to work tonight? Then I'd be stuck here once again, and the romantic day with Ridge wouldn't happen.

"Go," TJ said, watching me hesitate. "Before he sails down the Seine without you."

I snatched the love letter, which TJ had managed to read upside down, and shoved it into my pocket. "I'm going! Argh!" My stomach flipped, and I fidgeted nervously. We'd had a year of these reunions, but this one felt different.

I strolled out into the cool day, winding my scarf as I went, searching for Ridge. There was a small part of me that was worried I wouldn't recognize him, that when he kissed me or held me it wouldn't feel the same. It had been so long since I had felt his touch and I wondered, had too much time passed? Then I saw him. Up against a metal railing, he stood, looking every inch the suave sophisticate he was. His face broke into a smile, and he walked toward me. My heart hammered at the sight of him in tight black jeans, a navy knit sweater, and that smooth smile of his. His black hair was mussed from the elements; I wanted to run a hand through it, simply to touch him, and know it wasn't a dream. *He was here!*

He embraced me, his he-scent making me giddy, that particular Ridge smell, woodsy, spicy, and utterly male, and sexy as hell. "Sarah Smith, is this a mirage?"

"I was just thinking the same!" I gazed up at him as he cupped my face, and finally pressed his lips to mine. The thought that this man was mine made me woozy with love for him.

"Your chariot awaits." He pointed to a boat and sure enough a group of men holding violins and various instruments stood on the deck waiting to serenade us. His protestations of love were always over the top, and shamelessly romantic. "It's a private cruise, so that I don't have to fight anyone off when they stumble across you."

I laughed. "Is that so?" He always made me feel like I was the only girl in the world, and that men would fall at their knees at the sight of me. I didn't believe it for a minute, but I loved the rush it gave me.

"You are beautiful." He kissed the top of my head, and then took my hand. "Almost too beautiful for words . . . Will you join me?"

I nodded. "I'd love to." Any worries I had about us dissolved when he was by my side. Here he was making grand gestures, and it made the time I spent alone pale into insignificance. Two or three weeks of this would fill up my heart, until it came time for him to leave again.

Ridge helped me across the gangplank and it was hard to watch my footing when all I wanted to do was gawk at him. He'd changed since he'd

181

been away, his face was softer somehow, his eyes bluer, or maybe it was the lovestruck daze that hit me, blurring the edges of my mind. Even his hand in mine felt different, truer. I missed him so, and it was almost surreal, sitting together, in the front of the boat, him pulling a throw rug over us as we set sail along the Seine.

Gentle waves lapped at the hull as we made our way toward Ponts des Arts. Ridge wrapped his arms around me, as the musicians played Édith Piaf. Goose bumps broke out over my skin at the romance of the songs, musical notes drifting lazily into the ether. It was like the French kept her memory alive, or maybe it was a tourist-pleasing cliché, but either way, the evocative songs tugged on my heart.

"You seem to fit here somehow," Ridge said, staring into my eyes.

"It's that kind of place. When I'm wandering, lost and alone, I find something that takes my breath away. I've never had that before. I see why people get bitten by the travel bug." I was easily swept away by the ancient beauty of the city. Was home still where my heart was? Even though I still missed the simplicity of my old life, here, it was like I was someone different, almost French. Or at least, trying my hardest to tread softly, and become one with the place and people.

When I returned home, I imagined Paris would be like an old best friend, full of sweet memories, there to reminisce through rose-colored glasses. I could already see myself sitting down with the girls at home recounting a story that was a little shinier on the retelling, more vibrant, colorful, me exaggerating how brave I was, how I tried it all, but the real Paris would always be in my mind, the black and white, the gray days, the sepia of the past, and the fact that I loved the feeling I had wandering through the city, as if it welcomed me.

"Champagne?" Ridge asked.

"Please," I said, knowing the bubbles would hit my bloodstream and make me more languid, almost liquid in Ridge's arms. He poured two flutes, and I sipped, taking in the view ahead. As always, throngs of people walked on each side of the Seine. On the right bank known as *La Rive Droite* there was a market set up. Stalls of bric-a-brac, pieces of antique furniture, and clothing spanned along the one side.

Ridge nuzzled the soft skin on my neck, and my eyelids grew heavy. "How long does this boat ride take?" I said playfully, fighting the urge to tell them to turn around and deposit us back at the shop so we could race upstairs.

"An hour." He laughed. "And then, there's more . . . you, my little minx, are going to have to wait an entire day to rip my clothes off."

I guffawed. "Rip *your* clothes off!"

"It's obvious, that lusty look in your eyes, you can't hide it. It's written all over your face . . ."

I gave him a shove. "Is that so? Well, I've actually got to cover the night shift later."

His face fell.

"Joke."

He pulled me closer. "OK, I'm the one dreaming of a naked Sarah, but don't tell anyone. I'm trying to keep my cool, and do the right thing, showing her how magnificent the city of love can be when you're actually *in* love."

"I won't say a word." We kissed, his body pressed hard against mine, all thoughts of the view vanished and I wished the moment would last forever. Lost emails, and missed calls didn't matter so much with Ridge by my side.

Once off the boat, we strolled around the uneven cobblestoned streets of Montmartre, coming to the square filled with artists, sitting in front of their easels. The rain had slowed to a fine mist, turning the black of Ridge's hair silver under the gentle shards of sunlight that fought their way through the fog, casting a soft yellow hue above us, like an ambient glow.

Ridge stopped in front of a sketch. The lashings of smudged pencil brought out a deep sadness in the subject's eyes. Who was it in the portrait and what had made them so forlorn in this place, yet they'd still sat long enough for their face to be recreated on parchment?

He spoke to the artist in quick-fire French—

once again, I was surprised by how adept he was in any situation, from speaking fluently in French and managing not to butcher the silky rhythm of the language, to wandering around the avenues of Paris like he'd lived here his whole life.

"OK," he said, turning to me, his eyes lit with wonder. "Sit down, Sarah, and Remy will sketch you."

My cheeks flamed. It was all well and good wandering around, gawping at other people getting portraits painted or sketched but another thing for me to do it. I'd be under a spotlight and drawing the eyes of passersby, which made me cringe.

Ridge leaned close and whispered in my ear. "Please. I want a keepsake for when I'm not with you."

I battled with saying no, it wasn't my thing, and what if the girl on the page wasn't who I thought I was? But Ridge nodded, and shuffled me around, onto the stool, cupping my face. "Just be you. That's the girl I love."

It was hard to argue with that, so I tried not to slouch, and instead wrung my hands together, darting a glance at the artist as he took a seat in front of me, surveying me like he was already imagining me in black and white.

When tourists moseyed by, gazing at me full in the face, I smiled tentatively, and held my breath, hoping each stroke of the pencil would bring me one step closer to springing off the stool, and into a bistro for a glass of wine.

When the picture was done, I eased off the stool afraid to look at it. Ridge's face lit up, and his smile threatened to swallow him. "Now I'll have you wherever I am," he said.

I peeked at the portrait. The artist had captured the love in my eyes, and the difference in my face, from being in Paris. My cheeks were fuller—I blamed the macarons—and I didn't look so daydreamy anymore. But still, I blushed, being the center of attention as people openly stopped to look from me and back to the portrait.

I thanked the artist profusely, amazed at his level of skill with a pencil, how he could turn a few lines into a reflection of me.

Hand in hand we strolled around Montmartre. We turned and headed for the Sacre Coeur. The old church stood regally on top of the hill, the platform below a perfect vantage point to see the sprawl of Paris. We went to the railing and gazed out, the city a big, bustling maze from here. The Eiffel Tower was monolithic, dwarfing everything around it. It seemed so vivid, with the gray horizon acting as a backdrop to the city, and the mist floating gently above. There was a whole world out there like this, views that took my breath away, and I hoped I'd get to travel more in the future. As hard as it was for me to leave the comfortable routine of my old life—the safety, the regularity of every day—I knew now, seeing this, I wanted more.

Clusters of people took photos, and babbled in accents I couldn't ascertain. Ridge looped his arm around me and said, "Stunning, isn't it?"

I nodded. "It's like someone supersized the Eiffel Tower and plonked it down in the city. It's huge when you're standing under it, but from here, somehow it seems even bigger."

"There's one more thing I want to show you." Ridge took my hand, and we turned our back to the view. We dashed away, as rain fell harder, and I don't remember ever feeling so alive.

We wove our way through small laneways, and our breath came out fast as we tried to outrun the weather. Ten minutes later, and what seemed like a lot of exercise for a non-exerciser, we came to a little garden on the Place des Abbesses.

"What is it?" I asked.

"Come closer," Ridge said, pulling my hand. "It's *Le mur des je t'aime*."

I swooned at the French words spilling from Ridge's lips, a heady combination of want and need made me flush for him.

"It's the wall of '*I love yous*'," he said.

I edged closer, once people moved away. Up close, it was spectacular. The sentiment written in so many different languages. Dark tiles, glittering like the night sky. Some cracked and spaced, others perfectly aligned. Splashes of color were dotted here and there.

"The artist used the smudges of red to symbolize a broken heart, but tiled together again, the wall can reunite even the most damaged. It's about humanity, and generating peace in a busy world. A metaphor. But I prefer to think of it as all the ways I love you. In every language, Sarah."

My emotions were heightened from his presence, his silky words, and the way he *showed* me how much he loved me, even if he was away a lot. It banished the doubt I felt, the worry that things would be different between us.

As the sun set behind moody skies we wandered hand in hand, shooting glances at each other as if we were making sure this was real, and laughing each time we were caught out.

"So," I said. "When you're away, what's with the radio silence?"

He looked genuinely surprised. "I'm focused. That's all. There's so many things I want to do to set up our future and in order to make it happen, I have to work hard now, and hope it pays off. It's hard to hear the sadness in your voice too. It makes me second-guess my work, and all I want to do is be with you."

"I don't like it when we go so long without speaking. It feels like we're drifting apart."

He stopped, and pulled me close. "There's no way in the world that will ever happen, Sarah.

I've never felt like this before, and I plan on spending the rest of my life with you." He smiled. "If that's what you want too, of course. But first, I have to figure out how to make our two lives merge, so we both have the things we need."

He bent to kiss me, a soft sweet lingering touch that made me almost dissolve into the ground. When we were together, nothing else mattered. Days like this would recharge our love and make the time apart easier to handle.

"Now," he said. "I've booked a romantic dinner for two at Le Jules Verne, which is at the top of the Eiffel Tower."

My stomach growled at that very moment, and I blushed. Oceane had been to Le Jules Verne and said it was a super swanky restaurant with striking views of Paris. Imagine being in the heart of the Eiffel Tower!

"Shall we?" he said, and wrapped an arm around my waist.

A kind of dizziness hit me. We'd have two weeks of this! Wandering around under the filmy moonlight. Kissing in the rain. Leaning against each other beneath an umbrella while we went sightseeing. My Paris dreams were coming true: Ridge, me, and time in which to get lost in the most beautiful city in the world.

ELEVEN

We were tangled together in a deep sleep when the phone shrilled, not the usual trill of Sophie's cordless. Ridge's cell.

I pulled the quilt up and glanced at the alarm clock. Two a.m. shrieked in neon green.

Ridge groaned, stumbling from the bed, taking the top sheet with him and retreating to the bathroom.

When he returned ten minutes later, I was waiting, unable to fall back asleep, knowing instinctively what was coming.

"Where to this time?" I asked, groggily.

"Russia," he said, his eyes bright despite being woken in the early hours of the morning.

One lousy night. That's all he'd stay for? "Do you have to go? I thought . . ."

"I'm sorry," he cut me off. "I know I promised to stay longer. But I need to take the work when it's offered. If I refuse, those stories will be handed to someone else on a platter. I want to stay, Sarah, really I do. But I can't risk losing out."

I frowned in the semidarkness. "So, how long will this go on for?" I understood his motivations, but where did it leave us?

"Not long. You know there are quiet times.

Weeks in a row where nothing is going on. I'll be back soon."

"I'd prefer you stay now, though. Surely you can tell whoever it is that you will miss this one puny story? And that you'll be there for the very next call?"

"I can't. I haven't done it long enough to pay my dues yet. I'm still the rookie freelancer." He ran a hand along my back, sending shivers down my spine.

"Ridge, don't think that's going to distract me. In the light of the morning when there's an empty space next to me, I'll remember you stayed even less this time. One day?" It was hard not to feel insubstantial when Ridge practically bounded from bed to leave, as eager as a puppy, without a backward glance at me.

He laughed at the scowl on my face. "I love it when you're angry."

I took a pillow and lobbed it at him.

"One year of this, Sarah, and then I'm all yours."

"And whose are you now?" I said, annoyed despite his sexy smile that as easily as that he was leaving.

"I'm yours, Sarah. You'll see. I'm doing this for us."

I sighed. "Get back into bed. We can argue over the phone once you've gone." The fight left me; no matter what, I loved the godforsaken man, and

I wanted to wrap my arms around him before he was gone again. It had to last me however many weeks he'd be absent for.

There'd be no visits to the Louvre, no wandering around Père Lachaise to see the graves of the famous long since buried. Wintry picnics on the Champs de Mars would be spent alone, wrapped in a blanket, with my book— my most loyal and trusted friend. We'd had *the* most romantic of days together. The way Ridge expressed his love for me was the stuff of fairy tales, but was one day enough? The thought of four or five weeks alone, again, made me curl into a ball. Was I enough for him? Or more seriously, was he enough for me?

The day after Ridge left, it was teeming down rain. It drummed on the roof, and the scent of mildew was heavy in the air at the bookshop. I'd woken to find a pile of novels soaked when water seeped from above. Buckets were swiftly set down to catch the drips, while I pondered how water managed to wend its way through three levels. I hoped there wasn't a flood upstairs. Frowning, I raced up to assess any damage and curiously found the rooms dry.

Back downstairs, I reached for the phone and called the plumber, thinking it could only be another burst water pipe. The amount of money the building sucked up was horrendous. But I was also upset about the books being damaged. There they sat, patiently waiting for the next day, for the person who'd smile at the sight of their rosy red covers and pick them up to read them on the train to the Palace of Versailles, or in some dim corner of a bistro over a nip of whiskey. And now they'd be tossed into the bin, waterlogged, and dead.

Well, not on my watch.

Sophie didn't keep books whose spines were broken, or whose covers were missing. But I did. If the words were still legible they had value. I scooped up the soggy books, to find a warm place to dry them out. Perhaps I could have a table out front, of damaged novels who could be adopted. And all they had to do was promise to love them, raggedy pages and all.

"Has anyone seen the James Joyce *Exiles* first edition?" Beatrice asked, as she came rushing down the stairs.

James Joyce. My legs wobbled. "I sold one today," I said, my voice just above a whisper. "But I didn't know it was a first edition." Goddammit.

Her mouth fell open. "You didn't know?" she said, incredulous.

I blushed to the roots of my hair. I specialized in seeking out rare first editions for my online customers back home. How could I have made such a terrible mistake? I'd sold the book for a few euros! "I was rushing to serve. I guess it didn't occur to me to check. It wasn't wrapped or anything . . ." My feeble explanation sounded empty, even to me.

The first editions were locked away in a room with adequate ventilation so they wouldn't get warped by heat, or moldy from cold air. They were wrapped in a special type of plastic to preserve them. Customers had to make an appointment if they wanted to peruse those books. Gloves were worn, it was taken very seriously because of their worth. Thank God it wasn't a *Ulysses* I'd sold by mistake. That book was worth more than I could ever repay. Still, *Exiles* was worth a few thousand euros too.

But wait. "No one has been in the first edition room today. There's no way I could have sold it." There was only one key to that room, and it was looped on a chain around my neck.

Beatrice crossed her arms and narrowed her eyes. It was like she was weighing up her words before talking. It struck me again, how tightly she held in her emotions around me.

"A selection of books arrived a few days ago," she said. "From an estate sale. You were supposed to go through them and wrap the first editions. I did tell you, *twice*, that it was urgent."

I wondered, not for the first time, what I was doing here and if I'd be able to keep up without going insane or ruining Sophie's trust in me with her beloved shop. "Did you?" I asked, having no recollection of that conversation. "I can't believe I sold it without checking." Had I unpacked a box of estate sale books? I was more scatterbrained than usual, after the shock of Ridge leaving as well as trying to fit everything in each day at the shop I couldn't be sure . . .

I bit down on my lip. What a foolish thing to do. I should know better than that. I'd sold hundreds of first editions. Their scent was different to other books, earthier, ripe with the past. The cinnamon-colored pages curled slightly, fattening them. I'd have to tell Sophie I'd cost her more money, and hope she'd forgive me. Still, something niggled. I didn't remember Beatrice talking to me at all about an estate sale order. She'd just stared at me out the corner of her eye like I was an exotic animal that she didn't know how to behave around.

"Sarah," TJ said, interrupting my train of thought. "There's been an accident in the conservatory. You might want to go check."

I sighed. "OK." I was glad for the distraction, giving me a moment of pause to ponder my mistakes. And how on earth I was going to break the next lot of bad news to Sophie.

Upstairs books lay sprawled, covers open wide like arms flayed out, as if they'd had a party with too many cocktails and fallen asleep as the sun lit the sky. A shelf had collapsed, leaving books piled atop each other in a disagreeable jumble. It was just after nine a.m. and Paris was quiet. Torrential rain kept people indoors later, and the bookshop didn't get busy until after lunch. The calm was like a gift. I surveyed the back wall of the conservatory wondering if I could fix the shelf myself, or if I'd have to call yet another handyman in.

Dust motes swirled around as I stacked the fallen books into neat piles. Some pages were crinkled, and ripped, so I made another pile for novels that would need repair.

While I scrambled on the floor picking up as much as I could, Luiz walked in, his face pinched. "All that bashing at the keyboard has brought the shelf down," he said.

I laughed. The desk he usually sat at to write was covered in brick dust and rubble. Luckily the shelf hadn't come down when he was sitting under it. "Looks like it."

"Let me help," he offered as he knelt beside me and reached for some fallen novels.

The books in the conservatory were older tomes about gardening and horticulture, it wasn't a busy room. Customers didn't really venture this high, as the spiral staircase thinned, and darkened, it looked as though there was nothing above— which is what I supposed made this the perfect room for a writer to hide away in. Those who did brave it were rewarded with the brightest, most vivid room because of the picture windows, glass ceiling and the view.

"What's this?" Luiz said, holding a small case, almost like an old-fashioned beauty bag, with soft pink leather and a gold clasp.

"A travel bag?"

"By the layer of dust over it, I'd say it's been hidden for a while," he said.

"Or lost." I pictured someone wandering into this room and being spellbound by the sight of Paris from the window, high from this vantage point, where you could see Notre Dame's gargoyles, and all the way to the Eiffel Tower and the sprawl of the city.

I flicked open the clasp on the bag, and a stack of neatly folded letters spilled out.

The air around us hummed. "Whispers from the past . . ." Luiz said, sitting back on his haunches.

"We should reunite these with their rightful owner," I said, a grin splitting my face. I loved a good mystery and something about the letters called to me. They were soft with age, faded, scented almost citrusy somehow.

"I suppose we should," Luiz said. "Then we'd have to read them, it's the only way." His eyes twinkled with mirth. Luiz was rumored to be reclusive and after our first chat, I wondered if he'd warm to me, or retreat but here we were sharing in a discovery, both eager to know more. I had to catch myself from getting starstruck again. He was just a person, after all, I had to stop thinking of him as a celebrity. Oceane had worried I'd fuss over Julia Roberts if we saw her, but give me an author any day, and I was more likely to act like a loony. If I ever met Jojo Moyes, I would most likely scare the woman witless by babbling away wanting to know everything about her. She was my idol. And Luiz was a close second. So far I'd managed to keep my cool. Just. There were moments I wanted to say, go and write, I'll just stand behind you and watch the words flow from your extraordinary mind, to the keyboard, don't mind me. Luckily work was too busy for me to show my true writers-fascinate-me colors.

Without any preamble we moved to the desk by the window that was free from debris, and laid them out. They were written in French! Goddammit! It would take me far too long to decipher the language, especially with the loops and swirls of the cursive and I was impatient to know what they said. Luiz searched for dates, and found the oldest one. We'd have to start at the beginning to make any sense out of them.

Luiz took the first letter. "Get comfortable," he said, motioning to a high back chair. "I'll translate."

I couldn't hide my glee and did a silly jump clap thing. This old building, this beautiful city, I was certain we'd just uncovered something priceless, an epistolary story from long ago. Settling into the chair I curled my legs under me and pulled my cardigan together, ready to hear the story unfold.

Mon Amour,

I composed a piece for you today. I closed my eyes, and thought of you, that rapture, that fire. The memory of your love, it's like I've absorbed it all for the times we're apart, and it spilled from me to the ivory keys, my fingers a blur, as if the piece was already written, composed by the coupling of our souls. I had to force myself to stop playing, and write it down, but I knew I'd never forget that composition. It's as alive as you are to me. I know they'll say it's too progressive, it doesn't conform, but that's because what we have is greater than what's ever been before. Our love is an allegro, there's no light and shade, no slow start, and gradual increase, so the music cannot follow the standard rules either. And why should it? Why do I have to live in the shadow of someone else's ideals? They've never been in love like this before. Of that I'm sure. Until we meet again, my love, I'll play our song, and feel you with me, through the music.

Je t'aime
Pierre

" 'Our love is an allegro . . .' " With a hand to my chest, I smiled. "It's a love story!"

Luiz's smile widened. "Want to bet it doesn't end in happy ever after?"

I faux glared at him. "How can it not? He composed music for her! Progressive, dramatic pieces. We have to find out who she is! Maybe he'll say her name in one of them?"

"We better keep reading," Luiz said, his expression fervent as he reached for the next letter.

We only had Pierre's correspondence and I would have given anything to read the woman's reply to such a beautiful love letter. I pulled a rug over my legs and settled in to listen.

TWELVE

As weeks continued to pass the sales weren't improving as much as I had hoped. The new feature wall of books set in Paris and memoirs about the city had done nicely, pulling in the tourist crowd, but it wasn't enough. I had to come up with something unique if I was going to make this year as profitable as Sophie's last. The disappearing money was still a mystery too, even though it had dropped off some, we were still missing ten to fifty euros every couple of days and I had no idea how else to deal with it, short of doing a *Mission Impossible* stunt and hanging from the ceiling to spy.

I'd come to dread Sophie's phone calls. Nervously, I ran a hand through my hair, and got my paperwork in order so we could chat. The phone rang and I snapped it up, dread tightening my chest.

"*Ma cherie*," she said, her voice short. "What on earth is going on there?"

I grimaced. So she'd had time to read the reports I'd emailed. I almost laughed at myself—of course she had time, she was in the quiet, quaint town of Ashford, and in my cute little bookshop where nothing much happened unless you counted the adventures you read on the page.

"I'm sorry, Sophie. It's not like we haven't tried. We've implemented a buy one, get—"

She cut me off. "Sarah, these figures are abysmal. November should be double what you've done. Are you not unpacking the new stock quickly enough? What is it? What are *you* doing *so* wrong?"

The frustration in her voice and the tart way she emphasized the fact I was single-handedly ruining her business was like being scolded by a parent. "Well, that has been an issue, actually. I can't serve and be out the back at the same time, unloading stock—"

"Well, get someone else to do it!"

"Yes, as I was saying . . ."

"You need to take charge. I rely on these sales to last us through the winter when the tourist trade drops off."

"The staff—"

"Please, you must fix this, before it bankrupts me."

Frustration coursed through me, as she abruptly interrupted each time I tried to explain. I gave in, and let her say her piece, all the while feeling a fresh wave of anxiety creep over me. She hung up, without her usual sweet goodbyes, and I fell back, glad the call was over. I was working damn hard, and wondered if it was all worth it. I'd agreed to come here as a favor to Sophie, and then she heaped enough work on me to wear out the most savvy businessperson. And she was yet another person who wouldn't listen to me when I tried to speak up. If she'd have given me two minutes we could have discussed marketing strategies.

I wanted to throw my hands up and jump on a plane back to Ashford, or to call Missy, CeeCee and Lil, but how could I? CeeCee and Missy were so focused on gorgeous baby Willow, and Lil was exhausted from nights of broken sleep. I'd spoken to her a few times, she'd snatched moments between feedings and time zones and even though I knew my friends would be there for me, I couldn't burden them when they had far more important things on their own plates. So I turned to the only person I could and as soon as I heard his voice my worries tumbled out.

"Money keeps disappearing." I was rigid with anxiety. "Sophie is angry with me. Her complicated data entry is like something an accountant would do. There's someone here who's stealing because they think they can get away with it." I let out a half sob. "The sales are shrinking. I don't know what to do."

"You have to call them together and threaten them. They think you're a soft touch." Ridge's rough voice was exactly what I needed to hear, "Be fierce, baby. I know you have it in you. Don't let Sophie down by letting them play you."

I stared out the window watching the bare trees face off against the wind and felt the chill coming through the panes. I was too embarrassed to tell him I'd tried that and it hadn't worked—if anything it had been disastrous. "I wish you were here," I choked out.

"Baby, I do too. But you've got some friends there. Why don't you call Lucy and Clay? I know this is tough right now, but you're enjoying Paris. Don't let this work problem get you down."

Lucy and Clay were friends from back home who were here for a six-month stint while she took an art course at the prestigious Van Gogh Institute. I'd wanted to catch up with them, but hadn't managed to seize any time. Lucy studied long hours too, often into the night. Our Parisian lives had a tendency to swallow us up, it was a world away from the sleepiness of Ashford.

"I want *you* here. Is that such a bad character flaw? I can't help wanting to be with the guy I love."

He laughed, the usual Ridge response when he deemed me too girly, or too something he didn't quite know how to answer. It irked me that day, because I was reaching out to him—which I never really did, because I always had the girls at home and I knew he was running his own race. I'd read enough romance books to know I didn't want to be the girl who clung on and was needy, but I couldn't help be frustrated by his efforts to placate me.

Surely I was allowed to lean on him sometimes,

especially when we had barely seen each other in the last few months. Can any relationship survive on more than one day? I didn't think I was asking too much.

"Sarah." He composed himself. I closed my eyes, hoping he wouldn't say something banal. I felt a frisson of worry things would change between us if he shrugged me off when I wanted more from him. "Let this be the adventure of your life. You don't need me there to have that. I hate being away from you just as much, believe me. But for now, that's the way it has to be. I love you with every ounce of me. You suit Paris, it suits you. And once the exchange is over, things might settle down for both of us."

"So if I said please get on a plane, I need to see you, you'd say no?" I hated asking, but wasn't love being there if you needed them? Just this once I wanted him to choose me.

"You've had a crappy few days at the shop. Rise above it, baby. Me being there won't help. It'll take you away from the bookshop, when what you really need to do is fix the problems there before they escalate."

"Well, I guess, that's that," I said, deflated.

His voice came back soft, "You knew what my life was like, Sarah."

Had I expected him to drop everything for me? "And I remember saying big-shot reporters were a no for me."

There was a brief pause where we both registered what had been said, but neither of us took it back. Until he said, "I love you, and you know that. This is temporary."

After I hung up the phone, I sat at Sophie's window, watching the Eiffel Tower fairy lights flash in the distance on the hour. Moonlight shone down over the city, and rain drummed on the roof. Perhaps I could escape for an hour to wander along the Champs de Mars, to Les Invalides, around to the pyramid of the Louvre. Nighttime strolls through the city always lifted my spirits. It was the rest of the tangled web inside the shop that got me down . . . and Ridge. But I brushed him from my mind. Something had to change at the shop, and I had a feeling it was me.

"Luiz," I said. "No work today?" It was late, he hadn't arrived early this morning, which was unusual for him.

Luiz brushed a hand through his unruly waves. He looked every ounce the writer—messy too-long hair, a half-dazed expression as though he was only partly here, the rest of him lost in his mind with the characters he'd left back on his laptop.

Did those fictional people miss him? When his front door clicked closed, did they hold hands and jump from the screen? Perching on the keyboard, reading about their own lives, through Luiz's words? Crazy, kooky Sarah, my friends teased whenever one of these notions spilled from my mouth before I caught myself. But to me, books were alive, the words throbbed and pulsed, as important as a heartbeat, and I bet his books were just as real when they were half-written too.

"What are you thinking, Sarah?" Luiz cocked his head, a smile playing at the corners of his mouth. "I lost you there . . ."

I blinked, pulling myself back to the moment. "Oh," I said, nervous laughter escaping. "I was thinking about . . ." What could I say, I had a penchant for daydreaming? "Your writing, actually. Did you get the novel finished?"

Stepping forward, he folded his arms, and propped them on the counter. His eyes were dark and unfathomable against the slight tan of skin. "I did the first draft, at least. Now to leave it a while before I edit."

"A welcome break then?" It struck me, how little I spoke to writers despite being intrigued by them. There were a few I'd contacted through my blog, romance writers whose books I'd fallen in love with, but I hadn't met many face-to-face. Ashford was too small a place for them to venture, though I did have some visit for the Chocolate Festival eons ago, but they'd raced in and out, and I hadn't had time to chat properly. When the book club met back home, they would clutch their hearts and pretend to faint when I told them I'd met Luiz and become good friends. They wouldn't believe me, I was sure of it.

Luiz rubbed the back of his neck. "This novel, I will try and forget for a few months, and then read it again later, fresh. But I can't *not* write. My life is too lonely without fictional people crowding my mind."

"I would have thought you'd need a break, some time to catch up on sleep, and trashy TV . . ." If writing for him was what reading was for me, then I bet he wasn't a TV-watching type. Time spent in front of the box was time wasted in my opinion, there was always another story to fall into. My to-be-read pile sadly would most likely outlive me—though I tried valiantly to catch up with it, I'd never get there. The allure of new books, new writers, characters who beckoned to me would never wane.

Luiz laughed, his white teeth flashing under the lights. Ridge's teeth were also pearly white. How did they manage movie-star teeth? I couldn't help comparing the two men, Ridge's tall, dark, and handsome romance cover good looks, and then Luiz's blonde, blue-eyed movie-star features. While Ridge was forthright and dynamic, Luiz was quieter, more reserved, and only spoke when he had something important to say. Ridge was the one to take the lead of any conversation, directing it usually back to his work, the stories that drove him, giving people a voice who so desperately needed it.

"*Non, non*," he said. "Now, I wait for inspiration to find me . . . and it always does. Paris is the place for love. I walk around arrondissements, and see it everywhere. I wait for the flutter of the idea to turn into a heart-stopping bang, and I begin. And then *désolé*, I'm lost once more."

"Do you wish they were real?" I propped my elbows on the counter.

"My characters?"

I nodded.

"But they are real, don't you see?"

My stomach flip-flopped at the thought. Was there a place where characters hovered, brought to life each time someone cracked open the cover and read about them? Did they watch us, from some faraway place, as we caught up with their lives?

I smiled at the idea.

"They're part of you, a product of your imagination. You, the reader, make them four-dimensional, bring them to life in your mind, your heart, and your vision of them is unique, no two people read them the same way. So they're exclusively yours." Luiz's voice was soft, as if he was at that same place, the realm of half here, half there, in the gauzy shadow where characters came to life.

I raised my eyebrows. "I want to meet them for

a glass of wine, and quiz them about the choices they made. And grab some of them by the scruff of the neck, and say, WHY! Where's your happy ever after?" I couldn't help tease him.

He threw his head back and laughed, a deep baritone. "There's quite a few I'd like to toss into the Seine for not doing the right thing."

I smiled, imagining him doing just that with a character who was misbehaving on the page.

"Would you care to join me for an aperitif? There's a little bar on the Rue de la Colombe called La Reserve De Quasimodo. It's a secret though, only locals know about it, so you have to promise me you won't tell a soul or you'll end up in my next book as the one who cannot keep her word." His eyes shone with the joke. Everywhere I went with my new friends was a place no one else knew, a hidden door leading to a wonderland of mystery I loved exploring. It made me wonder if Parisians ever grew tired of their town being overrun by tourists, and hence kept so many places a secret.

"Will we run into the Hunchback of Notre Dame?" I said, fluttering with excitement at spending more time with an author I so admired. It was almost surreal to think that this man—who was so famous for hiding behind his book jacket, turning down interviews and shunning the press and adoring crowds—would want to spend time with me. I'd asked him so many questions and he had answered every one of them, but I couldn't help wondering about the sadness I still saw lurking in his eyes. There was a story, a secret, that in all of our conversations Luiz would sidestep, so I backed away from outright asking, wanting to preserve this new friendship. It hit me, that instead of Ridge being the one to fly to my side, I had Luiz, and it had certainly brightened up my time here. A platonic friend who liked me just for me.

"The hunchback may or may not be there. Just keep your cool," he joked. "Shall I steal you away?"

"Sure. Let me grab the love letters, if you feel like chatting about them?"

"I'd love nothing more. I haven't stopped thinking about them to be truthful. Of course, it's given me plenty of story ideas."

I smiled. "I'll just freshen up." I took my handbag from the counter, and went to the staff bathroom.

In my old life it was unheard of for me to give two hoots to my appearance. Before work I'd apply a bit of eyeliner, a sweep of mascara, and that was it. But here, I was taking pains to adapt, to be French—with those little touches that set them apart from the crowd. A slick of red lipstick, and a spritz of perfume, the technique of tying the scarf just the right way. Oceane had taken me aside and shown me the various ways in which it could be looped, and I felt a step closer to being Parisian, learning their ways. I gave my hair a cursory comb.

The phone rang. I dashed over to it. "Two secs," I said to Luiz. "Once Upon a Time," I trilled, hoping it wasn't TJ or Oceane calling in sick, they were due to relieve the casual staff and I'd have to cancel the drink with Luiz if they didn't turn up.

Luiz slid on his gloves, and I did the same while cradling the phone to one ear.

"Sarah Smith, at long last, I catch you."

"Ridge," I said, my surprise evident. "Where are you?"

"Still in Russia. Might be a while yet. Not ideal, I know. But I was thinking of what you said . . ."

Luiz glanced at his watch.

"Can I call you back later?" I cut him off.

"Sure, baby. But I might not be here. There's a group of us . . ."

There was always a group of them, usually with the background noise of a pub, or a party atmosphere. I'd spent too long cooped up in the shop, and I wasn't about to let down the one person who offered to take me from the confines of it. "I get it. You're busy. I have to go. Call me when you can." A week ago I would have dropped everything if Ridge called, but now, things had changed. My life wouldn't hover on pause anymore.

I clicked off. Ridge's voice had the ability to turn me molten with want for him, but all that was canceled out when I thought of the way he only deigned to call when it suited him and then went on to say he'd be busy so it was now or never. That was totally fine, and made it easier for me to say I was busy too.

Outside, for Luiz's sake, I shook off the angst, and kept my eyes straight ahead, taking in the Paris evening, the evocative filmy light. The Seine was silver under fingers of moonlight. Boats bobbed past, filled with tourists taking in a nighttime cruise, their champagne flutes held aloft as they cheered tipsily to pedestrians. The hulls of the boats were adorned with brightly colored tinsel, and flashing fairy lights, as Christmas edged closer. It was hard not to smile, and be caught up in the magic of the city, a place frenetic and alive.

"Was that your lover on the phone?"

Lover. It sounded so much more passionate than boyfriend and for a moment I understood the French attitude to love a little more. A lover was someone transient, someone you loved for a time before you moved on. A boyfriend . . . well, let's just say if Ridge was my boyfriend then those words were separated by a space that shouldn't have been there. "Yes."

"Where is he?"

"In Russia chasing bad guys, I guess." I hoped

my defensiveness wasn't clear in my voice. It was true, Ridge had to work that much harder than the reporters who over time had networked their way into top spots. He wouldn't settle for second best, it wasn't in his nature. But where did I fit into that equation? Once the bookshop exchange was over, I'd be back home, with the same routine, watching life tick on by. Even though it was demanding here, it had woken me up from the way I sleepwalked through life, and I knew I'd miss the drama of it all. And when I returned home, I wouldn't clock watch and wait anymore. That part of me was gone for good.

"It sounds like he's got a very dynamic lifestyle," Luiz said, his expression solemn. "It must be tough for him to leave you."

Ahead, the streetlights burned amber, their black nineteenth-century casings gothic, and wondrous, as they spanned down the bank of the Seine. "It's tough on both of us. I miss him."

"*Tu me manques*, do you know that term?" Luiz inclined his head, his hands deep in his pockets.

The words were familiar but I couldn't translate them quick enough.

"In French, instead of saying, I miss you, we say, *tu me manques*, which means you are missing from me."

The luscious phrase swirled in my mind. How did the French always get it so right? "I miss you" seemed like a lament, a sad wail, compared to "you are missing from me," which embodied a deeper, more visceral feeling. That's exactly how I felt when Ridge and I were apart. I could function, work, read, live, laugh, but it wasn't as bright, as real, unless he was there too. And yet, I'd just ended a phone call with him in order to step out into the inky Parisian night. And all because it couldn't be only him distancing himself—maybe if I took a step back we'd see if our relationship could handle the space that lay between.

"Three simple words, yet they conjure up so much," I said, as memories of Ridge flashed, the way he held me, the light in his eyes when he professed his love. Why had I fallen deeply in love with a reporter who traveled the globe? I knew we didn't choose love, it found us—but still, I would have given anything for him to be with me all the time. Especially here, under the twinkling stars in Paris. Luiz was a great friend to me already, but the man I wanted was in Russia.

Luiz took my elbow, and led me into the tiny wine bar, its ambient radiance like an invitation to relax. The tables were dressed in crisp white cloths, ruby red napkins triangled in wait. The walls were a deep ochre, and adorned with heaters that radiated warmth against the Seine wind that crept in.

The maître d' greeted Luiz, and we sat at a table by the window.

"Shall we start with a pastis?" he asked.

"Please," I said, having no idea what aperitif a pastis was but not wanting to appear unsophisticated. Nothing could compare to eating steak tartare with Oceane. Things could only go up from there.

Luiz ordered, and we sat in companionable silence. Outside, people strolled hand in hand, the rush of sightseeing through the day calmed by nighttime, when people tended to meander, taking things slower, their legs weary and their faces sated after full days.

"Aside from Ridge, what's missing from you, Sarah?"

The question took me by surprise and I coughed awkwardly, drawing stares from the elegant couple the next table over. "Sorry?" I said to buy time. Luiz had a way of reading me, despite my neutral expression. Maybe it was the writer in him that made him see beyond the obvious.

He surveyed me. "I don't peg you as the type to be waiting for a man to make you whole."

At least Luiz didn't peg me for the type of girl who couldn't cope on her own. "Being here, it's opened my eyes to the world. I was happy at home, but bored I guess, and now I know there are adventures to be had, even if I have to do them alone. I'd lived a pretty sheltered life before arriving here. It feels good to explore, try new things."

"Would you stay on if Sophie asked?"

I smiled. "A few weeks ago, I would have said a big, fat no. But now, I'm not so sure. The more I think of leaving here, the less I want to go. Don't get me wrong, I miss my friends and family badly. But here, caught up in a crowd of people as I saunter along soaking up the gothic beauty, and every single scent and sound, it's like nothing I've ever experienced. And I haven't seen enough yet to go home. Because what if I never come back? These memories will have to last me my whole life."

Our drinks arrived, the aroma of anise strong in the air.

He swilled the barely yellow liquid around his glass. "Paris is like no other place," he said. "If you stay here six months, Sarah, you'll find it hard to leave. It changes you. It gets under your skin, and no matter where you go, you'll dream of it forever. It's like a first love, one that breaks your heart but leaves an indelible mark."

I took a gulp of my pastis, feeling fuzzy from the heaters and the alcohol swirling through my body. "That sounds almost like a warning, Luiz."

He chuckled. "Maybe it is. I know people who've pined for Paris ever since they left. But life . . . it gets in the way, and no matter how determined a person is to get back here, sometimes it doesn't happen. And they miss it for the rest of their lives."

"Surely it's better to experience that, than

nothing at all?" Paris did have a particular pull, a magnetic feeling, like it was drawing you in, and I knew too, that once I left, I would sit in my own shop and dream of the fun I had here. I blinked back a rush of tears that sprang without warning. I didn't want to leave. My life in Ashford would always be there, and the more I discovered about this place, the more I wanted to stay.

"Yes," he agreed. "How can you appreciate love if you have never lost it?"

Ridge's beautiful face flashed in my mind. Was I losing him to his ambition? Were our two lives just too different? My heart tugged. Sometimes it felt like it, and how would I feel? Glad to have experienced it, or regretful because I knew what I was missing if our love ended? I pushed the morose thoughts away. Searching Luiz's face, again, I had that sensation that he'd had some great loss in his life. The way he wrote about love, and the haunted air about him. Again, I didn't ask, worrying it was too personal, or he'd shut down.

"I'd always choose to experience love," I said, playing with the stem of my glass. How could I not? My life had been lived inside the pages of romance novels, and it was only now—at almost thirty—that I'd experienced heart-stopping, real-life love with Ridge, no matter how rocky it'd been with the distance between us. Was what he was prepared to give me—a few days here and there—enough for me? I knew life wasn't like a romance novel, but I still held out hope it could be. Why shouldn't I strive for more?

We sat there in silence for a moment before Luiz broke the spell, his voice forcefully bright, helping to pull me back from my doubts. "Shall I read the next letter?"

I nodded, taking a sip of the aperitif, its sharp taste and alcohol strength warming me all the way down.

The tour is interminable. One country after the next flashes by, so that at times I have no idea where I am. My manager says I should be grateful because the world understands the music my peers said would fail. And I'm booking out shows in places I've never heard of. Bringing pianists back into the spotlight. Shaking off the dusty stereotype of what type of sound can come from those black and white keys. But it's hard to be anything other than melancholy. The only reason I wrote the compositions were because of you. What irony, that they catapult me into a type of fame I never imagined, taking me farther away from the warmth of your embrace.

My eyes went wide. "That's the worst kind of irony, he's right."

Luiz nodded. "His fame took him from her."

"Who do you think he's writing to? Sophie? Surely if they were her letters she would have stashed them in her own apartment?"

"Hmm," he mused. "I agree. They could be anyone's. The bag left by mistake, and packed away high on a shelf, forgotten after years of collecting dust."

"Do you think they got together in the end? Maybe his career quietened down, and he came back, they had a million babies, and settled down in the South of France to grow olives and make their own wine."

He laughed. "You and your rose-colored vision of love. No, I'm sad to say, Sarah. I think like so many others, it ended badly. To keep a stack of letters in a bag like this, like she was trying to hide them, or hide them from herself maybe, to save heartache. I think whatever happened, they went two different ways. Otherwise, if they were together, surely his letters would be in the bag too."

"No," I said. "Why can't it work out in the end? You're thinking of your own novels."

Maybe it was my own love life I was comparing the letters to. But I wanted the happy ever after for these strangers, as much as I wanted it for myself.

THIRTEEN

It was time to take the reins of my own life, and do the things I yearned to do. And that included being the boss in every sense of the word. No more was I missing out because things weren't panning out how I imagined they should. While the rain lashed down outside—the sunlight gone for good, hidden by thick gray clouds carrying the promise of winter—I made a choice. I would find the heart of Paris, I would do all those things lovers did, and to hell with it if I was alone. There was a certain beauty in my solitude, and I vowed to make the most of it. After all, it was something I actively used to do, be alone, but here in this bustling town, I'd just be one of the thousands wandering around awestruck by what they'd seen, and that suited me just fine.

Rummaging through the stacks of well-thumbed novels in the lending library, I found one that thrummed in my hand, and snatched it up, knowing it was the right book for me. "I'm going to lunch," I called to Beatrice, who nodded. The casual staff had appeared in their usual gaggle and I gave them a wave as I passed, determined to be friendly even if I didn't feel part of their world.

Once Upon a Time was so different to my

bookshop; when I stumbled out for lunch, Oceane's warning about being sucked into the place for all hours rang true.

Outside, I could breathe again. Putting some distance between me and the shop, and the overwhelming pandemonium of it, was my favorite part of each day. I footed it down an avenue, holding aloft my striped umbrella—which I'd picked up at a vintage stall along the river the week before—and headed deep into the 6th arrondissement. Even the pouring rain wasn't enough to pinch the sudden euphoric feeling that seized me. Wandering around the streets of Paris, alone, the wind in my hair, was a type of freedom I'd never experienced at home. I was one of millions who'd trekked down these very same paths, and I hoped I was following the footsteps of someone great. A writer who'd found inspiration here, or a reader who had fallen under Paris's spell.

On the corner was a pâtisserie, the cakes like works of art, so carefully constructed, that taking a bite out of the exotic creations would make me feel almost guilty.

Almost. But not quite.

I stepped closer to the window, the maroon awning concertinaing above, protecting me from the elements as I gazed at the perfection inside. Fruity tarts with sugary glazes were colorful under the lights. Chocolate opera cakes cut into rectangles proudly showed off their thin ganache and sponge layers. Mille-feuille slices with crisp puff pastry and creamy custard centers practically begged to be tasted. There were chocolate éclairs, and crème brûlées with caramel tops that I knew would make the most delicious sound as I cracked into the toffee shard. Shell-shaped madeleines and flaky *pain au chocolat* spoke to me in such a way, I had to go into the warmth of the pâtisserie and somehow select just one of the treats on offer. I loved rolling their luscious names on my tongue.

Inside, in a display fridge, there were quiches with buttery brown crusts and baguettes as long as my arm, stuffed with a variety of fillings. How did French people stay so slim? It was like being transported to foodie paradise, and any reservations about saving money went out the window, as my mouth watered in anticipation. So what if I went home the size of a blimp? I laughed, picturing myself ballooning out, and returning home with chubby cheeks, thick legs, and a hankering for crusty baguettes and rich cheeses that I couldn't break. From the *boulangeries*, to *pâtisseries*, and *fromageries*, my waistline was getting the most epic of workouts, emphasis on the *out*.

With the book clutched to my chest, I found a table at the back where I could read in the quiet. I unwound my scarf and snatched up the menu, though I knew exactly what I wanted.

"*Bonjour.*" A young waitress appeared wearing a tight fitted black skirt, and form-fitting shirt, from which a pink lacy bra peeked through. Her makeup was flawless, her eyes accentuated by smoky eyeshadow, and her lips painted nude. There must have been some kind of class in high school that taught French girls the art of style because I'd yet to see a Parisian in sweats, or dowdy in any way. Even the makeup-free girls had an aura of sophistication about them. Perhaps it was their accents, and their reserved nature, as though they held themselves together, poised and refined in such a way it was obvious to me who was French and who wasn't.

"*Bonjour,*" I replied, smiling at the thought that it was mere minutes until those delicacies sitting in the display were transported to my belly.

With pad in hand, she asked in French, "What can I get you today?"

"I'll start with a slice of the roasted heirloom tomato quiche, and then I'll have a *tartelette au citron*, and a slice of *Charlotte a la Framboise*." The plump red berries were too tempting to resist. She scratched hastily on the order pad. I managed once again to speak fluently, and I wanted to fist pump. God it felt good to pretend I was one of them.

"Oh, and a café au lait, please." I gazed longingly once more at the cabinet, and caught the waitress giving me a squinty stare.

"Is someone joining you?" she asked, indicating the empty chair opposite me.

"Umm, no . . . it's just me today."

"Just you?" Her voice was incredulous.

"Yes, just me," I said with false bravado. "I'm eating my feelings," I said with a shrug.

"Ah," she nodded. "Boy trouble?"

"Boy trouble," I agreed.

She gave me a sad smile. "Men, *merde*!"

I twisted my face into a grimace to match hers. "*Oui!* Men, who needs them!"

"Won't be long." She spun on her heel, and left me to ponder my relationships with the people I spent my days with at the shop, and Ridge's absence in my Parisian adventure.

At a table by the window, a couple kissed and canoodled. I looked away, but their happiness and downright togetherness made my heart ache. They were wrapped around each other in that new love kind of way, and I was envious of it.

Was Ridge over that initial spark of love? Did other women catch his eye, when I was nowhere to be found? I held my head in my hands, as my mind spun with it all. For me, that first burst of new love hadn't waned. How could it, when we hardly saw each other. And any other man paled in comparison to Ridge. But I'd begun to feel like an afterthought to him, an epilogue in his life.

To save my poor heart the agony of overthinking, I took another love letter from my purse, opening it delicately. It would take me an age to translate the words but that's what made it so special. I'd promised Luiz I'd read some of them and report back, while he went back to his own writing.

My only love,
Today there was a fuss over the violinist. Personally, I don't think we need her. They say she's like an introduction. A way to soften the crowd, calm them, before I walk on stage to my piano. Calm them? I'd screeched. What kind of audience did they think my concerts attracted? The people who flock to hear me play are subdued, studied, quiet people who respect music. A young, pretty violinist won't change that. Perhaps it's her beauty they've chosen her for, juxtaposed against my craggy, older face. I don't know. I've largely ignored her, with her eager, wide eyes, and parted lips, it's like she wants to speak to me but doesn't know how. Like a puppy, she follows me around. If only you played the violin. Then it could be you here. And if I saw your mouth slightly open, your full lips shiny with your red lip gloss, I would cup your face, and kiss you until you were breathless. Music be damned, I'd carry you to my room, and

never let you leave. Your body, naked,
slick after our lovemaking, up against
mine, is what I dream about. Three more
months. And I will be home. Until then,
I'll play until my fingers are numb and
hope it makes time go faster.

Pierre

I munched on pastry crust as I thought about
the letter. Perhaps I read too many romances but
I had a very bad feeling that his protestations
about the young violinist were false. Why would
he discuss her in so much detail? The way her
lips parted? It was too intimate to write that
about another woman who wasn't your lover. I'd
have to tell Luiz, who I'm sure would gloat, and
say I told you so. Still, I wanted to believe these
two fought hard to be with each other. And it all
worked out in the end. It had to.

FOURTEEN

My plan to find joy in the hidden parts of Paris was off to a flying start. Ensuring I got out of the bookshop for some time to myself, other than racing to the bank and the post office, had taken some of the pressure off and inspired me to tackle one problem at a time upon my return. Space to think, and plot my next marketing move, or a new way to handle the surly casual staff.

With a flourish, I pinned up the new roster. It had been worth the few days' work, hunting out the staff, talking to them alone so it wasn't mutiny, and asking which days they'd prefer in my effort to accommodate them all.

"I can't do nights. I told you that." Beatrice folded her arms, the abruptness in her voice startled me.

"It's not every night," I said. "But I need more help with the late shifts so I can go upstairs and do the paperwork. I can't be here all day and most of the evening and get it finished. I'm falling behind." I scratched the back of my neck. "Everyone is having to make a compromise or two, Beatrice. We need to work together for the benefit of the bookshop." There, I sounded professional and courteous.

She gave me a cool smile. "Your roster isn't going to work. Carlos can't do Saturday nights because he's in a band. Oceane and Fridays don't mix—you should know that by now. TJ won't work Mondays because that's when his poetry group meets. Half of these people don't even live in Paris anymore! Lois is in Thailand. Davey's back in Australia. God, you've even got Sue-Betty here—she left last year! Where'd you get your info from?"

I shriveled on the spot. What the hell? The staff had given me their details, or so I'd thought. "I was trying to make things easier . . ." I willed myself not to falter. "I can't pick up every shift when people don't turn up. I don't know what kind of people would play a prank like that." It was like being in school again. They sensed a weakness in me and used it for their own gain.

"Sophie always works extra shifts, and doesn't say boo about it. I don't know, Sarah, maybe the management job isn't for you." She shrugged and walked off, leaving me deflated once more. A part of me sagged, wondering if there was a kernel of truth in her words. Maybe things worked the way they were, all higgledy-piggledy when Sophie ran the place. No wonder she'd had enough. I teetered between fight and flight. After a moment alone, jaw set, I'd made up my mind. People stepped all over me because I allowed it. It was time to be fierce.

Wind from the Seine blew open the front door, and made the books shiver their discontent. By seven, I'd straightened skewed piles of books, and unpacked the new stock. With a groan I picked up pieces of the usual trash that was littered throughout. The late shift staff would be in soon. Dusk had become my favorite time in Sophie's shop. Most tourists headed out for dinner or to rest their weary feet. The crowds out front thinned, and I could lean on the doorjamb and watch the river flow under the murky sky. It was time enough to catch my breath, and revel in the beauty of the place, empty of bodies, a peaceful hush, only punctuated by laughter every now and then from the bistro down the road.

I'd stride through the shop, treading lightly on the once vibrant rugs, caressing covers, delighting in a rare find—a book tucked at the back of a disorderly pile, its pages browned with age, its scent a mixture of hope and anticipation, nutty and musky like a bouquet of old roses. Like a child misbehaving, I'd steal away with the forgotten novel, creep to one of the hidey-holes and read. Only able to snatch thirty minutes if I was lucky, before the mechanical doorbell would ping, announcing the next flurry of customers. And that was the cue for me to leave, and entrust the store with the nighttime staff.

When the casuals arrived that evening, I raced up the back stairs to Sophie's apartment my mind drifting to Ridge. It had been days since I had heard from him. To be fair, he was working on a story in some Siberian wasteland and rarely had phone signal, but that didn't stop me missing him, wondering where he was, what he was doing, if he was safe. On impulse I picked up the phone and dialed. I needed him, I just needed to hear his voice, hear him tell me that everything was going to be OK—not just at the shop, but also with us. Because for some reason I felt more uncertain than ever about our relationship. Maybe it was because I was so far from home, and my new normal was completely different.

"Hello . . ." I said.

"Hey, Sarah," a woman's voice at the other end of the phone said breathlessly, like she'd been exercising—or something less innocent, which I purged from my mind. "He's just stepped out. I'll tell him you called?" It was the photographer, Monique, who worked on assignments with Ridge. His cell phone was usually glued to his palm though.

Put out, and slightly miffed, I said "Yes please. And if he could call back as soon as possible?"

"Sure thing, sweet." She spoke with a Texan twang, and didn't seem the least bit bothered she was answering *his* phone and speaking to *his* girlfriend. "I can't say when he'll be back. You know what that man's like. But I'll be sure and tell him you were chasing him." She chortled away to herself, and I didn't have the heart to join in.

"Thanks," I said. And then thought to hell with it, I had to ask. "Why did he leave his cell with you?"

She laughed, a husky giggle that I thought only movie stars knew how to do. "He left it in my room last night. You know, we had a team meeting. Hoping like heck we can get this story done, so we can go home soon. I called his room this morning, but there was no answer. Probably at the gym staring at those muscles of his in the mirror!"

Right. A team meeting in her *room?* "I hope you wrap it up soon too," I said. "Just tell him I really need to talk."

"Sure thing, Sarah." She clicked off, leaving me with only the warmth of the fire for company. Why didn't he ever return my calls? We didn't so much play phone tag these days as phone chase . . . and it was me doing the running.

In the morning I went downstairs, headed to the kitchen and made a fresh pot of tea, delighting in the silence of the shop. It was just me and the books. Were they inching backward on their shelves, steeling themselves for another busy day?

Oceane arrived, her cropped hair sticking up at various angles, windblown and mussed. "Good morning," she said, rushing a hand through her hair. "Ugh, it's getting colder by the minute. It won't be long until Santa graces us with his presence!"

"What's it like here at Christmas?" I asked, reminiscing about the jolly festivities Ashford residents organized every year.

Back home we celebrated the season wholeheartedly. The town was decorated to the hilt, the best and brightest house competition so fierce that I bet you could see Ashford all the way from Mars.

Oceane smiled. "It's breathtaking. Imagine the town with a light dusting of snow, and a whole lot less people. It's magical, and blissfully quieter."

Time then for the books to take a deep breath, to recharge, just be, until the crowds thickened once more when the weather warmed up.

"What will you do for Christmas?" Did they all take vacations? Would I need to find more staff? My mind spun as I thought about my failure to lock down a new roster and remembered how lax everyone was when it came to turning up.

Her eyes sparkled. "We have a big orphans' party, don't you know! Lots of wine, French food, and a day where we completely sloth out in Sophie's apartment."

I couldn't contain my relief and did a little happy dance. "That sounds like fun!" I said, feeling the tension that had built evaporate. "But what about your family? Won't you miss them?"

"Oh, they're in Èze. A hilltop town on the Côte

d'Azur. I fly down after Christmas usually, and spend a week there."

"I bet it's stunning." I sighed, thinking about how far away I was going to be from my own parents for the first time. Christmas would be very different this year. I hoped they'd still celebrate—open presents by the hearth, sip on some eggnog, and sing along to carols.

Oceane continued, "The light is different there, gauzy somehow. It's the sunlight reflecting off the Mediterranean Sea perhaps. Better to visit in summer when bright pink bougainvillea creeps up walls, and sun bleaches the streets. But some paramour always whisks me away and I only ever get there over winter. And that is a beauty all of its own, the eerie wind off the sea, and days darkening early. We sit in front of the fire and read, my father nipping to the cellar whenever we need more wine. What's not to love?"

"What do you parents do?" I thought they must have subsidized Oceane's lifestyle, because she certainly lived extravagantly.

"They own vineyards," she said breezily, shrugging and picking up a pile of books to shelve. "So, this year, you'll be in charge of the Christmas party."

Oh, sweet Jesus, that I could do. Christmas was my favorite time of year, and I went all out for those I loved. "Do you decorate the bookshop?" I asked. I could picture it all decked out in full Ashford style.

At home it was hard to drive down the main street without being blinded by Christmas lights and walking into anyone's shop you'd be pulled in for a swift peck, as mistletoe was abundant, over every doorway. By the time you went home, your cheeks would be a fetching shade of various lipsticks, and your face would be sore from smiling.

"No, we don't decorate, save a tiny tree on the counter. Sophie has this fear that the place will catch fire if we so much as light a candle." Oceane shook her head as if the idea was preposterous. I poured two cups of tea and picked up a pile of books to shelve. "She's a bit of a Grinch with the whole festive season to be honest."

It baffled me, people who didn't adore Christmas. "Well, surely we can still decorate a little? It wouldn't be Christmas without glittery decorations and flashing fairy lights."

Oceane squinted at me. "I've seen how Americans decorate. We're going to have blinking candy cane earrings and warbled Christmas carols on a loop, aren't we?"

I laughed. "That's the spirit! I'm sure we can find some inflatable reindeers, and maybe hire someone to carve ice sculptures? It'll all be very French minimalist of course." Her face was a picture of shock, her mouth opened and closed while she tried to discern if I was joking.

"You see the French way . . ." she said before I interrupted.

"It's OK, Oceane. You can show me how you do it, and then we'll just step it up a teeny-tiny notch."

"We could visit Anouk for decorations, though maybe I should go alone. I'm not sure you're allowed to go out into the secret room yet."

The elusive other room where the real treasures were kept. I could hardly wait to step past those doors to see what Anouk kept back there. "Because I *can't* just waltz in there, it makes it that much sweeter. Maybe we can try for some Christmas presents first and see how that goes?" I said, putting the last book into place and surveying the shop. It was neat enough and ready to open.

"Good idea! She's got some lovely unique pieces your American friends would adore, but never, ever say that. Tell her they're for you," she warned.

"Why?"

"Anouk doesn't like her wares to leave the country." Oceane shrugged. "It's a quirk of hers. Thinks our antiques will be mass shipped out by consumerists. I don't know, it's just her way."

I frowned. "OK, but lying to her?"

"Saves her the heartache of worrying."

I would never get used to these idiosyncrasies, but still, they made me giggle.

FIFTEEN

The phone rang in the middle of the night, and my heart seized. "Hello?" I answered, my voice short, sharp.

"What's wrong?" Ridge's husky voice traveled down the line.

I sat upright. "It's two a.m. . . . . I thought, maybe . . ." A call at that time of the morning had the ability to make me freeze with worry that something had happened to him. He went to remote areas where there were wars, places riddled with conflict. "It's nothing. I'm glad you're OK."

He said, "I'm sorry I woke you. My body clock, and the time difference, and yet another country, it's addled me. I didn't realize it was so late for you."

"It's fine." I settled back on the fluffy pillows. "Is everything all right?"

There was a pause, and I frowned into the darkness. What was he calling for? It wasn't like him to mess up the times, he had every piece of technology known to mankind, when he was in range, and it worked. "I can call later," he said.

"No, let's talk now."

"Then you'll be tired tomorrow. Sleep, princess."

I almost huffed. "Ridge, the calls are few and far between. I'm awake now. We have time."

"Actually, I only have a minute. I'm supposed to be outside, the car's on its way."

"Did you call hoping to get my voice mail?" I couldn't hide the anger in my voice, because I *knew,* I could feel it. And what kind of relationship was that?

For the first time ever, Ridge was lost for words. My wordsmith, the one who spoke like poetry to me, was stumped.

"Well?" I demanded.

"Not exactly, it's just . . . I hate hearing the disappointment in your voice. I feel like a mug. I had a minute so I . . ."

I didn't wait for him to continue, just slammed down the phone. What was up with him? I get his life was busy, but so was mine. Calling to chat to my voice mail was just plain rude. And a bad omen of things to come.

Sleep was elusive, as I waited impatiently for the sun to rise.

The days were as routine now as they were in my shop back home, although a heck of a lot more frantic. I knew what I had to do each day, and managed my time well in order to get it all done. The promise of an hour or two to wander around Paris inspired me to work efficiently. Today, Beatrice and I worked well together, with no cross words. The aborted call from Ridge the night before was still swirling round my head—

what kind of game was he playing at? Pushing it from my mind I turned to the task at hand. Beatrice handed me a cup of tea before heading over to help a young couple at the till.

It was another dark day, where the skies refused to lighten. I was all set to head out for lunch when I spotted him. He was well dressed in loose fitting chinos and a white knit sweater with an all-too obvious designer logo that even I recognized. He didn't seem like the type who was struggling for cash. It was the way he darted glances over his shoulder that caught my attention. Leaving Beatrice behind the counter I inched my way closer to him, stealth-like.

After the drama of my bags being stolen, I felt capable of nipping this in the bud. I was done with thieves. Pretending to be a customer, I whistled to myself in an *I'm-on-holiday-in-Paris* relaxed kind of way. I pulled a book from the shelf in front of me, and flicked through it, watching him from the corner of my eye. With nimble fingers, he shoved a book up his shirt— so fast, I wondered if I'd imagined it. My chest tightened. I'd never confronted a shoplifter before! With a deep *you-can-do-this* breath, I squared my shoulders, and stormed toward him, holding out my hand. "Give me the book back." I surveyed his sweater; was there more than one book secreted up there?

He gazed at me with a smile in his eyes.

"Excuse me?" His face was a mask of innocence. Honestly, what was it with people stealing here?

Willing my voice not to shake, I said, "Give. Me. The. Book. Back."

His eyebrows shot up. "Which book?"

I folded my arms. "If you don't give me the book back, I'm going to holler the place down!"

He chuckled, he *actually* chuckled. What the hell was I doing wrong? I rearranged my expression and did my best steely glare. Just because I was short and unassuming didn't mean I couldn't be fierce.

Then suddenly I felt Beatrice next to me, I hoped that she was there to support me, but the air chilled at the tone of her voice. "Sarah, what are you doing?" she hissed through her teeth. "Can you help serve?"

My mouth fell open. All of our earlier camaraderie was forgotten. "Excuse *me,* Beatrice, I am actually in the process of catching someone—" I narrowed my eyes at the guy *"—stealing!"* The word came out like a shriek. I expected his face to fall, or him to dash out of the shop, books tumbling as he ran—but he didn't. A long, slow smirk settled across his features.

"Oh, for God's sake," she huffed. "You've just lost five sales from customers who walked out because they didn't want to wait, in order to catch this guy stealing one book? He'll bring it back when he's done! They all do!"

I stood there, openmouthed, heart hammering. Eventually I managed, "What?"

Beatrice shook her head, her red curls bouncing. "Could you be any more sheltered? Sophie turns a blind eye to book theft because she believes everyone should have the right to read, and just because they can't pay, doesn't mean they should miss out. I thought you'd been told all of this?" She rolled her eyes, and it was all I could do not to poke her. The gazing heavenward thing was getting old super-fast. She'd held off from doing it to me, but finally she'd cracked.

"That's ridiculous!" I said. "There's a lending library here! If they want books, why can't they borrow them the right way?" None of this made sense, it was like I was stuck in a parallel universe. Letting people steal? No wonder my bags had been taken if no one cared about theft!

With a huff she turned and apologized to the thief.

My face turned crimson. "Don't say sorry to *him!* Are you insane?"

"Look, Sarah. Things are done differently here, as you've been told a hundred times already! The lending library is full of *old* books. This guy—" she jerked a thumb at him "—no doubt wants something newer. It's not a big deal."

I glared at them both.

He laughed, and took another book from the shelf, giving me a wink as he walked blithely past.

"He'll bring it back," Beatrice said. "Serve now? Before we lose the rest of the customers to the bookshop around the corner."

Anger coursed through me. This was a flagrant abuse of Sophie's trust. There would be no stealing allowed while I was here. I was all for people reading, but there was a perfectly good lending library, and they could show some respect by asking at least. My mind whirred with ideas, we could easily update the library selection with newer books. I couldn't believe Sophie was that busy she let her books go, just like that? With so much emphasis on the bottom line, her complex computer programs for data entry, and the drive to make more sales, how could she let brand-new books walk out the door? It didn't make any sense. And yet another thing I added on the to-do list.

Later that day I was totting up the total takings, sipping coffee as the same heavy sensation settled in my gut by the continued drop in sales. I steeled myself. If books were being stolen, then that would definitely contribute to our bottom line. Without another thought I emailed Sophie and asked if she was free to Skype. A few minutes later a call came through on the laptop.

On screen, Sophie looked beautiful. Her time away had softened the worry lines around her eyes and the stiffness of her posture. She was so relaxed she was almost floppy, a stark contrast to me, coiled snakelike with anxiety.

"Oh, darling, your friends are like sunshine, the town is everything I imagined it to be and more. I never want to come home! Perhaps we should think of extending the exchange to a year?" I choked on my coffee, and managed to get hand to my mouth before I covered the computer screen with liquid.

Sophie frowned. "Are you OK?"

I composed myself, and managed a laugh. "I'm fine! But I think what we discussed originally is an adequate time to live each other's lives." Sophie was having a blast with my friends, and I couldn't contain the tiny bit of jealousy that crept up and tapped me on the shoulder.

I pressed on, "It's just, there was an incident today. A thief snatched a book, and Beatrice bounded over and told me you turn a blind eye to it. And it doesn't make sense to me. If you let people steal books, then no wonder the staff think it's OK to steal from the till."

Through the monitor, she gave me a patient smile, and I knew what was coming. Never in a million years would we be on the same page, of that I was certain. "Of course I allow people to take books! It's an unwritten rule, one we've had for years. It's for locals, students, people that will one day have their own names on novels in my shop, and will remember how we helped them . . . a long-standing tradition that started way before I took over."

My mind actually boggled—a pounding sensation, the beginning of a headache brewing. On top of everything else this felt like the final straw; I was exhausted, exasperated and I wasn't holding back anymore. "Fine! I'll let people steal, even though it makes no sense to me. But it's setting the standard, Sophie. I don't know which one of the staff is stealing, or if it's a bunch of them nipping euros out of the till, but how can you expect them to care if you give away books like that?"

Her eyes narrowed, as though she didn't like what I had to say. "Are you unhappy because of Ridge leaving, is that what this is?"

I reeled as if slapped. "No, Sophie, that's not why. You said your staff were a handful, you said the paperwork was monumental. Fine, I get that. But the pressure of covering shifts for lazy staff, and then staying up late so I can add everything into the computer, and then getting up bleary-eyed the next day to be told stealing books is OK . . . it's downright ridiculous. No wonder no one respects me here, when I try to do things the right way, and not follow some weak tradition from the past."

Her mouth fell open. She wasn't used to me having an opinion, especially a daring one like that. "You wouldn't understand," she said, sharply.

"Let me guess, because I'm not French?" I

shook my head. "Why can't they ask for a book instead of just taking it?" She went to speak but I held up a hand. I was going to say my piece this time. "I've been riddled with guilt working here. The thought of all that money missing kept me from sleeping. I've made stupid mistakes myself from being constantly woolly-headed. And I'm not taking it anymore, Sophie. While I'm here, things will have to change or I can't stay." The words fell from my mouth, before I could edit them. But it was time I stood up for myself, or I'd end up being run ragged by unwritten rules that made no sense.

"Fine," she said, her eyes hard. "But tread lightly, please."

We stared at each other on screen, and shared an awkward silence. "I will," I eventually said, feeling a tad victorious.

"The sales, though. That keeps *me* up at night, Sarah. Please, fix it. This is usually the busiest time of year, leading into Christmas . . ."

"I'm trying," I said wearily.

When I flopped back in my chair after ending the call with Sophie, I stared once again at my favorite view, knowing it would cheer me up. It was like falling in love. I curled up in the window seat and dialed Ridge's cell—it rang out, and his voice message kicked in. The smooth, silkiness of his voice made my heart race, but where was he? It'd been almost a week since we'd talked that horrible night when he hoped he'd catch me sleeping. Sophie wasn't right when she thought my issues with the shop were to do with Ridge, but I had to admit we were starting to have more bad days than good—or more days where I didn't hear from him. Was the gap getting harder to bridge?

Covered with a thin layer of dust, I was still only halfway through unpacking boxes of books that had arrived in time for the Christmas rush. TJ appeared, giving me a lopsided grin.

"It's never-ending, right?"

I patted a stack of books. "At least all this heaving and hefting burns the calories I'm consuming at the pâtisserie down the lane."

He grinned. "Between the sweets, and the cheeses, and the three course lunches, never mind all the wine, it's a wonder we're not huge." He patted his belly which was more concave than convex. "It's all the walking and, of course, the mad dash of the bookshop."

He moved boxes and made a makeshift seat, doing zero to help—but TJ had this way about him, just sitting and talking was compelling and more important than any work we might need to do. "Take a break. You've been in here for hours. We could wander down the Boulevard Saint-Germain."

"I shouldn't," I said, though the idea appealed. "I have a heap more to unpack."

"I'll help when we get back," he offered.

"OK." I ran a hand through my hair, hoping the black shock of it wasn't beige with dust and feeling excited about stepping into fresh air.

Opening an umbrella, we walked along the promenade to the bank of the Seine.

I enjoyed TJ's company at work. Nothing was ever too much trouble, and while he bickered with Beatrice, he wasn't malicious. I'd been worrying all night about who could possibly be taking the money from the shop, but I doubted it was him stealing from the till. TJ always wore the same beat-up, wrinkled suit, and only ever ate at the cheaper *boulangeries*, but more than that I trusted him instinctively because of his genuine nature, and warmth in his eyes. He'd be more likely to tell me he needed money, than steal it.

"Are you happy here, Sarah?" TJ grinned, and looped his arm through mine as we skipped puddles in the street.

His question caught me off guard, but TJ just had an aura about him, something that made me feel I could trust him with a confidence, and unlike some of the others from the shop, he was more empathetic. "I made the decision to come here so quickly, I don't know what I expected. I'm a small-town girl, so it's a sensory overload, sometimes. Though, stepping out into this—" I motioned to the vista, the river, the ever present Eiffel Tower "—makes up for it. I didn't know you could fall in love with a city. It'll be hard to leave, that's for sure. But I won't miss the politics of Once Upon a Time."

"It's a mammoth task running it." He lifted a brow.

I nodded. "I don't know how Sophie's managed it so long to be honest. She needs more staff, especially when it comes to the accounts," I said, as we dodged a couple swept up in the romance of Paris standing in the middle of the path and kissing.

"I hope this trip saves her from herself." His voice was full of hope. "She has to see that things need to change." While he hovered on the edge, like a silent spectator, I recognized that TJ saw it all, right to the heart of the matter, without being one of the people who added to the drama.

"Manu broke her heart. I can see why she'd flee. Following tradition is one thing, working yourself into an early grave is another." I couldn't hide the tightness in my voice and looked away from TJ, hoping he hadn't noticed.

He cocked his head. "What is it? Is it Beatrice upsetting you?"

"No, no, it's just me." The other staff didn't seem to have problems with her, and maybe I was being too sensitive. It was obvious that she loved the shop, and she had only been sharp when I'd made rookie boss mistakes. They must have thought I was some backwater hillbilly. "I guess being away from home." I gave a nervous laugh. "I've always felt like something was missing from my life. That I had to stop hiding. And for some reason, I thought I'd find it here. I'm not exactly a social butterfly. It's like my flaws are exacerbated here. Everyone is so charismatic, and bubbly, and I'm the girl with the silly ideas. When I do try something—" I blushed, thinking of the team-building idea "—it's considered bourgeois, or something."

Leading me into a café down a hidden alleyway, TJ moved us to a cozy table for two before ordering coffees. It was like that in Paris. Food or good coffee was a priority, and any crisis of the heart could wait until comfort was organized. "Traveling has a way of peeling back the layers of a person, leaving you exposed," TJ said, picking right back up where we left off, "When you're alone, miles away from all you know and love, that's when you find out who you really are."

"How did you end up here?" I asked, curiosity getting the better of me.

He smiled. "I was lost. My parents had this idea I'd work in the car factory, like all my family. That was as big as their dreams were. To be an employee for some huge manufacturer. When I said I wanted to write, they almost fell over backward with shock."

"Sounds bleak," I said. "Dreams are hard

enough to reach for, without anyone stomping on them."

The waiter arrived, depositing steaming cups into our waiting hands. "I knew if I stayed there, eventually I'd become a factory worker, and each day my poetry would be a step further away as monotony took over."

"So you just left?"

"I'd always been drawn to Paris, the city that housed The Lost Generation, all those bohemians who found a home here, and I knew it was where I was meant to be. I contacted Sophie and she promised me a job, so as quick as that, I left. When I arrived here, it was like I could breathe, great big lungfuls of air. I found my tribe, people who understood me. Didn't judge me. And I knew, I'd never leave. This city is my home, my heart, and I know I belong here. I might struggle to get published, might live on the brink of poverty, but it'll be worth it. This is the city of lost souls, and you, Sarah, are one of them. But that's the beauty of this place. It'll sweep you up, strip you bare, until *lost* becomes another word for *found*."

"You're such a romantic." I smiled. TJ's gentle chats always cheered me up. He was a sweet soul.

"Don't tell anyone. It'll ruin my reputation." He winked before motioning me to try my coffee. "It's the best coffee in Paris, but if you tell anyone I'll be forced to unfriend you on Facebook."

I laughed and sipped my coffee. The rich creamy brew was strong enough to make my eyes *boing* open. "It's pretty spectacular, TJ," I admitted. Paris really was broadening my experiences, whether it was a simple cup of coffee that heightened my senses, or gazing at artwork, and hearing haunting music that I felt right down into my soul. "I'm glad you found your tribe here." I said after a pause, "I have my own tribe back home, and I miss them."

"What about your parents, what do they say about you leaving everything behind?" He flicked a lock of black hair from his eyes.

"Like almost everyone, they're worried I won't be able to handle the big bad world . . . it's like people think because I bury myself in books, that I'm this fragile, delicate flower who can't cope." I explained about my twelve hour disappearance as a child. And that I'd developed night terrors and a stutter for most of my childhood. I'd always been the odd one out.

"So what happened? The kids bullied you?"

"They were merciless. And I just retreated, you know? It was easier to hide behind the cover of my books, and I found happiness there. Escapism at its best."

"But what about high school? Surely by then they'd moved on to bullying another kid? As horrible as that is."

I nodded. "I'm sure they had. But by then, I

was good at being invisible. I just floated into the background. Went to school, walked home, and spent my life reading. It wasn't all bad. On a whim I opened the bookshop when I was nineteen, and everything changed. I'll always be an introvert, but I have the best friends a girl could want, and a business I love, so I'm not that same girl anymore. But my family are overprotective, like I'm still a little girl."

"Kids can be cruel. I guess when they're that young they don't think their actions, and the repercussions of those can last a lifetime. When I announced I was gay, you can imagine how that went down. But luckily I had support from the school and they tamped down any bullying as quickly as they could." His eyebrows pulled together. "Paris will work its magic on you, of that I'm sure. And when you go home, people will see you differently, because nothing is ever the same once you leave a place like this."

"I hope so, TJ. You know I base almost everything on romance novels, like what would the heroine do? But the heroine wouldn't be like me, she'd be this bright young girl, with a clear plan, and a sassy attitude . . ."

"But this isn't a romance novel, Sarah. You're better than that, and you know how much I love my happy ever afters."

I threw my head back and laughed. TJ might have written poetry but he read romance like it was banned—eyes wide, shoulders hunched, while he raced through the story, exclaiming over plot twists.

After we finished our drinks, we bundled back up; scarves, gloves, umbrellas at the ready, prepared for the harsh winds as we stepped back into the cold. We came out onto the Boulevard Saint-Germain, a busy place, famous for its bohemian nature in the roaring twenties, and later a place where the likes of Hemingway hung out. Now though, it was more upmarket.

"Near the Odéon, there's a hidden little bistro who do the best croque monsieurs, and because they're hard to find, there prices aren't set high for tourists. Hungry?"

"Aren't I always?" I said, loving that TJ was just like me, always thinking of the delicious food that was abundant here.

"Instead of ham, they use smoked salmon and Comté cheese, and I promise you, one bite and you'll never want to leave Paris."

My mouth watered just thinking of it. It was great having TJ as a tour guide, because his budget was more in line with mine than Oceane's was.

"That's Café de Flore," TJ said, pointing to a café on the corner, as we crossed over. "Hemingway used to write there." No one was immune to bringing up famous names of the past. It was a thrill to think of people whose books I'd read, or artwork I'd seen in print form, once strolled these very avenues, just like us. Hemingway sat somewhere in that café, nursing a *vin rouge*, as a reward after a long morning writing. I shivered a touch, wishing that the enigmatic man was still alive. We wandered down small arcades, rain making the cobblestones slippery. It was like a maze, TJ led me left then right, and through doorways, so I was completely lost. No wonder it was a secret place, it would be impossible to find alone.

We came to yet another doorway—plain and indistinct. TJ rapped on it, and told me to wait as he stepped over the threshold. It was all very mysterious, and provoked a giggle as I stood, trying to keep the umbrella from blowing away.

A few minutes later, TJ brandished the fancy sandwich in front of me. "We're not eating in?" I asked.

He shook his head. "It costs more. Paris on a budget, that's me."

With buttery fingers, we chomped on our lunch and ambled through the streets, stopping each time we came to one of the *Bouquinistes*. They were booksellers, who sold antiquarian novels and vintage posters from little green boxes on the bank of the Seine. Awnings hung overhead, protecting their wares. They'd been selling old books this way since the mid-sixteen hundreds and it fascinated me.

How many thousands of books had been sold over the years, and who'd taken the sellers' places once they left this world? Did they keep them in the family? It was a romantic idea to own a tiny lockable bookshop by the river. The keepers were bundled up with scarves and gloves against the cold. They were the only thing that didn't change along the busy path—as hordes of tourists flashed by, they'd sit there some smoking pipes, others reading as they waited. What kind of special place was this that the River Seine was flanked by little bookshops? Perfection.

I rifled through the vintage posters, looking for gifts for the girls back home—conscious of the fact that Christmas wasn't far away. There were sketched couples kissing with the Eiffel Tower in the background, one of black cats perched atop a pile of books, and one full of petit fours and macarons in pastel colors. I selected a bunch, and then went through the books. With their red leather hardcovers, and golden French text, they seemed as priceless as a first edition, with a distinct book scent, earthy, timeless, like the Seine had jumped into the pages. When I was back home, I knew I'd pull these books from the shelf and inhale, with my eyes closed, to be transported back to this gray Parisian day, and I'd pine for it. And I knew that Paris—with its intensity, brooding clouds, and beauty—would be in my heart forever.

I paid the man, who nodded, pipe smoke swirling around his head, and we continued on. Our stroll had put a much-needed smile on my face and I felt that I had truly found another friend.

SIXTEEN

The shop had been madly busy for hours and the midmorning rush was almost over as crowds dispersed. Gulping down some water I checked the heating was still working and rewound my scarf tighter. The old building was drafty, and not even the roaring fires in each room could take the chill completely away. Beatrice hadn't turned up and I was relieved not to be faced with her, she always seemed to push me off balance. Instead of worrying about her I processed some online orders while keeping an eye on the door, only to find my humdrum day completely thrown off whack when a blur of familiar long blonde hair whirled into the shop.

"There you are! I've been waiting for you to call me back!" Lucy, my artist friend from Ashford, bounded over, her curls bouncing as a gust of wind blew in behind.

I ran around the counter to hug her. "Oh, my God, it's so good to see you!" She'd spent the last six months in my hometown, before being accepted to a prestigious art school and making a mad dash to Paris with her boyfriend, Clay, in tow.

She held me at arm's length and surveyed my face. "Why haven't you called? What is it?"

That was the thing about my friends, we knew each other intimately, and Lucy sensed on sight there was something up. She darted a glance around. "Look, can you leave for a while? Let's talk in private, yeah?"

"I'm just finishing up for today," I said, and went for my handbag. "TJ, can you cover the front?"

He dusted his hands along his suit pants. "Sure." He gave Lucy a lopsided smile.

She grabbed my elbow and we dashed outside. "Want to go to my apartment?" she asked, her blue eyes shining. She was a whirlwind of excitement and I was lighter just being near her. She seemed to glow from within and it was so wonderful to see.

"Sure. Are you staying with Adele in Montmartre still?"

Lucy laughed, and hooked her arm into mine. "No, it was a bit squashy being in a one-bedroom apartment with Adele, and then me and Clay. We rented a dodgy little place in the Marais. Dirt cheap by Paris standards. It's a little rougher than the 5th arrondissement, but we like it."

"How's Clay?" I asked about her boyfriend. He owned a maple syrup farm back in Ashford, and was staying with Lucy for the off-season.

She tried to hold in her smile, but it threatened to swallow her up. "God, he's amazing. You know, I thought he'd be bored here while I was studying all day at the institute, but he goes off, wanders around. He's made friends with all sorts of people. He's a different man to the one who left Ashford."

"Wow, that's one for the books." It was hard not to smile as widely as Lucy did. I'd never seen her so animated—her cheeks were rosy, her eyes bright, she was blooming like those newly in love, and I was happy for her. Her life hadn't been easy, and neither had Clay's. They deserved everything Cupid threw at them. I just couldn't keep out the little voice in my head that thought maybe I deserved a little bit of Cupid's attention too.

We took the Metro to the Bastille, Lucy an expert on navigating the crazy maze of train lines and platforms. She strode up and down stairwells with a confidence she hadn't had in Ashford, as if she'd been in Paris for years, when really it was only a short while before I arrived.

Holding my hand, Lucy led me through the streets, waving to people she knew, and pointing out places they'd eaten, and galleries that displayed her work. It was more labyrinthine here than the other quarters, and even though it had been renovated in the fifties, it still had a medieval feel to it, and a comforting bohemian vibe.

"Have you been to Village Saint-Paul yet?" Lucy asked.

"No, not yet." I took my well-thumbed travel guide from my bag. "I haven't quite made it this far."

She frowned, a small crease making her nose wrinkle. "I heard the bookshop is a bit like a ball and chain for you."

Flicking through my book, I was glad for the distraction, so she couldn't see my face. Lucy was thriving here, and I had floundered a bit. Trying to keep my voice measured, I thought up the best answer I could. "It's busy, so I haven't quite done as much as I thought I would. Including read."

She tutted. "I knew something was wrong. I should have dropped in sooner. I thought maybe Ridge was here, and you were caught up with him, and bookshop life, but I spoke to Sophie and she said things weren't going great."

"You spoke to Sophie?" I didn't even know Lucy and Sophie had met. I couldn't help feeling betrayed by Sophie. After all, I'd done this as a favor to her, and there she was, enjoying my life with my friends, and then talking about me behind my back. I couldn't find any reference for the village in my guidebook and had to give up the distraction of searching for it.

"The girls Skyped me, and she was with them. She didn't mean it badly, she just seemed to think you weren't as happy as she'd imagined you'd be here. It's a big change from Ashford."

I gave her a watery smile. "It's a huge change,

but I do love it here. The scent of the Seine from my window when I wake. The Eiffel Tower flashing at night, like it's exclusively mine. When I press my head against the glass of my window, I can see Paris as it sleeps. Maybe this trip is a great learning curve, that's all."

"Learning curves are good. Scary but good." Lucy draped an arm over my shoulder as we continued to weave down tiny lanes and I knew if I had to make my own way back to the train I would get horribly lost.

"I'm a tiny blot in a sea of people, and there's always something new to see. I've never felt so connected to any one place. It's almost like I've lived here before, and I'm visiting again, in another life."

"The magic of travel." Lucy grinned. In her old life, Lucy and her mom were wanderers, nomads who hotfooted it around the world. That was, until her mom got sick, and they had to stay in one place, the medical bills mounting up. Now, she was free again, able to follow the wanderlust in her veins.

"And Ridge?" she broached gently.

"He's been here all of one night," I said. "Work's hectic for him, but still, a twenty-four hour visit? Do you think he's trying to let me down gently?"

Lucy scoffed. "He's not like that, is he? Did you argue when he was here?"

We turned into another cobbled lane. It was like going down a rabbit hole. Some of the stones were green with moss, and slippery. "He showered me with compliments, and planned a whole surprise day—a river cruise, and a walk through Montmartre. Dinner at a fancy restaurant at the top of Eiffel Tower. A candlelit bath together when we got home . . ." I blushed, remembering the way in which we loved each other that night.

"Doesn't sound like he's letting you down at all. He's just that kind of guy, driven, and focused on his career. But then so are you, Sarah."

I frowned. "I wouldn't say I was driven." It was laughable. Unless you counted driven to read books all day.

"No?" she asked. "Your books are your life. Just because it hasn't taken you around the world until now, doesn't mean it's not as important. Your bookshop is a haven for people in Ashford. I think you're forgetting how important that is. And it's tough because you both love what you do, so I guess you have to find middle ground."

"I thought as our relationship progressed we'd get even closer, not further apart, that's all."

"It's only distance separating you. Not a fractured relationship. And that can surely be fixed." But I wasn't so sure. Ridge and I had barely spoken in the last few weeks and when we did it was strained and awkward. I hoped Lucy was right, but at the moment it all seemed a bit precarious to me.

We came to a stop. Under a window box was a wooden chair, its seat piled with antique biscuit and tea tins. "That's a sign." Lucy pointed to the chair.

"For what?" I asked laughing.

"For the secret entrance to the Village Saint-Paul. A marker, so you know it's this archway to go through." She put a finger to her lips. "They don't like anyone to know."

"Who's they?"

"The antique dealers . . ."

"Another hidden gem?"

She nodded, her face solemn. "Let's go. We can find some Christmas presents for the girls."

We walked through, my breath hitching. It was like another world. Medieval stone walls, courtyards and cobbled lanes. Fuchsia-pink azaleas were blooming, trellised above. The square was filled with tables of various collectibles, things salvaged from another era. Lace tablecloths, creamy with age. Bowls of bangles, in gold, silver and brass. Shoes, clothing, old telephones, the type you had to dip a finger in to dial. Vendors gave Lucy waves, as if she came here a lot. "Why do they like keeping it secret?" I asked, still amused by the way Anouk from the Little Antique Shop under the Eiffel Tower would only sell to people on an introduction from a trusted customer.

"I don't know for sure, but I like to think because it's even sweeter when you stumble upon a different sort of utopia that no one else knows about."

Storm clouds brewed overhead, but in the square, one ray of lonely sunlight shone down, highlighting the stallholders, their wrinkled faces, like markers of time. How long had they stood behind these rickety tables, selling odd and ends, and sharing flasks of coffee, the scent of freshly baked crepes an accompaniment to the day?

We meandered around the square, finding things that reminded us of our friends. I found a vintage teapot for Lil, with tiny gingerbread men along the bottom. And for Missy, an antique perfume bottle with an atomizer. Lucy chose an old French cookbook for CeeCee—instead of color photos, it had sketches, and was one of the most beautiful books I'd ever seen, its pages yellowed from age, and old oil splotches marking the passages of its previous owner.

We went back to Lucy's tiny but utterly Parisian apartment, and opened up a cheap bottle of rosé, clinking glasses to our success in navigating the French and their foibles, and admiring them for their determination in keeping their heritage alive. It was one of the first evenings I really and truly relaxed, letting the stress of the day ebb away as I enjoyed the company of a friend, someone who I could really be myself with.

December

The winter chill had hit Paris, the wind was whipping down the avenues and boulevards. It was a never-ending symphony of squalls, with snow drifting down and blanketing the city in white. Our customers were arriving windswept and looking for longer, complex novels that pulled them into different worlds, with their luscious descriptions and metaphorical prose.

Another week had crept up and I sat in the front window of the bookshop, trying to make sense of the sales figures, and get the end-of-month accounts up to date. I'd doubled-checked, and triple-checked, and still the numbers stared at me from the page, like they were disappointed in me. The sales were down. And not just by a small margin. What was I doing wrong? It seemed like the outgoing expenses were more than the incoming. How could that possibly be? Over the last week the nights had slipped into mornings, as I sat head bent over the computer trying to work it all out. My eyes hung out of my head most days; I was a walking corpse. Bookshop life had never been so mind-numbing. I hadn't read a novel in weeks, and I felt jittery without that down time. Mostly though, I was worried about letting Sophie down. We'd spoken a few times since our last Skype call and she was almost puce with anger.

This store was her baby, and I was starving it, no matter how much of myself I put into it.

Outside the pre-dawn was navy blue with swirls of moody gray clouds. Again I stared at the profit and loss statement, the figures had plummeted. I couldn't understand it. It was always so damn busy. I shoved all the documents back into the file. Flashes of homesickness grabbed me.

I couldn't help feeling that I wasn't cut out for this. Dealing with staff and their politics, trying to get them to turn up. Another attempt at a roster had been laughed at, and squiggled over. At times it was like I was talking to rocks. The habits the revolving staff had here weren't about to be broken.

Maybe I should just tell Sophie I was butchering her shop, and she should come back to Paris. I'd tried my damnedest to get everything done here, and it still wasn't right. The takings didn't balance, we were down a couple of hundred euros, and I'd re-counted so many times. The thief seemed to still be feeling bold enough to steal even though they knew I had noticed a couple of months ago.

I shook the maudlin thoughts away. Ridge would know what to do, but our phone calls had been infrequent—I spent more time talking to the robotic voice on his voice mail. Sometimes it all got too much for me, and despite being in this big, beautiful city, I'd feel very alone. Oceane and TJ had offered a casual sort of friendship but they were social butterflies, always fluttering from one party to the next, living so zealously that I struggled to keep up, and often refused their invitations because work called.

The doorbell chimed and TJ strode in, wearing the same crinkled suit, though somehow making it look dapper, with his impish grin and his windblown black hair.

"You're early," I said.

"Are you OK?" He cocked his head, twisting his mouth in concern.

I shrugged. "I think the dark skies have got to me. Everything is gloomier when the weather's broody. I miss my friends."

"You must do." His voice softened, "You're doing a great job here, Sarah. It's not an easy place to work."

"Thanks, TJ." It was just like him to see through the veneer of my faux smile and into the real me, in the way I supposed writers or creative types could. He was an observant and a compassionate soul, one of the people I could rely on here, without worrying he'd ditch a shift for a party and leave me in the lurch—like the rest of the staff did without any compunction.

Taking off his gloves he sat in the window with me. "I sneak in to write in the quiet," he said. "Hoping that the ghosts who haunt this place will inspire me."

"This place is haunted?" I love these little conspiracy theories the staff had of the shop. Everyone believed in something different, and took something unique away from their time here. Already we'd said goodbye to some casual staff, whose time as an exchange student had come to an end, and to travelers who had itchy feet and were off to the next place, waving farewell with tears in their eyes.

"I hope so," he said. "Sometimes I picture Hemingway wandering around with a glass of scotch, waiting for someone to talk to. Or Gertrude Stein leaning over me while I write, telling me off in that stern way of hers. They never really leave, those greats."

It was a fanciful notion, and one I'd thought of too, but it was the readers I envisaged. "Why don't they leave?" I asked.

"Because this *is* paradise, Sarah. Don't you know?" His face looked incredulous that I had even asked the question and I laughed.

"Not from where I'm sitting." I indicated the files I'd been poring over.

He scraped a hand through his hair. "Ah. The paperwork. A never-ending reel of hopelessness. The figures are down."

I sucked in a breath. "Yes. How did you—"

"The crowds haven't been as thick as you might imagine. There are new stores popping up all the time—they don't have the heritage this place does, but they decorate them to look like they've been there forever, and how's a hapless tourist to know the difference?"

A groan escaped me. "But I'm responsible, right? At the end of the day, sales are dropping while I'm here. What can I do to fix it?" I wanted things to go back to how they were with Sophie, our relaxed chats about bookshop life, and gossip about the latest novels we'd loved. Not the curt, abrupt, crushing anxiety-riddled calls of late.

He gazed outside, his dark eyes reflecting the view of the Seine. "If it helps, it's not you, Sarah. The shop has been on a downward spiral for a while. Sophie can't let go of the reins—something that always holds her back. Her father and her grandfather did everything themselves, until the day they died, so I think she feels she has to follow in their footsteps. But as you can see, it's too busy for one person to handle everything. Mistakes are being made because of it. And all because she refuses to change."

I could understand Sophie's links with her past, and that she wanted to uphold tradition, but it wasn't working. A generation or two ago, they wouldn't have had the crowds they did today.

I let out a long sigh. "Well, what can we do, TJ? Surely between us we can come up with something?"

"Sure. Let's go for a walk."

Paris under the cover of darkness was almost

eerie in an ancient gothic way. Even the apartments looked like they were slumbering, with their shutters like eyelashes—closed against the morning chill.

"OK," he said. "Firstly, author readings. Can you imagine? In spring we'd get hundreds of people sitting by the Left Bank. This time of year, we can squirrel them into the piano room by a roaring fire and a glass of mulled wine. It's not only about sales, it's about supporting the reading and writing community. Giving people the opportunity to be involved with the shop, become a part of it."

"That would be so much fun." I said nodding, starting to see his ideas take shape and finally feeling like we were getting somewhere. "It's easy enough to make flyers. Do a Facebook event? But which authors could we approach?"

His breath blew out in front like fog in the bitterly cold morning. "Oh, I know plenty of authors, lots of poets too. That's the easy part."

"OK, great. What else?"

"A book club," he continued, his face animated, his hands a blur as he gesticulated. "A revolving club, full of locals, tourists, anyone who wants to discuss the novel whether they're transients or not. True bibliophiles always buy books, and that's what we need. Sophie does turn over a tidy profit usually, but the upkeep on the building is sky-high. This summer the entire top floor had to be rewired. Walls crumbled, it all had to be replaced. Add into that wages, theft, and dead books, it makes for some tight months."

I groaned, worried for my friend. I'd seen invoices for plumbing work, and electricians, plasterers, and building surveyors, to make sure the place wouldn't tumble down around our ears. I'd had to call a fair few myself, when disaster struck—pipes bursting, electrics shorting. "OK, a book club. What else?"

"Merchandising. Bookmarks, book bags, and gift packs. Everyone wants to take a piece of Paris home, why not a collection of nostalgia from Once Upon a Time? There are so many old photographs of the shop, each marking some point in its rich history. We could print them on postcards. There's the correspondence that goes all the way back to the twenties. It should be cataloged, made into a book. There's so much history and it's all locked away in a cupboard."

"Great idea, TJ." I could imagine little book bundles, and tote bags filled with postcards, and vintage-looking posters. Though the correspondence was personal, and I thought an ambitious project like that would need to involve Sophie—it was her heritage, and I could only imagine how special it was to her.

I continued: "The correspondence will have to wait until Sophie gets back, but let's do the other things you suggested." Maybe this would galvanize the staff to help more, be proud of the heritage of the shop, and not be mere travelers in the midst, who took more than they gave.

"Sure," TJ said as we walked back toward the shop, the sun beginning to peek blearily through the gray skies. "Thanks for letting me have a moment to shine. Words, and the celebration of them, are all that matter to me." He scratched his chin. "I want to look back on my time here and know I added something to the history. We all leave our mark, our footfalls bow the wooden steps, our fingertips leave oil on the pages, we're woven into the tapestry of the place, but I don't just want to mar it, I want to make it better."

There was something unique about Once Upon a Time, people fell in love with it, wanted to protect it, cherish it. The love people had for the place, like it had a soul, and was a real and tangible thing. All I had to do was tap into that yearning. That was how I would rouse the staff and turn everything around at the shop. Talking with TJ had spurred me on—I knew what I had to do now and nothing was going to stop me with my newfound enthusiasm.

SEVENTEEN

"Beatrice." I motioned her over. "This customer would like to see the music books, he's looking for a particular novel . . ."

"It's right through there," she pointed, and gave the man a cool stare.

I grimaced. "Can you *show* him the way please? Help him *find* the book?"

"Serving," she said blithely, and went behind the counter. The man, frowning, shook his head and walked out of the shop. Another sale lost. This was the problem. They'd relied too long on the shop's popularity. That had worked for a while, but no one helped customers, they just directed them to the right room and hoped for the best.

"Beatrice, that just cost us a sale! You weren't serving, you were stacking shelves!"

She gave me a slow dismissive once-over. "How many sales did we lose when you were prancing around helping that Spanish guy to find the book he wanted?" She glowered at me, I guess because I'd insisted she work the weekend. Now she was doing what she did best—arguing about something ridiculous. I'd reworked the roster so I could have one measly day off, and no one was happy about it, least of all Beatrice.

I damn well earned it, balancing the books every evening, running to the bank twice a day because Sophie didn't trust anyone else with the takings, covering shifts when the staff got a better offer. No more. One day off, and I was taking it.

I knew that's why she was being difficult but still I bit back at her remark. "I was *helping* him, and that's what you do when someone asks for a specific book. Did you ever think people other than tourists would shop here, if they had some assistance when they asked for it?" Her attitude toward me was verging on rude, and I was at breaking point with her. "Look, you've managed to shirk most weekends. It's your turn, and that's that."

She cocked her head, her red curls twisted tight like coils. "I don't have to work weekends, Sarah. And you can't make me. I have other responsibilities. Find someone else."

I clenched my jaw, wondering what would happen if I pushed her. They'd all taken it in turns to work weekends, except her. "Bad luck, Beatrice. Work this weekend, or don't work here at all. And that's final." I stomped off, all at once feeling triumphant I'd said my piece, and hotfooted it away so we didn't dissolve into an argument. I was in charge, and she would listen, or she would be fired. No more would I play the role of shy, small-town bookworm.

Rain lashed down as I left the shop, leaving Beatrice to pout over working the weekend. Paris was misty—like something out of a ghost story. The stormy weather made me feel like I was the only person outside, my visibility reduced to a few steps ahead because of the thick fog. It sat perfectly with my mood. TJ said Ridge had called when I was in the middle of the row with Beatrice, and I was too fired up to call him back. Anything he said, I'd probably shoot him down. Better I wait until I was calmer.

Each step away, I felt that same lightness take over. I'd never been a walker back home, but here it was my main mode of transport and a way to clear my head. I wound my way to the Luxembourg Gardens. The place was empty, no soul brave enough to walk in the heavy downpour. It was a gift, having the huge expanse of garden all to myself. With my hands thrust deep in my pockets, I sloshed along, thinking of all the famous writers, long since dead, who'd walked these very same steps, and picturing the verdant lush gardens in the summertime—people clutching books, their feet resting against the tip of the fountain like I'd seen in so many photographs.

When I came to the fountain, I sat on the cement edge, gazing at the cloudy water. Raindrops fell like kisses on the surface. Taking my e-reader from my bag, I switched it on, having downloaded Ridge's latest article. It was a story he'd worked on months ago, that had only just been published, about the right for patients with epilepsy to be able to use medicinal cannabis as a way to stop seizures, especially in children who sometimes had hundreds a day. Modern medicine wasn't working for those kids, but the medicinal cannabis was, yet the Australian government had made it illegal to be administered in the home.

He went into detail about one family's struggle to make it legal, so their child could get the help it afforded, to curb the damage the seizures caused every day. Without the law changing there was little hope. My heart broke when I read the account of the suffering of their innocent child. Ridge highlighted the difference between the drug cannabis that people smoked, and medical cannabis, two completely different things. Reading the story, I was so damn proud of him. Shining a light on an issue that needed to be told. What he wrote about was important. How could I ask him to veer away from that simply to stay by my side? I could embrace being alone, and enjoy that time. I'd spent most of my life that way, only being dragged out when the girls back home insisted. But once I'd fallen in love with Ridge, that solitude wasn't so ideal any more. How could I not want him there all the time? He made me laugh, showed me how to love and enjoy every single second of my life. So when the brightness of his attention was gone, I floundered in darkness. But that was a choice. And it could be changed.

I thought about TJ and what he'd said about those who flocked here. Was Paris a beacon for people like me? It certainly seemed like a place where you could reinvent yourself, or even just be yourself, and you'd fit in among the hordes of people here who were all searching for something too.

Pulling out my notebook I made notes about our new plans for the shop. TJ's ideas had been brilliant and I knew they would work, but we needed more concrete marketing plans. Proper signage made, the staff all kept in the loop. Book recommendations and reviews had helped, we just had to step it up a notch. I wrote down all the ideas that flashed through my mind. There were so many things we could do to turn curious onlookers into customers.

I marked mid-December for the launch of the author events. It would be a great way to draw in more customers—who didn't love getting a book for Christmas?

A man came sloshing along, catching me unawares. He was dressed in a black slicker and plastic boots. "*Bonjour*," he greeted me. "Would you like to see the bees?"

Bees? "Pardon?"

"The hives. The bees are protecting their queen. *S'il vous plaît.*" He motioned with a gnarly finger to the south of the gardens. His ruddy, lined face and hunched shoulders, made me think of an old weathered farmer. I was intrigued, despite being alone with a stranger who wasn't making much sense to me. It all struck me as very Parisian. I thought maybe something was lost in translation but I followed him anyway. From a man offering to show me the bees to Anouk only serving customers who had an introduction, the Parisians were certainly an eccentric lot.

My mind whirled as I followed him. We trudged through the wet grass, his breathing labored until we came to a semicircle of beehives made from what looked like old chests of drawers, with steel pitched roofs on top. I wouldn't have stumbled on them without the man telling me. Paris had so many marvels, hidden here and there, you just had to know where to look.

"See?" He smiled, his teeth were tobacco stained, and he was missing a molar, which only added to his rugged beekeeper appeal. "They cluster around the queen in winter, to keep her warm. They live off their own honey, for energy. You come back in the springtime, and take a beekeeping class. I will show you how, and you can try the honey. We must respect the bees." His expression was solemn. "You see the bee has to fly around, flitter from flower to flower, but he will always come back to his queen."

I double blinked.

He has to fly around.

He always comes back.

EIGHTEEN

The next evening, the shop was strangely quiet. The rain had disappeared and heavy snow fell, sending tourists scuttling back to their hotel rooms and leaving the streets of Paris silent and blanketed in white. It was like a picture on a postcard—dark flashes of gray and black, with the white snow like hope. I could have stared out the window all day just watching the landscape change.

With the shop door firmly closed against the bracing weather, I tallied the takings discreetly behind the counter. The numbers didn't match. Again. We were down a hundred euros. I checked the desk for any handwritten notes, in case someone had borrowed an advance on their wages, but there was nothing. I resisted the urge to bash my head against the wall.

Beatrice wandered over and pulled her jacket from the hook. "I'm leaving," she said, her voice brusque.

"Wait," I said, "The takings are down again. Any ideas why?" I asked, hoping that perhaps she'd borrowed some money and forgotten to leave a note.

She huffed, though she tried to mask it by coughing. "I have no idea, Sarah. It's not my job to balance the takings, is it? If there's nothing else?"

"Beatrice, I'm not messing around. This is happening regularly now, and from what I can gather, it's always when you're here."

She shrugged, feigning disinterest. "Are you accusing me?"

Why was she so cool about it? Wouldn't you be angry if someone suggested such a thing?

Was it Beatrice stealing? As far as I could see she didn't live extravagantly like Oceane. But then, I didn't know much about her, except her reading habits.

"Do you think it's odd that it only seems to happen when you're here?" I threw the question back on her.

"Not at all. You know staff pop in when they want books. They're not likely to steal on their own shift, are they? Too obvious."

I shrugged but I just didn't trust her. "I'll have to tell Sophie, and see what she says. It can't keep happening. Just so you know." Would that scare her? I wondered if Sophie would threaten them all with being fired, or if I should? But after the last time I had brought it up I knew that the culprit wasn't going to raise their hand and take the blame.

"Good idea. And while you're speaking to her, maybe tell her about the first edition you sold for almost nothing." And there it was. I wasn't imagining her hostility. The passive aggressive way in which she spoke to me. Blurting something out, and then softening it with a smile or an innocent shrug. I felt more than certain now it was her. Her masked threats made it obvious.

"She knows," I said. "I haven't kept anything from her."

She did that same smug grin that I'd come to hate. "Well, perhaps you should worry about what you're doing to make the shop more profitable before you worry about some loose change going missing."

"It's not loose change and you know it."

She raised a brow. "Oh?"

I narrowed my eyes, certain Beatrice was behind the so-called mistakes I'd made. When I thought back to the boxes from the estate sale with the first editions, there were no Joyce books there. I'd sold one that day, but I doubted it was a first edition. They almost hummed, those types of novels, and were hard to miss. I suspected someone had taken it, and the only person who knew it was there was Beatrice. But I couldn't prove anything. "See you tomorrow night," I said, dismissing her by going back to my counting.

"I can't work tomorrow night, it will have to be the day."

I sighed, my patience wearing thin. "We agreed on some nights, Beatrice."

"Yeah, well it's not as easy for some of us.

And you're lucky I even told you. No one else would have." It irked me that she was right. The staff treated any idea of a roster like a joke, and no matter how I tried to enforce one, it always ended up the same. But for the first time in a long time I felt like I was onto something—not only were the plans for the author events and book bags coming along beautifully, I might just have solved the thieving problem too.

Tyler approached me, the same mutinous look on his face as the day I'd called the staff together about stealing. He was only a casual staff member, and like a handful of them only deigned to work when it suited him.

I gave him a wide smile. "Nice to see you, Tyler."

He glared at me in response. "You can't tell me what to do!" Spittle flew from his mouth as he held a piece of paper aloft, waving it in front of me.

"Excuse me? I think I *can* tell you what to do. And if you don't like it, Tyler, feel free to give notice and leave. I have Sophie's permission, and I will pull this bookshop into the twenty-first century if it kills me." I couldn't help but feel a thrill of satisfaction as his face fell. "No more, *the roster is just a suggestion,* or, *they'll work when they want.* I'd never heard of anything so dumb in all my life. You'll work when I say so, or trot on down to the bookshop around the corner and apply there." The tension was palpable, as Tyler gave me a stare that would have had me shrinking in on myself before, but not now. "Got it?" I asked him.

"Got it," he eventually mumbled and stalked away.

Do not fist pump, do not jump for joy.

Internally, I did a kind of happy dance. Shy, reserved, mousy Sarah was a thing of the past. Even if I was talking about myself in third person. It felt damn good.

"Right," I said to the staff who had edged closer, a willing audience to a confrontation they thought I'd lose. "Does anyone else have issues with the memo about the shifts and what's expected of you while I'm in charge?"

They mumbled noes, and cast their eyes to the floor. The thrill of victory hit me anew, so I poured that excitement into the next thing on my to-do list. "Now, as I have you all gathered. Christmas is around the corner, and I'd love you to choose your favorite festive reads, and for you to write a little note about why you liked it, without spoilers. We're going to display the books in the front window, with a bunch of gaudy, flashy, American-esque decorations. And you will be required to sing 'Jingle Bells' on occasion," I smiled, hoping they knew I was joking to soften the mood. Well, sort of joking. Who didn't like singing "Jingle Bells"?

"Personally, I can't wait to get merry," TJ, ever the supporter, said.

"I will adopt a little Americanism if it kills me." Oceane smiled, and gave me a wink.

"This is going to be amazing. Sales will soar, and I will throw you guys the most epic end of year party. We just have to pull together to make it all happen."

The rest of the motley crew gave me small smiles, and I knew they'd come around. Once the basic rules of working were set in stone, we'd find some harmony. And we'd sell a truckload of books, if I could help it.

"We can start by wrapping presents!" I said, to their startled faces. "Well they're faux presents, for under the Christmas tree when it arrives. And a couple of real presents to send home to my parents."

Oceane picked up a book I'd selected for my dad. *"The Gargoyles of Notre Dame."* She lifted her brow. "Good choice. They have an interesting history. What'd you get your *maman*?"

I opened a shopping bag, and took out the small box I'd found in one of the flea markets along the Seine. "A music box?" she asked. It was tarnished with age, and its velvet lining was worn bare, but it had so much soul to it, and once you twisted the button the music notes drifted out. " 'La Vie En Rose' . . . It's always that song," she laughed. "Your *maman* will love it."

She would, I think. My mother had never ventured far from her little patch of the world, and I'd been so much like her—content to stay in one place, doing things mechanically, regularly, keeping up the farce I was happy. Stepping away from my own inadequacies and coming here had been one of the best choices I'd made. And I suppose I hoped giving her the music box, burnished and bruised with age, but a treasure, nonetheless, she might understand. Instead of putting it in the dresser with the plates we weren't allowed to use, maybe she'd wind it up and listen to the haunting song, and dream about a different sort of life. And that would be enough.

Later that night, the phone rang and I snatched it up, hoping it was Ridge.

"Sarah!" Lucy spoke loudly. "Get dressed. I have a spare ticket to the launch of a huge art exhibition! And yours truly has a couple of paintings included!"

A rush of pride hit me. Lucy had been so nervous in the past about sharing her work, she deemed it her heart on the canvas, and here she was exhibiting it. "OK," I said, surveying my pj's. "I'll grab a taxi to you?" Everyone caught the Metro here, but I still avoided it at every cost. Getting lost on a train to nowhere in the middle of the night didn't appeal. What a change in circumstance! Instead of snoozing my life away I was burning the midnight oil and loving every second.

I'd been half asleep the next morning when I'd opened the bookshop after Lucy's exhibition. I'd marveled at her skill with a paintbrush. She was right when she said it was her heart exposed bare on the canvas. You could see her passion, her skill, the way she captured the emotion in each canvas. She'd taken me on a tour, explaining her pieces, and those of the other artists—what the dark and murky brushstrokes meant to her, and then asked me what they meant to me. I supposed it was like two people reading the same book. We each read a different story, even though the words were the same. The paintings were like that too. We took from them what we needed.

I was putting the final touches to our Christmas plans; I had ordered fairy lights and real Christmas trees to put up in the corner near the children's section, and one on each of the three levels. My belly flipped-flopped at the thought of a real Parisian festive season. Perhaps I could bake some gingerbread treats for customers? If we were a little more welcoming, rather than the book factory method of serving, customers might return instead of visiting only the once. Spontaneously I Skyped the girls back home— they were the experts on baking, and I was itching to clamp eyes on baby Willow again.

The call was answered and CeeCee's shiny brown face came into view.

"Cherry blossom!" she cried. "Were your ears burning? We was just not two minutes ago talkin' 'bout you!"

I laughed—as always, hearing the warmth in her voice. "And what were you girls gossiping about me for?"

"Lil here was sayin' how jealous she was about you bein' in the city of food and all." She hemmed and hawed. "I tried to tell her it's the city of love and romance, but would she listen? No. That's 'cause she don't read enough books."

Lil pushed her face on screen. "I read books!"

"Cookbooks don't count," CeeCee said.

Lil lifted her eyes to the heavens, and gave her a shove. "They do so! Lotta love goes into each and every recipe!"

They could have talked over the top of each other all day, and I would have happily sat there and listened but a gaggle of tourists wandered in so I said, "Speaking of food, I need your best gingerbread coffee recipe, and also a gingerbread man one . . . something I can't mess up."

They bustled around, lifting their latest creations to the screen, and emailing me recipes from Lil's phone. While I watched their performance on screen, laughing, I thought how amazing modern technology was—my friends weren't that far away, not in spirit.

"OK, girls, I have to cut to the chase because the shop is filling up. Where's that baby? I need a visual on her, or I won't be able to focus . . ."

Lil held up a swaddled little bundle and it was all I could do not to blubber. She was the sweetest thing with her chubby cheeks, and one tuft of blonde hair sticking straight up into the air. "Aww," I said. "I love you, baby Willow!"

She let out a little gurgle that almost made my heart explode.

NINETEEN

"You're sure you need all of this?" Oceane asked, nodding toward the boxes of Christmas decorations that had finally arrived. It would feel more like a real Christmas when I'd strung up fairy lights, and draped tinsel on every available surface. Baubles glittered red, green and gold, and a wreath for the front door twinkled with little crystals, and had a huge red bow on top.

"I'm sure," I replied, doing my best to keep my face straight. "These bells will go nice by the front door, yes?" I held aloft a cluster of golden bells that made a heck of a lot of noise.

"Bells ringing every time someone blows through? I can't see any reason why that wouldn't work . . ."

I laughed. "TJ, come and help!" He was behind the counter trying his best to look inconspicuous.

"Let me guess, you want me to hang the mistletoe by the front door too?"

I scoffed. "You guys are amateur. I want it hung above every doorway! That's what this box is." I pointed.

They tried very hard to feign disinterest but I could tell they were excited. "Admit it," I said. "You want to go dig out your ugliest Christmas sweater."

TJ pulled a face. "We do. In fact we might go home now and see what we can find. What do you say, Oceane?"

"Not so fast. You, my friend, are going to carry the trees up to each level for me. And if you're good you can put the star on top once we've decorated them."

Oceane pouted. "I want to put the stars on top!"

"That's the spirit!" I said, laughing.

Together, we strung fairy lights across the beams above and then looped tinsel through. By the counter we draped *Merry Christmas* bunting.

"So where should we put the inflatable Santa?" I asked and was met with their jaws dropping and total silence. I guess they were serious when they said Sophie didn't get festive. "Kids section it is," I trilled.

Customers strolled in, smiling when they saw the flashing lights and sang under their breath to the carols that played through unseen speakers. It struck me how much fun I was having. I lifted a finger. "Christmas sales! We need to get some banners printed and get some books sold!"

"That I can do," Oceane said. "Leave it to me."

The nights were getting longer as darkness descended earlier. I'd survived winter in Ashford, but I'd never lived by the bank of a river. The blustering wind gathered momentum, bringing with it an icy chill as it whipped into the shop, making me shiver. I pulled my scarf tighter, bundling myself up and wishing I had a pair of fingerless gloves to pull on—at least they would keep my palms warm, and leave my fingers free to type on the computer and work the till.

We were preparing for the full Christmas rush; I had just received a special-express delivery from the Gingerbread Café full of recipes and a premade mix for the gingerbread men I wanted to make. My own attempts had been photographed and laughed over good-naturedly on Skype with the girls. I never was going to be a world-class baker and now I finally had the proof.

"Well," TJ said, breaking me out of my reverie. "It's quiet. I say we close up and head out for drinks. YOLO, right?"

We fell about laughing at TJ's attempt to use modern lingo. It was at odds with his ill-fitting suit, and his serious gaze and usual verbose way of speaking.

"YOLO is right," I said. "Let's hit the town and please say where we're going has a heater!"

"Oh, my two little bookish party animals," Oceane said in a faux proud parent tone. "When you say hit the town, don't tell me you mean the Bibliothèque nationale de France?"

The French library. Luiz had promised to show me around its cavernous halls later in the week, to read more of the love letters. I couldn't get them out of my head, the romance was so intense and I was desperate to know how it would turn out. For some reason, I thought if their love managed to weather the storm of international travel, and so much time apart, then mine would too. Ridiculous, of course, but I was a romantic at heart and a lover of words so I couldn't help compare our stories.

Oceane continued after a small pause, "Please say you actually mean a place where liquor is served. The harder the better."

"Haha. I mean a place that sells liquor with nary a book in sight," TJ said, throwing the front door open dramatically and gesturing out into the night. "It's Friday, time to shrug off the weekday, and get sozzled."

Oceane and I looked at each other and grabbed our coats, ready to brave the night to see just where it would take us.

We sat under the flashing lights of the Eiffel Tower, on a rug, wrapped in dense puffer jackets against the cold. We had the place to ourselves. As if the spectacle, the immense theater of the flashing lights above, was just for us. We must've been crazy, sitting on the snow-covered grass, but it was worth it to have the view to ourselves.

TJ had bought a few bottles of cheap wine, some cheeses and a baguette, which he placed down on the rug. A nighttime picnic in Paris. A magical experience with friends I'd come to feel secure around, enough that I could just be, and live in the moment. Away from the shop TJ and Oceane were exactly the same people, kind, caring, and trustworthy. They both loved Once Upon a Time as much as I did, and I felt a real connection with them, despite our different personalities.

"How do you afford to live the way you do?" I asked Oceane, slightly brazen after a couple of glasses of wine.

"Trust fund, darling," Oceane said, laughing.

TJ and I gasped. "I knew it!" he said. We'd shared the better part of two bottles of wine and our stories were spilling just as fast as the burgundy was.

She shrugged. "I tried to play the bourgeois card, but it's impossible. Everyone knows my family, so everyone knows me by default. When Sophie hired me I told her I was a struggling waitress from Èze with a penchant for reading, but I don't think she believed me. I didn't think she'd employ me if she knew who my family were."

TJ laughed so hard he began to choke on his wine. "So you're saying Oceane, thirty-three, from Èze, romance reader, man-eater, flower aficionado, isn't true?"

Giggles spilled out from me at TJ's shocked expression.

Oceane fell back on the rug laughing. "TJ, your people dossiers are sweet. It's all true. But my parents are super wealthy. They live in Èze, have vineyards in Provence. They export wine all over the world. I'm not actually the man-eater I've portrayed myself to be. I can always swing us entry into most places, because people know my family, and when I was in my early twenties I worked in Paris as a representative for my parents' business. I got to know the place well."

"So you hid your wealth because of Sophie?" Somehow I couldn't see Sophie worrying about what kind of background a person had, as long as they loved books.

"At first, because I thought I'd ruin my chances of working at Once Upon a Time. I'd been a customer there for years, and saw the staff, dressed like riffraff, struggling artists who somehow fit better among the books than I did. I wanted to do one thing on my own, get a job that wasn't given to me because of who my parents are."

"I really thought you were a man-eater," TJ said sadly.

Oceane gave him a playful shove. "I've had everything handed to me my entire life. I love words, and I wanted to be surrounded by them. I thought I could be a regular employee, but too many people know me here. They know my family. So I had to invent that man-eater persona."

TJ was right. Paris was a haven for lost souls. A

place for reinvention. The type of city that would keep your secrets like the most loyal friend. I lay back on the rug and stared up at the stars winking at us; the fairy lights and Christmas decorations reflected in the Seine made a spectacular light show just for us. "What do you want from your life?" I asked Oceane, feeling like we were in a bubble where any question, no matter how strange, was there for the asking. "You don't want to continue at your family business?"

"God, no. It's absorbed my family for generations. While I love the lifestyle it provides, I don't want to join. My siblings can run it, and bicker between themselves. I'm happy here." She gestured with her wine glass, slopping a little onto the white snow.

I sat up and took another sip of wine. "What do your parents say?"

"They think I'm doing some literary course. If I even mentioned Sophie's shop they'd set out to buy it or something over the top. They think of me as their crazy daughter, the one who floats through life without a goal." Her eyes widened. "But they just don't understand that I'd rather sell books than sell wine. They feel I should strive harder. If I want to read, let's buy a string of bookshops! They don't get *me*, they don't get *it*." She sounded so passionate, so sure of herself I was in awe. Had I ever known what I wanted to do so clearly? Other than my beautiful little bookshop, the last thing I had felt truly passionate about was coming here, to Paris. And the man mountain, but that wasn't at the forefront of my mind as much now.

We were all here in Paris, searching for something tangible, something that would fix us. I would never in a million years have thought that Oceane wanted to be a different person to who she was. I supposed it was easy for her to shrug off any family pressure, and be who she wanted to be, even if that meant bending the truth about what she was doing in Paris. She exuded a confidence I hadn't seen in anyone else—nothing bothered her, she'd simply wave away conflict, or roll her eyes dismissively when she disagreed with someone, and continue chasing the things that made her happy.

"What about Beatrice?" TJ asked, pouring more wine into his glass and snagging a purple grape from the basket. "She's not who she says she is either."

"What do you mean?" I asked, surprise making my voice squeak. Whatever insight TJ had, I tended to trust his instincts, because so many times he'd seen beyond the veil of what I'd meant to outwardly show the world.

"Have you noticed sometimes her posh accent slips away when she's mad? It's more Liverpudlian . . . She's always dashing off somewhere, a watch checker, like there's something else that takes up her time outside the shop," he mused, and I felt Oceane leaning closer, enthralled by the story he was spinning.

"Maybe she works two jobs?" I said. I was still suspicious after I had accused her of taking the money, and this made me more so.

TJ ran a hand through his hair. "What do we know about her? Beatrice Lockhart. Twenty-five. Loves literary fiction, but doesn't actually read it. Hates people. Huge fan of eye rolling. Claims to hail from Paddington, central London. Father is rich banker type, mother is a lawyer. Vegetarian and staunch coffee addict. Anything else?" He'd been ticking details off on his fingers, Oceane and I nodding in agreement. It struck me that I really had zero idea about who she was, and what made her tick. Guilt gnawed at me, as it always did. Should I have made pains to get to know her better? Just as TJ and Oceane had with me. There was something that had held me back, like there was an invisible wall between me and Beatrice, but maybe I should have tried harder to climb it.

"That's very thorough, TJ," Oceane said. "But after a year of working alongside Beatrice, I still don't know anything about her. She runs hot and cold with me, but doesn't give much away. Anyone else would have invited themselves when we drank a bottle of wine by the Seine. But not her, she hurries off like she's got somewhere else to be."

"So if she's hiding who she really is, the question is why?" I asked.

TJ threw his hands up. "I can't help feeling disappointed that my very in-depth dossiers are actually missing some crucial elements . . . like the truth!"

Oceane reached over him to sling her arm around his shoulder. "TJ, you're too much of a sweetheart to see the lies, that's why!"

He snorted. "Aren't writers supposed to be able to read people? Is that why I'm not published yet? I have one major flaw?"

I patted his arm. "You read people just fine. Besides, your characters are fictional, so as long as you know them inside out that's all that matters."

"So we're saying we have a stranger in our midst? Beatrice is not the girl she appears to be," TJ said. "Who is she, then? And more importantly, why the charade?"

We sat in silence, wondering about her, watching the pretty lights dance in the water, and the beauty of the Eiffel Tower. "Maybe, like all of us, she came here to change an unhappy situation." The thought made me feel slightly sympathetic toward her. There were times I saw genuine anxiety in her eyes. "Paris has that quality about it. You can shed your past and start again, and no one would ever know."

"She's the thief, right?" TJ asked.

I bit my lip. This was the one issue I knew neither Sophie nor myself could stand for anymore. If Beatrice was the thief I would have to confront her, or worse—fire her. "I think so," I mumbled, feeling regret in each word. How had I gone from disliking her to almost pitying her in one evening? I looked at TJ and Oceane. We had left Beatrice out, again. I couldn't remember a time when I had asked her to play tour guide. Or for a coffee. I remembered when she asked to speak to me the day Ridge arrived and I'd blown her off. My own actions weren't innocent either. If this was Ashford, I would have made the effort to get to know her, and if she was prickly, I would have got to the bottom of it, and found a resolution. In my busy daze, had I become selfish?

I felt a touch sad and wholly responsible for how we had excluded Beatrice, but TJ and Oceane pulled my spirits up, packed up our picnic and got me laughing again. I had time to fix things with Beatrice—time to find out if she was the thief and see if there was anything behind it. In a fit of giggles we wandered along the Seine, having drunk too much wine. We looped arms, and zigzagged our way across another beautiful Parisian bridge.

"We'll walk you back," Oceane said. "You can protect me from Eiffel Tower keyring sellers, can't you, TJ?" She giggled, gesturing to the ever present clusters of men who sold cheap keyrings and bottles of water to tourists. I'd heard sometimes they were a little desperate for a sale, and trailed after you offering one, then two, then three keyrings for a euro.

"You're safe with me," TJ said, pulling his collar up. "We'll speak French, and they'll know we're locals."

The air chilled and I shivered under my coat. Our footsteps echoed in the late night, bouncing around as if there were dozens of us.

A solitary figure appeared in front, his head bent, hands thrust deep into the pockets of his long, black coat. His walk was familiar. As we got closer, he lifted his face.

"Luiz!" I said, my breath floating in the air like smoke.

He turned toward us and mock bowed. "Good evening."

"That's Luiz?" TJ hissed. "The writer?"

"Yes. He's been writing in the shop for years, and none of you ever noticed," I whispered back.

I laughed and gave TJ a shove in the back, pushing him forward. "Well . . . wow . . . I . . ." he sputtered. Seemed Luiz had the same effect on all of us, his fame, and our love of great fiction, turned us into incoherent fools.

"Are your characters misbehaving?" I asked, wondering if he walked when the words wouldn't come.

Luiz chuckled. "A brand-new book and they're already being difficult. I'm giving them the silent treatment, and hoping that makes them rethink their actions."

I cocked my head, surveying Luiz. The soft skin under his eyes was bruise colored, like he hadn't slept for days, but he still had a certain vitality, the wind making his cheeks ruddy and his blue eyes luminous.

"So," Luiz said. "It's nice to see you all enjoying your time away from the bookshop."

"We almost have frostbite but it was worth it," TJ said, his eyes lighting up like he just had the best idea. "And we were just discussing our new project—author readings." He made a show of rubbing his chin like he was contemplating. "Just trying to knuckle down some writers we know and love. They can't be just anyone . . ."

I held in a laugh at TJ's obvious hint. But it was a brilliant plan—and who knew, Luiz might even say yes. We could use a big name like his on the list. It would bring in readers from all over France, not just Paris. An exclusive reading from the elusive Luiz Delacroix would put Once Upon a Time on the map again! I stared at him and crossed my fingers behind my back—if Luiz said yes, it would be an omen of good things to come.

"I'd love to," Luiz said, making us all gasp simultaneously, which we half-drunkenly tried to mask with coughing and clearing our throats.

He gave Oceane a shy smile, and something in it made me wonder, especially when she cast her eyes to the ground, which was very unlike her.

"Great!" TJ said, "I'll make some arrangements next time you're in the shop." TJ tried valiantly to appear relaxed, but he fidgeted with his coat, and stared openmouthed at Luiz.

"I better go," I said. The cold had seeped into my bones, and as much as I'd dreamed of chatting books with Parisians and foreigners alike, the midnight hour crept up and I wanted desperately to plunge into a hot bath and warm up.

"I'll walk you back," Luiz offered. "To make sure you're safe. Paris at midnight is no place to wander alone."

"Thanks, Luiz," I said. Paris at night was beautiful, but somehow each road and boulevard took on another character and I knew I would get lost trying to find my way back in the dark.

"We should head home too." Oceane reached over to hug me. "TJ, you can escort me, *non*?"

We hugged our goodbyes, which went on forever in our tipsy states. I smiled to myself when Oceane's gaze lingered a touch too long on Luiz, and the slight blush it provoked on him. If I didn't know better, I'd say Cupid was back and hovering somewhere above. Eventually we headed different ways in the inky night.

"Would you really consider doing a reading at the bookshop?" I asked as we walked with quick steps through the slithers of mist swirling around us. He didn't usually do interviews, or book signings, preferring to be as anonymous as possible, even though he was instantly recognizable from the picture on the dust jacket of his novels. Though, I didn't know it was him until he'd introduced himself. It was the icy blue of his eyes—intense, driven, deep like pools—that made women and men swoon. But everything I'd read about him, so far, had turned out to be utterly false. He was honest and open, and fun to be around. There was no hint of a reclusive writer who shunned the limelight.

He wrote about heartbreak in such a way that people wanted to seek him out, and fix him, offer him their heart, because it was easy to confuse fiction with reality, because he wrote it so well.

Back home, when the Wednesday-night book club gathered to discuss their latest read, there'd been many a woman, hand on her chest, claiming Luiz wrote such melancholy love stories because he hadn't found The One yet, and the chatter would become animated as everyone stuck a hand up, offering themselves to the writer, who then was a million miles from my life. Their cackles would ring high and loud into the musty air of the bookshop.

Luiz turned to me, even in the dark of night his gaze was penetrating. "Of course, I'd love to do a reading. I owe it to Sophie and Once Upon a

Time, since I've written so many novels there."

I smiled. This night had been full of surprises. Not only did I have a new plan for dealing with Beatrice, our author reading event was going to start with a bang! When I first arrived in Paris I had only ever pictured a romantic stroll with Ridge, but now here I was spending an evening with friends and having more fun than I'd ever imagined. With Christmas around the corner my time in Paris felt like it was going so fast, I wanted to drink it in and make the most of it. I turned to look at the Eiffel Tower. It flashed in the sky and I felt that just for that one moment it was winking at me—so I winked back.

TWENTY

"Why haven't you called? I've been worried." Ridge's voice had an edge of rebuke to it. It was early morning, and I was still a little light-headed from the amount of wine I'd consumed at the foot of the Eiffel Tower with Oceane and TJ the night before.

I leaned back against the damp wall at the bookshop. The walls had a mildewy, river Seine smell about them when you were up close, like over the centuries the river was being absorbed by the brickwork. "I wanted some time to think, without being wooed by a gift in the mail or the promise of a visit that doesn't eventuate." In actual fact, I'd been enjoying myself so much Ridge had worryingly been far from my mind.

"It's not like I *plan* to let you down. I hate not being reliable, and knowing you're going to be upset with me when I cancel. You knew this year was going to be tough."

"I did." He'd warned me often enough.

"So what are you saying?"

Ridge could focus on his job, but he had to make time for us. He wasn't the president, or a neurosurgeon on call. He was a reporter, who deserved downtime just like anyone else. "I don't know," I said, truthfully.

His sigh came down the line. "I love you, Sarah, and I know those words sounds empty. But the thought of losing you . . ." His voice petered out. "I won't let it happen." And with that the phone went silent. Did he lose signal?

I'd get a card in the mail full of promises. Backed up by an email letting me down gently. I sighed. You couldn't lose something you didn't have. I made a Christmas wish as I stared outside; I wished things were black and white so I knew where I stood in the game of love.

"I bet you're all ready for Christmas, and the town's lit up like a spaceship," I laughed down the phone line, picturing the wintry scene.

"Golly, sure is! It's been that way for a month or two now. You know what we're like, no harm in starting early." CeeCee's loud voice filled the room, and the laughter in her voice made me smile.

Lil and CeeCee started decorating a month or so earlier than most. Their display window was an edible Christmas delight, and they took great pains in making it more spectacular every year. "Is Lil back in the café?" I asked, wondering how she could drag herself away from Willow, but she'd no doubt strap her onto her with one of those baby wraps and work anyway.

"She's still resting up at home, playing with that gorgeous baby o' hers—I practically have to lock her in the cottage to keep her away from here. But we made one allowance that she could bake on Saturdays when Damon was home. I think she'd go crazy if she couldn't."

I smiled. Lil loved her business something fierce. Wild horses would have no chance of stopping her from visiting the café if she had her heart set on it. "I miss you all so much!" I exclaimed, picturing CeeCee stirring a gingerbread coffee and munching on a cookie with her feet up in the café. But it was easier to say now, and know that it only meant I loved them, and that I wasn't feeling that need to rush back. Homesickness had packed up its bags and retreated when winter came. I straightened my new sweater, smiling as I remembered the ugly Christmas knits that Lil wore with pride every day in December back home. She'd sent me a Kermit-green one that read *kiss me under the mistletoe!* It was knobbly, itchy, and so bright it almost glowed—everything an ugly Christmas sweater should be.

Back on the screen, CeeCee's eyes grew glassy. "Ain't nothing changin' here. We miss you too, sugar plum, but you be home soon enough. It's not the same sharing these big things with one o' us missing. We know you're having the time o' your life though, so we happy."

"Aww, Cee. It's been up and down for me here, but I've fallen in love with the romance of the place." I took a big breath and knew that I just had to talk to her. CeeCee would know exactly what to say and what I should do. "The only downside is Ridge. I don't ever see him. Paris was supposed to be this big romantic getaway for us, but my tour guides are my new friends, or my own two feet."

CeeCee grunted and sipped her coffee. "That boy love you, you know that. He said this year was gonna be tough after he quit *The New York Herald*."

I trusted Cee's opinion about people because she was always right, with her sixth sense and all, but she had a soft spot for Ridge and could overlook any fault of his. It was time for me to be completely honest and own up to all the worries I had. "We've spent a grand total of one day together, Cee."

"Oh, sugar, that is hard. Three months and only one day, but don't you forget that relationships don't come easy. If they was simple we'd meet Mr. Right every day." She was a little teary, and held her hands up like she wanted to reach through the screen and squeeze me tight. "But you mark my words, things'll change. You'll see."

I smiled. CeeCee was taking the lead from her sixth sense and I had to put my trust in her. I went on to change the subject and stop myself going crazy thinking about Ridge and my future. "How's Sophie going with the festivities?"

"She tried to avoid it all at first. Wasn't going

to decorate your shop, that kinda thing, but we marched over there and 'fore you know it, carols were playin' and the Christmas tree was lit up, and in the display window! I don't think she's in any rush to return to Paris . . . Think she's hoping you'll stay on for spring."

Winter already held us in its clutches, and I relished the idea of seeing the landscape of Paris transformed to spring. Could I stay though, even longer? What would it mean to be here and not go home? How would it affect my relationship with Ridge? But I felt a shiver as I thought of all the exciting plans TJ and I had been cooking up—our authors events, the merchandise—getting to see that succeed and grow the business was a gift I wasn't sure I could resist. The sales had not so much risen as cannonballed their way into the atmosphere. Our marketing plans, after much tweaking, had *finally* worked, and Sophie was back to being the dear friend from the past. It was like a huge burden had been lifted, and I felt a new optimism in the air—the promise of success in whatever I chose to do.

"What about you, cherry plum? You think you'll come back before spring?"

The bookshop exchange was supposed to end as brightly colored bulbs pushed themselves from the earth. But I felt a pull for Paris. And seeing it in riotous color, with fragrant blooms and clear blue skies . . . could I miss that?

"I haven't decided yet, Cee. Depends what Christmas brings. But I want you to kiss baby Willow for me, and tell everyone how much I love them. I've sent you off a bunch of presents, but you aren't allowed to open them until Christmas day! I got baby Willow the cutest little fur-lined boots, and Missy some makeup that she'll shriek over. And for you and Lil, well, that's a secret . . .."

Christmas was just around the corner and Luiz and I were cloistered upstairs in the conservatory reading through the love letters. They were mesmerizing and I felt this urge to find out exactly who Pierre was, then perhaps we would discover who the letters were addressed to. They were so beautiful I knew if they were mine I'd want to have them back, even if the love affair had ended badly, like Luiz continued to suspect. "Let's go to the Bibliothèque like I promised. It'll be deserted because everyone's Christmas shopping. We can read the letters there."

"OK," I agreed and packed them away. It was my so-called day off, but I usually stayed close by in case the crowd thickened with the promise of Christmas. There were extra staff working, and if a customer asked for a book they went and helped them find it. It was like I'd found a simple yet effective cure for the bottom line. Simple customer service with a smile went a long way, and I only hoped they'd continue it when I went back to Ashford.

The Bibliothèque nationale de France was an imposing building that made me feel the need to take two large steps backward in the attempt to take it all in. I couldn't wait to dive headfirst into the stacks and sniff all the books when no one was looking. OK, I admit, I was a closet book sniffer. Outside Luiz's scarf flew sideways and he shrugged deeper into his black coat. "Let's hope we don't get blown away," he said, his words carried away by strong winds.

"Let's head in," I said. We walked through the hallowed halls and Luiz whispered to me, "So who is this guy? If he's this grand pianist shouldn't we be able to find him pretty easily?"

Pierre Someone-or-other, in a city where I had met more Pierres than I had ever dreamed of—from the chef at the corner café, to the new baby of the resident on the second floor. I wanted to laugh. "We could Google piano players, but that takes the fun out of it! And I want to find out who *she* is too." Luiz stared at me full in the face when I talked, like he was invested in every word that poured from my mouth. Even when I spoke of something inane like the weather, he looked like he was reading every nuance of my expression to get past the usual chatter, to the heart of what I was trying to say. The girls back home were like that, while they chatted as much as anyone, when you had something important to say, they stopped their fussing and listened up.

"Can't rush a good story. You're right," he said and motioned to a seat.

"That's it completely. And we can't skip chapters either. It's bad enough we don't have her letters. We have to rely on his. OK, next . . ."

Luiz cleared his throat and read quietly:

My love,

Another season has passed, and I'm yet to return to Paris. The shows sell out as quickly as we announce them, so they add more to the tour. Like I'm a robot, or a trained monkey. They're simply thinking of their profits, not about me, and what I want. Each night is spent in a different bed, on a different pillow, where I rest my weary head and dream of you.

There are times I want to flee. To wake up before dawn breaks, pack my bags, and fly home to you. Hide out. Pretend I am no one. But, when the calm light of day shines through dusty curtains, I know I would miss the music too much. My fingers would cramp without their release on those ivories I love so much. It's as though I have two great loves, and somehow they entwine. I couldn't live without either of you. Yet it's the piano I

*spend all day caressing. I'll come home
soon, that balance must be restored.
Christmas without you, is there anything
sadder?*

My heart, my love.

Luiz put the letter down, and went for another.
I double blinked at the realization of how similar
these letters were to my predicament. Pierre was
separated from his love because of his music, yet
he yearned for her, almost wanted to give up his
career for her. Ridge and I were apart because of
work too. Did these lovers manage to find their
way back to each other?

Luiz held the next letter, the parchment shell-
colored with age. "Don't you think it's selfish
he never asks about her? He pines for her, but he
never once asks how she is."

I cocked my head, having been so caught up in
their distance that I hadn't thought past that. The
lyrical writing had swept me away. "I guess, but
it's like he's only focused on the music because
he wrote it for her, and that's what catapulted
him into success, and it's the reason they're not
together. He says they're both his great loves,
but I think underneath it all, he resents the fact it
worked out that way. I wonder if he'd have been
happier if he was never famous? He'd still have
her, and his piano, and wouldn't that be enough?"
I mused, leaning back in my chair and surveying

Luiz to garner if he felt the same sense of loss as I did from the letters.

Luiz chuckled. "We're reading these differently. You think he's a romantic at heart, whereas I think he's self-absorbed. I understand he has to tour, you only get one shot at that kind of fame, if you're lucky enough at all." He waved his hand as if to sweep his statement away, before continuing. "He proclaims his love for her, but how does he show it? Shouldn't he ask if she's OK? If she needs anything? We don't know one single thing about her because he only speaks of himself."

I pondered Luiz's observations. He was right in a way and it only made me more intrigued because we were hearing the exact same story, but getting two very different ideas about it. "You just want it to end the way your books do. Admit it."

He shook his head and smiled. The haunting sadness I'd seen in his eyes when I first met him had slowly dissipated, and if I didn't know better, I'd say he was in the early stages of love himself. His cheeks were flushed, and the blue of his eyes brighter. "Actually," he said. "Perhaps a happy ever after is on the cards for my next book . . ."

"And when are you going to spill the beans?" I asked.

He frowned. "Beans?"

"The good news," I laughed, the term getting lost in translation. "About you. Don't think

I haven't noticed the spring in your step, the sudden *joie de vivre* you've got."

This time the blush crept up his neck, turning him scarlet. "It's nothing," he said softly. "Not yet, anyway. She doesn't see me even though I'm right there."

"Luiz. You're *Luiz Delacroix*." I used air quotes to emphasize to my friend how special he was. "I'm sure if you ask her on a date, you won't have any troubles with her saying yes."

He shrugged. "She's out of my league."

My eyebrows shot up. "I don't think so, Luiz. I think any woman would be lucky to have you. What are you waiting for?"

He smiled. "The reading. I wrote a story for her."

I almost did a happy dance right there, having an inkling I knew who he was in love with. And their future flashed in my mind—I could tell already, they were a match made in heaven.

"Well, that just made it even more amazing than it already is."

He threw his head back and laughed. "Then we will see. It will be she who decides which way the story ends."

I rubbed my hands together. "I'm one step away from chanting HEA."

"You're more confident than me."

I smiled at the fluttering of his hands, the nervous way he kept blinking, and felt a pang of envy about that new love feeling.

TWENTY-ONE

At the morning food markets in the Upper Marais, old women dragged shopping bags on wheels, stopping to point to fresh herbs and vegetables, the sellers picking up each item as gently as if it were a newborn baby. Food, and the preparation of it, was treated differently here. No one haggled over prices, but they insisted on buying the freshest carrots, or garlic, pointing and gesticulating, until with a look to the heavens the seller would scramble to a secret box under the table and bring out their very best produce. Lucy had taken me here on one of our walks, and I'd been visiting ever since.

The markets were like a kind of street theater and I enjoyed wandering down the uneven pavement and watching the locals perform. As Christmas was fast approaching, it was even busier than usual, as people rushed to stock up for their festive feasts. I did a lap, and then returned to select some cheeses. Wheels of brie, wedges of blackened, pungent Roquefort, jars of *chèvre* marinated in garlic and lemon. Today I was here to scope out what I'd need for the orphans' Christmas party. I wanted it to be perfect. And totally French. Lucy had taught me the art of making a *jus*, a delicate sauce to pour over turkey, and I wanted to get it right. The French used mounds of butter, lots of garlic, and bunches of fresh herbs in almost everything, so with that winning combination in mind, I eyed the stalls greedily. I had to get supplies for the author reading too, and my mouth watered as I dreamed of all the possible combinations I could buy.

"*Oui?*" the man from the *fromagerie* stall said.

I pointed to a wheel of camembert that had already been cut, its creamy filling oozing out, just begging for a piece of torn baguette to scoop it up. "*Petite,*" I said, holding my thumb and index fingers apart to show the size. He nodded and cut into the semicircle. Cheese was different here, better quality than what we shipped in at Ashford. That triangle of camembert was just to tide me over while I decided about what I'd choose for the reading.

"Here." He smiled, handing me a chunk of baguette. "You scoop." He cut another generous portion and nodded for me to try it. A month ago I wouldn't have had the same treatment. I was almost giddy with delight at becoming one of them, one of the locals here.

"I need some cheeses for a party," I said between mouthfuls. "And some terrine perhaps?" I pointed to the one I liked.

I could easily live off the food from the markets. The terrine was beetroot and capsicum, with pork and chives. For someone who ate frugally, the markets were paradise. Everything was fresh, and you only bought the size you wanted. And returned the next day to do it all again.

He smiled. "You have the brie, it's won many awards. We only sell to locals."

I grinned like a fool. Yes! Even though he knew I wasn't a real Parisian, he'd recognized me from my jaunts. I was getting the goods from the secret box! "*Merci beaucoup*," I said, nodding and trying my best to act cool.

"I'll choose you a selection of cheeses, and be very careful to match the right wine, OK? Otherwise, it will ruin their flavor."

I nodded solemnly, wondering who'd know enough about wines to pair them. Oceane! "I know someone," I said. "Her family own vineyards."

"*Très bien.*" He wrapped my goods carefully, and gave me a half smile. The appreciation of produce here was something I'd take back home with me. Instead of going to Lil's just to fill up my plate, I'd get my hands dirty in the kitchen with her. Learning here how seasonal produce was worshipped, I swore I would make my former life of microwave meals a thing of the past.

With thanks, I paid and headed for the *boulangerie* to buy fresh bread.

There was a line-up at the bakery, which was

a sign it was one of the best. While I waited, I people-watched. This area wasn't as fancy as the 5th or 6th arrondissements. Apartments were smaller, washing hung limply from balconies, rubbish littered the pavement. And people weren't dressed as well, but that's why I liked it. It was more authentic, as though the rest of Paris was on show, but here real families lived in a more cosmopolitan way, between the chugging of rubbish trucks and the noise and bustle of people going about everyday things. There were fewer tourists, more graffiti, and I liked it warts and all. The prices reflected it was more for locals, and it suited my budget.

Once I had my baguette safely stowed, I wandered slowly back to the Metro. The screaming trains didn't scare me anymore, and I'd see a lot more of Paris by jumping on the Metro, and being deposited farther away than I could walk. Turning a corner, I realized in my daze, dreaming of a cheese-filled breakfast, I had wandered up the wrong avenue. The sight of a little boy with short red curls caught my attention. He was sprinting along enjoying his taste of freedom. I looked around, but couldn't see a parent. Was he alone?

I stopped in my tracks, as the little boy giggled and ran on. He was almost at the end of the laneway, too close to the road, where the traffic whizzed by without a care in the world.

He was quick considering he was staggering but he was so close to the cars whooshing past my pulse sped up. When his little foot stepped off the curb, I dropped my shopping and dashed for him, my heart in my throat. Two great lunges forward, and I had the wiggling redheaded boy in my arms, the sound of blood pumping in my ears.

Around the corner came a cry, "Marc, MARC!" I froze, as the toddler squirmed in my arms. That voice, I recognized it. There was such anguish in it goose bumps broke out over my skin.

Chest heaving with adrenaline, Beatrice screamed around the building, her eyes wide with fright. As soon as she saw Marc was safe, her hand flew to her chest, and her eyes closed briefly. When she opened them they were shiny with tears, and then she noticed me.

She stopped short, and composed herself before moving to take the child from my arms.

"*Maman*," Marc cried, his thin arms reaching for Beatrice.

Maman? She took him and swung him expertly onto one hip, her face coloring.

"This is your son?" I couldn't manage to hide my surprise.

"Yes," she said, frowning.

"Why didn't you tell anyone?" I burst out, my mind whirling. What the actual hell? Why would she keep this to herself?

Her lip wobbled, probably from fright, and the fact that someone had discovered the secret she had obviously wanted to keep concealed. I couldn't help staring at her, my jaw practically on the floor. It was so alien, the idea that Beatrice—so cold and aloof—would have a child. My brain pinged so hard I was almost blinded. This explained a lot.

"Can we discuss this at my apartment?" She inclined her head to Marc, who was doing his best to wiggle free from her embrace.

"Sure." I grabbed my shopping from where I'd dropped it and followed her around the corner.

Once inside she said, sarcasm heavy, "Home sweet home."

"It's . . . cozy." I looked around and tried to hide my shock at where they lived. The apartment was just one tiny room. There was a bed taking up most of the space, a kitchenette, and an armchair in the corner covered in a patchwork quilt that was well loved. Marc's toys were piled up, their clothes hanging on a hook behind the front door. On the kitchen bench a few Christmas presents were wrapped and stacked neatly. You couldn't hold your arms out and turn in the space, I was sure of it.

"Yeah, super cozy," she laughed, as she turned into the kitchenette and put the kettle on to boil.

I sat on the edge of the bed, and clasped my hands. Marc went to his mom, pulling at her legs until he was rewarded with a biscuit and I marveled at how natural it all seemed.

"Are you going to tell Sophie?" she said, shaking me from my scrutiny of them.

"Why? Is it a secret?" I said and held a hand up to her protestations. "You're a mother, Beatrice, what do you think Sophie's going to do? Send you away? You should know her better than that."

Beatrice busied herself grabbing mugs and making up a plate of biscuits. "Sarah, you don't understand. She hired me under the pretense I was a single girl, ready to work my butt off for the shop. If she knew I had a child that would've changed everything. I wanted, *needed,* the management position to survive here. I don't speak to my family back home—things blew up, and I vowed I wouldn't have Marc around that kind of lifestyle. I have no backup plan if things don't work out. And where will that leave me and Marc?"

"So you left the UK to try your luck here with a baby in tow?" It seemed like such a huge risk.

"I thought we'd have a better life here. Isn't that what Paris is? The place where dreams come true?" She looked so wide-eyed and innocent. So unlike the woman who had challenged me at work and made me doubt myself.

"Why didn't you tell me you had a child? I wouldn't have changed your shifts around if I'd known you had Marc to care for." And now like a puzzle, all the pieces snapped into place. Why Beatrice hadn't wanted to work nights, or weekends. She wasn't out partying like the others, she needed to be home to care for little Marc.

"How could I? I'd built a life of lies here, and painted myself into a corner—fear being the driving force. But here, where no one knows me—no one knows my past, my parents or the tumultuous time I had growing up—it's the type of freedom I always wanted. It's so hard money-wise, but I love it here. Books were my savior, the only thing I had growing up that couldn't be taken from me, but now I have this place. A fresh start. A new life."

Beatrice had transformed herself and made a life here for her and her son. And how could I begrudge her that? Hadn't I been looking to do something similar?

She sighed, and rubbed her face. "When Sophie had the trouble with Manu, I knew she'd leave Paris. For months, she'd been toying with the idea of taking a break from the shop. I thought I'd get my chance to take over, run it for her, show her I could manage the place. But then she breezed in and said you were coming . . . just like that I'd been usurped by some stranger. And any hope of extra money—so we can find a better apartment, live a bit easier—was gone." She handed me a chipped mug of tea.

"I bet my arrival wasn't a happy day for you then."

She gave me a rueful smile. "No. I wasn't looking forward to meeting you. Sophie said you were a small-town girl, and the pace here might be too much, because you had a dreamy little shop and a quiet life. I thought a few rough weeks, and you'd leave." She sighed and I felt some sort of kinship with her, despite her doubts about me in the beginning. Beatrice wasn't a bad person, she just had dreams—like I did—and she wanted to make a better life for her son. "Sophie has dangled the management position in front of me since I started and the extra money would've really helped. I'm barely managing to feed and clothe us, with the money I pay for sitters, and rent."

"And I suppose you made it that much harder for yourself because Sophie thinks you're a rich kid from London."

"Bingo."

"So is that why you don't mingle with everyone? And why you're outright hostile to TJ?"

She flopped on the bed and held her head in her hands. "It had to be that way. I loved it there, and enjoyed chatting about books and bookshop life but then came the *let's grab a drink,* or *I'll walk you home,* and I couldn't risk it. I couldn't lose my job. They'd have seen Marc, my secret would've been out." There was a sadness in her eyes I hadn't seen before. "I would have loved to tag along, and share some wine by the Seine and chat about books, and whatever else you all talk about—but I couldn't."

I took a deep breath, and asked the one question I knew I needed to. "Have you been stealing the money?"

Her skin paled, and she gave me such a beseeching look my heart went out to her. "I tried to talk to you, but you were just about to dash out to see your boyfriend. I was going to tell you, and ask to borrow the money instead of taking more. The guilt has almost killed me. But with having to work those night shifts, and the weekends, I had to pay for a babysitter, and I couldn't afford it. I've been slowly getting further behind, and the only thing I could think to do was take the money. I was desperate."

It didn't take long for me to assume some of the guilt was mine for ignoring her pleas—no matter how distracted I'd been. I should have made more time to get to know her, and offer friendship, giving her a person she trusted to confide in when things got tough. "And the first edition I allegedly sold?"

She shook her head. "I sold it. I unpacked the estate sale books. I'm so sorry, Sarah. It's unforgivable."

I let out a long sigh. "You know I'll have to tell

Sophie, right?" I dreaded the thought, but I would reason with her, and ask her to give Beatrice a second chance. We'd all made mistakes and even though Beatrice had gone about it the wrong way I knew she deserved another chance. It was Christmastime after all . . .

"I know. I can't even begin to imagine what she'll think of me, and that hurts more than anything."

I'd been so lucky in my adult life, having great parents and amazing friends. By the sound of it, Beatrice didn't have that, and also had a child to care for. It must have been a worrying time for her, with no one to call for backup if things went awry.

"If we're completely honest with Sophie, I'm sure she'll see reason. You might even get that management job, after all. It's true, Sophie wants some time away, and I'm not staying forever."

A groan escaped her. "I don't know. I've broken her trust badly."

"Leave it to me," I said. "I'll be straight with her, and convince her you're worth it."

"Why though?" Beatrice pulled her eyebrows together. "Why would you help me after all I've done?"

"That's what friends do, Beatrice. They forgive and forget."

Her eyes were glassy with tears, and it was all I could do not to follow suit. I stood up and hugged her tight. She was a mom who'd been pushed into a corner. I would be there for her, and she'd always have someone on her side, who was prepared to help out.

TWENTY-TWO

The next day, Beatrice arrived early. "What did Sophie say?" she asked, the quaver in her voice evident.

I motioned for her to sit down. "At first she was angry. She never in a million years thought it would be you who took the money."

Beatrice covered her face, her shoulders squaring as she steeled herself. "I feel horrible," she said between her hands.

I patted her shoulder. "But once I told her about Marc, and the issues you faced when I changed the shifts, and things, she came around. She wants to trust you, Beatrice, but you're going to have to work for it."

Beatrice glanced up sharply. "She's not going to fire me?"

I smiled. "Nope. And if you play your cards right, you might just get that management position after all. But until then, we'll rearrange your shifts so you don't have to pay for sitters."

She moved to hug me. "Thank you, Sarah. For everything."

I waved her away. "Are you coming to the Christmas party?"

"I guess, if I can bring Marc."

"Of course! We're a family of sorts now, no

matter how we all fit into the equation. I better make sure we have some gifts for him to open on the day. What does he like?"

"Books of course," she said with a smile and I realized it was the first genuine smile she'd ever given me.

Watching Beatrice bound out of the office and to the till, it was like she was a different person—now she could be herself. I was proud of her for being honest and admitting her mistakes. It couldn't have been easy for her alone here, with a toddler to care for, and her future was much brighter now the truth had come out. And perhaps her Christmas would now shine a little brighter.

Later on that morning, Beatrice wandered over, her face pinched.

"What is it?" I asked.

"I thought I better apologize to everyone," she said. "Explain myself a bit . . ."

I gave her arm a reassuring pat. "OK," I said, smiling. It wouldn't be an easy thing for her to choke out, and I was proud of her. "I do think it'll help. They all know something's up." You couldn't keep a secret in a bookshop. Staff sniffed out gossip and, like a game of broken telephone, by the time it got back to me it was so far-fetched, I could only laugh. Better then, if Beatrice was honest with them all. "You can gather them all in the office if you want. I can stay out here and serve, unless you need me in there too?"

Her face colored a little, but she shook her head. "I'll be OK. But, thanks."

She went to them individually, tapping their shoulders and motioning to the office. They seemed to respect her, maybe out of fear, but that wasn't really who she was, and I thought she'd handle the place and the staff well if she got to be the manager.

I served a sea of customers who were buying cookbooks, and children's books, and the odd romance or two, asking about what books were popular for Christmas presents. Ten minutes later, the staff went back to their stations, seemingly nonplussed by Beatrice's confession. I knew TJ and Oceane would have something to say later, but I hoped now to include Beatrice on our little excursions, even if it meant we went somewhere child-friendly so she didn't miss out.

Oceane, her face blanked against the news she'd just heard, said, "Let's fix these decorations. We need more tinsel, you're totally right."

I couldn't help but laugh. "I thought you said tinsel was gaudy . . ."

She giggled. "It is, but it's your big thing, so why not?" We giggled as we restuck the decorations that had blown down each time the door flew open.

• • •

That afternoon it was hard not to smile. The bookshop was lit up like the Fourth of July. Christmas lights flashed and pulsed in the front window, merrily glowing red, green, and golden. By the front door we had a small sleigh that Oceane had practically prized out of Anouk's hands. It was so old, the red velvet of the seat had faded to a russet color, but it was charming, with its ruddy-faced Santa and collection of reindeers.

On the low-hanging wooden beams, garlands of tinsel, crisscrossed back and forth, a web of shiny color.

"You know Sophie would have a coronary, seeing the place like this, don't you?" TJ said. "Like she'd literally clutch her chest and fall to the floor, screaming."

"Thanks for painting that so vividly," I said. "But she won't know, will she?"

Sophie wasn't a fan of Christmas and the thought made me smile, because in Ashford, there was no escaping the festivities—she was being dragged into them, no matter what she did to avoid it. She'd be drinking a cup of gingerbread coffee and singing "Jingle Bells" with the girls, there was no question about it.

Beatrice swanned over, draped in tinsel, and wearing a headband with bobbles that spelled out *merry xmas!* "Turn up the carols!"

"Done," TJ said, giving us a woeful look.

"Honestly, I won't be able to spend the next week listening to 'Silent Night' without killing you all off in a poem, just a heads-up."

I gave him a shove with my hip. "Oh, we've got ourselves a Grinch."

He lifted me up and swung me around, my shriek scaring the customers.

"Service? Anyone?" Oceane asked. A queue of customers had materialized, catching us unawares.

I went to help all the while thinking of Ridge, and wondering what he was doing. I'd found a few presents for him, but had no idea where I'd send them. So they sat forlornly upstairs in the apartment.

Once we caught up, I went out front to survey our new Christmas romances in the display window, and the megawatt fairy lights I'd added. You'd certainly know the bookshop was here, no matter which side of the Seine you were on.

"An American in Paris, you'd never guess." I turned to the laughter.

"Too much?" I asked, facing Luiz. The shop almost hummed with the amount of voltage from the lights.

"I imagine the tourists will feel right at home."

"Come in," I motioned. Winter was in full swing, the cold air shocked the breath from my lungs.

Inside, we stood with our backs to the fireplace,

avoiding the pockets of cold in the store. "Have you heard from Ridge?" he asked.

I forced a smile, but it felt like a grimace. "Nope," I said. "I'm going to concentrate on my first Parisian Christmas. Everyone has high hopes for the annual orphans' party, as they so dub it."

"Infamous around here, those parties of Sophie's. Too much champagne, and a whole lot of warbling, or so I've heard."

I laughed. "Well, I hope we manage to outdo the previous years for the loudest and most ear-bending singing ever! I do a mean rendition of 'Amazing Grace,' seriously, it's enough to get you crying into your eggnog," I laughed. "And that's not the emotion of the song, it's the ear-splitting way I sing."

"So I'll get the staff earmuffs for Christmas. Thanks for the tip."

I scoffed. "They will plaster on a fake smile, and watery eyed, watch me until the last note is sung."

He folded his arms. "You wouldn't sing in front of a group of people."

I laughed again. "True. It's on my bucket list though." It wasn't so lofty an idea these days. Singing, if it meant living in the moment was something I just might do with my newfound confidence.

"Well, if you do I hope I'm there to hear it. TJ called me," Luiz said. "To confirm the reading Friday."

Luiz would be a huge draw card, not only because he was a fantastic writer, but because he never did readings. And locals were out and about more in pre-Christmas buying frenzies. "You're sure?"

"I'm sure. I've fallen in love with the new story, and I know I'm not supposed to admit that." His eyes twinkled. "But it's time *this* story was told."

I rubbed my hands together for warmth. "I can't wait to listen to you read it!"

"Great," he said. "Tell TJ I'll be here at seven on Friday." He kissed my cheek platonically and walked out into the brisk night. His story would be a revelation, I knew it from the way he flushed. I bet it had a happy ever after!

TWENTY-THREE

"You're a good person, Sarah, to fight for her like that." Luiz's words came out in puffs of fog in the snowy day.

"Once she explained her reasons, it was a no-brainer," I said. "Don't you think everyone deserves a second chance?"

"Depends what they've done. What about the love letters? Now we know he slept with the violinist, do you think she should continue their love affair? Is it even worth it, when he's wrapped in someone else's arms, never on home soil because his career is far more important to him?"

I shivered, recalling the last letter we'd read together. Pierre admitted he'd found solace in the young girl's arms, but tamped it down by saying she meant nothing, it was something to pass the time. Sex for the sake of release and nothing more. I was enraged at the casual way he'd written it to the mysterious girl he supposedly loved above all others. Did Ridge partake in affairs on the road, assuaging his guilt by not mentioning it? Was Monique the photographer a willing partner? The idea made me queasy. "I disliked Pierre after that letter, the way he brushed off the violinist's feelings as if it were nothing, and to tell his real love in such blunt terms. But we don't have her response. We don't know what she thinks. Surely it would have ended after that?"

"There's one more letter," Luiz said. "But the French, they think differently about affairs. There's love, and there's lust, and sometimes they go looking for both. It's excused here, as a pursuit of happiness."

"But then how is it real love? If you search for something else with another person?"

"In terms of our love letters, they were apart for almost an entire year. I'm not excusing it, but I'd say that had a lot to do with his reasoning."

"Do you think all men do that?"

Luiz turned to me. "You're thinking about Ridge?"

I nodded, my mouth downturned.

"It's hard to say—I only know him from what you've told me. But it seems his passion lies with his work, like Pierre's did. The difference is, all we got from Pierre was how *he* felt—what *he* missed, what *he* wanted. I don't think your guy is like that," Luiz said, eyes ahead as we walked toward the Notre Dame. He'd arrived at the bookshop early, found me curled up like an ampersand, head pressed against the cold glass window, and urged me to join him for a walk. Once again Ridge and I had missed each other, swapping voice mail messages in the night.

It was only a week before Christmas and the shop had been hectic. I'd been racing around, wrapping presents and wishing and hoping that Ridge would walk through the door. He'd said he wasn't going to lose me, but where was he?

"Maybe it's the wrong time for us," I said. There could be a time Ridge would want to settle down, when the bright lights of a foreign city didn't call to him, but when would that be? And who would I be then?

"You'll see, Sarah. Remember, *tu me manques*. This is when you'll find out if that's true, if you can live without each other or not."

"I don't want to live without him," I said, tears stinging my eyes. Christmas exacerbated my feelings. I wanted my near and dear close. "But how can I compete with his lifestyle? It's what he runs to first, and it's like I'm always coming second to that. I never used to think like this . . . but our visits were regular, and the brief times spent with him quelled any doubt. But three months in the city of romance, with just a quick one-day visit . . . it feels like he's already gone, and he doesn't know how to tell me." The love I felt for Ridge threatened to take over sometimes. It was a heady feeling, an intense need for him that couldn't be assuaged with anyone else. But was the same true for him?

Luiz glanced up sharply. "You think he's trying to break up with you?"

I shrugged. Ridge wasn't like that, the Ridge I knew, but who was he really? On location he was the cocktail drinking, party in the bedroom type of guy. That lifestyle was a million miles away from what we did when we were together. A dinner party with my friends was as exciting as our social life got. Was I being unreasonable?

"Why else would he not visit?"

Luiz's expression was pained, as if he was absorbing some of my sadness. "No man would do that to you, Sarah. You don't see how spellbinding you are, how vital. You may not be the one who dances on tables at a party, or the type to speak up first in a group, but that's what makes you special. You're different, starry-eyed, and romantic, an old soul who has ideals, and you stick to them. It's rare. And it's beautiful." He spoke so softly, almost like he was describing someone else. The compliments provoked a blush, nevertheless.

I laughed to cover my nerves. "I'm too whimsical. Too much of a daydreamer, I see that now. Being here, I see that my lack of ambition is at odds with everyone else, and that's what's missing from my life. Some kind of goal, or direction."

He shook his head, his hair catching under the streetlights as we got to the front of Notre Dame. "Why do you have to compare yourself to anyone? If you're content with your bookshop why should you change?"

"Because shouldn't I want more?"

"Why? Wanting something you can't have is a heartbreak of its own."

Had Luiz lost someone he loved? His voice was thick with a type of ache, a loneliness. "I've always felt like the odd person out. Let's face it, I'd choose a good book over a night out, nine times out of ten. Growing up, my friends were books for God's sake. And I loved them all. Who chooses to live in a fictional world, even as an adult? Surely I can't always hide between the covers, as life passes me by." Even as I said it though I knew things had changed for me for the better.

"Sarah, what you describe is paradise. How many people would swap lives with you in a heartbeat? To be able to snuggle in one of the coves of the bookshop, pull up a throw rug, and read as the light darkens when day turns to night. If you make enough to live on, why do you need more?"

Luiz wasn't like most men. He was introspective and observant, he only spoke when he had something to say, not to fill a silence. "I suppose you're right. Being here though, I wonder what else the world has to offer. I could easily jump on a plane to the next place . . ."

We came to the front of the Notre Dame, its facade spectacular under the somber sky. It had so much presence it was almost alive, its gothic style intricate and otherworldly.

339

"You'll know soon enough what you want, Sarah. If Ridge loves you, he'll prove it. And you deserve a man who worships you." Turning to me, Luiz caught my hands and stared into my eyes. "And *don't* accept anything less."

Ridge. Even just hearing his name was enough to set my heart racing. The thought of never being in his arms again almost made me dizzy with sadness. And I knew I would never love anyone the same as him.

The rain grew heavier, so we sought refuge in a café. In a quiet corner, I sipped the black bitter coffees the French favored as rain lashed the windows, making them shudder.

"Ready?" Luiz asked, taking the last letter from his satchel.

"Ready," I said, bracing myself.

My love,

She's pregnant. She told me last night, her face wild with a sort of joy I can't recognize or feel myself. I never meant for this to happen. It was a way to warm the bed at night, to forget the ache in my heart. To ease my loneliness. Taking a lover, as we've both done, to find comfort where we can, until we're together again. And now this. It's as though my world has collapsed. I cannot be the man who walks away from his child, even though I would give anything

340

to make you his mother instead. I must do the right thing, by her, by this child who's due in the wintertime. I don't know how I'll live without your love. Your letters. Your laughter. But I must. My heart is broken. Be free, my love, and may you find someone who loves you even half as much as I do, which is almost too much to bear.

Pierre

"What!" I yelled, drawing attention from café patrons. I gathered myself and said, "Well . . . wow." The letter made me think of Ridge. He was faithful, wasn't he? Or did he think finding comfort in the arms of a stranger was acceptable?

"Do you think it's common for people with long-distance relationships to fall into the arms of a willing partner?" I cringed at the betrayal of even asking in a roundabout sort of way again. Did people go about and do that kind of thing without any thought of the consequences?

"Some," Luiz said. "Everyone's different. For some it doesn't mean anything. It's a means to an end. From these letters we know they subsisted on only a couple of weeks a year together because his schedule was hectic. So I guess the other fifty weeks they were lonely, and accepted they'd both see other people, but it wouldn't mar what they had. They were honest about it. It's not like they hid it from each other."

Was it because Luiz was French that he viewed love differently to me? How could you say you love someone, yet fall into bed with another person? That kind of reasoning made no sense to me. "I guess," I said, trying to wrap my head around the notion. I didn't begrudge them finding someone to ease the loneliness, but I could never do that. And surely what he'd done ruined their chance of true love that might have lasted a lifetime. "And that's how the letters end. I never would have expected that. It's too sad to even contemplate." Despondency sat heavily in my heart. The mysterious couple didn't find their happy ever after, and I wanted to sob for them.

Oceane held my arm as we walked rapidly. Snow dusted the bare trees on the Left Bank, and our breathing quickened as we picked up the pace to keep warm. "You're never too old for Santa," I admonished her.

My life was a hell of a lot brighter now that the whole issue with Beatrice was sorted out; the shop was a much happier place with a set roster, and sales targets that were achievable. Each dawn, I was up early, stealing time to languish in the quiet and read before my day started in earnest. There was space now to go Christmas crazy. I had been desperate to drag Oceane to see the man in red, pestering her for a week now. Finally, finally, she said yes!

She clucked her tongue. "Santa's village is for *enfants*," she said, though I could tell by her smile she wasn't being truthful, and was just as excited as me to see the spectacle.

We arrived at Boulevard Saint-Germain, sparkling fairy lights pulsing along each side of the street, brightening up the dark evening, and bringing the magic of Christmas to the fore.

Stalls were set up, selling everything from hot chocolate and crepes, to more robust French cuisine that made my mouth water. Roasted chestnuts enriched the air. There was a stage with a manger and we stopped to ogle it. French Christmas carols played from unseen speakers, and it was a moment of pure bliss. The French did do Christmas just as brazenly as Americans! On a small podium Santa sat proudly on an oversized red chair, listening to children as they delivered their wish lists. I pushed Oceane into the line, ignoring her cries of *Non, non, non*.

"Don't be such a spoilsport. I want a photo with Santa, and you're going to tell him what you want for Christmas."

She rolled her eyes dramatically. "I'll never live this down," she groaned while I laughed.

Santa's eyes lit up when Oceane perched on his lap. She sat stiffly, pretending to be mortified before speaking quickly to him, and it took me a full minute to untangle her words. Something about a man she loved, who didn't know she existed . . . I couldn't fathom any man not noticing Oceane. She was striking, and vivacious, and very hard to miss. When the photographer nodded to me, I sat on Santa's other knee and grinned like a fool knowing this picture would be displayed on my mantelpiece back home, and I'd remember the scent of freshly baked crepes, the snow tickling my face, the laughter, and shiny faces of the people here.

Once our photo was printed we were each handed a candy cane, just like back home. I thanked them profusely before we moved on, coming to a stall selling gingerbread. I gasped when I saw some in the shape of an Eiffel Tower, and knew I had to buy one for each of the girls back home. It was too perfect a present to pass up. I just hoped they'd survive in the mail . . .

"You're such a tourist," Oceane said, but her tone was mellow, and she forgave me my foibles what with it being Christmas and all.

We giggled, fetching cups of warm *vin rouge* and sipping while we drank in the Christmas spectacle, all with the Eiffel Tower shining in the background. Could I really leave all of this? My beautiful new friends, my life on the Seine . . . It was becoming more than just a place I loved, it was almost becoming a home. There was just one thing I was missing . . . and my heart ached for him.

We wandered out of the market and into an

avenue, coming face-to-face with a Christmas carousel. Reindeers moved slowly up and down, making their way around in a never-ending circle. "We have to go on there!" I said.

Oceane scoffed. "*Enfants!*"

It was true, there were only children clutching the wide-eyed reindeers, but still, that didn't put me off.

I paid for two tickets and waved them at Oceane. "Don't offend Rudolph," I said, enjoying teasing her. She rolled her eyes, and tipped her *vin rouge* back. "Fine. Only for you," she said with a shake of her head, laughter spilling out of her.

"Get the chairs from the attic," Beatrice barked her orders, her face shining with concentration. "Please," she added with a sheepish grin.

TJ let out a theatrical sigh, but bounded upstairs as he was bid.

Oceane was busy serving customers. Charming them with her delightful French accent, and inviting them to the reading, which was only an hour away.

"I'm nervous for him," I said to Beatrice, moving piles of books, so we could make room for more chairs.

"Don't be. He's going to be a crowd pleaser. That voice, and those mesmerizing eyes of his. We're going to sell out of all his books," Beatrice said. "It'll have the whole of Paris talking. You watch tomorrow, it'll be in the papers, and we'll be overrun. Women will flock here if they know he writes upstairs, so we'd better keep that to ourselves."

There'd been plenty of speculation about Luiz and why someone as visually appealing, who wrote so succinctly about love, was without it. I'd read countless articles online and even some fan sites—gossip was rife and sometimes laughable. But even though I knew him as a friend, I still didn't know much about his deeper feelings. What was his past? From that one moment where I had asked him about whether his life had inspired his writing, we had avoided the subject, talking about love and life but never about his.

"Do you ever wonder if he was in love himself?" I asked, a little dreamily because of the happiness of a full bookshop of real buyers.

She nodded, untangling a microphone cord. "I heard he lost his wife in an accident."

"What? Who'd you hear that from?" I said, shocked. It was too heartbreaking to imagine.

She shrugged. "One of the regulars here, an artist named Sally. She paints upstairs in the study sometimes." Beatrice stepped closer, lowering her voice. "Says it was ten years ago, and they were newly married. And that's why he can never write a happy ever after."

My skin broke out in goose bumps. "Wow, that's so sad, but it makes sense."

"Gets worse," Beatrice said, leaning in closer, not wanting to be caught talking about Luiz. "His wife was seeing another man behind his back . . . and that's the reason she was driving so fast in bad weather, to get home, before he knew she was gone. But the snow had come early that year, and her car skidded off the road."

No wonder Luiz couldn't write about love ending well. That kind of tragedy would cast a pall of grief over anyone. "How did he know where she'd been?"

"There was a letter in her handbag. She was breaking up with him." Beatrice looked as heartbroken as I felt.

"You got all of this information from Sally who paints upstairs?" I couldn't imagine Luiz confiding all of this to someone.

Beatrice's eyes were solemn. "Sally was his wife's sister."

"Oh, my God."

"I know. So he stopped writing for a few years, but really he'd just stopped getting them published. And each novel became that little bit grittier, darker, tangled love that can't ever work."

We both stood stock still for a while, the enormity of what she had just said breaking over us in waves. I was so surprised, but then, when I thought about it, it all made sense. Luiz had suffered a real devastating heartbreak. With a situation out of his control that had skewed the course of true love and left his vision of it cloudy with hurt.

I walked around in a sort of daze, sorting out books, organizing a few nibbles and pouring glasses of wine for those who wanted something to sip on during the reading. My mind was on Luiz. Before I knew it the time for the reading was upon us and the staff were running this way and that causing total commotion in their excitement for the first author reading at Once Upon a Time.

"Turn the carols off!"

"Lock the till!"

"We need more wine glasses!"

"Move!"

Nerves made us panic, before we eventually bumped into one another in our haste, and burst out laughing.

"OK," I said, "let's just take a deep breath. If we look like jittery wrecks, it'll make Luiz nervous. Paste on a smile, hand out glasses of wine—TJ, in ten minutes once everyone is settled you introduce him."

"Go, team," Beatrice said, her eyes blazing like we were about to play sport rather than listen to a book reading.

I walked toward the front of the shop, stopping to help direct people to their seats, and then found Luiz.

"Ready?" I asked. He was relaxed, and smiling, sipping a glass of white wine. I studied him under my lashes. Had he really lost his wife like that? Luiz seemed so grounded, and honest, a good friend to me, and fair when I confided in him about Ridge. Had the love letters we'd found brought the memory of the one in her purse back for him?

"Ready," he exclaimed, holding his drink aloft. "Excited by it, actually."

TJ walked over, pulling at the lapels of his crinkled suit. "Everyone's seated, and they've spilled out into the other rooms, so I think we should start."

Luiz nodded, and I gave him a quick hug. "Good luck! I better find somewhere to stand."

TJ picked up the microphone. His eyes darted around the room, and he licked his lips nervously. "Welcome to Once Upon a Time." His voice wobbled slightly. "We're thrilled to have Luiz Delacroix here with us to kick off the first of the new author readings we'll be hosting here. Today he is here to read the first chapter of a book he's currently working on. Ladies and gentleman, please welcome Luiz."

There was thunderous applause as Luiz took the microphone and nodded to the crowd. "Thank you for inviting me here. I've never done a reading before, because I'm usually crippled with fear that my words don't matter, that what

I've written isn't right, and I'd see that reflected in the faces of the crowd, and I'd lose any ability to write again." There were a few laughs in the crowd that were immediately shushed, but Luiz smiled. "Dramatic, yes, but that's the conflict I face every time I finish a book. This story, however, is different. It's real, it's my heart on the page, and that fear of failure has vanished with this one story. I hope you like it."

The room was silent bar the crackle of the fire, as all eyes were on Luiz as he read. The story started with a man wandering around the streets of Paris, the scents, the sounds, and the feeling he was alone in the world, so alone that sometimes he felt life was passing him by. He'd fallen in love with the wrong girl, and she was gone, and he felt a certain level of guilt at the events preceding it.

My heartbeat hammered. He was writing about his own life. Somehow, I knew this would be a groundbreaking novel for him. That once he'd dealt with the past on the page, he'd transform.

He continued on, about a tragic accident, a breakup letter hidden in her purse. Coming face-to-face with her lover in the gloom of the hospital room; as she took her last breath, it was *the lover's* name on her lips, not his. And he knew, in that instant, she'd ruined him. Her death, his sadness, his trust broken, and only himself to pick up the pieces. Endless days and long nights ahead where he nursed a broken heart that he knew would never heal. And even though she'd done that to him, he missed her. He had loved her with everything.

Until one day, he met a girl, in a bookshop. And he felt a small thrill, like he could love again. She didn't know he existed. He'd been going to the same shop for years. And the idea that she didn't know, that it was his secret, gave him hope. It was enough to admire her from afar.

A grin almost split my face when I worked out who he meant. It had been right in front of my face the whole time.

But the time had come, he said, to tell her how he felt. She loved words, so he wrote her a book.

I nudged TJ, who stood beside me, and indicated with my head to Oceane, whose cheeks were flushed. A smile threatened to swallow me up, as I thought about Luiz making his way upstairs every morning to write. Was that just so he could get a glimpse of Oceane as he passed? When we'd met on the bridge that night, they'd cast admiring glances at each other.

I closed my eyes and wished they'd find happiness together. That Oceane wouldn't have to waste time with any more Mr. Right Nows, and that Luiz would step from the shadows of his past, and into the light of new love. Maybe this would be the one book of his that ended in a happy ever after. I almost squealed at the thought.

The bell chimed, and I cringed—I was meant to have to turned it off. I mouthed a sorry to Luiz, and dashed behind the counter to halt its pinging.

And there he was. The veritable man mountain, his shoulders dusted with snow, his eyes reflected with concern. My heart beat so fast I thought I might pass out. Everything around me faded as we locked eyes. His face was lined with worry, his jaw tensed tight.

"Ridge." I wanted to run to him, but I held myself back. It had been too long, I wasn't sure how to act. Still hurt about radio silence, and broken promises.

"You're busy," he said, indicating to the crowd, his voice a murmur.

"A little." He could have called, told me he was coming. But like always, he'd hung up and let me wait. I spent my life waiting.

I wanted to hear Luiz's reading, but I couldn't help feeling that I'd soak it up better reading the inky-black words myself when it was published. Or maybe that was just an excuse. "So?" I said.

"I'm so sorry," he said, his brows pulled together, and he took a step closer. "When you said you weren't sure how you felt it hit home how my choices were affecting us. I don't want to give up my career, but I don't want to lose you either," he whispered.

"Let's go outside." I grabbed my scarf and coat, and pushed open the door, Ridge close behind.

We went to the little garden on the corner, standing close for warmth's sake. Being near him, the familiar he-scent, the planes of his face, which I'd stroked with the pad of my finger so many times, made my heart hurt. Because what if it ended here? I'd never kiss those lips again. Never feel his breath on my skin when he took his time, teasing me, caressing me, making me feel wholly alive and in the moment. But I'd had enough. I couldn't be a stopgap. I had to come first, or at least equal with his other love, his work. He could at least promise me that much, or it was *c'est la vie*.

"If only you knew how much I loved you, Sarah." His voice was plaintive, sad.

"But how can we go on like this? Months apart . . . missed phone calls. No communication? I can go weeks, but I can't go months." Each word was like a razor blade falling from my lips, cutting me to the quick. I'd never understood heartbreak, until that very moment—my chest seized, the pain real. I put a hand to it, hurting badly.

"Let me explain." His eyes were murky, like he was ravaged inside. He ran a hand through his hair, disturbing snowflakes that drifted lazily down. "When I left *The New York Herald*, I thought my career was over. And I've worked so hard to make it in that world. You know how competitive it is. All I'm asking for is twelve months to make a name for myself as a freelance reporter. That only leaves us with six months left of this . . . lull between visits. Can you not try and understand? It's not forever. I have plans after that. Plans that may keep me in Ashford full-time, but first I have to prove myself in order for that to happen." His worry lines deepened.

I crossed my arms—even bundled up, my bones still felt the cold. "Will that year turn into two? Ridge, it feels as though I'm waiting for something that's always just out of reach."

"I promise, not long, and I'll be free." He inched even closer, his presence having the ability to make me melt. I squared my shoulders, not wanting to give in to the familiar. "I have investors lined up for a venture. I wasn't going to tell you in case it didn't pan out. We're looking at starting up a digital magazine with me as the editor—and I can edit from Ashford, Sarah. I can edit from anywhere. Be wherever you are *full-time,* if this takes off."

My mouth fell open. "You'd stay in Ashford for good?"

He laughed, the sound carrying into the air above. "That's the plan. One of the reasons I've been taking so many assignments is to find reporters who'll sub to us. It's been a lot of work, and I know it's still not right, that I let you down, but it was all because my long-term goal was to be with you. I know I should have confided in you, kept in better contact. But it was like I was racing against time to make it all happen. I didn't want to lose another set of investors. I didn't want the idea to go belly-up. I was so driven, I almost lost my mind. And what a wakeup call, to think I'd lose you, in my efforts to get this financed, to be with you all day, every day."

"I wish you'd told me. It would have saved a lot of heartache." The similarities with the letters hit home. What we did for love, and got lost on the way. "You shouldn't have kept it secret. What did you think I'd do if it didn't work out?"

"It was more that I wanted it to be perfect. To tell you, and then never leave your side again. I'd have felt like the biggest failure if it hadn't worked out."

"I don't want there to be secrets between us."

"There won't be."

"OK," I said, still unsure what all this meant for us.

"What about you, Sarah? You used to be content to live in Ashford, being at home—and now, here you are running a business in a bustling city . . ." He trailed off. "Where do I fit with the new you? You've changed so much in these few short months, from your clothes, the way you speak, your confidence. Even the emails you send are different."

"Paris has changed me." I smiled up at him, his dark eyes sparkling, snow falling on his broad shoulders, the Eiffel Tower a winking reminder in the background. "I couldn't keep waiting to live my life. I'll always love my hometown. But I couldn't be a passenger in your life, or even my own any more. The waiting, that wanting, only I could find it. And here it was the whole time. Inside of me. I'm not the same person I was, because she needed improvement. A little pizzazz, and a hell of a lot of confidence injected into her. The bookshop, with its bevy of drama, brought that out of me. I had to speak up to be heard, and now I'm speaking up with you."

"You're my everything, Sarah. And I would gladly give it all up, if you asked me to choose. My reasons were pure. I should have just told you, and we could have hoped together."

He gathered me in his arms, shivers coursing the length of me. Back in the embrace of the man I loved, who loved me too. The worry of the last few months ebbed away. My heart was light, and I knew if we spoke openly like this from now on we could get through anything—together.

"I wasn't certain it would happen," he mumbled into my hair. "We've had investors pull out, and advertisers cancel. It was only a week ago we got confirmation that another corporation would help finance for a share of the business. It's been one big ball of stress, but I can finally say, fairly confidently, it should all go ahead. We plan to launch it next summer. My motivation was you, Sarah. I love my work, and the competitive nature of the industry, but I love you more. And this way I can have both."

I leaned on tiptoe to kiss him, not trusting myself to speak. I thought of the love letters, and how Luiz said the pianist was self-absorbed, only ever mentioning himself, his work, his upsets. And here was a man who loved me, who knew what he needed to keep that fire in his belly, and keep me, and he'd done it. Solved the problem of our vastly different lives. He'd still have the drama and the action of his job, being at the helm of the digital magazine, and he'd be able to come home at night and tell me all about it. I knew deep down, we both needed our passions to keep our love alive—his was reporting hard-hitting stories, and mine was reading romantic fiction, in my own easy, sweet little shop. Where there wasn't a spreadsheet to be found.

"But now I'm concerned," Ridge said. "You've fallen in love with Paris. Will you stay?"

I shook my head. "No, I won't stay," I said, thinking of Beatrice and the job she so needed. "I'll be back to visit though. Oceane's promised me summer on the Côte d'Azur, so how could I resist?"

"You couldn't. You're irresistible." Ridge lifted me up, I wrapped my legs around his waist and kissed him again, more deeply and with all the pent-up passion I had for him.

"I love you, Ridge Warner."

"And I you, Sarah Smith."

• • •

Ridge slept, jetlagged to the hilt and exhausted from our night of no sleep as we remembered how to love one another. I dressed quietly and snuck out of the apartment, heading for Anouk's shop for some final Christmas presents, if she agreed to sell them to me.

In the snowy day, her shop was like a beacon, warm light spilling from the lacy curtains. With a deep breath, I set my shoulders and pushed the door open. She was at the counter polishing jewelry with a delicate cloth. She was made-up, every inch the forties glamor puss. On anyone else it would look as though they were trying too hard, but on Anouk, surrounded by relics from bygone eras, it suited her.

"*Bonjour*, Sarah," she said, giving me a once-over.

"*Bonjour.*" I tried not to cringe under her scrutiny.

"You're looking for Christmas gifts, *non*?"

How did she know? She just knew—like the ring she'd found for me, which was perfect. And it had been a lucky charm, as she subtly hinted that long-ago day.

"*Oui*," I said, remembering Oceane's warning too late. I was not to tell her they were for my friends back home. She didn't like her wares leaving Paris. But she must know I was leaving eventually.

"Some things I can sell you, some I cannot."

I nodded complicity. "I understand. Some books are like that for me too."

She smiled, and it transformed her face. She was breathtakingly beautiful once she dropped the haughty demeanor. "He might like these," she pulled a box from the display that housed antique cufflinks.

"He?" I couldn't help but ask. How did she know who I was shopping for?

"Customers are easy to read," she said. "You just have to know how."

I didn't push for an explanation, knowing I was still on a sort of probation period even being allowed to enter the shop without a long-time customer acting as a go-between. "The cufflinks are perfect," I said. She indicated to a golden pair, simple and elegant, and I knew they'd suit Ridge. "May I?" I asked.

She nodded.

I took the delicate cufflinks and held them in my palm.

"They belonged to a writer once," she said solemnly. "A very famous man. He was American, but he lived in Paris. I'm trusting you, Sarah. These cufflinks are tied very heavily with the past, and they must be cherished."

They almost pulsed in my hand, and I squeezed my eyes shut to see if I could imagine which famous writer they had belonged to. Hemingway? Faulkner? Ezra Pound?

My eyes flew open. "I promise they'll be treasured. Perhaps when I wrap them, I'll include a book too. What do you think of . . . *Tender is the Night*?"

She laughed, a husky, deep chortle. "Good guess, Sarah. I think he'll like that very much." Anouk took the cufflinks from me, and used the polish cloth to shine them. "Next time you visit here, I'll take you out the back."

I nodded, doing my utmost to hide my joy. I hid my hands behind my back, lest I start fist pumping, and simply said, "I would love that. Thank you, Anouk."

I strolled outside with my purchase in hand and let out a little shriek of happiness. I'd been accepted by Anouk, and it meant a lot somehow. Like I'd passed some really complicated test.

Grinning like the happy fool I was, I slipped on the icy ground in my rush. TJ had asked me to meet him by the city hall, a beautiful nineteenth-century building I'd passed many times. When I arrived out of breath, laughter tumbled out of me. There he stood holding two pairs of ice skates, and motioned to an outdoor ice skating rink set right outside the hall. "I'll break my legs, I'm sure," I said.

"Give your shopping to the girl to stow and get these bad boys on your feet. You haven't lived until you've ice skated in Paris at Christmastime."

Snow drifted down under somber skies.

Christmas lights twinkled even in the daytime. It was magical. And if I did break a leg at least I'd have a great story to tell.

"OK," I said. "But don't you dare sneak photos of me when I'm face-first on the ice."

"Seriously? But my Instagram would go wild with a picture like that."

I laughed and gave him a shove.

TWENTY-FOUR

The table was laid with bright red cloth, and Christmas crackers sat atop plates. Cutlery shone under the lights, and the wine glasses sat waiting to be filled with French champagne. Christmas carols played chirpily overhead, while I made the final touches to the apartment, plumping cushions and adding more wood to the fire.

I switched on the Christmas lights, which twinkled brightly, making me think of my friends back home, who'd still be sleeping, but would wake to have breakfast at Lil's and open presents together, including the ones I'd sent which thankfully had arrived the day before, just in time.

I had presents for my Parisian pals too. They were wrapped in gold foil, so I spent some time writing in the cards. I wanted everyone to know how much they meant to me. Each person from the bookshop had touched my life in some unequivocal way, and they probably didn't know that. Even Tyler, the American who'd led the charge against me, had a place in my heart. Without his surliness, the way he'd put me on the spot, I would have still been the girl who never spoke up, the one who so desperately wanted to be heard.

I was sentimental and a little emotional, them

all having left a mark in my life—one I would never forget. I knew nothing stayed the same, and all I had was this moment to thank them. When I came back in a year, maybe two, for a visit, I knew most of the staff would have moved on. Real life called for those transients, and what we'd shared—the ups, the downs, the arguments, and the laughter—was part of our journey, and nothing could change that.

Over time, I'd reflect back, and with the hazy light of memory, I'd remember the fun times, more than anything else. It was hard to say goodbye in those cards, knowing each person would flit off around the globe to somewhere new that became home, and we'd never see each other again. For some of those staff it would be a forever goodbye, so I had to make it count. Maybe one day, a book would arrive at my shop, one of their names blinking from the cover, and I'd shriek as I unwrapped it, and think of them fondly. I hoped all their dreams came true. Because I felt as though mine had and they'd contributed to that.

I couldn't hold back tears when I wrote to TJ. He'd been like a protective big brother to me, and I loved him so. His words were art, and I knew he'd make it with his poetry. The world just had to catch up to him. One day he'd have a wardrobe full of suits, rather than one crinkled promise.

And Oceane. She'd found The One. It was

early days, I knew that, but I could tell. Real love shines more brightly, and they were almost blinding together. Luiz was a great man, and I knew he'd cherish her, like she deserved. He'd been hiding too, and now it was time for him to step back into living and follow his heart.

I wrote to Beatrice with a flourish, telling her she now had family. A backup plan. Everyone deserved to have friendships as special as I had with the girls back home, so I told her she'd never need to feel alone again. If things didn't pan out, and she needed help, I was a phone call away, and whatever it took we'd fix it. I asked her to consider visiting me in Ashford one day, knowing she'd be fussed over by the girls, and made to feel loved. And she needed that, to know that there were people other than little Marc who cared about her.

For Luiz, I thanked him for his friendship. His light in those dark days when I was missing home so badly. And for the way he translated the letters, and what we learned about love from those whispers from the past. I knew, no matter where I was Luiz and I would always remain firm friends. I loved his quiet nature, his brilliant mind, and the words that he wrote.

"The champagne is cooling, and the table is set," Ridge said as he walked from the kitchen, looking every inch the sexy man he was, dressed in a crisp white shirt and tight jeans.

"You're a minx dressing like that right before everyone's about to arrive," he said.

I lifted a brow. "This old thing?" I joked.

He ran a hand over the fabric, dropping his palm to the small of my back. "You're a siren in red."

It was one of the dresses Oceane had found for me on the Champs-Élysées when the insurance had come through. It was scarlet-red jersey fabric, and fit over my body like it was tailored for me. I'd splurged, feeling glamorous and sophisticated and totally French, but hadn't had an occasion to wear it until today.

The doorbell sounded just as Ridge was nuzzling my neck. He groaned. "To be continued."

I laughed and answered the door to Oceane, who held Luiz's hand. My heart just about burst at the sight of them together.

She put down her bag, and pecked Ridge on the cheek. "So you're the hero in her story. I see . . ." She winked at me.

TJ arrived, finding the door ajar. "Ridge," he said, formally shaking his hand. "And Sarah." He enveloped me in a hug.

When Beatrice and little Marc arrived, Ridge popped the champagne and handed everyone a glass, and ducked to the kitchen to get Marc an apple juice.

"Who's going to toast?" Oceane asked. She

looked utterly ravishing in a deep blue dress, her short blonde hair slicked to the side.

"To Paris," TJ said. "May we all be as happy for the rest of our lives as we are now." His eyes glittered with unshed tears, and I knew the sensitive soul that he was, he understood that we'd all move on, lives would get busy, and this would be a distant memory so we had to soak up every minute.

"To Paris," we said and clinked glasses. This was a magical time in our lives, and no matter what had happened I would always look back on the time at the bookshop as something marvelous, something bold and brave that I'd done.

"I'd better check on things in the kitchen," I said. Rosemary peppered the air, and the rich scent of roast turkey wafted lightly through the apartment.

"I'll help," said Oceane, digging the heel of her palms into my back, practically tripping me into the kitchen.

With a tea towel in hand, I took the roasting pan from the oven and basted the crispy meat, while Oceane knocked back her champagne. She was jittery and flushed.

"OMG!" she said. "He's *The One,* Sarah. I know it already." She gave me a wide smile. I'd never seen her as beautiful as she was right at that moment. Her blue eyes shone with happiness.

"I knew it!" I said, giving her a quick hug. "I

want to be invited to the wedding, don't forget."

She giggled like a schoolgirl. "Of course! Obviously, he hasn't proposed yet, being only a few days into it, but when he does you shall be my bridesmaid!"

Imagine a French wedding, Oceane-style. It would be a grand affair, with all the trimmings.

"I would love to," I said.

"Right, what do we need to do for lunch?" she asked, surveying the bench.

"Get the foie gras on a plate, and I have some *chèvre* to go with it."

With capable hands she plated the appetizers expertly.

"I attempted a *buche de noel*, with coffee buttercream and ganache. Do you want to take a look, and tell me if it resembles a yule log?" We all knew baking wasn't my forte but I'd had a few practice runs with the cake leading up to today, because it was a traditional French Christmas dessert.

"Sure." Oceane opened the fridge, and gasped. "You did not make that yourself! You bought it from a pâtisserie!"

I laughed. "I did so make it myself!"

"I'm joking," she said, deadpan. "I can see that. I'm sure it tastes a lot better than it looks."

I flicked her leg with the end of the tea towel. She let out a yelp, and fell about laughing, like she was on some kind of lovestruck high. "So you and Ridge?" she raised an eyebrow.

"Desperately in love," I smiled. "And a pact to be more forthright in future."

"I'm happy for you. And he's *sooo* handsome," she said, sing-songy. "Right, everything is baking nicely, let's take out the appetizer and some more champagne."

"Let's do presents?" I said. Little Marc was racing around the room with a paper plane, and I couldn't wait for him to open the gifts we'd bought. Knowing he and Beatrice had had it tough made buying presents that much sweeter. I'd dithered over what to choose for them, wanting to get it right. There was a stack of a dozen, brightly wrapped with his name on them.

"Marc, I do believe St Nick left you a few things here under the Christmas tree. You must have been an incredibly good boy this year."

His solemn brown eyes widened and he said with the sweetest, lilting accent, "I've been very good. Ask Maman."

Beatrice and I exchanged smiles.

I knelt with him by the Christmas tree, and everyone gathered around, their faces lit up by the sight of a child with an expression of unadulterated joy on his face. The magic of Christmas was still so new to him, and a thrill to watch. I took one of the biggest parcels. "This one has your name on it."

Without hesitating he ripped the foil off, and screeched. The box on his lap almost dwarfed him. Everyone had wanted to chip in for his presents, and we'd made the right choice by the look of it.

"A real train set! Can I open it?" he asked, suddenly shy.

"Of course," I said. "And we have batteries so you can play with it while you're here."

Ridge knelt down beside us. "Would you like some help putting it together, buddy?"

Marc nodded. My heart swelled watching Ridge sit crosslegged with the little boy, patiently helping him take each piece from the box. There were plenty more for Marc under the tree but he was content with the biggest one, as all little boys probably are, when they get their first serious piece of machinery. "I don't know who's having more fun," I said, kissing Ridge on the cheek before taking another present from the tree. "Beatrice," I stood and handed her the gift.

She opened the card first and read slowly, her eyes welling with tears. She took a moment to speak, her lip wobbling. "Thank you, Sarah. For everything."

"Go on," I said. "Open it." I wasn't too far away from a blubber-fest myself so I tried to keep things on track and leave the happy tears for later.

She ripped off the foil a lot more delicately than Marc had. "No!" she said, a small sob escaping. "Airline tickets?"

Ridge had graciously added to my dismal

savings in order to buy the tickets. "They're open, so you can either fly back to the UK whenever you want, or you can come to Ashford for a holiday." I didn't want to press her, but I thought maybe once things improved for her here, she may want to mend the bridges with her family. None of us knew what had driven her away, but at least she had the means to get back if she wanted. Selfishly, I hoped she'd visit us, and bring little Marc, and a piece of Paris too.

She promptly burst into tears and Oceane moved to hug her, handing her another gift. "You may as well get all your tears out at once," she said, laughing.

Beatrice opened the next gift, a bunch of navy blue clothing, suspiciously small, like Marc's size. "What . . . ?"

"Marc's uniform for nursery next year. We couldn't resist when you said you'd enrolled him."

Beatrice's eyes filled with tears. "Thank you. They're so adorable. Look at these little vests!" She bit down on her lip, and hugged the uniforms to her chest. "I don't know what to say. After everything I did, you guys do this?"

TJ said, "You haven't opened my gift yet."

She took the proffered gift, which was wrapped in newspaper. She ripped it off and smiled. It was a book with a serious black cover. "Your poems?" she asked.

"Yeah, I'm not so much unpublished anymore, as well . . . published."

We gasped, and crowded around TJ, hugging him and throwing up high-fives. "When did this happen?" I asked.

"A few weeks ago, but I only just got my author copies. And, FYI, you're all getting the same Christmas present."

I hugged him tight. "No guesses who the next author reading will be performed by! If you're not too famous to hang out with us now?"

He shrugged. "You'll have to talk to my people, I have no idea what my schedule is like these days. Getting mobbed by fans, and men and women falling over themselves to get to me . . ."

"Yeah right, Romeo," I said. "I want boxes of your books sent to Ashford, so I can sell them at my shop."

"Sure," he said. And handed us all our copies. I flicked to the first page—the dedication read, *The nights by the little bookshop on the Seine, spent with word lovers, and other lost souls, this is for you. Paris swept us up, and made us whole, may we never wander alone no matter where we are.*

He knew. We all did. That what we'd had was something special. It was like someone had sprinkled fairy dust and made all our Christmas wishes come true. After mammoth hugging and a few tears I said, "Shall I finish preparing lunch?" The rest of the bookshop crew were coming at various times after they'd caught up with other friends. And Lucy and Clay were dropping over after they'd had a feast with their art crowd. There were murmurs of yes, so I smiled and wandered back into the kitchen.

My nerves fluttered at the thought I'd burn the turkey and serve raw potatoes, but Oceane was a brisk assistant and added more oil to the trays, and basted the meat once more. I trimmed the green beans that were so fresh they made a satisfying crack. I added them to a pot of water and parboiled them.

"Once they're done," Oceane said, "I'll toss them in a little butter, and top with some roasted almond slivers and some chopped parsley." The French knew how to cook, even the most basic dishes they fancied up with different herbs and the essential dollop of butter that accompanied everything.

We sat down to eat, everyone complimenting the meal and managing to hide their grimaces when the *jus* I'd made tasted sour enough to pucker their lips. I don't know what I did but it had split, and tasted all sorts of wrong. I played along, "Anyone want more of the *jus*?" I lifted the gravy jug in the air.

Ridge coughed. "I wouldn't want to appear greedy."

"None for me," TJ said. "I have another party later. Don't want to overdo it."

Beatrice rolled her eyes. "Sarah, it tastes like

vinegar. I don't think you can call it a *jus* just yet. But well done for trying."

I laughed. "I was waiting for someone to say it! I have a way to go before I can call myself a French cook."

Oceane raised an eyebrow. "When you arrived here, Sarah, you couldn't boil an egg. You've come a long way." And I had. Not just with my kitchen prowess either.

"My life of microwave meals are over."

We finished the meal, and the guys cleared the table and stacked the dishwasher. "I could get used to this," I said, watching them work from the comfort of the sofa.

Oceane sat beside me. "Me too. I have a present for you." She took a small gift from her handbag. "So you don't forget about us whenever you decide to leave. And so you remember how much fun your first Paris Christmas was."

"I'll never forget," I said. I took the paper off and it was my turn for tears to prick my eyes. It was a photo of us all around the Christmas tree in the bookshop, taken the night before when we'd closed the shop, and opened a bottle of wine, exhilarated about a few days off. We were pulling silly faces, and our eyes shone with happiness, in that pure, free way you have when life is truly the best it can be. "The frame Anouk says belonged to a formidable woman who collected art, and scribbled some books too. You might know her as one of the lost, who wasn't lost at all."

I gasped. "Gertrude Stein?"

"The very same."

"I'll treasure it," I promised. I went to the tree and grabbed Oceane's gift.

She gave me a wide smile and opened it. "It's perfect," she said, placing the necklace over her head. I'd searched everywhere for the girl who has everything and eventually stumbled on a tiny market that sold bookish gifts. The pendant was a pile of golden books and by chance the top one was engraved with Once Upon a Time. "I absolutely love it!" We gave each other a quick hug, delighting in our presents and what they represented.

The guys wandered back into the room and filled our champagne glasses. We pulled the Christmas crackers, laughing at the silly jokes that were written on the parchment inside.

Evening came too quickly, the rest of the staff coming and going, cheery and smiley and leaving for other parties around the town.

"Should we go for a walk before the Sandman comes for Marc?" I asked. His blinks were getting longer, the excitement of the day catching him. "We could take him to see the Christmas lights." Almost every avenue was lit up, whether it was the trees along the side of the road, to balconies above circled with fairy lights and glittery decorations.

"He'd love that," Beatrice said, smiling.

Luiz nodded and said, "Shall we leave a

note on the door in case the other staff arrive?"

"I'll stay back, and wait," TJ said, waggling his eyebrows as he clutched an unopened bottle of champagne. "Now I'm a proper published writer I think I'm supposed to develop some bad vices like drinking too much or smoking?"

Oceane laughed. "I don't think so. But for today, you can do whatever you want."

Ridge wandered over and sat on the edge of the sofa, taking my hand in his, giving me that special look, one that said so much with just a raise of his brows. Having him so close made my heart lift, and I knew if we were separated again for work or anything, I wouldn't overthink it. I wouldn't second-guess myself. Our love was real and we could deal with anything. I was overjoyed he'd eventually work in Ashford full-time, but if the shine wore off that, I'd understand. This exchange had opened my eyes to so many things, and my future wouldn't be spent in one place anymore. Perhaps vacations would be the order of the day and that would be enough for me.

Outside, the Eiffel Tower pulsed and flashed on the hour. Fireworks burst in the distance, making us stagger to the window in haste to catch the spectacular sight. The merriment from outside drifted up. Full boats chugged down the river, people milled along, waving, and the Notre Dame in the distance had a crowd of people lining up for a Christmas concert.

There was a knock on the door. "Must be another reveler," I said, moving to answer it.

"*Oui?*" I said to the man who stood there. His face fell when he saw me.

"Where's Sophie?"

"She's in America, on . . . a sort of holiday. Can I pass on a message?"

His gaze flicked behind me, as if he didn't believe she wasn't really there. "Tell her that Pierre called for her, and I am hers now. If she wants me. Tell her . . . that I've always loved her."

I gasped, recognizing his name. "Why don't you phone her and tell her yourself?" I said, my words coming out in a garbled rush. The love letters . . . Of course, it was Sophie! I felt blind for not seeing it now. The piano room! A legacy to the man she loved and lost. Luiz nodded to me, a small smile playing at the corners of his mouth.

Pierre blushed with so many sets of eyes on him as Luiz welcomed him into the apartment. I yelled out the phone number while Luiz practically dialed the cordless phone for him, before pushing him into the bedroom for some privacy, and shut the door.

I was frozen to the spot. Ridge stood next to me and pulled me in for a hug. "My reporter sense is tingling," he said, laughter in his eyes. "But you can tell me later. For now, I want to stroll through Paris with you and watch your face light up at every little thing you see."

"Yeah?"

"Yeah. I've been thinking long and hard about things, Sarah Smith. And I think we should stay in Paris as long as you want. Will you miss your bookshop too much?"

"You're going to stay?"

"Every minute, every hour, until you cluck your tongue and want some space."

"But the . . ."

"The investors confirmed this morning. We're good to go, and like I said, I can edit anywhere."

"So I'll be your tour guide?"

"I hope you'll be all that and more . . ." He kissed me so softly on the lips and I swooned. Actually swooned like they do in the books. Here he was, my book boyfriend come to life.

We were interrupted by Pierre rushing from the room, his face shining. "She said yes!" he said. "She has always loved me. It's not too late for us. This time the music will *not* get in the way!"

I smiled. He'd chosen his career, which led to a lover and a baby. Ridge had chosen me. But Pierre got a second chance and my heart lifted with happiness for Sophie getting her happy ever after, finally.

Ridge wrapped his arm around me, pulling me close. We gazed at each other, the rest of the world fading.

It was true. Real love always finds a way.

If you loved Sarah and Ridge in The Little Bookshop on the Seine, *turn the page to read about how they met in the charming bonus story,* The Bookshop on the Corner.

The Bookshop
ON THE CORNER

ONE

Snuggled in the cozy bay window of the book-shop, I looked up from my novel as the first golden rays of sunshine brightened the sky. Resting my head against the cool glass, I watched the light spill, as though it had leaked, like the yellows of a watercolor painting. Almost dawn, it would soon be time to switch on, and get organized for another day at The Bookshop on the Corner.

Every day I arrived at work a few hours prior to opening to read in the quiet, before customers would trickle in. I loved these magical mornings, time stolen from slumber, where I'd curl up with a book and get lost inside someone else's world before dog-earing the page and getting lost in mine. Sure, I could have stayed in bed at home and read, but the bookshop had a dreamlike quality about it before dawn that was hard to resist.

I turned back to the inside of the shop to watch shards of muted sunlight settle on piles of books, as if it were slowly waking them. The haphazard stacks seemed straighter, as if they'd decided when I wasn't looking to neaten themselves up, dust their jackets off, and stand to attention. Maybe a customer would stumble across one of them today, run a hand lovingly across their covers, before selecting a book that caught their attention. Though my theory was books chose us, and not the other way around.

The bookshop was silent, bar a faint hum— were the books muttering to each other about what today would bring? Smiling to myself, I went back to my novel, promising myself just one more chapter.

When I looked up again the sun was high in the sky, and I'd read a much bigger chunk than I'd meant to. Some stories consumed you, they made time stop, your worries float into the ether, and when it came to my reading habits I chose romance over any other genre. The appeal of the happy ever after, the winsome heroine being adored for who she was, and the devastatingly handsome hero with more to him than met the eye tugged at my heart. And I'd read about them all: from dashing dukes, to cocksure cowboys, I never met one I didn't fall for.

The sounds of the street coming alive filtered in, roller shutters retreating upward, cheery shop owners whistling as they swept their front stoops. Lil, the owner of the Gingerbread Café across the road, arrived, hand in hand with her fiancé, Damon. They stood on the pavement in front of her café, and kissed goodbye, spending an age whispering and canoodling.

I tried to focus on my book, but couldn't help

darting a glance their way every now and then. Each morning they embraced almost as though they'd never see each other again, yet they worked only a few short steps away. It was as if they were magnetically drawn to each other; one step backward would draw the other person forward. I bet they couldn't hear the sound of shops opening or cars tooting hello. They had their own kind of sweet music that swirled around them as if they were in some kind of love bubble.

Feeling as though I was intruding on a private moment, I swiveled away from the window and padded barefoot down to the back of the bookshop to make more coffee. My feet found the familiar groove in the wood; the path was so well trodden it was bowed. The feel of the polished oak underfoot with its labyrinth-type trails exposed around stacks of books was comforting. It'd weathered traffic for so long it was indelibly changed by it.

Taking the pot of coffee to the counter, I poured a cup, and sipped gingerly. Lately, I'd felt a little as though I was at a crossroads. You know that frustrating feeling of losing the page in your book? You didn't want to go too far forward and spoil the surprise, and you didn't want to go too far back, so you kind of stagnated and started from a page that didn't seem quite right, but you read it a few times just to convince yourself . . .

that was how I felt about my life. A little lost, I guess you could say.

Ashford was buzzing with good news recently, love affairs, weddings, babies, but I was still the same old Sarah, nose pressed in a book, living out fictional relationships as if they were my own. I was waiting for *something* to find me. But what if that *something* never came?

What did heroines do when they felt like that? Broaden their horizons? I imagined myself swapping Ashford for Paris, because of the bookshops and the rich literary history. But really, I'd never ventured far from my small town, and probably never would. My bookshop was a living, breathing thing to me, and there was no one to look after it even if I did want to do something spontaneous. Should I take up a hobby? I'd be the girl stuck line dancing with the octogenarian. Instead of dreaming of the impossible, I set about opening the shop, and shelved that line of thought for another time.

With a feather duster in hand, I ambled around gently tickling the dust off book covers. The dust motes floated up briefly before landing back on each tome to settle until the next morning, when I'd wave the duster around again as though it were a magical wand.

I turned when I heard the familiar click-clack of high heels. Missy, my best friend and owner of The Sassy Salon, strutted into the bookshop in a cloud of sweet-smelling perfume. Her formfitting scarlet dress lit up the sepia-toned shop. She was all bouffant auburn curls, and thick Hollywood-esque makeup, and the type of person that made you smile just by setting eyes on her.

"Good morning, my gorgeous friend! You're looking as pretty as ever, I see." Missy had a tendency to speak loudly, and peppered her dialogue with compliments. In her hands was a bunch of pale pink roses. "These are for you," she said, handing me the flowers. "I walked past them in the garden this morning, and it was like they yelled out, 'Take us to Sarah!' So what's a girl to do? I hurried back inside and got my best hair scissors and lopped them off, not feeling as glum as I would normally since they expressly asked for it."

Times like this, I realized Missy and I had a lot more in common than you'd think. Her roses spoke to her and my books spoke to me. What a pair we made.

I buried my face in the delicate petals and inhaled. They smelled fresh as a summer's day.

"My books thank your lovely roses. They sure will appreciate their wonderful perfume."

"Pass on my thanks to your lovely books," Missy joked. She was vivacious, and charming, but there was so much more to her than that, an inherent goodness, that made me appreciate our friendship every day.

"Will do," I said and kissed her cheek, before retreating to find a vase.

I ambled back to Missy and propped the vase on the counter. I admired the roses once more before tapping the stool next to me. "Get comfy, you still have a while." Missy didn't open until ten so she usually came into the bookshop for a quick chat and a cup of coffee. Her salon was as lively as she was. It sat on the opposite corner from the bookshop, and was like a beacon in the street. The rest of our shops were old colonial style, lots of red bricks and timber, but Missy's shop was painted in lemon yellow and pink stripes, which somehow looked glamorous rather than gaudy.

Missy settled herself on the stool, and swung her legs like a child. "Would you take a look at them . . . ?" She pointed across the road to Lil and Damon. "Ain't love grand?" she boomed.

"Sure is. I've been trying not to watch them, but it's like seeing a romance novel come to life with those two. It's utterly captivating."

She must have heard the wistful tone in my voice because she turned to me and said, "You'll find your plus one, you know. It's only a matter of time."

I laughed. "My plus one?"

She fluffed her curls, before responding: "Well, you know, with all the weddings coming up, namely the lovebirds across the way."

Would I go to yet another wedding unaccompanied? At nearly thirty I couldn't keep up the pretense that *love was just around the corner*. Maybe some people were destined to be alone. But, I reminded myself, you're never alone if you read. I had my books; they took me to extraordinary places without having to leave the comfort of Ashford. Nope, I wasn't lonely, I was just minus a plus one. I was never good at math, anyway.

We watched them for a beat, before Damon finally stepped off the curb, and headed to his own shop.

"Can you imagine," I said, "how beautiful their wedding will be?"

Missy rubbed her hands together. "And even better, Lil said I'm allowed to cover her face in gloop, and put a host of overheated hair-torture devices near her scalp—her words, not mine."

I raised my eyebrows. "She's going to let you do her hair and makeup? That really will be a Christmas miracle!" Lil's wedding was taking place in December, the perfect time for a winter wonderland setting. But Lil wasn't a fan of makeup or torturing her hair, as she saw it. Classically beautiful, she didn't need to primp and preen, but I was glad Missy was going to help on her big day.

"She's going to look as pretty as a picture. All that blond hair, and those bright blue eyes of hers . . ." Her words trailed off as they often did when Missy was caught up picturing how a person would look after she got through with them.

Missy was the only hairdresser in town, aside from a barber who was purely for men. She had a steady business, but, like most of us, could always be busier.

"Are you booked up today?" I asked, thinking about my bangs, which seemed to grow overnight, prickling the tops of my eyebrows each morning.

"Not really, but I've got Rosaleen and her daughter in first up." Missy rolled her eyes. Rosaleen was the town gossip. Every town had one, ours just happened to be particularly good. "Wonder what tidbits I'll find out today," Missy said. "I thought hairdressers were meant to be the ones who gossiped like crazy."

I laughed, and shook my head. Missy would never get into a game of broken telephone, but I guess she was inadvertently privy to it when people like Rosaleen patronized her salon. "Tell her gossip makes your hands shake, and you'd hate to lop off an extra inch or two of those purple curls of hers."

"You know, that just might work!" She laughed and picked up a lock of my hair and scrutinized it. "Come by later. I've been thinking of a new style for you, and I can sort those bangs of yours out."

"You read my mind," I said with a smile. "But

you only just gave me this style." I indicated my bobbed hair.

She held her hand up. "Trust me, you're going to love it," she said, silencing my concern.

"Okay, okay, a new style, why not?" I wasn't a person who took change well, preferring the rhythm of what worked, but Missy had a way of making me step out of my comfort zone with her dynamic personality.

"Until then . . ." she air-kissed me " . . . I better go see about a little sugar to start my day. You want anything from the café?"

Missy claimed she needed sweet treats to keep her curves voluptuous. She was more fifties screen siren, with a saunter that accentuated her figure. "I might pop over later. I can't keep away from the chocolate truffles. Sometimes I wish I'd never suggested the chocolate festival."

Over Easter I'd orchestrated a chocolate festival in Ashford. Lil and CeeCee from the Gingerbread Café had been the focus but all of the shops along the main street had been involved, including my bookshop. It had been a huge step for me to jump out of the shadows and try and woo some new faces into town, but our businesses had needed a boost, so with that in mind I'd pushed the fear of failure out of my mind and set to work. It had been a lot of fun, and made me appreciate our small town once again, and how well we worked when we banded together.

Missy glided to the front door, and turned to me. "That was the best weekend of my life! I'm still paying for it though." She grimaced as she surveyed her hips.

"Hardly," I scoffed, watching the way Missy exaggerated her saunter, indicating the weight she'd supposedly put on.

"Stop past at lunch, sugar," she said with a backward wave.

TWO

"The Bookshop on the Corner." I cradled the phone with my shoulder, and glanced at my watch. Almost time to head over to Missy for my appointment.

"Who am I speaking with please?" asked an elderly voice.

"This is Sarah. Can I help you with anything?"

"Sarah . . ." He spoke my name slowly as if he was trying to place who I was. "I'm Gerald. I hail from Chicago." Gerald's voice was squirrelly with age, and tinged with something . . . sadness perhaps? "I have a business proposition for you, Sarah, if you have a moment to discuss it?"

Intrigued, I replied, "Sure, Gerald. Fire away."

"I have a wonderful library full of books that I think you might be interested in. They're special books, very special indeed . . ." It wasn't unusual for me to receive calls from people wanting to sell their book collections because I advertised far and wide in an attempt to find stock, though lately I'd reined in my budget a little out of necessity.

"Any first editions?" I asked, thinking of my out-of-town clients who collected them.

"No, nothing like that. You see, these books are extraordinary, but maybe only to folk like you and me. Most of them are brown with age, and their covers are spiderwebbed from use. But they tell a story, you see. They tell *our* story." He paused as if weighing up where to begin.

"My wife, Gloria—Glorious Gloria, I called her—spent a lifetime acquiring this collection. Books written in various languages, books so old the pages are loose, but she loved them. The scruffier the book, the better." His voice dropped to almost a whisper. "A lifetime, she sought out books to add to her shelves. Like some kind of mysterious algorithm, she chose books based on what? I never knew. There was no rhyme or reason. There are books about boat building, and gothic horror—they're so varied, I sometimes wonder if even she knew why a certain book appealed to her. Sixty-five years spent on this hobby of hers. Finding bookshops that were tucked down narrow alleyways, or great big houses converted into a book lover's paradise—I've seen them all."

It sounded like bliss to me.

Gerald continued: "Do you believe in magic, Sarah?"

I replied instantly, "In the magic of books? Yes."

"So did Gloria. If only I could explain how she looked when she found the book she would take home. Her eyes would light up, she'd speak in this beguiling hushed tone, her face full of wonder like a child on Christmas morning. It was like she was finding something priceless each and every time, yet to anyone else they would be nothing but a book destined for the penny bin out front of these small shops."

It was as though I knew Gloria, understanding the happiness of stumbling across a book as though it were burnished gold. How lucky she'd been to find a man who was obviously besotted by her. But he spoke about Gloria in the past tense and tears pricked my eyes when I realized I'd never get to meet her, another person who lived to find lost and forgotten books and give them a new lease on life.

"I know exactly how she felt," I said. "There's a certain pull books have on a person if they listen hard enough."

Gerald chuckled. "I have found the right place, then," he said. "You know, Sarah, we visited The Bookshop on the Corner a long time ago. I wonder if you remember . . ."

Closing my eyes, I thought back for a moment. Surely a couple like that I would remember? I would have recognized a kindred spirit in Gloria. "When?" As soon as the word left my mouth, it came to me. It was winter, and snowing hard outside. The bookshop looked as romantic as ever that day; snow filled the squares of wood on the windowpane outside. I had the fire in the reading room stoked up casting an orange hue in the small space. An elderly couple spilled through the door, laughing as they dusted snowflakes from their clothing. It was Gloria I pictured, wearing a cerulean-colored coat, vibrant, and chic. But there was something in her eyes that made her seem timeless, almost ageless.

"Do you recall us?" Gerald asked.

"Yes," I said, smiling at the memory. "Gloria bought a sci-fi novel—something wacky. You stayed in the reading room sipping tea while we watched the snow fall through the windows and talked about books for hours." How could I have forgotten them? They came in a few years back. Gloria had a quiet grace about her, but also a zany sense of humor that had me in fits of laughter. When they left, I remembered thinking I hoped I'd have a relationship like theirs one day. They just seemed to fit, perfectly, like two pieces of the same jigsaw.

"What happened to her?" I asked before it dawned on me I could have worded it better.

Gerald sighed, and took a moment before replying: "She passed on, Sarah. Not too long after we came into your bookshop. It was sudden. I woke up one morning, and she was gone. But you know what? She'd just that last night finished the book she was reading. And I think that was a sign especially for me—that she knew what was coming somehow and it was okay. God chose the right moment, at least, in that respect.

She would have given Him hell if He'd taken her halfway through a book." He laughed softly, but it sounded hollow.

"Which book was she reading?" I wanted to read that book, and wonder what she might have thought about that last night when she went to sleep.

"It was *The Notebook*, by Nicholas Sparks . . ." Gerald sniffed, and I gripped the phone tighter, hoping he wouldn't end the call just yet. I wanted to hear more of their story. "You know, I read the book afterward," he said, "and it seemed fitting. Right, somehow. I've never told anyone this, but sometimes I read passages from *The Notebook* aloud, pretending she's there, and is listening, with that glorious Gloria smile on her face. It makes me feel close to her. As though she's just stepped into the other room for a minute . . ." His voice trailed off, and it took all my might not to cry into the phone. They'd exuded this radiance, and that kind of shine only came from real, once-in-a-lifetime love.

"I'm so sorry, Gerald. I can only imagine . . ." Anything I could say would only seem trite in such circumstances, but I tried desperately to think of something to say that would comfort him.

"It's okay, Sarah. I'm doing better. I know we'll meet again, so I live for that. I live for her, because it's what she would want. But it's time for me to move now. There's too many memories in this big old house, and I'm too old to be tending gardens, and wandering around waiting for her to come back. Which brings me to the books. I want you to have them. I know they aren't worth anything money-wise, and even if they were, it's not about that. I want them to go to someone who understands their value, albeit sentimental."

I exhaled quietly, trying to keep my emotions at bay. "Are you sure? There's no way you can take them where you're going?"

"I'm sure. I'll keep a few that hold an extra-special memory, but the rest, I would like to ship to you, if you'll have them."

Light spilled into the small hallway from the reading room off to the side of the shop. It was a small room with a few high-back chairs that had seen better days, a fireplace and bookshelves around three of the walls. It was a space for customers to read when it was cold, and a room the local book club used for their monthly meetings.

"Gerald, I'd be honored to have them. But I won't sell them. I'd like to put them in the reading room, the room you used when you visited, and then they can be enjoyed the way they're meant to be."

Gerald didn't speak immediately. I sensed he was crying, and trying to quell the tears before responding. I pictured Gloria's books arranged along the shelves in the reading room, including the one she bought here all those years ago. They'd have another life, those books, and Gerald could move along with his.

"Thank you, my dear. From the bottom of my heart. Gloria rhapsodized about you and your bookshop all the time. You've made an old man very happy."

"I hope you find comfort in your new place, Gerald. And if you're ever in town, come by and say hello."

We finished the call; when I hung up I let the tears flow. And I knew right then, that was what I was missing in my life . . . a love affair like theirs. I wanted someone who knew books were more than just words on paper. Someone who understood my introspective nature and didn't try to change me. I dabbed at my eyes with a tissue, ruminating about the fact that there was no one like that in Ashford. I could see the type of man I wanted: quiet, bookish, and introverted, someone who wouldn't make me feel that reading all day was weird. And someone who'd snuggle right up next to me and read too.

My last thought before heading to Missy's was that I hoped Gerald would find his way without his Glorious Gloria.

"Hey!" Missy said, snipping away at a manic pace on a client's hair as I wandered into her salon. "Busy morning?" she asked, her voice as loud as her clothing.

"I wish," I said and sat heavily on the pink sofa. The bookshop figures had been dwindling each week. I had my out-of-town clients who sought hard-to-find books, and without them the bookshop wouldn't survive, but worryingly they weren't ordering as much these days either. My walk-in traffic had increased over the chocolate festival but not enough to stop the worry that seemed to plague me.

I rested my head against the back of the sofa, recalling the conversation with Gerald. "I had a lovely gentleman call and offer me his wife's book collection for my reading room. She's passed on . . . " My voice broke as I thought of Gloria.

Missy eyed me for a moment and said softly, "Must be a mighty fine collection all right—only the best go into that room."

The reading room was my own personal library. It was filled with books that meant something to me, or that had changed the way I viewed the world. Anyone could sit in there and read, but the books weren't for sale. Now, though, I'd take those volumes home and Gloria's books would take pride of place.

"Yes," I said. "It's time for a shake-up. I thought I might rearrange the shop, maybe organize a weekend away or something. I just feel like . . . change."

Missy arched an eyebrow, and stopped her furious scissoring. "Whoa, whoa, whoa. Did you just say you'd rearrange the shop?"

"I did."

"And the *C* word? Change? What's brought this on? I know you, and change isn't in your vocabulary."

I laughed at Missy's reaction. Change was so alien to me, it was almost another language. I was a staunch fan of the "if it's not broke—don't fix it" mentality. Missy ran her hands through her client's hair, fluffing it up. "I'll just blow-dry Lettie's hair, and then we can have a proper girl chat—what do you say?"

Lettie piped up. "Don't mind me, gals. I'm enjoying this."

Missy threw her head back and hooted. "I'm sure you are, Miss Lettie. Shame I'm about to drown out any conversation with this little beauty." She winked at me and pulled out a hair dryer. The whooshing sound prevented us from talking, so I walked out back and made a pot of tea. When I returned Lettie was gone and Missy was sweeping up piles of golden-blond hair from around the chair.

She rested the broom against the mirror and said, "What's this really about?"

I poured tea in two dainty but mismatched cups, and handed one to Missy.

"The gentleman who called told me the most incredible story about his wife, and their relationship . . . and seeing Lil and Damon every morning, kissing like their life depends upon it, I just feel a little lost. Dormant. Maybe nothing happens to me because I don't try hard enough." The words fell from my lips before I could edit them.

Missy clucked her tongue. "Oh, Sarah, you don't need to *try*. You're perfect just the way you are, and the quicker you see that, the better." She sashayed over to me and joined me on the sofa. "I think broadening your horizons is a great idea but don't go changing who *you* are."

"I won't," I promised. "It's time for this little bookworm to scramble from the pages for a few days, at least."

Missy leaned in to hug me. "Who knows? Maybe you won't need to. Maybe change will blow in on the wind under the guise of a six-foot-tall, dark, and handsome stranger."

"You romantic, you," I said, and rested my head on her shoulder.

Later that day, I was finishing an order for a client who collected old comics, when Mary-Rose, a regular, walked in. She worked down the street a way, selling aromatic candles and beautiful bath products.

"You literally smell like peaches, Mary-Rose," I said.

"I've just made a batch of peaches-and-cream

bath bombs. The whole shop smells divine!"

Mary-Rose made everything from scratch using natural products; often the scent would wend its way down the street, having us scurry up to see what concoction she'd made this time. "I'm still in love with the marshmallow bath bombs. They make my whole house smell gorgeous for days after. You're an alchemist."

Mary-Rose grinned. "That's what I keep telling Paul, but will he listen? No!"

Paul was Mary-Rose's husband, who originally told her it was preposterous opening up a bath shop in Ashford. That she'd go broke before the first week was out. But she hadn't. It seemed the townsfolk of Ashford adored her products, and what girl didn't like smelling as if she'd just bathed in a tub of peaches?

"Paul will work it out eventually, once you're sunning yourself in Spain, a holiday paid with the profits!"

"Wouldn't that be something?" she said longingly before shaking her head. "Must not think of Spain. I'll get the worst hankering for tapas and I'm not likely to find them around here, unless I get Lil to expressly cater them for me. Now, I'm looking for a book."

"What kind of book?" I moved around the counter.

Mary-Rose scratched her chin. "It's got a red cover."

I tried to keep the grin off my face. "A red cover, right. Do you know the title?"

"Hmm, no."

"The author? Or genre?"

Mary-Rose crossed her arms, and gazed around the shop. "Well, no . . . I think it might be classed as romance, but it could also be family saga."

It never ceased to amaze me when customers inquired about a book they wanted purely based on the color of the cover. As though there were only a few books in all the world with a red cover, and it was just a matter of narrowing it down.

"Family saga, well, let's start there," I said. "Come to the back, Mary-Rose. I think I have just the book you're after."

I'm sure the books rustled in anticipation, and somehow we found the mysterious red-covered volume Mary-Rose was searching for. That was the inexplicable magic books held over us mere mortals.

After a long night at the kitchen table poring over the paperwork for the bookshop, I'd eventually given up, and gone to bed with a regency romance. Debonair heroes were just what the doctor ordered, and I'd ended up finishing the book just as midnight struck.

I'd fallen into a restless sleep, dreaming about my life and how to make the bookshop a little more successful. Words flashed through my mind, until I plucked a couple from my dream. *Book blogging.* It couldn't hurt to start a blog, discussing my love of books, and what the bookshop had in stock. Maybe I'd review books as I read them. Start discussions on the latest trends, including the popularity of the ebook. I knew there were a lot of books being published that were only in digital format, and, being a voracious reader, I didn't want to miss out purely because they weren't in paper form. Either way, a daily blog post could only help the bookshop, and who knew what might come of it? Energized, I got up in the predawn darkness and dressed for another day at the bookshop.

"Book blogging?" Missy cried. "That's about the greatest thing I've ever heard of! I follow a bunch of lifestyle blogs, and they're great! I can't believe we haven't thought of this before." Her forehead furrowed. "At any rate, it's not too late. And, you know, you can have a link to your online store too."

I'd been waiting all morning for Missy to arrive to tell her my plans. "Right, well, today The Bookshop on the Corner blog will be born!"

Missy sipped her coffee and then said, "The possibilities are endless. You can do a monthly book club, or monthly discounts, book bundles, all sorts of things . . ."

I inched forward on the high-back chair in the reading room. "Guest authors, interviews, I'm in heaven just considering it."

Missy stood, and kissed my cheek. "Let me know when it's up, sugar, and I'll send it out to my veritable treasure trove of online friends."

THREE

The Bookshop on the Corner blog took off moments after I sent the link to clients old and new and my friends in Ashford. It seemed people loved to read about daily life in a secondhand bookshop. Within a month, I had over three thousand followers, and the numbers grew daily. I'd met a community of other book bloggers who were supportive, and funny, and felt like real friends.

Orders poured in for vintage Harlequin romance books, so I'd been busy scouring my usual sources trying to find more. I was as busy as I'd ever been, and this new venture had given me a major confidence boost. Women emailed me daily with stories about their lives, and how books had been there for them when times were tough. It reminded me of the Ernest Hemingway quote, "There is no friend as loyal as a book." And this new cluster of online friends made me cherish our shared passion, always and forever—reading. I'd found people who were just like me, and it made me feel as though I could do anything, and be myself, and that I was enough. It changed me almost overnight, giving me a sense of self-assurance I'd never had before.

The cloud of feeling lost that had hung over

me the weeks before had vanished as quickly as it had come. For the first time in ages I was invigorated, and felt that the world—albeit virtually—was opening up to me, as I tried to open up to it.

After scheduling my blog post for the morning I gave in to temptation and settled behind the counter with my book, promising myself I'd only read for ten minutes. Twenty if I finished on an odd-numbered page. Thirty if I was stuck halfway through a chapter. Okay, I'd stop when a customer walked in.

A silhouette loomed through the open doorway blocking out the last vestiges of the summer sun. The half shadow seemed rugged, masculine. A second later, a man stepped over the threshold of the bookshop dipping his hat. The girl held her breath, hoping the stranger would be as handsome as his powerful saunter implied. She gulped as he stood in front of her; the orange glow of the overhead light lit up his face, highlighting his chiseled cheekbones, and piercing gaze, making her mute with desire . . .

"Excuse me, miss?"
The book fell from my hands as the presence

of a man startled me. There he was, the rugged stranger with chiseled cheekbones, and a look in his eye that screamed *take me to bed!*

It took a moment for my brain to unscramble and realize I was not in fact living out the scene I had just read. Actually, it took *far too long* for me to understand that I was staring at him, my eyes wide, jaw hanging open, like some kind of fool. Gathering my thoughts, I coughed, clearing my throat, and donned my professional bookseller face.

"Can I help you? Let me guess, you're looking for a book on . . ." I took in his appearance: tight denim jeans, casual white T-shirt, tight around the bicep region—I mean, wasn't that uncomfortable? The sleeve of his tee looked as though it were practically cutting off the blood supply. I dragged my eyes back to his face, and my breath caught. I hadn't seen a man so good-looking except in my imagination.

"On . . ." he prompted, raising an eyebrow.

Damn! No more romance reading during work hours.

I coughed again, this time more forcefully, to pull myself together and focus on the job of selling books. "Right, a book on, er . . ." It was a gift of mine to be able to garner what book a person was looking for just by their dress, and their mannerisms, but this guy had me stumped. All I could imagine was that little man crease thing, right where his jeans hung. Note to self: stop dropping gaze to his nether regions.

I was doing it again. The mute, bamboozled, mouth-open thing.

"I'd say you're a thriller man." There. Done.

He shook his head. "Wrong."

Folding my arms across my chest, I said, "What do you mean 'wrong'? You have thriller written all over you."

He made a huge show of looking for the word *thriller* on his clothing; he pulled his T-shirt out, and, oh, good God . . . his six-pack rippled, exactly as it did on the hero of a Harlequin cover.

This time I shook myself as though I'd just come out of the ocean. I couldn't keep clearing my throat and coughing; he'd think I was sick, or worse *contagious,* or something.

"Are you okay?" he asked, tilting his head.

I moved from behind the counter, and headed toward the front door. It was steamy in here all of a sudden. I made a mental note to open some more windows in future. And maybe stock an ice pack or two.

"I'm totally fine. Just a little hot." I needed some space. This guy had me dreaming Harlequin, and I didn't know how I was supposed to do that and keep the giddy, dreamy look off my face.

He followed me, leaning against the opposite doorjamb. "Let me guess, you're more of a romance reader?"

I double blinked and hastily said, "I am not!" *Please tell me I didn't say out loud his abs rippled.* "I mainly read true crime. And horror. The gorier, the better," I big-fat lied. For some reason he looked like the kind of guy who'd belittle romance readers, and I didn't want to give him the satisfaction of knowing.

He gave me the once-over, a very slow up and down, that made me shrink under his scrutiny. "You look more like a romance reader to me."

I squared my shoulders. "And what *exactly* does a romance reader look like?"

"Let's see." He scratched his chin as if he was contemplating. "She's tiny, like a doll. Has perfectly cut black bangs, which highlight her mesmerizing doe eyes. Nervous around strangers, unaware that her hands flutter like the wings of a butterfly when she's thinking things she doesn't want anyone to know . . ."

I gasped, and put my hands behind my back.

"Her voice is husky, betraying her desires . . ."

"Okay, stop. What's with all the flowery prose? Are *you* a romance writer? Are you one of those men who moonlight as Cindi Lovenest, or something, to help sell more books?" I narrowed my eyes at him.

He laughed, throwing his head back, and showed his perfect white teeth. No actually, this *wasn't* a romance novel, let me adjust that—he laughed, throwing his head back, and showed his perfect white teeth, which would one day in the near future, possibly ten years or so away, be not as white. There.

"I am a writer. Just not a romance writer. I'm a reporter from New York."

"A reporter from New York, hey? Aha, let me guess, you want a self-help book? How to have it all? How to avoid living the cliché? No, wait, how to make every minute count?"

He put a hand to his chest and scoffed. "I detect sarcasm! Do you think us New Yorkers are that bad, really?"

I shrugged. "I only know what I read."

"Which is romance."

"Bloody, gory, zombie-loving horror with chain saws, and ninja stars, and a little true crime, remember?"

"Liar."

It was not like me to be so extroverted, and I didn't usually think so . . . *lewdly*. This stranger had some weird kind of pull over me, eking out a different Sarah from the one who actually existed. Gone was the girl in a corner, nose in a book, somehow replaced with a girl expertly flirting, using fast-paced banter with someone who was *definitely* not my type. Too handsome was *too* hard.

But he smelled good. Not of the tree-bark, glorious man-sweat, musky he-scent, rather I've-doused-myself-with-some-male-perfume-that-smells-a-little-like-cotton-candy, and spice, making me consider taking a quick nibble of his skin. This was of course highly inappropriate and a little weird.

He ran a hand through his dark too-long hair. See, too-long? He was the epitome of a romance-novel hero. And it wasn't a cliché, it just *was* a little too long, in that it curled around his ears in an enticing way that would make women want to tuck it behind for him. It was a ploy, and I bet he knew it. He looked around midthirties and had examined what women read about, and, I'd bet, copied the brief, right down to, well . . . his briefs. I had a twenty-second battle with my eyes, which were trying to drop their gaze to see if his underwear was the usual hero style.

"Anyway . . . Mr.?"

"Ridge."

"Mr. Ridge—"

"No, it's Ridge. Ridge Warner."

I snorted, which I tried to cover with a fake hiccup. I hated that I couldn't control my snorts. "Your name is Ridge? Like from *The Bold and the Beautiful*?"

"Maybe my mom was a fan of the show? Who knows?" Mirth danced around in his blue goddamn sexy hero eyes.

"Ridge," I managed to sputter. I couldn't stop laughing. I just couldn't.

"And what's your name?"

413

Internal sigh. Could it be any plainer? "Sarah. Sarah Smith."

He pursed his lips. "Sounds like an alias to me. I mean, is this really a bookshop or a front for your spy business? Are you CIA?"

"FBI, actually." I grinned at him, before catching myself. This little exchange was fun, but I wasn't foolish enough to believe a big-city reporter would be interested in me. That would only happen in a fairy tale. "So, what can I help you with, Ridge?" I was almost certain I managed to hide the lip wobble by clamping my teeth down, and looking away. *Ridge.* I had to stop thinking of his name or I'd never compose myself.

"Have you got any Keats?"

"A poetry man—color me surprised."

I was about to amble to the poetry section when he caught my arm. I tingled from his touch, but tried to mask it by whistling. Whistling? He must've thought I was cuckoo.

"Also, I'd like to interview you. I'm doing a story about Ashford, the little town making waves with its specialty shops."

My eyebrows shot up. "A New York paper wants a story on the shops in Ashford, Connecticut? Is news that slow?" Our tiny town wouldn't even be on the radar for ninety-nine percent of New Yorkers.

"Yep, seems there's a lot going for this town.

What with the Gingerbread Café, and the recent chocolate festival. The shop that sells furniture made from the wood of old boats. It's a feel-good piece. You never know, it might just bring some tourists to your quaint little shop."

Quaint. I didn't know why, but he made the word sound dusty. A little secondhand.

"And which paper is this?"

"*The New York Herald.*"

Gasping, I brushed my hand along the top of a book, while I pondered. *The New York Herald* was one of the biggest newspapers in the world.

"And you, Sarah Smith, with your suddenly successful blog . . . largely about romance books." I colored. Of course, he knew about the blog, hence the romance-reader banter. And he knew my name, though pretended he didn't. He'd researched, and then gave me textbook *lines*. And I'd fallen for it.

"What's the angle for the story?" I asked huffily.

"Little town makes good, something like that. Why?" He laughed, a deep rich sound. "You seem suspicious. Is it your FBI training that makes you question everything?"

Oh, boy. Why did he have to be so disarming, and funny?

"I just know New Yorkers, that's all. And more often than not, in my experience, they don't come to small towns and heap praise on them. They stick to their huge city, with their indefatigable spirits, and try and cram as many things into one day to be able to call themselves successful. It's like a competition to see who's better. Every. Single. Day."

He cocked his head, his small smile slipping. "You've been to New York?"

"Well . . . no. I have no desire to be crushed in the throng of people racing through their day. I'm a small-town girl, always will be."

"Not everyone is like that. Maybe I could show you around NYC sometime?" His megawatt smile was firmly back in place.

I let out a "hum" that sounded slightly strangled. It wasn't as though I didn't understand the appeal of big cities; it was just our cozy little town was so easy to live in. And perfect for people like me who were happiest hiding in a book nook with their fictional friends.

"So, can I interview you for the piece?"

I shook my head. "A secondhand bookshop? I don't think so. And my blog is a place where women feel comfortable talking about things that are of no concern to fast-living men. Why don't you ask Lil and Cee from the Gingerbread Café? They're the ones who are trying new things, and putting Ashford on the map."

Lil owned the cute-as-a-button Gingerbread Café across the road, and worked alongside CeeCee, the most effervescent human on earth.

They'd built the tiny café up over the years into a successful business.

"Fast-living men?" he continued. "I can't decide if that's a compliment or an insult. I've just come from the Gingerbread Café." He patted his six-pack. "They plied me full of sweets. Fun girls. But what about you? This shop . . ." He turned to survey it, and I wondered for a minute what he must make of it. I tried looking through a stranger's eyes at the books haphazardly piled on the floor. The shelves were double stacked, and skewed. It was gloomy, and musty, and smelt like old parchment. And that was what I loved about it. It wasn't shiny and new and filled with light. It was a place for words, and a place for quiet. A harmless little alcove where you could loll on a faded half-empty beanbag, pull over a garish-colored throw blanket and while the afternoon away reading. It wasn't unusual for me to stumble and trip over a boot of someone snoozing, as they had read themselves to slumber.

He sighed softly, bringing me back to the moment. "It's similar to a timeworn Parisian bookshop. Like there's buried treasure here, if you just spend some time hunting for it."

I held in a shriek of yes! Mr. Rippling Abs had it spot on. It *was* like a Paris bookshop. An old, forgotten, hidden little gem of a place, where time stopped, and the only thing that mattered was a good metaphor, or an awe-inspiring paragraph. A sentence that made you close the book and think of the way twenty-six letters could be arranged to make something so miraculous, something that *spoke* to you, almost as if it were written especially *for* you.

He looked deeply into my eyes as if he was trying to read me. "Aha. So Paris is okay in your books?"

Wistful, I said, "Of course—doesn't every girl dream of Paris?"

He inched closer and said, "Some dream about kissing under the Eiffel Tower, and strolling along the Champ de Mars . . ."

I gulped, and held back a sigh of longing as I pictured myself strolling hand-in-hand along the cobblestoned streets of Paris.

"Sarah . . . Sarah?"

"*Oui*?" I blinked the fantasy away and felt myself color. *Oui*? I couldn't believe I just said that! This man was making me go completely loopy.

He laughed as I retreated back to the safety of the counter. "*Mademoiselle*, you won't change your mind about being interviewed by *moi*?"

I threw him a dark look and fiddled with the books stacked precariously on the desk before muffling a reply. "I'm very busy, actually. So if you'd like a poetry book, you'll find a stack near the beanbags at the back . . ."

His face dropped, but I couldn't tell if it was

because I'd said no to the interview or the fact I couldn't quite meet his gaze. I wasn't brave enough to. The way I was thinking, I'd have us married off any minute. And men from out of town were a big no. No matter how ruggedly handsome, and sexy smelling, and funny, and flirty, and downright edible, and—

"Shame, you would have made an excellent subject."

"Yes, a frightful shame. A very good morning to you. Good day." Oh, dear, I'd gone from bumbling romantic to posh Londoner. I fought the urge to laugh at my awkwardness. Once Ridge left, I was going to be meeting Missy at the Gingerbread Café. I'd replay my woes to her and the girls and see what they made of it. And I'd eat my weight in chocolate while I was there.

He tapped the top of the counter, and gave me a questioning look. "People don't usually say no to me."

"Is that so?" He looked truly baffled at my rejection. I guessed big shots like him always got their way. "You know what they say: every no brings you one step closer to a yes. Try someone else." I smiled benignly.

"You are one in a million, Sarah," he replied, grinning. "Here's my card, in case you change your mind, or if you want a tour of New York one day."

I looked under my lashes at him—because that

was what girls did in books when they weren't sure how to act—and took the proffered card. "Nice to meet you, Ridge."

"I'll be back." He winked, and walked out into the sunlight.

Once he'd gone I tried to pretend that the last ten minutes weren't something extraordinary in my habitually quiet life.

FOUR

"You said what?" CeeCee screeched, her forehead wrinkling.

I shrugged, and fell back into the softness of the couch. "He made me feel a little unhinged, demented even, so I just kind of said, well, that New Yorkers were a little shallow. I didn't actually use the word *shallow* . . ."

CeeCee slapped her leg, and let out a guffaw. "Oh, Sarah, good Lord, you don't see what he seein'! He was probably tryin' to ask you on a date, and you mock him over livin' in a big city?"

"I suggested a few self-help books—that's all. Is that bad?" I covered my face with my hands.

CeeCee hemmed and hawed to herself. "Lotsa people have long-distance relationships these days, you know. There's that Spacebook, and Tweeter . . ."

I giggled at CeeCee, and nodded. "Ah, yes, Spacebook, of course. And long-distance relationships? I think you're jumping the gun somewhat, Cee! I am not interested in him, at all." No siree, Bob. Zilch, zip, nada. But the visions of his man crease . . .

Lil wandered over with a tray of drinks. The Gingerbread Café was empty of customers after the lunch rush. I'd waited for it to slow down before I wandered over from the bookshop, leaving a Back in Ten sign on my door.

"So," Lil said, plonking down next to me. "You must admit he's one fine specimen of a man."

Laughter barreled out of us. "He's too good-looking. And he knows it."

CeeCee groaned and patted my knee. "You know, Ridge asked an awful lotta questions 'bout you. Seems he came to the chocolate festival way back when, and *suddenly* he's back again today. All he wanted to talk about was the girl from the corner bookshop . . ."

Lil nodded in agreement. "I got the feeling the article was a ruse. I think he's smitten with our resident book-lover."

I gave her a playful shove. "Oh, please. He's just nosy—it's the reporter in him."

CeeCee tried to stare me down with this arched-eyebrow thing she does. "Nosy? I don't think I'd call it nosy—more like infatuation."

"How could he be infatuated with someone he doesn't even know, Cee?" I smiled. "Nope, that man is one hundred percent New Yorker, you mark my words. He's after something, and it isn't me."

Lil harrumphed and leaned into me, nudging my ribs. "Are you free Friday night?"

I rolled my eyes. "No, I have a hot date with my book boyfriend. Why?"

"Damon and I are having a little dinner party to try out some recipes for the new catering menu, and we thought you might like to join us? CeeCee'll be there, and a few others."

I inhaled sharply. "Do you even have to ask me? If there's food involved I'll drop that book boyfriend like he's hot!" So I was fickle with my literary loves. Lil's food was good enough to tempt the devil himself.

Lil giggled and said, "So it's a definite?"

I tilted my head. "Yes, of course."

They both sputtered into their hands.

"What? What's so funny?"

"It's just Ridge is comin' up from New York, see. So we figured you could sit next to each other—"

"Why is he coming back here?" I interrupted. It was Monday, and I'd figured Ridge was interviewing people for his article today, and then we'd never see the likes of him again.

"We just happened to mention our pretty little book-lover was going to attend the dinner party," Lil said matter-of-factly.

I lobbed a cushion at her. "Oh, you're as subtle as chili in the eye, you pair of matchmakers. I thought I was going to come here for some sisterly understanding, but all you want to do is set me up with some swanky, swishy reporter, who's perfected the come-hither look . . ."

"Someone's been bitten by the lovebug," CeeCee said, drawing the words out like a child in a singsong.

"Cee," I said, "you sound like you're five!"

"What the heck's going on in here? I can hear your laughter all the way down to my shop!" Missy stood in the doorway with her hands on her hips, grinning.

"Oh, you know," I said, looking up at her perfectly made-up face, "these two girls are bored or something so they're trying to play Cupid."

Missy sat down on the couch next to CeeCee and said, "Again? Cee, didn't you learn anything last time?" She winked at me and fluffed her auburn curls.

CeeCee folded her arms. "What you mean last time? The last time that I remember was when that fine-looking thing, Damon, strolled into town and I had the second sight about him and Lil here. Was I wrong? No, I most certainly wasn't! They about to get married!"

"I'll give you that one. Damon and Lil are a match made in heaven," Missy said. "But the *last* person you tried to fix up before them was poor Sarah, when you set her up with Crazy Old Lou's second cousin's half brother. Or was it the first cousin's half brother?"

I shrank down into the couch and groaned. "It was Old Lou's neighbor's cousin's half *sister* if I remember correctly!"

We cackled like a coven of witches remembering that fateful hookup.

CeeCee tried to compose herself and said

between chest heaves, "Well, what kinda name is Billy for a girl?"

Missy pulled a cushion into her lap. "It's Billie, with an *ie*. S'pose it could have happened to anybody!"

CeeCee clucked her tongue. "It was a small misunderstandin', that's all, but Sarah still had a good night, right?"

I giggled at the memory. Billie with an *ie* and I had stared at our spaghetti, mutely, while I pondered how I'd been set up with a girl when I was heterosexual. We were both too polite to say anything, so we ate a silent dinner, watched a silent movie and then went our separate ways— silently. And that was the last time I'd agreed to step outside my comfort zone in relation to dating.

"Anyways," CeeCee said, "let's put the past behind us and focus on Ridge for a second."

Missy's eyes lit up and she scooted forward on her seat. "Yes! Tell me about this hunky man who's got you girls giggling into your aprons. Did I not say a change might blow in on the wind?" She looked pointedly at me. Distracted, I noticed Missy's cheeks were rosier than normal, even with the amount of rouge she always wore. And she had a quiet kind of sparkle about her. She was always the bubbly, animated one of the group, but she seemed more contained today, different somehow. I made a mental note to ask her later what was going on.

CeeCee and Lil went on to explain every minute detail about reporter Ridge, while I sipped my gingerbread coffee and wondered if Ridge was just a handsome face. Or if there was more to him than that.

After plying me full of pecan truffles, which made me slump into a sugar coma, the girls convinced me that the dinner party on Friday night would be fun, and that it wasn't intended as a setup for Ridge and me. It was a blatant lie but I agreed because Lil wouldn't hand over the rest of the chocolates until I said yes. I threatened her with all manner of things before she capitulated with the truffles.

FIVE

Damn! I was late. Dashing to my car, I cursed and muttered to myself. For some inexplicable reason, I couldn't sleep last night. Instead I'd stayed up far too late reading under the dim glow of the bedside lamp, often getting to the end of a page and having to start over because I hadn't taken a word in.

It was that blasted reporter.

The hero in the book I'd been reading reminded me of him, so instead of focusing on the words in front of me I'd become lost inside my mind, etching out my own visions with hero Ridge as the misunderstood big-town reporter set on stealing my heart—I mean the heroine's heart.

Did most people put themselves in the place of their heroines? Picturing themselves going through the trials and tribulations of the character? To me it seemed a completely normal habit, but maybe I was bonkers. No time to contemplate; I made a mental note to blog about it as I jammed the key in the ignition of my hatchback and set off for work.

I parked out front, and rushed to the bookshop. "Sorry," I hollered out to a courier waiting on my stoop.

The man looked at the small box he held and then asked, "Are you Sarah Smith?"

"Yes," I replied, pushing a tendril of hair from my face.

"Delivery for you." He motioned to an electronic gizmo for me to sign before giving me the small box.

I thanked him and rushed inside to open it.

There was no return address, I noticed as I delicately picked off the tape. The only packages I ever received were big boxes of books, nothing as small as this.

Opening the box slowly as though it might detonate, I stifled a giggle when the embossed title of the book stared out at me.

New Yorkers: How to Live the Dream.

I flipped open the cover and a small note fell out.

Dear Sarah, AKA Covert CIA operative.

I'm beginning to think you might be right about New Yorkers. But don't tell anyone I said that. I have a reputation to uphold as a swaggering, jocular, cocky scribe who's making his way, by whatever means possible, up the corporate ladder in this dog-eat-dog town. Or am I? It was great to chat to you yesterday, would still love to interview you if you change your mind.

Ridge

Oh, he was good. That was exactly what I would expect from a reporter. I scrunched the note and aimed for the bin; it hit the metal edge and bounced to the carpet.

I couldn't comprehend why he'd want to include my bookshop in an article. And all jokes about matchmaking aside, I didn't think he'd go to all that trouble just to get a date with me. I could see the angle for Walt's beautiful handcrafted furniture, yes, and the glorious food at the Gingerbread Café, definitely. And I guessed my blog had proven to be popular, but for some reason I wanted to protect it, and keep it for those who stumbled upon it organically, joining because they truly loved books, and not because some showy reporter wrote about it.

First up, I needed a strong coffee to get my addled brain to switch into gear after such a late night. I went through the back to the small kitchenette and filled up the coffee plunger. I tried hard not to think about all the sweet treats across the road. Instead, I opted for an apple, and took my cup back to the front of the shop.

I'd just settled down to read when Missy strutted in, wearing a leopard-print miniskirt and matching high heels. Her fashion sense was zany, and would look silly on anyone else, but it suited her. "Oh, my Lord, what did you do to your hair?" she said, tutting.

"Nothing. Like literally nothing. I was running

a tad late today." I stroked it back in place, having completely forgotten about it, and looked down quickly to make sure I had in fact dressed myself this morning, in my haste. Skirt. Check. Sweater. Check. Phew.

"Never mind, I can fix it later when you come for your appointment."

"I don't have an appointment, do I?" I said, knowing if Missy said I did, then I had no choice in the matter. She decided when my locks needed attention, not I.

"Honey," she said, "you have a hot non-date Friday—what do you think? Of course I need to fix up your hair!"

Shaking my head, I replied, "The non-date, right. I'd forgotten all about it. Surely, though, since it's not a date, it doesn't matter what my hair looks like?" I couldn't help but tease.

She gripped the edge of the counter, and started counting.

"What are you doing?"

"I'm just counting to ten and hoping by then I've calmed down somewhat and can pretend you did not just say that which is unspeakable!"

This was the Missy I knew, all over-the-top dramatics, and hilarious to boot.

"Which part? The bit about who cares what my hair looks like?"

She let out an indignant wail. "Don't make me wash your mouth out with soap, young lady!"

"Okay." I laughed, picturing Missy chasing me around the bookshop with a bar of some fancy-smelling soap that probably cost a fortune.

Tugging at her skirt, she cast her gaze around the bookshop as if she were searching for something.

"Are you going to spill?" She seemed fidgety all of a sudden, as if she wanted to say something but didn't know how, which was out of character for Missy.

She pasted on a wide smile, and tried her level best to look innocent, but when you'd been friends as long as we had it was easy to see through the charade. We were opposites, and that worked in our favor for our decade-long friendship. I guessed I originally intrigued Missy, being this quiet girl who would rather read than socialize. And Missy would rather spend time chatting away until the early hours of a morning.

"What?" A smile played at the corners of her mouth.

"You closed up early yesterday and rushed off. I was all set on grilling you about that glow on your face, and the slightly high-pitched way you seem to be talking."

Her face broke into a huge grin. "That's just the cocktail of vitamins talking. I need a book."

"I know you have a secret. The book is the clue, right?"

She shrugged. "I thought I'd take up reading—what's so strange about that?"

"Absolutely nothing. Go on, what kind of book are you after?"

"Oh, you know, something on pregnancy, but nothing too horrific. I want one that glosses over the whole labor part . . ."

I shrieked and skipped from behind the counter. Enveloping her in my arms, I jumped up and down with her. "Wait," I said. "I don't think you should be jumping like that!"

Missy laughed and said, "That's why I need the book! I have no idea what I'm supposed to do here!"

I giggled and held her by the hands. "Congratulations, Missy! What does Tommy say? I bet he's pleased as punch he's going to be a daddy."

Missy's expression softened. "He sure is. He's already thinking about names, and color schemes for the nursery. But you know, it's all a bit scary. You think forty-five is too old to be a mom?"

My eyebrows shot up. "You're thirty-five, remember!" I joked. For the last ten years come April we had re-celebrated Missy's thirty-fifth birthday. She said she was sticking with that number for at least another decade.

She flounced over to the stool at the counter. "Well, I got to keep up appearances, don't I?"

"You don't look a day over thirty!" I said mock-seriously.

She clapped her hands. "And that's why I love you! But truthfully . . ." her brow furrowed ". . . do you think we're too old? Tommy is nearly fifty. Who would've thought it would happen this late?"

Behind the sunny façade Missy had hidden her anguish about not getting pregnant like a pro. Every now and then we'd be lolling on her porch having Friday-night cocktails and she'd confide in me how much she yearned for a child, but almost instantly she'd back it up with a positive spin, and tuck the conversation away for another time. To think her wish would finally come true after all these years made my heart almost burst with happiness. "You're going to make great parents! And you're only as old as you think you are, right? Thirty-five is the perfect age for a mom." I squeezed her hand, before sitting on a stool next to her.

"I have no idea how it finally happened when we'd put the thought out of our minds for good."

"Babies come when they're ready. Maybe this one—" I patted her still-flat belly "—was waiting for the right time."

Her eyes were glassy with tears. "That's what Tommy says. Maybe we are finally ready. You know me, always a little slower to catch on than most," she said self-deprecatingly.

I hugged her curvaceous frame tightly. "This baby is special. She's been searching for the perfect mom, and now she's found her." Missy would make a wonderful mother. I could already picture the baby, dressed in a gorgeous outfit, snuggled up in an elegant fluffy blanket.

"She?"

"Of course! You can't really dress up a boy with bows and ribbons, can you?"

She wiped her tears away, and laughed. "You know, I thought the very same thing, but I am sure I could work out some way to outfit a boy a little snazzier."

"I don't doubt that for a minute. How far along are you?"

"Nearly ten weeks." She placed a hand on her stomach protectively. "We found out for sure yesterday. It was so hard not to tell you, but I didn't want to make a big deal of it in case it was a faulty test, or something. We saw Dr. Lewis yesterday and he confirmed it. I'll tell everyone else when we get to twelve. I'm not usually superstitious, but, in this case, suddenly I am."

"Lil and CeeCee are going to be crazy with excitement. There'll be parties, baby showers . . ."

"I can't wait!"

"Let's find you that book," I said.

"Nothing with pictures. I don't want to be traumatized."

I giggled at Missy again, and promised I'd find her a book that guaranteed a smooth delivery.

SIX

Missy stockpiled books for expectant fathers and one glossy upbeat book on maternity for herself, before heading back to her shop with promises of meeting for lunch. I tried to get back to my novel, but my mind was as scattered as the leaves on the pavement.

I was overjoyed my best friend had this wonderful news to celebrate, but it did bring me crashing back to earth with an almighty thud. My singledom at almost thirty made me feel like some kind of failure, as if there was something wrong with me. I tried to shrug it off and get back to my book but the text on the page in front of me blurred. It was one of those moments where you knew you were about to have an epiphany, something miraculous, if only you'd listen to your subconscious . . . I gasped when the words formed in my mind.

Was I being too fussy about men?

Only wanting to settle for someone as dashing as a hero in one of my books? I cradled my head in my hands and groaned; maybe that kind of man simply did not exist. Was I expecting the fairy tale, and thus eradicating any chance of love?

Something niggled at me. What if the fairy tale

did exist? A man as buff and suave as any hero, with brains and brawn, and a sexy smile reserved only for me. No; I lifted my head, pulled my shoulders back. I wasn't going to compromise. I wanted the guy in the books. The book boyfriend must come to life. Otherwise there was no point.

Instead of picturing the buff hero of my future I saw cats circling my ankles, waiting to be fed. I shook the thought away. I didn't even own a cat, and for that very reason I vowed to never buy one—just in case.

Coffee would soothe the erratic beating of my heart. Or speed it up. The phone rang, catching me midway between the kitchenette and the counter. I jogged to answer it, plopping myself back on my chair.

"Sarah from The Bookshop on the Corner."

"Did you get it?"

Ridge.

"Who is this, please?" I tried to keep the smile from my voice.

"It's your friendly New Yorker, calling to check in. I've budgeted so many minutes of my day for this call, so you better make it worth my while."

"Oh . . . Ridge, is it?"

"Very funny."

A silence hung between us, probably because I was picturing him at the other end of the line, wondering what he was doing, what he was seeing. Was he looking out of a big glass window that faced the gigantic city skyline, surrounded by black furniture, and lots of objets d'art that were sleek in their simplicity?

"I'm guessing you're snuggled up in that little alcove you have behind the counter." He sounded as if he were lost in a dream, his tone mellow and sleepy.

"Did you install cameras?" Heat spread through me as I fought to sound jocular.

"Yes."

I laughed in spite of myself, while internally screaming, what was this? Harmless flirting? Something more? Nothing? And what did I want it to be?

"Did you get the book?"

"I sure did, thank you. Stiffens my resolve to stay away from big cities."

"Well, in that case, the big city will come to you."

"Are you referring to yourself as a big city? Is that some kind of metaphor?" Again I was bowled over by my confidence with Ridge. It was so unlike me, but he had a way of making me say the first thing that sprang to mind.

He let out a big belly laugh, which took me by surprise. I'd only heard him be all soft, and practiced charm. "It was kind of corny, I'll admit."

"I'll forgive you this once."

"So I'll see you on Friday?"

"Let me guess—CeeCee's made friends with you on Spacebook?"

"Tweeter, get it right."

Oh, boy, here we went again. Why was the back-and-forth banter so easy with him? It was as if we'd read these lines so many times they fell from our lips as though they'd been memorized.

"I'll be at Lil's for the food, and, just so you know, I'm not one of those lettuce-munching, skinny eaters, so don't mind me if I don't talk all night. I'm more interested about what's on my plate than socializing."

I could hear him accept the challenge, as if the little cogs in his brain were turning ever so slightly.

"Me too," he said. "I'm not one for people really. Much rather be snuggled up in a little nook, next to a roaring fire, with a novel . . ."

"Yeah, right, Romeo."

He scoffed. "Are you calling me a liar?"

I exhaled down the line dramatically so he'd know how completely uninterested I was. "Yep."

"You're right, the picture is incomplete. I'd rather be snuggled up in the little nook at the back of your bookshop, next to a roaring fire, with a novel in one hand and *you* in the other."

I dropped the phone as if it were scorching. Dammit! As I struggled to pick it up the dangly cord caught around the books at my feet. *Not* well played, Sarah. Now he'd know his words had affected me.

Finally, with shaky hands I put the receiver back to my ear. Note to self: get a cordless phone—at least *try* to keep up with the bare minimum of technology. Sometimes the "if it's not broke" mantra had a lot to answer for.

"Excuse me, I missed that, er . . . I have a customer . . ."

"No, you don't." He was all throaty desire.

I coughed. Oh, I coughed! I had to stop coughing. "Hello there . . . er . . . Doris, be right with you . . ." I said to the books in front of me, before mimicking the fictional Doris in a high-pitched granny voice, "No worries, dearie . . ."

He laughed again. "You are something special, Sarah. I'll see you on Friday. If I have to climb on top of your plate to get your attention, I will."

The phone clicked off. I slumped, exhilarated yet exhausted.

"What are you doing?" Missy bellowed loud enough to make the books on the shelf above me rattle. Fine, I'd admit it, I was snoozing in the back. And it wasn't because of the picture Ridge had painted in my mind about us earlier that day. Blame it on the lack of sleep the night before.

"Missy, you scared the bejesus out of me!"

"You're asleep? At noon? You're supposed to be selling books, not sleeping with them."

439

I laughed and cuddled the book tight on my chest. "I love them, and I won't hear a bad word about my book babies."

She shook her head, and grinned. "Why are you sleeping during the day?"

"I'm probably low on vitamin D and need some sunshine to perk me up. This sleepy, love-struck haze is clearly a medical condition that warrants some attention . . . not love-struck! Dumbstruck," I corrected quickly.

"Excuse me—what have I missed here?"

I yawned and rolled over, hugging my book. "Dumbstruck by the words in these pages, that's what I mean. The written word, it can be downright mind-blowing, sometimes."

She kicked my boot. "Don't think you can turn away so I won't see the truth in your eyes."

"I'm not turning away. I'm simply resting until the next flurry of customers arrive." Lassitude had me in its embrace. It was so weird—I felt weak, woozy.

"Ha! Really? Are you going to make a pregnant woman scoot down there?"

I groaned and covered my head with a limp European pillow.

She tapped her foot. "In my delicate condition?"

I didn't respond.

"At my age?"

I let out a, "Pfft."

"With this amount of morning sickness . . ."

I sniggered and sat up. "Okay, okay. Are you really suffering from morning sickness?"

"No, but get up anyway, and tell me what's making you drowsy as a cat in sunshine."

I dragged myself up and was trying to pat my hair back into submission when Missy gave me the evil eye and shrieked, "You are love-struck! I knew it!"

"I am not!" I folded my arms across my chest. "And what makes you say that?"

"You're all sparkly-eyed, and sheepish. You're flushed red like a rose. He called, didn't he?"

"Who?"

Her eyes lit up. "He did!"

I fell floppily into her arms for a quick hug. "If you mean Ridge, yes, he did. He sent me a book about New York, and a little note, so I guess he was following up on that."

We strolled near the bay window of the bookshop where a small oak table stood, the only space that wasn't covered with dusty books.

Missy sat on a chair and leaned forward. She cupped her face as if she was rapt. "And . . ."

"Well, he said this kind of weird thing about being snuggled in the back with a book in one hand . . ."

"How sweet!" she interrupted.

"And me in the other."

Missy whooped so loud people on the street

stopped to look. I waved at them, and watched them walk by before turning back to Missy.

"He likes you!" she said.

"Yep, me, a quiet little bookworm from smallsville," I said, the sarcasm in my voice evident.

She clucked her tongue. "You say that like it's a bad thing, when it's actually the opposite. What's not to love?"

"True, I am the whole package. Beauty, brawn, brains."

She slapped my arm playfully. "Brawn? You're so skinny you need to run around the shower to get wet!"

I shrugged. "There's a lot of muscle underneath this scrawny frame."

"You're lithe. Not scrawny. Now—" she rubbed her hands together "—let's talk about what you're going to wear on Friday night . . ."

If I didn't know better I'd say I was about to be struck down by some kind of killer plague. I was lethargic, and restless, and found sleep at nighttime a suddenly impossible feat. I'd spent the better part of the week double blinking and stretching to try and keep my heavy-lidded eyes open.

However today I felt a strange sense of buoyancy. Could it be because it was Friday, and I was going to taste some of Lil's delectable food? Upon reflection, it was definitely about the food. There was simply no other reason for my sudden euphoria.

After a busy few hours, packing orders for the online store, I pulled the shop door shut, and flicked the sign to Closed. My favorite part of the day was when the noise of the street was blocked out and I was alone in the quiet. The sun was sinking, casting an eerie glow through the windows, landing on the stacks of books like fairy dust. I imagined the books exhaling, stretching their bindings, as they relaxed, not on show anymore. And once I left for the night, I pictured them moving around the shop, their pages fluttering, as if they'd come to life. Until morning, where I'd walk in and find them not quite where I'd left them the previous night.

Batty, that was what Missy said I was.

I ran my hand along a stack of books and watched dust motes float to the ground. The tomes sat silently while I wandered around searching for a novel for the weekend. I came upon a stack of vintage magazines and flipped through them. One of them was about forties-style weddings so I put it in my backpack for Lil. Finally, as though it were calling to me the whole time, I found a book that looked just right. Switching off the lamps, I paused at the door, glancing at the books, just in case today was the day I'd catch them moving, before smiling ruefully and heading to my car.

SEVEN

"Where are you?" Missy screeched over the phone.

Glancing at my reflection in the mirror, I sighed. "I'm just about to leave, but my hair is sticking up all over the place." I was a "set and forget" type of hair girl. Usually it fell in a straight line, and that was good enough for me, but somehow after Missy's extensive hairstyling I'd ruined it.

"What? You didn't wash it, did you?"

Oh, whoops. "It smelled kind of dusty from a little cleanup I had at work."

She groaned. "Sarah, you were supposed to leave it be. That's why I put all those products in it, so you wouldn't have to!"

I ruffled my hair, which Missy had cut shorter at the back, making me flinch when cold air hit my naked neck. "I'll wear a hat."

She huffed. "You most certainly will not. You just hurry up and get here, and I'll fix it as best I can." She lowered her voice, and muttered, "Ridge is here already, and one of the Mary-Jos is flirting up a storm with him."

I laughed. "Sounds like he'll have his hands full, then." The three Mary-Jos, cousins, were experts on the art of flirting.

"Well, they're about to leave, anyway. But just hurry up!"

"I'm leaving right now, Missy Bossy Boots."

She guffawed. "*Missy* Bossy Boots, oh, that takes me back to school. See you in five."

"Geez, Sarah, did you stick your finger in a power socket?" Missy said as she combed her fingers through my hair.

"I tried to tussle it, like you said."

"*Tousle,* like this." She demonstrated a slight wiggle of her hands through her hair. "Not *tussle* like this." She mimicked a tug-of-war.

"Right." I nodded. "I can see the confusion there." Ah, the foibles of the English language.

She pulled out a clip of bobby pins and went to work securing my hair. "There, that'll have to do. Your gorgeous face makes up for it anyway. You're like a little French ingénue, with your rosebud mouth and big innocent eyes."

"Wow, poetic, Missy. Thank you."

She took my hand and pulled me inside as though we were escaping a fire.

Lil's cottage was similar to the Gingerbread Café in that it was cozy, and always smelled as if something delicious was being cooked.

Missy marched through the small entrance, and into the kitchen, dragging me like a naughty child.

"You're here!" CeeCee bellowed, enveloping

me in a hug. With the breath squashed out of me, I muffled into her shoulder, gasping until she loosened her grip. Lil came over and gave me a gentler hug and a peck on the cheek.

Catching my breath, I said, "I have gifts." And groped in my bag for the bridal magazines and handed them to Lil.

She flicked through the crinkled pages, and sighed softly. "Thank you, Sarah. These must be the nicest wedding dresses I've ever seen. I've got goose bumps just looking at them."

Missy piped up, "That style would suit you to a T, Lil. That understated elegance . . ."

"Maybe it's time to start looking for dresses," Lil said. "Any takers?"

I looked quickly at Missy, expecting her to jump up and down with joy; instead her lips twitched in an effort to keep her features neutral. "I could possibly help," she drawled. And then continued: "Oh, I can't be that person!" She whooped loudly, startling us, and her words poured out of her mouth in a rush. "I've got lots of ideas, and I know of these great shops, but we can also get it tailor-made—Bessie has the most gorgeous silk, not that I've asked her or anything, I just happened to wander in there one day."

Bessie ran a little haberdashery shop in Ashford and tailor-made clothing by order.

Lil hugged Missy, and said, "Oh, you just *happened* to walk in?"

Missy replied, "It was like the silk beckoned me, and I need to know what kind of dress you're wearing so I can match the hairstyle."

Lil wiggled her eyebrows like a slapstick comedian, taking nothing seriously, and said in a low voice, "Sounds like we've got some serious shopping to do."

We giggled at her play-acting. Lil was a sweet soul. The idea of a wedding would flummox most people but she was having fun contemplating what kind of style they'd like and how to make it magical. Simplicity was key, and the forties style was glamorous yet understated, a look that would suit Lil, a non-makeup wearer, or hair fluffer, perfectly. I loved that Lil was the opposite of highly strung, and I knew there would be no Bride-zilla moments leading up to the wedding.

"Anyway," Lil said. "Let's get back to Sarah for a minute."

To avoid any conversation about the highly illogical setup I rummaged through my bag for more gifts. "Cee, I have a bag of bodice rippers for you."

"Thank the Lord, I was gettin' low." She took the paper bag full of secondhand books, and peered in. "Historical—what you tryin' to say?" She winked, and kissed me on the cheek.

Missy craned her neck and looked into my bag. "And?"

"I nearly forgot," I said, delving in one last

time. "For you, Missy, fashion magazines." I had a whole bunch of baby magazines too, but couldn't give them to her until she'd shared her good news with the girls.

"You're always spoiling us. Now," Missy said, rubbing her hands together. I knew right away she had something up her sleeve. No doubt to do with me and Ridge. "Let's go out back. Everyone's on the porch."

The trio looked at me for a reaction and it was all I could do to control my snort laugh. "Girls, you couldn't be any more obvious!"

Lil frowned. "But we acted this out before you got here."

I arched my eyebrow as the snort eventually escaped. "Acted what out?"

Lil laughed into her tea towel until her shoulders shook, causing Missy and CeeCee to join in. Once everyone had composed themselves Lil said, "Well, it does sound kinda dumb now, but we set the boys up outside, and planned how we'd go about casually walking you out there like it was just another night . . ."

"It *is* just another night."

CeeCee clucked her tongue. "You ain't seen the way that man is dressed. Or how he smells. What *is* that smell? It's like heaven itself. He got this little hair flick thing he doin' and it's mighty distractin' even for an old woman like me."

"That's it, Cee," I said. "It's back to nonfiction

for you. Now, ladies, if you could try to pretend you haven't set me up that'd be great. So forget how you acted it out because your expressions give you away."

Missy grabbed my arm, and led me to the back door. She whispered loud enough for Lil and CeeCee to hear, "It was their idea." Prompting them to hiss back all kinds of blame leveled at Missy, who waved them off and tried to stop the giggles that escaped her. "Stop it, you two," she hissed. "Now let's do this just how we planned it."

"Excuse me, am I invisible here?" I whispered. "Let's just try and pretend we're normal, just for one night."

Lil stopped, and doubled over laughing. "Wait, wait," she said between breaths.

Missy said, "You heard Sarah. Pretend we're normal, and this is any other night. Think of your taxes or something, if that helps."

It was CeeCee's turn to start hawing. "I'm too old for this carry-on," she said, laughing.

There was no way the guys outside couldn't hear us. We were loud enough to wake the dead.

"Right," Missy said, pulling down the hem of her saffron-colored miniskirt. "It's go time."

I walked out into the cool spring night, smiling because of my friends and their good intentions—until I locked eyes with the man mountain that was aptly named Ridge. Oh, good God, he was leaning against the banister with one arm up high holding the capping on the porch, and, sweet Jesus, his fitted cotton shirt lifted with his stretch, exposing the man crease. Yes, it was everything I expected it to be. I was caught short, not wanting to stare at it but unable to drag my gaze away.

"Oops, sorry," Lil said, pushing me square in the back. With one quick wobble on my heels, I went flying. With a silent cry of *yes-s-s,* I fell into the very man crease I vowed not to stare at. My cheek was pressed firmly against said crease, my heart stopped, and I moaned softly, before arguing with myself, Do not lick the man crease—you *do not* need to taste it.

But . . .

Before I could decide if *accidentally* licking him would be obvious, Ridge pulled me into his arms and steadied me.

I turned to glare at Lil, all the while feeling slightly electrified being so close to Ridge. And the crease. I was leaning on him as a surfer would his board. And because it was an accident, I didn't hurry away. After all, I was still deciding if I'd been hurt in the fall.

Lil smiled, and shrugged. "Sorry, Sarah. Must have been those heels of yours. The deck is a little uneven."

The girls giggled into their hands, and it became clear just exactly what they'd acted out.

"Are you okay?" Ridge asked, staring deeply into my eyes.

Please don't say something inane. "Fine. Just dandy." Dandy? Where was I getting this vocabulary from? I extracted myself from his clutches, albeit slowly, and smoothed down my hair. *Do not cough. Do not whistle.*

"You look great," he said, tilting his head, giving me the hot-guy appraisal. He'd certainly mastered the book-boyfriend mannerisms.

I blushed, hoping he wouldn't notice, hoping instead I just looked as if I had a healthy glow or something. "So," I said, "what brings you back to Ashford? Quite a hike for you." *Smooth, Sarah.*

Lil ambled over and handed us each a glass of wine. I prayed to the wine gods to make their magic work a little quicker, so I'd feel more comfortable in Ridge's hulking presence.

"You, Sarah. *You* bring me back here."

Holy moly! Was this a dream? I chugged back a great gulp of wine and had to look away when it threatened to come out of my nose. Swallowing the mouthful finally, I said, "I don't want to be in your article, remember?"

Without me realizing it, the others had gone inside leaving only Ridge and me on the deck. Oh, they were cunning with their methods.

"The article is all but done, Sarah. I'll finish it off in the next few weeks, and it'll be published in July sometime."

Interesting. Maybe he wasn't just here for the article. Call me cynical, but for some reason

I couldn't quite shake the fact Ridge was a reporter, and one who'd stumbled upon Ashford and found it newsworthy. It didn't add up, but maybe I was reading too much into it.

He continued: "So rest assured I'm not here to grill you."

"I see." Why did words fail me in times of need?

"Can I ask you on a proper date, Sarah? A walk through the woods, and a picnic tomorrow?"

A date! If I stopped second-guessing everything, I had to admit, the attraction between us seemed to sizzle, and, as whimsical and reserved as I might come across, even I couldn't deny there was something magical in the air. The way his hands hovered, when he stared into my eyes, as if he wanted to hold me. It was just that Ridge was all practiced charm, and too smooth. How did I know that he didn't treat all women this very same way?

I knew my voice would come out like a choked sob in my nervousness, so I took some time pretending to consider the offer, by scratching my chin, and looking, I hoped, contemplative. Or perhaps like a science professor. That was attractive, right?

Stalling for time, I said, "You're staying in Ashford tonight?"

He nodded. "At that little B-and-B just outside of town. Pretty picket fences, lots of lace, and floral-covered everything, you know the one?"

I laughed, imagining Ridge ensconced at Begonia Bed-and-Breakfast. To put it politely, the B-and-B was stuck in a time warp. Rose, the owner, was everything you could imagine her to be: seventy, smiley, a really bad cook, and immensely lovable. "Yes, cute place."

"So?" he pushed, arching his eyebrows like a man-model. *Do not start picturing him in Y-fronts.* White Y-fronts, with one finger resting behind the fabric, with the sun behind him in an empty room with wood floors . . .

I did the I've-just-run-out-of-the-sea shake to push the semi-naked vision away. "I'll think about it." I managed to sound casual, though my heart was racing, and my hands shaking. It had been years since I dated, except for the silent dinner with Billie; there had been no one who had interested me. Ashford wasn't exactly teeming with men. As dramatic as it sounded, I just felt like a fool when it came to love; when you were so far gone with someone, and you couldn't switch it off like a tap, then how could you protect yourself? It was easier to live vicariously through books.

"Okay, I'll wait. As long as it takes."

I took a deep breath in, turning away in case my nostrils flared like a dragon. I could do this. One date. Just to prove he wasn't the right guy for me. One date.

He ran a finger along my arm, and I was grateful my face was hidden so he didn't see my eyes widen. "Let's go inside. I think they're waiting."

The clatter of cutlery wove its way to us. "I'm starving," I said. Ridge clasped my hand as if we were already a couple and pulled me through the doorway.

CeeCee pointed to a chair. "That's your seat, Sarah." She smirked at me as I sat next to Ridge's heavenly scented presence.

"You two lovebirds need any help?" CeeCee boomed, pulling me back to the present. For a second I thought she meant Ridge and me and I went to speak, catching myself just in time.

Damon and Lil buzzed around, filling platters with delectable morsels they conjured up as though it were a simple thing, and not food that had taken most of the day to prepare.

"These," said Lil, carefully placing a ceramic dish on the dining-room table, "are baby sweet peppers, stuffed with a mix of pancetta, and ricotta and parmesan, and a few secret ingredients for some wow factor, so go on and try them and tell me what you think."

The baby peppers were the color of traffic lights: red, orange, and green. The vibrancy of them with the oozy goodness inside had me reaching for the plate before anyone else. I knew some girls couldn't eat in front of men when they were feeling somewhat gooey, but I wasn't like that. Especially when it was Lil's food.

Damon said, "If they get your vote they'll be on the new catering menu, along with some other recipes you'll try tonight."

Between mouthfuls, I said, "They get my vote!"

One thing was certain: there wasn't a lot of chatter while we ate. Lil and Damon were harmonious in the kitchen; they fluttered around each other, stopping every now and then for a brief kiss, before laughing their way through the preparation of the next dish. As a couple they were certainly something to aspire to.

I tried hard not to notice Ridge's leg directly next to mine. I was conscious of not touching it with my own leg, which had me sitting stiffly, hyperaware of his proximity. So what if our legs touched—would it be that bad? I tried to look serene as I slowly allowed my body to relax. If in my relaxed state my leg touched his, so be it.

"Are you okay?" CeeCee asked, frowning at me.

I tensed up, and become toy soldier–like again. *Do not cough.*

"Yes, Cee, why do you ask?"

"Oh, it were nothin' really, you just looked—"

Missy interrupted, "I think she's just contemplating the meditative effect of the food, right?"

I threw her a grateful glance. Maybe I wasn't being as subtle as I thought. Okay, no leg touching. Unless he touched me first.

"So," CeeCee said, leaning forward. "What brought you to Ashford originally, Ridge?"

And here it went: let the interrogation begin. I sank back in my chair, and wondered if my friend's questions would make him squirm. After all, he had to pass the friend test if I was even going to think about a date with him.

"Well," he said, "somehow I stumbled onto the chocolate festival Facebook page, and thought that sounded like a nice event to attend. My job allows me to travel for a story, so I figured I'd see what the town had to offer, and I'm mighty glad I did. I found something unique here, something special, that I wasn't even looking for. Serendipity—it's a wonderful thing." He turned and stared into my eyes. Oh, boy. I coughed. Twice.

As the evening progressed we got a little rowdier after each course. The wine was flowing, and the food plentiful. Ridge charmed everyone with stories of his travels, and all the excitement he'd squished into his thirty-five years. He'd sure seen a lot of the world, and not just the pretty sunny things, either. He'd traveled to developing countries, and helped in orphanages. Flown to places after natural disasters and got his hands dirty trying to assist with rebuilding small communities. Maybe Ridge was deeper and more compassionate than I'd given him credit for. CeeCee and Missy goggle-eyed him as if he were Prince Charming; it didn't take a genius to work out he'd won them over.

Lil ambled over with the last dish of the night. The third dessert. I groaned as I watched her set down miniature ice creams.

"These are creamy margarita popsicles with a circle of salted lime on top."

"I'm fit to burst," Missy said, and handed her popsicle to her husband, Tommy, who'd arrived at the dinner party late after being held up at the dairy he worked at.

"More for me," he said. "I got a bit of catching up to do."

Missy had dodged wine all night, without anyone noticing, a miracle in our small group, and had now managed to refuse the alcohol-soaked ice cream. Usually CeeCee would sniff out a secret within minutes with her so-called second sight. There was nothing like a newcomer to distract everyone.

As full as I was, the ice cream before me looked so creamy, and fresh with the verdant lime, there was no way I wasn't going to consume it in three bites. I made the mistake of glancing at Ridge. And there he was. Holding onto the popsicle and licking it. With his tongue. His perfectly pink tongue. Until that moment I had never realized how a tongue could be so . . . sexy. Heat flooded me as I watched him enjoy the popsicle. The thoughts that swam through my mind were somewhat risqué, for me.

"Sarah?" Missy said.

My head felt leaden as I dragged my gaze to Missy. "Mmm?"

She lifted a hand to her jaw and mimed closing her mouth. Oh right. My jaw had dropped open somewhat dramatically. I took a deep breath and picked up my popsicle. Focus on the food. Just the food. The flavors were fresh as a summer's day, but all I could think was . . . Ridge. Ridge and that no-good tongue of his.

Tingling, I felt Ridge peering at me. Did he see me staring at him like a fool?

"You have a little bit . . ." he leaned close " . . . here." He traced my bottom lip with the tip of his finger. And then promptly put it in his mouth. "Tasty," he whispered, winking.

Speechless, I dabbed at my mouth with a napkin. And then dropped my hands to my lap. Everyone else was seemingly preoccupied talking about their weekend plans, but I was lost in a bubble. The only thing I could hear or see was Ridge; everything else felt like white noise.

He clasped my hand under the table, rubbing his finger along mine.

Oh, boy.

There was no way I could fall for a fancy-pants reporter from an enormous city, was there?

"A date, tomorrow?" Missy said, letting out a squeal of glee.

Ridge had said his goodbyes after dinner like a true gentleman, giving us all a peck on the cheek. We girls had retired to the front porch, soaking up the moonlight, and pondering life's great mysteries. Damon and Tommy had skedaddled to watch Friday-night football.

"A picnic," I said, and filled them in on what Ridge had proposed. I'd only just managed to get my equilibrium back. Sitting so close to Ridge and all the gamut of emotions had sapped me.

"Well, I can't see why you wouldn't," Missy said. "He passed our inquisition with flying colors. I don't think anyone's ever scored so high on the friend test before."

CeeCee said, "Damon came pretty close with Lil, and look how that's turned out. That Ridge, he's a keeper, all right."

"Oh, girls, please, you forget he's a journalist," I said, finally finding my real voice, and not the husky, half-dazed sound I used when Ridge was next to me. "He knows how to grill people under the spotlight—you don't think that translates into him knowing how to act when the situation is reversed?" Once Ridge wasn't around, the smidgen of doubt crept back up and tapped me on the shoulder.

CeeCee shook her head. "Ain't no one can pass our test, unless they genuine. It's foolproof. I tell you somethin'—that boy in love with you. It's as obvious as icing on a cake."

"Sarah, you should have seen the way he was looking at you." Missy's voice softened. "Like you were some kind of prize. I found it impossible not to watch him watching you."

"He's smart, and funny, and considerate. Not to mention extremely good-looking. You could do worse." Lil stopped swinging on the love seat and jumped up. "Let's toast to new beginnings."

I wondered just how often they'd discussed my singledom. The way they were acting you'd think I was about to marry the guy, not go on a harmless picnic.

"Wait." CeeCee held up a hand. "Missy hasn't got a drink. Go on in, Lil, and get her a glass so she can toast, too."

Missy grinned at me and shrugged. It was inevitable they'd find out.

"Hang on, Lil," Missy said. "I don't need a glass. I'll toast with my water."

Lil stopped abruptly and surveyed Missy. "Wait a minute, you're the one who toasts something as simple as the sun coming up, and you're not—"

CeeCee cut her off. "She's pregnant!"

Missy nodded, and was swept into CeeCee's arms. Lil embraced them both in a group hug.

Once everyone settled back on their chairs, the girls plied Missy with questions.

I watched them talk animatedly, and thought there must be nothing as special in the world as having friends like these. And I giggled to myself, because they'd forgotten all about my date with Ridge, leaving me time to think about what it all meant, and how I really felt.

The girls' chatter fell away, and suddenly all eyes were on me.

"Don't think you're gettin' away with not tellin' us everythin'," CeeCee said, using her particular brand of stare-down tactic.

Hand on chest, I said, "Who—me?"

"Let's hear it, honey," Missy said. "I need my beauty sleep, and I want to know *all* the details before I go."

Their gazes bored into me, and I knew they wanted me to be open to the idea of love. I'd put up so many barriers, and made so many excuses, but they could see through them.

"When I close up tomorrow, he'll be there to whisk me away to the woods, so let's hope this is more of a romance and not a horror story, don't you think?"

Lil laughed, and said, "Maybe it's more of an erotic story—you ever think of that?"

I blushed to the roots of my hair. "If I had a cushion I would lob it at you now."

She giggled. "And that's exactly how I know

it's crossed your mind. When you become Sarah shot-putter."

"You know me so well . . ." Our words floated off into the moonlit night, like stars.

EIGHT

When I arrived at the bookshop the next morning, it was blanketed in darkness. Predawn there was a bite to the air. I peeked through the window as I always did to try and catch the books fluttering about.

In the shadows the shop looked asleep, no movement, no color. It was a beautiful sight, made even more perfect by the fact the books were mostly secondhand and had that loved feel about them. Hardbacks with brown leather covers looked like austere grandparents perched alongside a pile of colorful paperback chick-lit books.

I opened the door, and let the musty scent of the shop wash over me. Old book scent, it should be bottled. Treading quietly, I scanned the shop to see if there'd been any changes since I'd left the day before.

A thin dog-eared novel hung slightly over the edge of one of the shelves, as if it wanted to be found and read again. As if it needed more love after a lifetime of its pages being turned and bent by the pads of so many fingers.

Most booksellers frowned upon dog-earing a book, but that was how you knew it was special. It had lived, and been reincarnated again with another owner; there were notes on the margins, and words highlighted. With a book like that, when you gently pried open the cover you could hear whispers from the past float out from the pages.

I took the little book that craved another reader and popped it in the front bay window, to read once I'd made some coffee.

Shuffling through to the kitchen, I switched on the kettle. A steaming cup of coffee and a few chapters would do just fine until the sun rose. Quiet time, when the streets were deserted, and the birds still slumbered, was like a panacea for me. Time to revel in reading and fire up my blood with caffeine before I became bookseller Sarah, and not so much whimsical Sarah.

The kettle whistled for attention, so I filled up the coffeepot and wandered to the front of the shop and set myself up in the bay window. Sipping my coffee, I rested against old pillows, and had just opened my book when a movement out of the corner of my eye startled me.

Shrugging down so I couldn't be seen, I glanced out of the window. Holy moly. It was him. The sexy reporter. What was he doing . . . running? His athletic frame whizzed by one side of the street and back down the other. Was something chasing him, or was he doing that for fun? Earplugs sat inside his ears; he certainly looked decked out for exercise: shorty shorts, tank top, and sneakers.

His man bulges pumped on opposite sides to his stride, and when I say man bulges, I mean those mammoth biceps of his. They were like footballs, they were so big. Okay, maybe not that big, but they were rounded and much more sticky-outy when not covered up.

He was out of sight, having crossed the street and moved past the Gingerbread Café. I went back to my book, only managing a few words as the need to glance out of the window distracted me. Where was he? By now he should have turned and been headed past the bookshop again.

I leaned closer to the window, and looked to the right. Footsteps pounded against pavement, so I shrank back covering my face with the book.

After a beat, I peeked above the book, gazing at his retreating frame. Who knew calves could be so appealing? Spellbound, I watched him until he was out of sight.

A fine sheen of sweat had broken on my upper lip. Exercising was hard. I was waiting for him to appear across the street, when he stood in front of the window, surprising me. I let out a yowl of fright. "You scared me!"

He stood with his hands on his hips. "I saw you watching me."

I scoffed, and held up the book in front of my face. "I was reading, I had no idea you were there."

He cocked his head, and grinned. "I could see

your reflection in the windows across the road. Your face was pressed firmly up against the glass as I ran past. Were you checking out my butt?"

"Oh please. As if! Hardly. I am not that kind of person," I lied.

He wiped his brow, and said, "That sounded very defensive, and usually defensive means guilty."

"Oh that was *you* running past just before? I see! Okay, that makes sense, I actually thought you were some kind of burglar. A robber even. A crook. A shys—"

He cut me off. "Liar."

I feigned disbelief. "We are extremely community minded in Ashford, and when we happen across someone running at six in the morning we immediately look for either an army of angry spiders chasing the person, or if that person is carrying a duffel bag with Aunt Pam's best silver. It's just a neighborhood watch thing."

"Neighborhood watch? Is that what you call it?"

I nodded slowly, in a way I hoped made me seem very believable. Trustworthy. "Yes."

He laughed. I couldn't help notice his particular man-sweat did smell a little like the books described—I'd thought that was a myth. An earthy, lemony scent, punctuated by the laundry fragrance that still hung on his clothes. Oh, boy.

"Only six hours to go," he said, fingering the buds of his earphones.

"What, until you're finished running? Wow, you New Yorkers really commit when you commit."

He flashed a smile. White teeth, God love 'em. "Funny. Six hours, until I whisk you away, and let you decide what kind of story it is, right?"

Oh, my God. "What?" I sputtered.

He grinned. "Horror, romance . . . erotica."

My mind reeled. How did he know that?

"CeeCee's Facebook," he said.

She had embraced technology and run with it. I cleared my throat. "I'm sure the post you're referring to is *actually* about books."

"I can read between the lines. I'm a reporter, remember."

Note to self: tell CeeCee to make her Facebook posts a lot more ambiguous. "Sometimes you may just read too much into things, you think? You know, looking for a story when there isn't one there?" I crossed my arms across my chest and pursed my lips for good measure.

"You look adorable when you do that pose."

A smile twitched at the corners of my mouth, but I controlled it as much as I could without making my nostrils flare. "Adorable?"

"Adorable."

He glanced at his watch. "Five hours and fifty-five minutes."

The morning was hectic, which didn't leave much time to think about the impending picnic with Ridge—a good thing. The less time I had to worry about the fact he wasn't the right man for me, the better.

I was packing a huge order when Missy strutted in. "Need help?" She raised a perfectly plucked eyebrow.

"There will be no book heaving from you, Missy."

"That sure is a big stack of books. Are they for Tomlinson?" She giggled.

Tomlinson was one of my best customers. We didn't know anything about him, really, except that he went by the moniker Tomlinson and his tastes for literature were mainly erotic. I scoured the globe looking for first editions of Anaïs Nin and Henry Miller novels, plus a wealth of other erotic literature that would make even the more sexually liberated person blush. But, hey, reading was reading in my book.

"Sure is. I found a very early *Kama Sutra* translated into French. I think he'll like that, don't you?"

Missy sighed. "I guess so. Do you ever wonder about him? Like why he collects only erotica?"

I shrugged, and blew my bangs out of my eyes. "Maybe he's writing a thesis or something? Maybe it's a lifetime investigation into what makes people tick in the bedroom. Who knows?"

"Could be. We live in a funny old world."

I had lots of customers like Tomlinson. People

468

who collected certain genres, or hard-to-find books. No matter what their proclivities, I respected them because they respected books. They prized them. And these clients always intrigued me. Since I mailed the books, and they paid online, I never got to meet them. But that didn't stop me imagining where they lived, or what they did with the books. Were they on display? Did they arrange them in alphabetical order? Or size order? Color order?

In Tomlinson's case, did he hide them? Were they locked away in a vault because of their worth, and their subject matter?

I had another regular customer who wanted only books with handwritten dedications. It didn't matter which book or what the message said, but she wanted books that had been given as gifts. I'd found two for her earlier this morning.

Mexico on a Budget: Derek, Don't have too much fun without me! I'll love you always, Tina xoxox.

Judy Blume classic, *Are You There God? It's Me, Margaret*: I read this book when I was your age, I hope you cherish it, love Mom.

I can understand her wanting to collect books with dedications. Can you imagine what stories these little snippets tell? Especially if you weave the title of the book around their words. Why wasn't Tina going to Mexico with Derek? Why did he give the book away? Did they stay together, or did he meet someone in Mexico? Did they trade this book for a later edition and go back to Mexico together years later?

Did the young girl find solace in Judy Blume's words? Why didn't she cherish the book as her mother hoped? Was it because she was a grown woman now, and maybe kids of today considered this book old-fashioned? Would you not keep it for memory's sake?

So many questions, all the markings of a life so different from mine. These books told a story, and not just the one written on the black and white pages.

I placed the last of the books in the box for Tomlinson, and taped it shut.

"So-o-o," Missy said, weaving her way behind the counter and perching on the stool. "Are you nervous?"

I considered lying for a moment but then thought better of it. "Extremely."

She tutted. "No need to be. There was practically steam coming off you two last night. You were downright sizzling sitting there next to each other."

I ran a finger around the collar of my sweater. Gosh, I was literally hot under the collar just thinking of last night. "Do you think he noticed my gawping thing when he was eating his ice cream?"

Missy threw her head back and laughed. "I

don't think so, honey. Plus, he was certainly making a show of it. The mind boggles at what a man could do with an instrument like that."

"Missy! Oh, my God." I stifled laughter out of pure embarrassment. Maybe the chemistry between Ridge and me at dinner hadn't been as subtle as I thought.

"What? Oh, come on, we were all thinking it."

I groaned. "Really?"

"Mmm-hmm. That man was making a play as if he were trying out for major league baseball. You must be the big time."

"Baseball metaphors, Missy?"

She grinned. "He can hit a home run with me any day."

I covered my face and howled with laughter.

"Come on," she said. "He's not going to strike out, is he?" She bit her lip to keep from laughing. "Do you want football metaphors?"

"Stop." I held up a hand. "I'm going to pull a muscle in a minute." There was nothing like a few minutes with Missy to make you laugh as if you were fit to burst.

"Anyway, all jokes aside, I came to tell you I think you should just try and enjoy today. Don't read too much into it. Don't compare Ridge to the heroes in your novels—though saying that he'd probably beat them hands down. That man is seriously hot! His eyes actually twinkle. I didn't know eyes could do that."

Yes, his eyes.

"I saw him running this morning."

Missy's forehead wrinkled. "From what?"

I giggled again. "I think it's a fitness thing."

She scrunched her nose as if the thought of running for fitness was foreign to her. "Okay . . ."

"He caught me staring."

Missy guffawed. "So you mean to tell me he ran up and down this street like some kind of show pony? He wanted you to stare at him!"

"At six in the morning? He wouldn't know I get here that early."

Missy shook her head. "Honey, of course he knows. He gave Lil and Cee an inquisition about you that day in the café. You're the only one who doesn't get it. That boy, sorry, that *man,* is completely entranced by you!"

The same niggle of worry stopped me jumping up and down in excitement. "Missy, he's gorgeous, sexy, funny, charming, the whole package. I get that. But I just don't see how, or why, a man like Ridge would be interested in me. He seems the type to go out with those swan types."

"Swan types?"

"You know . . ." I stood up and flicked my hair, and proceeded to swan around. "Think long lily-white neck, tall, graceful, mouth perpetually turned down."

"Sometimes I worry about you," Missy said,

laughing. "At any rate, you can swan with the best of them. And Ridge clearly isn't looking for wildlife—he's looking for love. Honest to goodness love with my little bookworm."

"Okay, say hypothetically we were both interested in one another. He lives thousands of miles away, in a city teeming with people. I live here, a tiny town, where nothing much changes. How can it work?"

"Sarah, this is what I mean when I say don't overthink it. Why can't you just let it run its course? See what happens?" She sighed, and paused to fluff her curls. "What if he takes his shoe off today and he has a huge big toe and that turns you off completely?"

A snort escaped me. "A huge big toe?"

Missy giggled and then said, "Well, you know what I mean. I'm just saying you might not mesh once you're alone together, but what if you do? What if you're perfect for one another? Things like distance and differences don't matter when it comes to love."

As I shook my head it dawned on me. I was completely obsessing over something that might turn out to be nothing. Maybe it was a self-confidence thing. A flashy reporter, who looked like a hero from a Harlequin book, was interested in Sarah Smith from The Bookshop on the Corner. It could happen . . . in a romance novel.

Missy put a hand on my arm and searched my

face. "Will you put down those barriers? Just for one day? And see what happens?"

I nodded and tried to arrange my features into something akin to nonchalance. "What's the worst thing that could happen?"

He could break my heart into a million pieces, and never even know it.

NINE

I'll admit it, by the time noon rolled around the sweet butterflies fluttering in my tummy had morphed into a rogue swarm of apocalyptic moths, churning my gut until I had to sit down and pretend it was just another day. My hands were inordinately sweaty. How could hands produce moisture in such a quantity?

With a few minutes until Ridge was due to arrive I clutched a tea towel between my sweaty hands and blew out breaths as they do in Lamaze class. That was supposed to calm you, right? I was mumbling to myself, "Keep calm, keep calm, keep calm," when someone tapped me on the shoulder. I stopped my gibberish and closed my eyes, not wanting to turn around. I knew from the he-scent it was Ridge and he had just heard my crazy ramblings.

"Meditation?" he asked.

"Ommmm," I said, and dropped the tea towel, joining my index finger and thumb together as if I were a yogi.

He laughed, that same sexy sound. "If it makes you feel any better I'm quite nervous myself."

I turned to face him. "Nervous? Me? You're mistaken. I was just in a trancelike state. I can get er . . . Zen-like fairly quickly." I clicked my fingers to show just how fast it could be.

"Is that so?" he said, raising a perfectly shaped man-brow. "Why don't you teach me, then?"

Oh, good God, I could only focus on his lips, which smiled in that lackadaisical way of his when he found me amusing.

"Cat got your tongue?"

I coughed. "I wouldn't be able to teach you, I'm afraid. It takes years to reach my level of, er, enlightenment."

"That so?"

"Uh-huh."

"Shame, I would love to do the downward dog with you."

Oh, my God. "We are talking yoga now, aren't we?"

"Talking positions, yes."

We smiled and stared at each other. I didn't trust myself to speak, knowing it would come out completely wrong. But curiosity got the better of me.

"You don't have an unsightly big toe, do you?"

He cocked his head. "Is that a yoga rule? No, I don't. My little toe, on the other hand . . ."

I slapped his arm playfully. "It's okay. We won't take our shoes off."

"Not yet, anyway," he added.

After closing the bookshop, we strolled up the street, every now and then bumping hips, and giving each other a sheepish apology. I glanced over my shoulder and saw Lil and CeeCee peering out of the window of the café. They had goofy smiles on their faces and gave me a thumbs-up. Holding in a giggle, I waved them away and turned to Missy's shop. She was standing near the front door, on her cell phone.

Ridge hefted his backpack to his other shoulder and clasped my hand. Before I could say anything he said, "She's faking that call, isn't she?"

How did he know that? Though looking at Missy, who was gesticulating wildly, it did look a little farcical. My heart swelled for the love my friends had for me. My guess was they thought I'd chicken out of the date, and then they would have dragged me kicking and screaming to meet Ridge for the picnic by the water's edge. "I'd say so, yes," I admitted. "Looks like a prop." I thanked my lucky stars she wasn't talking into a hair dryer.

"You've got great friends."

"Yes," I mumbled, suddenly remembering my sweaty palms, one of which was now encased in Ridge's strong man-hand. Was it noticeable? Surely he would let go if it was? Would he now think of me as the sweaty-hand girl? I blinked my angsty worry away. I was acting like a teenager on her first date.

Ridge squeezed my hand gently, bringing me back to the moment. "Ashford certainly is a nice town," he said, his voice reflective. "Your friends made me feel very welcome."

He didn't seem to notice anything untoward with our hand-holding, so I replied, "Even with the third degree they gave you?"

"Of course, they're looking out for you. And any man would think twice if he wasn't serious when CeeCee does that special look of hers."

If he wasn't serious.

I nodded. "She's got that look down to a fine art. It's taken years of practice."

"It's like you all value your friendships, you look after them, so they last forever. I guess that's the beauty of a small town."

His comment made me wonder about what kind of friendships he had. A place as big as New York City you could have hundreds of friends and literally never bump into them. Whereas here, we cherished the people in our lives because they were all we had. We lost townsfolk every year, mainly teenagers who'd finish school and head out to university, and on to greener pastures. The people that stayed banded together like a family, as such.

As we neared the edge of town the rolling meadow came into view. The grass was soft and lush from the spring rains, and waved slightly in the breeze.

"Should we set up here?" Ridge asked, pointing to a shady patch under a sugar maple tree.

"Yes, there's just enough sunlight poking through the leaves." From here we could see the small riverbed, the sound of lapping water a perfect accompaniment to the bright day.

Ridge took a checkered rug from his backpack and flicked it open on the grass. It occurred to me I hadn't packed anything for the picnic. No wine, no cheese, not even a book, which was unlike me. Lazy days under the shade of a tree with a hot man or no, I would *always* carry a novel.

"What's wrong?" Ridge asked, his forehead creasing.

Who went on a picnic *without* the picnic? What if he thought I'd come here expressly for some kind of raunchy encounter?

"It's just in the rush of the morning, I . . ."

He kept his eyes trained on me while he pulled a bottle of wine and some glasses out of the backpack. "Yes?"

"Oh, well, it was so busy and . . ."

He sat on the rug and leaned the wine bottle against the gnarly trunk of the tree. Out of his seemingly endless bag, he rummaged and pulled out a small hamper of food. Phew.

"Sit down," he said.

I gathered my skirt in my hands and sat on the rug.

"You've thought of everything," I said, indicating the picnic, which would now be a picnic and not some first-date shag-fest. Not that I was thinking it would be.

"Try this." Ridge held a chocolate-covered strawberry to my lips. I took a delicate bite, not wanting to clamp down on his fingers in my haste to eat.

I made a show of nodding and expressing my delight over the strawberry so he wouldn't know what my turncoat mind was imagining.

"It's not too early for a glass of wine, is it?" he asked, popping the half-bitten strawberry in his mouth. For some reason, the gesture seemed wildly erotic, us sharing the tiny red fruit.

"It's never too early for wine." My voice sounded thick. Who knew desire could make a person come across intoxicated? Maybe the wine *would* help.

"There's all sorts of delicious treats in here, so I hope you're hungry."

Hungry for love. What? It was as though someone else had taken over my mind. Someone a little more adventurous than me. I tried to ground myself and focus on Ridge. "You've been to see Lil and CeeCee, I take it."

He nodded. "I wanted the picnic to be perfect."

His movements were slow and precise, as if he'd been here before. I felt as if I were the stranger to this town. Everything at once appeared different. The white clouds were fluffier, and the grass softer. A diaphanous light blanketed everything.

Handing me the wineglass, Ridge stretched out

beside me, propping his chin in his hand. "So, Sarah Smith, what do you think?"

I took a hasty sip. "Umm, great tannins, complex fruity flavors, maybe blackberry, a hint of pepper . . ."

He laughed. "I meant about us in general."

I blushed. *Nice one, Sarah!*

"I'll add wine aficionado to your repertoire, and what else does Sarah Smith enjoy?"

Where to start? Would telling him about the real me seem inordinately dull? "I live and breathe books," I said, deciding on honesty, because, really, who cared what he thought? He'd be gone from our lives soon enough. "My bookshop is everything to me, and I can't see myself ever venturing far away from it."

He searched my face. "Really? But on your blog you talk about wanting to travel to bookshops around the world, to meet like-minded owners . . ."

I frowned. He must have read a number of archived posts to find out that little gem. Why was he so interested? Again the feeling that he was looking for something other than a date made my skin prickle. "It's a pipe dream. I'd love to travel but my bookshop is my income, and there's no way I could entrust anyone with it. My friends all have their own businesses, so it could never happen."

He sipped his wine, sloshing it around his mouth. "But you said yourself on your blog, it's your online business that sells the most. Surely you could continue that wherever you are? You order the books in, they could be shipped direct to customers instead?"

He was thorough in his research of my blog. I wondered why he'd read so much of it. A man who'd scoured the globe probably thought I was some kind of bumpkin for never having left Ashford or its outskirts.

"I suppose I could, but it's not as simple as that."

He brushed a lock of my hair from my face, distracting me for a moment. "I understand," he said. "For some reason I can visualize you traveling, marveling at bookshops around the world. I'd just love to see your face when you wandered into Shakespeare and Company in Paris . . ."

He reminded me of Gloria and Gerald, searching for forgotten bookshops together. What a sweet life that would be. And he was right about Shakespeare and Company. I spent a lot of time trawling through the internet looking at photos of the iconic bookshop where Hemingway and a host of other literary greats hung out all those years ago. Would I ever leave, if I stumbled into that rickety, glorious bookshop that hummed with memories of the past?

I did what I did best: coughed and changed the subject. "Where to next for the roving reporter?"

He ducked his head and fiddled with the stem

of his wineglass. "I'm off to Australia. Two weeks traveling around big brown land in a four-wheel drive, in the remote north. It's an outback-adventure-themed travel piece, so think camping, and fishing and whatever it is Aussies do."

My eyes went wide with surprise. Australia. It was practically the other side of the world. Wasn't it dangerous there? Snakes, and crocodiles, and killer kangaroos at every turn?

"Sounds like a once-in-a-lifetime experience."

He shrugged. "It will be. A few weeks ago it would have been the highlight of my career so far, but now . . . things have changed."

"What's changed?" I asked.

"You'll think I'm crazy if I tell you."

"Everyone thinks *I'm* crazy so you're in good company." I couldn't make eye contact while I waited for his reply, so I gulped my wine, and swished it around my mouth before remembering it was red wine, and my teeth would no doubt now be a shade of burgundy.

"Well . . ." He paused, fiddling with the stem of his wineglass.

Silence hung between us like a page break.

He continued: "When I first came to Ashford for the chocolate festival it was like coming home. I don't know why. I'm born and bred in a big city but the place touched me. I don't know how to describe it without sounding cheesy. And then, at the festival, I saw you."

I wrestled with his words, surprised and confused as to how I felt.

"I shouldn't have said anything," he said, rubbing his chin with jittery hands. "I know how it must sound. You haven't even seen my big toe yet—that could be the deal breaker."

"You said it was your little toe." My voice came out as a squeak.

He laughed, and pulled me down next to him on the rug. Wine sloshed out of my glass, so I let it roll onto the soft grass. Ridge turned on his side and faced me. We were so close I could feel his breath on my face.

"Did you ever feel like you were on the brink of something, something indistinct, but like there was something missing, you just didn't know what?"

Yes! I wanted to scream YES! But I lay mute, ogling him, wondering when I was going to wake from this dream.

He said, "I've always felt like that, like I was one step away from finding out whatever it was . . . and then I saw you. And it clicked. You intrigue me, Sarah. I've never met anyone like you."

Were these mere words? We hardly knew each other, and yet something had changed when I first met Ridge, too. The old me, pre-Ridge, would be running for the hills right now, but I stayed, because maybe this *was* something extraordinary. Maybe after a whole life of my reading romance novels, the love gods decided to drop a real-life hero into my world. And who was I to fight it?

"So, you see, going to Australia doesn't seem all that enticing anymore."

He was going overseas. To a country so far away they were practically living under a different sun.

"But that's your job, Ridge. You'll always be on assignment, won't you?" It was easier to talk about anything other than what he'd said. I wanted to hide from the words in case he took them back.

"Yes, but that doesn't mean one day I won't want to settle in one place. I do have a base in New York, and that base can be anywhere."

His suggestion hung in the air above. I couldn't help thinking if this were a romance novel any minute there would be a plot twist. Something to upset the balance. Before I could rethink my actions, I leaned forward, put my arms around Ridge's neck, and pressed my lips against his. He gathered me in his arms, and kissed me back softly, our legs falling over one another in a jumble. Desire spread through me, making me feel lush and alive. Instead of dreaming up an embrace with a hot hero, I was actually enmeshed in the real thing. Finally.

TEN

After a languorous afternoon beside the riverbed discussing our varied lives, Ridge had walked me home, and said his goodbyes. He was going to pick me up for dinner at *L'art de l'amour*, a tiny French bistro just outside Ashford.

A longing for sleep overcame me. I wandered into my book-laden bedroom, and fell into bed. My reflection in the dressing-table mirror stared back at me and I gasped. The girl in the mirror had wide eyes that kept a secret, her cheeks were rosy, her hair a tangled mess. She looked older, and self-assured. Huh. I pulled the quilt over and lay back against the pillows, too tired to even read.

As night fell I finished tidying up the front room for Ridge's benefit. I wasn't a neat person; I subscribed more to disorganized chaos. Time cleaning was less time reading, so I usually just did the minimal amount, and left it for another day, a day that would never come.

Whistling as I dusted, it occurred to me I was strangely confident. Maybe it was the wine from the picnic still buzzing around my bloodstream. Or the way in which Ridge had made me feel adored. When doubt tried to crawl its way in I pushed the thought away and instead focused on Missy's advice: not to overthink things.

Car tires scrunched over the gravel of my driveway. I rushed to the mirror in my room to double-check my appearance. My hair was shiny, and untangled, and my kohl-rimmed eyes looked bright.

Spritzing on perfume, I tousled my hair once more, hearing Missy's stern advice in my ear, and headed to the door.

"Sarah." He said my name as though it were something magical.

"Ridge." I knew I had a cheesy grin plastered on my face, but how to contain it?

"You look beautiful." He gestured to my dress. A little black number that Missy assured me was perfect for a second date, before adding a quip about the second-base metaphor, and then saying it would be acceptable to hit a home run if I so desired.

"Thank you. You look handsome too." And there it was. Handsome? You look handsome? Urgh. "Would you like a drink first?"

"Sure." He strode inside, breezily as if he regularly dropped in to visit. He was dressed casually in dark jeans, and a white shirt, that somehow looked fancy. Maybe it was just him. He made everything look good.

"Sit down." I motioned to a recliner. "I'll bring you a glass of wine."

Returning with two glasses, I found Ridge bent forward, peering at the books on my shelves. "Not a romance reader?" he said, pointing to an entire numbered collection of Harlequin books.

I handed him the glass, and laughed, which unfortunately turned into a mini snort. "Well, never say never is my motto."

"Where's the bloody gory zombie ninja books you said you love?"

"Oh, they're around here somewhere," I said, pretending to look for a bunch of books that didn't exist.

He smirked and said, "I'm sure they are. Shall we go? I know you well enough now to guess you're probably ravenous."

"I have a fast metabolism . . ." And one that would probably catch up with me in the coming years.

"One day, I'll entice you to New York. You would love the food there."

Again, he was on about traveling. I tried not to feel as though he was expecting me to be someone I wasn't.

"Don't think you can bribe me with food. It won't work."

He edged close and put a hand on the small of my back. "Then I'll send photos of bookshops."

"You know my weaknesses."

We put our wineglasses on the mantelpiece and headed out into the moonlit night.

. . .

We arrived at *L'art de l'amour* and the maître d', Jean-Pierre, showed us to a small table in a dimly lit corner of the restaurant. A tea candle threw shadows that danced around the white tablecloth. Ridge ordered a bottle of champagne, and we settled back to talk.

"Will you stay in touch while I'm in Australia?" Ridge asked. There was something vulnerable in his eyes; his usual composure was missing for a moment.

"That depends," I said.

"On?"

"If you have Wi-Fi where you are."

He grinned, and relaxed his shoulders. "I know you think I'm forward, but I like you, Sarah. And I want to get to know you properly. I asked about you traveling at the picnic earlier because I had this crazy notion of enticing you to Australia. I could protect you from errant snakes, and randy redback spiders . . ."

It clicked. He wanted me to travel *with* him. And there I was thinking he'd pegged me for this two-dimensional girl, too staid to want to explore the world.

Jean-Pierre bustled over with the champagne in an ice bucket. It gave me time to imagine the scenario Ridge painted. Did he expect a girlfriend to globetrot with him? Follow him blithely while he worked? Jean-Pierre popped the cork and expertly filled our flutes without spilling a bubble. We thanked him before turning back to each other.

"It sounds nice in theory," I said. "But we hardly know each other, and my bookshop doesn't run itself." I'd always been discounted by men for living in a fictional world, and it seemed as if Ridge was no different.

He shook his head. "I didn't mean it that way. I only meant a holiday, and after we talked today I realized it wasn't possible. And before you think I go and ask every woman I've just met to come on assignment with me, I don't."

He had this uncanny ability to read my mind, but in all likelihood he must have read the expression on my face. "Then why me, Ridge? As much as I like this whole wooing thing, it does seem so fast." Even a dating dummy could see that.

He shrugged. "It's crazy, I know." His voice drifted away as he groped for more words. "I can't even explain it myself. I just feel as though I don't want to be away from you. Not for a minute."

My breath caught. Could it be real? I'd read enough books to know it did happen, but I never imagined it could happen in real life, not to me anyway.

Ridge ran a hand through his dark hair. "I wanted to show you what my job is like. The excitement of a new country, a new place.

Meeting the locals, and learning their customs. Sometimes it makes you appreciate how easy we have it here, and other times the place makes me yearn for it, long after I've gone. Some towns can get under your skin . . . just like a great book, and I selfishly wanted to show you that. Open that part of living up to you so you'd think of me as someone who added another layer to your life, and so you wouldn't think of me as a roving reporter, but as someone who searches the world to get to know myself better. Every time I go somewhere, I learn more about myself. The man I am, and the man I want to be. So, you see, locking eyes with the girl from The Bookshop on the Corner at the chocolate festival didn't seem like such a random thing. It felt like coming home."

I picked up my champagne flute with shaky hands and held it out. Ridge clinked his glass against mine and said, "To finding what you've been searching for."

In that instant I decided to live in the moment. Whatever the future held, I'd take the risk and enjoy it right now.

"Would you look at her?" CeeCee boomed. "All folded in on herself like she's got a secret." I was sleepy, and sitting on the couch at the Gingerbread Café, my legs tucked in front of me, and my arms wrapped around them.

Missy giggled, and said, "I know you're not one to kiss and tell but we beg you to make an exception, because, well, we need to know."

Lil wandered over with a tray of gingerbread milkshakes. She knew I loved them and drinking one would be akin to downing truth serum. "And," Lil said, setting the tray on the coffee table, "Rosaleen's already stopped in here today, saying she might have seen a thing or two as she walked by your front porch late Sunday evening."

"Glory be," CeeCee said. "I don't know how that woman does it. She has some kinda radar, or somethin'."

I groaned. If Rosaleen, the town gossip, knew about me and Ridge, then it wouldn't be long before everyone knew. I thought back to Sunday evening, and saying goodbye to Ridge on the porch: he'd lingered, kissing me briefly in the moonlight. I colored, thinking of Rosaleen somewhere in the inky night stumbling on us.

"So," Lil prompted. "How did the weekend go with the sexy reporter?"

I told the girls what had transpired.

"I knew it! I knew that man were perfect for you," CeeCee said. "When you gonna see him again?"

I took a sip of the gingerbread milkshake and was momentarily lost for words. How on earth did they make a milkshake taste like comfort itself, like a warm hug on a cold day? "He's going to Australia for two weeks, so some time after that. I really do like him," I said. "And he's so fervent about me—I guess I kept waiting for the punch line, like it's some kind of joke. Honestly, girls, a man that gorgeous, well, I thought he'd be shallow, but we talked for hours, and hours, about so many things. I got swept up in the end. And I figure, this once, I will let go of the mind-bending fear of being heartbroken, and see what happens."

Missy sat quietly opposite me, shaking her head and crying softly.

"Missy, what is it?" I asked.

She waved a hand at us. "I'm just so happy. Proud like a momma, or something." She plucked a tissue from a box. "You're radiant, beautiful, Sarah. Love suits you. I know you've held out, only wanting the boy from the books, and now you've found him." She broke into full-fledged sobs.

I went to her and hugged her tight, trying to contain my laughter. "Thank you, Missy. I don't know if I'd use the *L* word yet, but it has been nice." I sat back on my haunches and studied her. It was the first time I'd ever seen Missy cry. "You sure you're all right?"

Dabbing at the smudged black mascara under her eyes, she said, "Don't you worry about me. It's those pregnancy hormones everyone goes on about." She was laughing and crying in unison.

493

"Cherry blossom, come here." CeeCee hugged Missy, squashing her perfect mane of hair against her ample bosom as a grandmother would do. I waited for Missy to protect her hair, but she continued sobbing while CeeCee patted her back and hushed her.

"You might need to invest in some o' that fancy waterproof mascara, Missy," CeeCee said.

Through her tears, she said, "I'm going to buy cartons of the stuff! Now, never mind that." She looked pointedly at me. "Tell me about Ridge again. I got myself all worked up and missed the best part. What did he say about finding the missing piece?"

It was too good to be true; that was how it felt. We hardly knew each other but maybe love at first sight wasn't just a trope used in stories. "He said when he saw me it clicked, the 'something' he'd been searching for . . ."

ELEVEN

The week went inordinately slowly. I spent a lot of time lying on the chaise lounge by the back door, staring out of the big window and into the garden. A fragrant summer breeze blew through the screen; the scent of roses wafting inside made me think of love. My real-life Harlequin love affair.

I couldn't concentrate on anything that usually made my days whole. Reading, the words blurred, and doing paperwork I ended up doodling pictures of flowers and hearts, like a teenager in the throes of puppy love. A sort of listlessness overwhelmed me; it was unlike anything I'd experienced before. I was lonely, but didn't seek out my friends, because there was something special about the feeling. A kind of rapture that could only be assuaged by Ridge returning. I'd never felt time march so slowly; it didn't march as much as hobble.

Deeply buried longing had finally been unearthed by a man who I'd thought would never see anything in me. A real man, who looked and acted like the fairy tale.

For once, I couldn't eat. Lovesick. Who knew that was real?

The computer pinged with an email. I jumped up, hoping it was from Ridge.

Sarah Smith,

In the afternoons once everyone is beat after a day of 4WDing, I wander away from the campsite and sit on a red rocky outcrop nearby. Quiet time alone to think of you snuggled in the bookshop, busily packing up books, or reading with that beautiful sleepy look on your face. The thought of you being so far away makes me ache. It's as though the clock never turns over, and the days stretch on. Tonight, I've managed to find an internet café, but from tomorrow they say we'll be out of range for a few days. This wide brown land is ruggedly beautiful and I often wonder what you'd make of it. Snakes abound, and crocodiles too. But so far, not close enough to do any damage. I'm sure I could wrestle a croc to the ground if need be—do I sound like one of your heroes now? In truth I'd probably run the other way.

Until next time,
The roving reporter.

I replied to the email as quickly as I could in case Ridge was still sitting in front of the computer.

Dear RW,

I'm sure you could wrestle a crocodile! I bet as soon as he locked his beady eyes on your biceps, he'd scurry away as fast as his little reptilian legs could take him! Work is piling up at the bookshop because I've been stuck staring out of the back window into the rose garden for some inexplicable reason . . .

Only one more week, until RW returns to the good old US of A, and back to the land of plenty. Until then, I'm thinking of you,

SS

Distance made everything that much sweeter. I missed Ridge, and he missed me. I was falling into the abyss of messy, manic love. And it was divine.

Midmorning the following Friday, I'd finally managed to catch up on all my orders, blog about my all-time favorite romances and unpack boxes of stock that had arrived, including Gloria's motley collection of secondhand books. I'd left Gerald's neatly packed boxes until last so I could linger over each book, before I lovingly shelved them one at a time in the reading room. The books seemed to swell with pride as they sat solemnly on the old wooden shelves. They knew they were going to be well loved here, and read again, maybe a few times, in the years to follow.

An ephemeral waft of cool air hit my neck as I placed the last of Gloria's books on the shelf. Smiling to myself, I said out loud, just in case, "Thank you for your wonderful collection, Gloria. I'll treasure them always."

A faint "you're welcome" rustle came from the magazines on the coffee table.

I hoped one day Gerald would visit and sit in here and feel the magic too.

Ridge returned a few days later. I knew he was back, but wasn't expecting him for a few days. He strolled into the bookshop as if he were merely a customer, and not someone who made my heart skip a beat. And then skip again, until I was gulping for air.

"Thirsty?" he asked, and walked to me . . . that he-scent. How I lived without him for two weeks was beyond me.

"Not thirsty, just, um, out of breath from unpacking boxes. Of books. Out back."

He pulled me into his arms and said softly, "Liar."

"*Moi*?"

"You're not dusty."

I looked up from his embrace. "Busted! Tell me all about Australia."

He withdrew his arms and pulled me to the

table near the window. "You would have loved it, I think. The Aussies are a great bunch of people. So strikingly different from New Yorkers, you would have appreciated them. They have this laid-back attitude, and everything's a joke. It was fun. I'd love to go back and explore some of the bigger cities. We were lost in the bush for most of the time."

"Somehow, I can't picture you with your perfect smile, and immaculate clothing, lost in the bush . . ."

He clasped my hand across the table, and laughed. "You know I did get quite a bit of grief for being a 'pretty boy.' It wasn't long before I was dressed more casually and wearing thongs, which are flip-flops, not a type of underwear."

My eyebrows shot up. "Well, I'm glad you clarified that for me."

His smile slipped. "I came to tell you I'm going away again. Soon."

My heart dropped. Would this be how it always was? Just when I was excited to get more time with Ridge, he'd jet away, to somewhere exciting. How long before the shine wore off the girl from the bookshop? I shook the thought away.

"Where to this time?"

"The Philippines. I'm doing a report about the effects of the typhoon and how the towns are coping now."

I couldn't understand how he could go from a fluffy piece about Ashford to such a serious story about the ravaged state of the Philippines.

"You sure cover a lot of topics. When will you be back?"

"A week, maybe two?" He smiled, baring those lovely white teeth of his. "You wouldn't consider coming, would you?"

I dropped my gaze to our clasped hands. "Not this time, Ridge. But keep asking."

As time wore on, maybe I would consider it. One week away, I could probably do. So the bookshop would stay closed. I was sure the books could talk amongst themselves for seven days without incident.

"So there's hope," he said. "But in the meantime can I take you out for dinner tonight?"

"As long as you order something I like in case I want to switch."

"Deal."

We did that super-sweet new-couple thing where you just smile goofily and stare into each other's eyes.

Ridge stayed in the Philippines for three weeks. He sent me flowers by way of Missy's garden; she was only too happy to chop off her gorgeous roses when Ridge asked.

"He is missing you fiercely," Missy said, handing me a bunch of scarlet roses.

"Oh, Missy, thank you. I know how you hate cutting them."

"What's a girl to do when a man like that is pining for his love? He emailed me when he realized there was no florist in Ashford. How you holding up?" she asked, settling herself on a stool at the counter. Her belly had a slight swell that never failed to make me smile. I itched to run my hand across it. I'd felt the baby kick for the first time last week. It was such an intense feeling— Missy and I had bawled like babies ourselves.

I couldn't fight the urge any longer, so I perched on the stool next to Missy and ran my hand across her bump. "Yoo hoo, baby, it's your adopted aunty here."

Missy put her hands on her hips and jutted her belly out. "Get him to wake up, will you? Then he might not kick me all night when I'm trying to sleep."

"Oh, he's keeping you up?" I asked and then gasped. "Wait . . . he?"

Tears filled her eyes and she pulled a tissue from her sleeve. "We found out this morning. We're expecting a little boy."

"Missy!" I choked back another sob; seemed this hormonal baby crying was contagious. "Congratulations again!"

"Tommy has gone into overdrive. He's repainting the nursery. On one wall he's sketching a huge mural of a steam train. I think secretly he'd hoped it was going to be a boy, though I'm sure he would have been just as happy with a little girl."

"What about names? Are you up to that stage yet?"

She swallowed hard, fighting back tears. "We like the name William. Or Jaxson. Maybe William Jaxson, or Jaxson William. What do you think?"

"I think they're great names. Strong. They'd suit a boy of yours perfectly."

"They just stuck. So that must be a sign, right?"

"Right. And flip a coin to see which order you choose."

She stood up quickly. "Oh, you're a genius! That's exactly what we'll do!"

I filled up our cups with decaf coffee, only stocked since Missy got pregnant.

She continued: "So you didn't answer my question—how are you holding up with Ridge away all the time? He sounded like a lovesick teenager in his email. It must be hard."

I shrugged halfheartedly. "It's hard, but I guess it's the way it is, and I knew that. It's kind of nice falling in love slowly. No matter how fast our feelings have developed, the assignments put the brakes on it, and make those brief reunions all the sweeter."

Missy pulled out another tissue. "Don't mind me," she said in a high-pitched voice. "You should be used to this emotional seesaw from me now, but that is the loveliest description I've ever heard. You know, you really are living out a romance worthy of the books."

I rubbed her arm. "It does seem like it, doesn't it?"

TWELVE

A few weeks later CeeCee ran into the bookshop, startling me by knocking a pile of books from the windowsill straight into my lap. She waved around a newspaper. "What are you doin'?" She stopped abruptly, taking in the spreadsheets on my lap.

"I'm seeing if there is any viable way I can pay for an employee at the bookshop, and still afford to give myself a wage."

CeeCee guffawed. "An employee? Do you mean to say you're considerin' goin' on a jaunt with Ridge sometime?"

I tried not to look coy, but it was damn hard. "Maybe. It'd be a huge step for me to leave my book babies."

"Oh, you should do it!" she said. "Surely we can all pull together for a week or so and help you out."

I waved her away. "CeeCee, if you and Lil help any more people out you'll have to close the café. It's okay, I think I can find a way."

"Ain't nothin' we can't manage. The offer is there. Anyway, lookie, it's here!" She handed me the newspaper. "None of us have read it yet—we wanted you to read it first."

I sat upright. "Is it the article, already?"

"It surely is." Out of breath, she plonked down on the chaise beside me and said, "There's a picture of the Gingerbread Café! Wait, I need my glasses."

Placing her glasses on the bridge of her nose, she began reading aloud. " 'The town time forgot. Ashford, a small town in Connecticut, is a place where people don't change much. In fact, they still use colloquialisms like *color me surprised*, and *glory be . . .*' Oh, that's me, I say glory be!" CeeCee said.

I stiffened, thinking back to the first time Ridge walked into the bookshop. What had he said?

"Have you got any Keats?"

"A poetry man—color me surprised."

CeeCee was still reading. My heartbeat raced as I heard more of the article.

" '—The town itself looks like it's been stuck in a time warp dating back to the early nineteen hundreds. There's a tiny bookshop where everything is stacked in disorderly piles on the floor, where a girl with a simple name and an eager smile will banter with you about what kind of book suits you—' "

"Stop, CeeCee." I couldn't believe it. The article was focused on me, after I explicitly asked Ridge not to be included.

She looked over her glasses at me. "What is it?"

I exhaled, anger making my hands quake.

"What kind of article is this? He's belittling the town, Cee. Making a mockery of us. The town time forgot? Stuck in a time warp? You don't see it?" I asked. I crossed my arms over my chest. How could he do that? I knew it was too good to be true, a man like Ridge loving me. All the while he was memorizing things I said and using them for his own gain.

CeeCee mumbled to herself as she kept reading. "No," she said softly as if she was trying to convince herself of something. "Maybe I'm reading it wrong. Yes, that's it. Maybe he's saying it's quaint, *it's cute*. We haven't moved with the times 'cause we don't want to!"

I shook my head, and stood up, pacing back and forth in the small space.

She read the rest of the article silently, and then turned to face me. "I just don't understand it, I don't. You want to read it?" she asked, holding out the paper to me. She looked shocked; her face had paled.

"No. I don't need to read any more about what kind of hicks we are in Ashford. I told Ridge I didn't want to be in the article, and yet he used direct quotes that came from me, and ones that make me look silly."

CeeCee frowned. "He goes on to say a whole lot more about all of us. Maybe I'll show Lil, and see what she makes of it."

I was so upset my shoulders shook as great big

chest heaves racked my body. The one time I'd allowed a man to truly know the real me, and he abused the privilege, for what, one article, when he traveled the world reporting on bigger, better things anyway? It didn't make sense, and made me wonder if Ridge was play-acting the whole time. I was mortified that my friends would know he was a phony.

"Sugar plum, I'm goin' to show Lil, and see what she thinks. There must be some explanation."

I watched her amble off, shaking her head all the while.

Later that day the phone rang, but I knew it would be Ridge. It rang out, and the answering machine picked it up. I glared at the answering machine when I heard his deep voice croon lies into the recording.

I shut the shop early because I couldn't face any customers. I'd been played for a fool and everyone would know it.

Slamming the cash register shut after counting the takings, I heard the familiar click-clack of Missy's high heels. The back door squeaked open and in she strutted.

"Are you okay?" she asked, squinting at me.

"No, not really. Why, Missy? Why would he be so hurtful? You can't tell me Ashford is newsworthy enough to spend all that time with me just to write an article? It doesn't make sense when he gets paid to go from one exotic location to the next. I'm hurt. I can't believe I trusted a man like that."

"There must be something else going on. Maybe it's . . ." She stopped when she saw the fury in my eyes.

I scoffed. "What else could it be? Missy, please. The title was *The Town Time Forgot*. If that's not an insult I don't know what is!"

She sat down on the chaise, and spoke gently. "I know it reads badly, but no one, especially not someone as good and true as Ridge, would do that. We know him, we do, Sarah," she said, beseeching. "I agree, the sentiments in the article are not nice. But please let him explain before you push him away forever."

I sat next to her, and closed my eyes. "There's no disputing the fact I asked him not to mention me. I wanted him to focus on the café, and Walt's furniture shop, for their sakes. Instead there's a great big picture of the Gingerbread Café, and nothing about Walt's shop, and then he's pulled the mickey out of all of us. Wait, do people still say 'pulled the mickey' or would he use that against us too? I should have known better, Missy. Men like him do not come to backwater towns like this for no reason."

Missy put an arm around me. "You're the one calling Ashford a backwater now? Honey, let me tell you this straight, because I know you better than anyone. I think you're looking for something to use as an excuse so you can run back to your book cave and hide. You can't bookmark your life, Sarah. As much as it's easier to live in a fictional world, you can't live there forever! You finally stepped outside your comfort zone, and it scared you. But, please, just ask him, just do that one thing for me."

"Missy, don't you see? Ridge is a walking cliché. I trusted him, I did. And look what happened."

She shook her head. "I've got a shop full of clients with bleach burning their hair, so I have to go. But I'll let you think a while. We sat with him over dinner—he's not that kind of man. He's not." She hugged me and walked away without another word.

There was no way I was going to talk to Ridge and listen to another pack of lies. Instead, I found my favorite book, one that I'd read so many times the pages were loose, and started from the beginning. At least books could never let you down. They'd been my refuge, my go-to place in times of need, and nothing had changed. This particular book felt familiar, like an old friend. The characters drew me into their world, and I blocked out mine for the rest of the afternoon.

It was after dark when I made my way home. The town was empty, the shops shut as I drove past.

Arriving home, I was suddenly ravenous; trust my good old appetite to return once the love buzz had diminished. I pulled out a frozen dinner, and shoved it in the microwave. I found my old stuffed teddy bears and threw them back on the couch with various threadbare blankets I'd hidden away. There. It looked more like me again.

The microwave beeped and I flicked the TV on hoping for a soppy chick flick I could watch while I ate. Just as I was opening the microwave there was a pounding on the front door.

"It's me, Sarah. Open up."

Ridge.

I faltered for a second; I hadn't expected him to drive here.

Squaring my shoulders, and taking a deep breath, I moved to the closed door. "What do you want this time, Ridge? Another off-the-record quote?"

"Sarah . . ."

I closed my eyes against the sound of his voice.

"Let me explain . . ."

"Was that your plan all along, Ridge?" My voice cracked and I hated myself for it. "String a girl along so you could make fun of the way she speaks, and the small town she's from? And even worse, her friends who trusted you?"

He sighed. "I wasn't making fun of you, Sarah, or your friends. Not at all. Can you let me in so we can discuss this?"

I rested my head against the door. I wanted to pretend the article had never happened. His voice, his presence did something to me, but I stood firm.

"No, Ridge. I trusted you and you used me for a stupid article."

"You know we're living out the storybook misunderstanding here, don't you?"

I rolled my eyes, even though he couldn't see me. "Don't try to charm me with book talk."

His Ridge laugh rattled through the door.

"Do you think this is *funny?*" I huffed.

He dropped his voice. "Rosaleen's out front, so unless you want the whole town to hear you'd better open the door."

That woman! I did a little angry dance, and shook off the rage before flinging the door open. And there he was. Why did he have to be so downright good-looking? He stepped over the threshold, forcing me to move backward. His dark hair shone under the moonlight and, like the textbook Harlequin caricature he was, he ran a hand through it. I narrowed my eyes at him. I bet he'd been studying romance books his whole life to make women swoon.

I yelled over his shoulder, "Rosaleen, it's dark out—you shouldn't be walking around town alone."

"I heard a commotion, that's all," she said, not moving from my driveway.

I shook my head, and shut the door.

Ridge, the man mountain, stood before me, his eyes shining with that goddamn sparkle that no one else seemed to have. He probably used twinkle–eye drops or something for that effect.

"Did I interrupt dinner?" Ridge said, glancing at my microwave meal that had dried to resemble cardboard.

"What is it you want? Because I have other obligations tonight, Ridge."

"Like what?"

"Like what what?" I said, slightly forgetful because of the way he smelled. I was really going to miss that.

"What are your obligations?"

"I'm up to book three in a five-part series, and once I commit, I commit, you see. Not like some people." I raised my eyebrows as high as they could go, and nodded to him.

"You think I don't commit, when I commit?"

"Can you please stop repeating me? It's a very archetypal reporter defense, and, *this time,* I can see straight through it."

He moved to the couch, and picked up a teddy bear before sitting down. "Cute."

I snatched the droopy-armed teddy away. "So?"

He stretched his arm across the back of the couch and said, "You didn't answer my phone calls."

"Yes, I didn't want to end up in another article

I didn't give you permission for." I crossed my arms, and then uncrossed them. I didn't quite know where to put myself.

"I can explain. And I hope you'll listen. That wasn't the article I wrote. My editor changed it last minute. He couldn't get hold of me—I was out of range covering another story, as you well know—so he used my notes and, as he said, 'jazzed it up.' "

"Jazzed it up?"

Ridge sighed. "His words."

I stood up and paced in front of the lounge. "Hang on . . . he used *your* notes . . . so you *did* write all those nasty lines about us hicks in Ashford?" I would pay to see his notebook; scratch that, I would probably hide for the rest of my life if I read any more of his vengeful insults.

Ridge pinched the bridge of his nose. "Yes, he used my notes. But he spun them into something they were not. He took them out of context for the sake of the story. And it's unforgivable."

I stopped pacing and sat on a recliner opposite Ridge. "I specifically asked not to be in the article so why did you write notes about me, anyway?"

He looked down, and toyed with the tassel on a cushion before responding. "Because I didn't want to forget the things you said. I was spellbound, still am. When I'm away I flick back in my notebook and read those passages, and conjure up the memory. What you were wearing, what you did. Those fluttery hands of yours . . ."

I wanted to believe him but it was all too neat. Like something out of a movie. For once, I wanted real life. Nonfiction.

He gazed at me, his look a mix between remorse and resignation. "Sarah, I'd never chase a girl for a story. I have more integrity than that. I want you to believe me. Your friends who invited me into their home have been hurt by the article, you're devastated, I'm at a loss what to do, and I want you to know I would never do that, ever."

He continued: "My version of the article said how in this huge world of ours you can stumble on a little town where nothing changes, and the people are happy with their lot. *Time forgot Ashford because Ashford forgot time.* No one hurries here. Every moment is savored, from having a twenty-minute conversation when you buy a loaf of bread, to shutting up shop two hours late because you got to talking. Don't you see? I was saying we could all use some of that old-fashioned goodness in our lives. You're right about New York: it's a race against time to get everything done. Most of us don't even *see* a real person when we go through the checkout at a supermarket—we use an automated machine and scan our groceries ourselves." Ridge stopped and pulled out his phone. "I can show you the attachment I sent to my editor with my article. It has the date and time so you know how I originally intended it to be." He stood up and handed me the phone.

"I *also* said that I thought I'd found paradise, especially when I locked eyes with the girl from The Bookshop on the Corner. I'd found her, the girl from my dreams, the one who stood in shadows when I slept at night, the girl I knew I would one day find and recognize immediately."

The staccato rhythm of my heartbeat drummed in my ears as I read Ridge's article. It was sweet, and made all our eccentricities seem like something to aspire to.

I exhaled all my frustrations. "But, Ridge, the twisted version of the article is still out there for the world to read. I don't see how I can forgive that."

He searched my face, before standing close enough to me that I tingled from expectation. "Agreed. I can't forgive it either. It goes against every moral I have. Every ethic. That's why I've quit, and asked for a retraction otherwise there'll be a lawsuit from me about using sources that were off the record." He spoke in a rush, his words hitting me hard.

He quit? The job that inspired him? That made him grow as a person?

I frowned. "You quit? Just like that?"

He folded his arms, and laughed suddenly. "Just like that. And it felt good! I can't work for someone who does that. And if I lose you because of it, there *will* be hell to pay for that paper, trust me on that."

I was completely lost for words. I expected Ridge would be upset at leaving a job he loved but he seemed . . . happy, ecstatic even.

"What will you do now?"

He smiled, the big toothy smile of his. He must get them polished to be so bright. I made a mental note to ask him about his unnaturally white teeth and his sparkly eyes.

"I'll freelance. *That,* I can do anywhere. And I'll travel for holidays, instead of for work . . ."

"I see."

"Do you?" He cocked his head.

"Yep."

"So . . ."

"So, what?" I was buying time to work out how I felt about this new development. In parts I felt guilty that he'd left his job, and worried about his future, but mostly I realized I was relieved the man I loved still loved me. And was prepared to put his career on the line to prove it.

"Talk about a plot twist," I said, smiling.

"How are we going with the resolution?"

I threw my head back and laughed. Imagine spending a lifetime with someone who got you. So what if I lived in a fictional world ninety-five percent of the time? He'd just have to meet me there.

"If this *were* a romance novel, and I was the

dashing misunderstood hero, and you were the ultra-sexy heroine, what would happen now?" Ridge asked, pulling me into an embrace.

"Depends what genre the novel is," I said, arching my brow.

"Pretty sure it's erotic," he said and winked.

Ridge and I held hands as we made our way to the Gingerbread Café the next morning. It was time to explain to the girls. I'd spent some time mulling over what Missy had said about bookmarking my life and realized she was right. It was so much easier to hide behind the covers of my books because there was no chance of being hurt that way. Books were my sanctuary, my escape, and a place to dream without judgment or criticism. Maybe Ridge would be *my* happy ever after, and maybe he wouldn't, but there was simply no way of knowing unless I threw caution to the wind, and lived out a real romance.

"There they are!" CeeCee bellowed, waving us into the café. "So you lovebirds have sorted it out, I see?"

I laughed, and pulled Ridge to a table. "We have. And we're here to tell you what happened."

She brushed the comment off. "Never mind that, let me call Missy. She's been sobbing her little heart out over the fact that you were going to end up a lonely old cat lady. I tried to tell her you don't—"

Lil walked over and put a hand over CeeCee's mouth. "Save it for Spacebook, Cee. Morning, you two. You look like you could use a warm drink." She winked at me and bustled off to make us something delectable.

CeeCee stood in the café doorway and yelled down the street, "Missy, you need to see this!"

Ridge and I held hands under the table and waited for Missy to come click-clacking down the pavement.

She strolled into the café, her mascara leaving black traces under her eyes. "Missy, what is it now?" I asked, jumping up to go to her.

"It's these damn hormones; even magazine advertisements make me cry! Hi, Ridge," she said, leaning down to peck him on the cheek, before giving me a tight squeeze. "You sorted it out?" Missy asked between choking sobs.

Ridge smiled. "We did. And I owe you all a huge apology; you see, what happened was—"

CeeCee interrupted. "Ridge, you save your explanations. If Sarah's happy, we're happy. We knew it musta been some kind of misunderstandin'."

My friends sat at the table with us, and started gabbing. CeeCee held up her hand and said, "Wait! Wait! Hush up for a minute." She closed her eyes, and shrieked, "I seen it!"

Lil shook CeeCee. "Don't go and scare him off now."

CeeCee opened her eyes wide. "You going to live in Paris awhile, oh, yes, you are. The two o' you. Not right now, but soon." She slapped the table hard. "And I ain't never been wrong yet!"

Ridge threw me a questioning glance. I shook my head. I'd tell him all about CeeCee's second sight later. I melted into Ridge's shoulder as we listened to CeeCee talk animatedly about our future as if it were mapped out as sure as the stars.

I squeezed Ridge's hand under the table and when I closed my eyes I could see us strolling down the streets of Paris toward a bookshop that wasn't my own. I'd nuzzle into Ridge's arm as he recited poetry in French, the wind carrying the exotic words away before I could grasp their meaning.

Maybe it was time to step out of the shadows of my books, just for a little while, and see where love would take me. Paris, the city of love, seemed a good place to start.

Books are produced in the United States using U.S.-based materials

Books are printed using a revolutionary new process called THINKtech™ that lowers energy usage by 70% and increases overall quality

Books are durable and flexible because of Smyth-sewing

Paper is sourced using environmentally responsible foresting methods and the paper is acid-free

Center Point Large Print
600 Brooks Road / PO Box 1
Thorndike, ME 04986-0001 USA

(207) 568-3717

US & Canada:
1 800 929-9108
www.centerpointlargeprint.com